George Johnston was bor working-class parents. At the age of sixteen his career as a journalist was launched with the publication of several articles in the Melbourne *Argus.* By the time the Second World War broke out, Johnston was already an established journalist. He became Australia's first official war correspondent, and wrote for *Time* magazine.

Towards the end of the war he met Charmian Clift, who was also an accomplished writer. They married, and in 1951 left Australia with their two children and moved to London, later settling on the Greek island of Hydra.

During the 1950s Johnston contracted tuberculosis, the disease that led to his premature death. He returned alone to Australia in 1964 for the launch of *My Brother Jack* which, along with *Clean Straw for Nothing,* won a Miles Franklin Award. The last few months of his life were concentrated in an effort to finish the third novel of the trilogy, *A Cartload of Clay.* He died in 1970.

Also by George Johnston
and available in Imprint Classics

MY BROTHER JACK

IMPRINT CLASSICS

CLEAN STRAW FOR NOTHING

GEORGE JOHNSTON

An imprint of HarperCollins*Publishers*

AN ANGUS & ROBERTSON BOOK
An imprint of HarperCollinsPublishers

First published in 1969 by
William Collins & Sons Pty Ltd
Published as a one-volume edition with A Cartload of Clay *in 1989 by*
William Collins Pty Ltd
This Imprint Classics edition published in Australia in 1991 by
CollinsAngus&Robertson Publishers Pty Limited (ACN 009 913 517)
A division of HarperCollinsPublishers (Australia) Pty Limited
Unit 4, Eden Park, 31 Waterloo Road, North Ryde
NSW 2113, Australia

William Collins Publishers Ltd
31 View Road, Glenfield, Auckland 10, New Zealand

Angus & Robertson (UK)
77-85 Fulham Palace Road, London W6 8JB, United Kingdom

National Library of Australia
Cataloguing-in-Publication data:

Johnston, George, 1912-1970
Clean straw for nothing

ISBN 0 207 17100 9.

I. Title.

A823.3

Cover painting by Sidney Nolan
Printed in Australia by Griffin Press

5 4 3 2 1
95 94 93 92 91

Drunk For a Penny.
Dead Drunk for Tuppence.
Clean Straw for Nothing.

A London sign in Gin Lane in Hogarth's time

AUTHOR'S NOTE

Since this is, in a sense, a continuation of an earlier novel, *My Brother Jack*, I feel it necessary to point out that it is a work of fiction. I emphasize this because after publication of *My Brother Jack*, which was a largely autobiographical novel a great many readers seemed to find it imperative to give factual identity to all the characters, some of whom were vague composites and others wholly imagined. As this sequel is obviously to some degree similarly pegged to a background of actual autobiographical experience I should like to reiterate that it is a very free rendering of the truth; to an even greater degree than in the previous book characters and incidents, more often than not, are no more than what I have composed in my imagination.

I should like to express my very deep gratitude to the Australian Commonwealth Literary Fund for the award of a Fellowship which enabled me to write this novel.

My hope is to do now one more novel to complete the Meredith trilogy.

SYDNEY, 1968

'I'll tell you why I'm not writing,' I said.

But his attention had begun to wander, as it does with too many people in a small room, and since he was no longer listening the way he had to listen if I told him, I didn't tell him. Couldn't tell him, to be honest, even though there was no doubt that he had attacked me in an oblique sort of way from behind the creamy pale skin revealed by his having shaved the neat Carolinian beard he had grown in the Simpson Desert while directing his little film for television. He still wore the tight cord pants and heavy ski sweater he had bought to go with the beard, but he would have been wiser to have kept the beard and sent the clothes back.

Earlier he had been more emphatic, involved in some way, even secretly angry I thought, and had spoken with an urgency as if he cared whether I went on writing or not. 'Look,' he had said, intending to make some point, 'I'm thirty-five,' and Cressida had smiled across at him and said, 'Already?' and this checked him on the point he wanted to make and raised a small laugh among some of the others, that sort of approving laugh like a tick made on a formal questionnaire that went with the smart anachronism of a Queen's Birthday holiday party in a tweely restored little mid-Victorian cottage in one of the in suburbs, drinking red wine out of flagons and watching Ginna, his continuity girl, stirring the minestrone in a plastic apron over a mini-skirt that showed white net stockings to eight inches above her knees.

It was very much that kind of a party, and I remember thinking it could never have happened in earlier years. Not in this part of the world. Cressida wore a Mary Quant thing, black and white with a hood that made it look a bit like an academic gown, and her net stockings were black, and Sue wore tights and a very short white dress made up out of a crocheted Hong Kong tablecloth, and Edda a Marimekko shift, and Martha tight pants and ruffled shirt in a kind of batik. There was a hint of flagrancy about their sophistication. They were all married women, or had been, although some of the present associations were not quite clear, and there were two late-arrived babies, desperately conceived, rolling on the hairy rug where the Siamese cat stalked mewling. All four women dressed just a bit younger than they really were. But smart with it. Attractive women still. They all wore interesting rings on their fingers, original rings, not acquired hurriedly, rings denoting distinct experiences, cosmopolitan travel, peaks of admiration.

I had not met Martha since London, over seventeen years before, when she had been a top mannequin there, and she still had all the style and the looks and was threatening more than half seriously to get out on the catwalk again, in her middle forties, and show the young ones. You felt she could, too. Edda was from Trieste, and she too had been a model in London, and a notable beauty, but that had been after Cress and I had packed up and gone off to Greece. One of the babies on the floor was hers, and she was married now to Steve, who was trying to get rid of a cattle property he had up north in the brigalow scrub and talked, as he had talked for years, of writing a novel.

The men were all smart too in a casual holiday way, checked shirts and hacking scarves and sweaters and fine socks—Giovanni from Alitalia dreaming of white and cubic towns spewing down the hillsides in Reggio Calabria, and Harry who dealt in old houses, restoring them with sandstock brick and white paint and filigree balconies of cast-iron, and Peter the grazier who had once stayed on the Greek island with us and who dreamt melancholically of selling everything up and going back to Europe to live. He had in his middle fifties fathered the other baby on the rug, but there had been no solution in this and he no longer lived with Sue of the Hong Kong tablecloth-dress, although they continued an intermittent social rapport among their friends. He drifted around art openings and film society shows and lived, alone and dispirited, in a beautiful beach house twenty-five miles up the coast. He had recently built a darkroom into the house where he developed and enlarged his photographs and made his own colour prints of his one long and hopeless sojourn abroad. Earlier the emptiness had left his eyes when he had been talking of trying Ibiza or buying a small vineyard on the coast south from Barcelona. A year before it had been the Dalmatian coast, the year before that a Greek island.

That was what had started Jeremy off—Jeremy of the recently shaven beard—because he was working and saving towards his first trip abroad, and perhaps he had felt a bit out of it with all the talk about London and Paris and Athens and Messina and Majorca and Amalfi and Porto Ercole and Hydra—bored and irritated by other people's verbal colour slides—and he said to me, 'Why did you come back to Australia from overseas?'

'I suppose because it's easier out here,' I said, since it was not a question one could answer simply and this was a way of summarizing it truthfully enough.

'Then why go away in the first place?'

This was even more difficult. I thought about it for a while, and felt that this place and this group of people and this question had almost no relationship at all to what had happened, and I had no intention of dishing up some satisfying little titbit of reason and passing it around with the caviar and the smoked oysters which Giovanni and Peter were handing down from the makeshift bar, and then he said, 'I mean, you haven't written anything since you came back, have you? That's well over three years. Anything worth while, I mean. Why come back at all if it stops the flow, if it buggers you as a writer?'

That was when I said, 'I'll tell you why I'm not writing.' But I didn't tell him. Ginna was bending down to sprinkle Tidykit into the tray the Siamese cat used and you could see the join of the net stockings running all the way up to the white cups of her bottom.

A quite eminent zoologist has just brought out a book in which he theorizes that the females of our ape-ancestors when we walked on all-fours developed those unique fleshy hemispherical buttocks as a sexual come-on for the males, and so when we began to walk upright women had to develop those unique fleshy hemispherical breasts as an erogenous compensation or mimicry to make sure of attracting men from the front. Looking at Ginna's bottom, I mused for a while on the redundancy of evolution. Buttocks were all right too, I thought, and these reflections absolved me from any further discussion with Jeremy.

SYDNEY, 1968

I shall have to try to work it out somehow. It isn't the stopping writing, anyway. Everyone gets to the stage, or should get to it, where it's more important to stop doing things than to keep on trying to do them. The bonus of being in one's fifties is the relief of not having to try, not even wanting to try, any longer. But why work it out for bloody Jeremy? Someone who'd only been a twelve-year-old when the war ended, someone who'd never be able to understand anyway. Even to me it had fallen back into a time of lost history, jerky and blurry like old film. Grey, too, and spotty. Half the truths lost, and the lies, the little ones and the big ones, and the self-deceptions, honed down by time into valid truths. Another of time's little bonuses. Once you've traded in experience for the memory of experience there's no difference any longer between the lies and the actualities: you might as well have it the way you would have liked it to have been: given enough time you'll come to believe genuinely that this was the way it really did happen. Which is very good for the soul, especially when it's showing signs of shrivelling a bit.

If I try to set it down in a kind of random journal, it won't really be going back to writing. Just trying to work it out, rather, to get it straight before it is too late. Before falsification and delusion take it all over, like a lulling anaesthetic blandly easing one into the desired oblivion.

Bugger Jeremy.

MELBOURNE, OCTOBER, 1945

It is hard to believe that this is the same city that went to war in a vernal exuberance of bells and bands, the pretty girls lively in their dresses, the young men zesty with new excitements, a spring contagion touching everyone with dizzy delights and restless exhilarations spreading out of a unique promise of futures unpredictable. It was jaunty then. There was a smell of brown boronia in the streets.

But six other springtimes have intervened, black ones and bright ones, and the first sere summer of peace is still to come, and it will be as nervy and exhausting and as hard to get along with as a hot northerly, and after that the southern autumn will move in cold and squally with sluices of rain mulching red leaves against grey paving stones, and peace will still be creeping and cringing back, shuffling among us for a long time, uneasy in an exuberance that can only be artificial.

It's funny that there are no labels pasted across the place bearing the boldly printed word PEACE, like the pointers in the newspaper cartoons. The last time I was back on leave there had been lithographed posters everywhere which still said WAR—and thrift and sacrifice and security and aid and effort and co-operation. These are the posters one still sees, fading, peeling off the hoardings, marked over with the names of girls and servicemen and with telephone numbers and crudely delineated charts of the ways to places.

I often find myself stopping to examine these sad *graffiti* of an explosive and by now exploded time. 'Olga Troughton, redhead' and then a telephone number: 'ask for Max, Cicero Mansions'; 'Chuck K. Vandegger, APO 362'; 'ALL YANKS ARE WHORING BASTARDS'; 'Phil T., British Pacific Fleet, June 1945'. I see how Melbourne was trampled on in my absence. By GI's, Marines, the British Pacific Fleet, by Task Forces, the returning AIF divisions, the Free French from Noumea. God knows who else. Prisoners, of course, and the Dutch from the East Indies. There are times when I feel like a Crusoe coming across a million footprints.

I spend a lot of time aimlessly tramping the streets. For one thing I don't want to go home and face Helen. But also I must keep my hold on instability. I must try to retain this gleam that is still on me from far places and suspended responsibilities. I want to stay identified with a dilemma, because this makes me part of what is unorthodox and unstable; it retains me in a world which is still out of balance. One must at all costs prevent this from tilting back into the static dullness of the conventional picture.

What helps is that there appears to be almost as many men and women wearing uniform as before, when the war was still on, although a good many of these uniforms are green now instead of the old khaki, jungles having long since supplanted deserts, and the men usually have gaunt faces jaundiced by too much atabrine. Most of the faces carry marks of experience and suffering, and usually a kind of bitterness too. Nobody looks particularly triumphant. There are also many unrepatriated foreigners about, which gives a kind of basic strangeness to the town, and street traffic is still being stalled by already anachronistic convoys of drably painted army vehicles. Sometimes long tragic trains come into Spencer Street with emaciated men from the Japanese prison camps. I feel the anachronism strongly in the road convoys, but hardly at all in the trains.

Melbourne is hateful, really. Butter and steaks are on the black market, and bottled beer, and cigarettes kept beneath counters, and taxi-drivers are churlish, remembering the free-spending time of the Yanks, and the city grins its rapacity and greed stalks through the town with a smirk on its face. Petrol rationing is worse than ever and the cars still lumber about with those grotesque charcoal burners built on behind, fouling the air. In the smoky swill of crowded pubs returned men force beery arguments and fights around their own roles in forgotten skirmishes, involved in loud lies and terrible uncertainties. This is a sour, cynical, nasty city. The night places are filled with costly and illicit shadows, where restless men and women promulgate anxious gaieties. A powerful tide of human dilemma runs beneath the skin of everything. I must stay within this tide, for it will move me along.

It is well past midnight by the time I get to my wife's flat. I pay the rent for it but I have not yet come to think of it as my flat, or even as ours.

The night has been much like all the others since I got back. Leaning on the granite coping near Flinders Street, where the attenuated palms sullenly survive the slow asphyxiation of train smut and the chill discouragement of the wrong climate, I watched the engines of the goods trains in the yards breathing white like old men on frosty mornings, and looked down on lovers welded in sculptural lumps in dry archways, and up from there a little where the bridge crosses the river I saw the rain placing coin-spots on the Yarra's turbid slow tide and spent quite some time working out the pattern where the spots turned into swirl at the prow of the stone piling. The effect was of little lizards trying to get away somewhere. Earlier I had drunk beer convivially with two army nurses on their way to Adelaide for demobilization, then stayed on to talk to the waitresses at Costa's grill, wandered up Little Bourke Street to smell the Chinese smells and along past the locked-up Eastern Market through the smell of damp secondhand books, down again to run the gauntlet of the streetwalkers around Little Lon, and here the smell thing again because the women traffic in the heavy iodoform smell from the big grim red-brick hospital which takes up all the block. When it gets late at this end of town the only lights that stay on are in the hospital and the brothels and the police station around the corner. When it gets late in a city and you are alone smells and lights seem to achieve a special significance.

Ordinarily I would have taken a taxi to her flat, but tonight, after not being able to talk to the prostitutes—it's funny, but it's only in Asia that I am able to talk to whores—I went on up to the top of Swanston Street to wait by the City Baths—a distinct smell again here, but stale and unpleasant—so that I could ride in the all-night tram that rocked and meandered through dull dead suburbs, taking home drunks and shift-workers and men from the newspaper offices.

She is in bed with the lights out, and she has packed the bolster down beside her, underneath the bed coverings, jammed between her long slender body and my side of the bed. 'You needn't have bothered, you know,' I say, after I have switched on the reading lamp. 'I intended sleeping in the lounge.' I had intended no such thing, but the absurdity of it offends me.

She switches on her own light then and sits up and arranges a mauve bedjacket of padded satin around her rather graceful shoulders. Her eyelids are tired and heavily drooping, with an oily smear of some lotion across them, not unbeguiling, and a fine golden hairnet solidifies the heavy blonded casque of her hair. There are lines, dimly marked, as if by a very sharp pencil, at the corners of her mouth, and a faint bruising at the cheekbones which could be fatigue, and that tired terror I have begun to notice in her eyes, an apprehension perhaps of a curtain falling on something that never really added up to what it might have been. The moody odour of her cosmetics has a stale pungency in the over-bright room.

'You're very late again,' she says, without rancour.

'I had things to do. People to see.'

'Mr Brewster rang you around nineish. He wants to see you tomorrow, something about your China articles. He said ten-thirty.' She lifts manicured hands—her hands are very lovely—to touch the set of her hair. 'You're going to South America?'

'Quite possibly. It's under discussion.'

'You might have told me.'

'Yes.'

'Especially on such a long assignment. Mr Brewster said two years. Why didn't you, David?'

'What?'

'Tell me.'

'You might have wanted to come.' I have a sense of confidence, a sudden wish for total candour.

'Yes, that was rather what I told Mr Brewster. He seemed quite surprised. That I hadn't known about it, I mean. Whom were you with tonight?'

'Nobody.'

'You just said you had people to see.'

'They weren't anybody. Why don't you toss that silly damn' thing out of the bed? It's all right, *I'm* not coming in with you. It's just so bloody ludicrous. As if I've surprised you practically in the act and you've got your lover skulking there under the blankets. For God's sake be your age, Helen!'

'I put it there simply because I'm tired of your coming in at all hours, more than half drunk, smelling of liquor and of other women.'

'What bloody nonsense! I'm going out to make myself some coffee.'

She has had this suspicion in her mind, of course, ever since that stupid Fred Kentish called at the flat on the Sunday evening, drunk as a lord and wearing his raffish licentiousness as if it were part of his DFC ribbon and his air force uniform, with two chorus-girls from the Tivoli in the cab outside. He had tried to talk me into going out on the tiles with him and the two girls. When I refused he sent the girls away and later tried to make a pass at Helen, then ended up spewing in the hallway and making a mess of everything. Helen wouldn't forget that evening. And I can't blame her, really. Kentish is a bastard of a problem. Only a few days after this shambles I saw him brawling in the bar of the Royal George with his old squadron-leader, who'd already been demobbed and was in civilian clothes. It was all to do with the squadron-leader having had an affair somewhere with Kentish's wife. It was an ugly, vicious brawl, but when it was done they embraced and clung together and wept all over each other, remembering all the other things they had shared besides Kentish's wife, and what they had been through.

What a bloody time and place to come back to, I muse to myself, thinking about this in the kitchen. I tip the coffee down the sink without drinking any, and when I go back I see she has pushed the bolster down to the bottom of the bed.

'David,' she says, looking at me wearily. 'David Meredith,' she says, and shakes her head slowly. 'How much longer do we intend to go on like this? Hasn't it gone on long enough? Isn't your resentment satisfied, not even yet? This time you haven't even tried, have you?'

I hesitate. I have to try to judge the angle of her attack. 'Have you?' I ask.

'I think I have. As much as you'd ever allow me to. I thought this place might work, the flat. I knew how you detested the house we had in Beverley Grove, although I always liked it there . . . and so . . . well, while you were away that's why I exchanged it for this flat. I thought when you came back the war would be over and you'd like it here, with your own study and everything, and you would try to settle down and make an attempt. But you haven't even begun to try. You haven't, have you?'

'I don't *want* to settle down.'

'The war is over.'

'What this war has done, my sweet, won't be over in your lifetime, or mine. For Christ's sake, you don't think I'm unique, do you? This whole bloody city's a caravanserai. People passing through. People—*just—passing—through*!'

'So I have just been informed. Indirectly, of course. If you don't mind my saying so.'

I look at her carefully, hating the way she drops into clichés like that. She sits up very straight, the way she walks, her head tiredly tipped back against the figured walnut headboard. She holds the padded bedjacket tightly around her as if she is cold. The chintz bedspread stiffly moulds the elegance of her legs. Her eyes are dull and steady and plead for nothing.

'There are a hundred thousand blokes in this town who don't want to settle down,' I say to her carefully. 'I'm not the only pebble on the beach.' (I use clichés too, I realize.) 'Blokes who've come back to something that wasn't here when they went away. The whole world a bloody mess of disillusion. Of anxiety, sexual betrayals all round, uncertainty. And this place is a damned sight worse than the others because it hasn't suffered as well. It hasn't *been* hurt. It's just done it to itself. Half these chaps who are rattling around the town . . . I bet you they wish now the war had just gone on and on. Do you know why? Because they had a place there. A *place*, do you understand? And now they're scared because they haven't got one. Nerves shot to blazes, kids shoved out into it at eighteen, straight from school, to fly fighters or bombers, and five years of that, and the looking after, and all the heady glamorous stuff that went with it, and now they're all shoved back here wondering what the hell has happened, what they're going to do now, why the—'

'Like your friend Kentish?'

'That's right. Like my friend Kentish.'

'A fine example!'

'That's right.'

'You weren't a fighter-pilot, David. You don't have a war neurosis. I hadn't thought so, anyway. In fact, in some ways I guess you had a fairly comfortable and probably a pretty pleasant war. Certainly an exciting one. *And* glamorous. After all, you were a war correspondent. *The* war correspondent.' I note the emphasis. 'You got around everywhere. You wrote your books . . .' She pauses, seeing me looking around. 'Cigarettes over there,' she says in the voice of habit. 'The ash-tray's beside you. I think I'd like one too.'

'And aside from all that—' I am watching her as I speak over the flame of the match, close up to her now, seeing the tired lines in her face—'we were better for each other when we were a few thousand miles apart. It suits us. We don't get in each other's hair so much. I write you regular fond letters, and—'

'I burnt them yesterday. All of them. They made a lot of smoke, David, but very little flame.'

I assemble the right sort of smile. 'I was also going to say I send you lots of presents. Nice things, too. Nothing tizzy.' She is not smiling back at me. 'All that stuff there in the lounge.'

'You were going in there, weren't you? Why don't you? You can go in and gloat over your gifts and go to sleep. Why don't you, David?'

'Because you are the one who is demanding explanations of why I haven't tried . . . to . . . to *what*? Patch it up? For God's sake, let's just skip it. Don't worry. I'll send you gorgeous things from South America.'

'I don't want gorgeous things from South America. I just want you to look at the set-up with some sort of . . . of honesty, and fairness.'

'Helen, it isn't something new between us.' I say this as gently as I can. 'We've both known it for years, darling. We grew out of each other a long time ago. And then there's been the war. It's changed us. We are two different people now.'

'Maybe this could change us back again. Peace, I mean. If war could do it, peace should be able to, shouldn't it? And this place. Us. If you were prepared to try. I'd be prepared to try.'

'Look, we're just parts of a thing that's happened, that's still happening, all over the world, all over this city. Why go on pretending?'

'We're not going on pretending. Come to think of it, that is something neither of us thought of trying. No, I just hoped . . . well, it doesn't matter, I suppose.' She moves her pillow down and kicks the bolster away. 'Why don't you go into the lounge, David? You're such a selfish bastard. And I'm terribly tired. I'm putting my light out now. I want to sleep.'

In the lounge, curled up uncomfortably below the Tibetan mask and the Japanese scrolls on the wall, among all the exonerating trivia I sent to her from distant places, I find some things becoming clearer. I do feel pity for her – not love any longer, nor desire, hardly even kindliness (for that could become a trap), but certainly a kind of pity. She has her journey in front of her now, out beyond the time of bravery and banners. As I have, too. All of us.

I think of the Chinese straggling across the Szechwan plain. It is now important, I tell myself, to cling to the improbable continuities.

WEST CHINA – JAPAN, 1945

Nothing has seemed quite real since we flew out of Chungking from the grassy, treacherous strip beside the Chialing. The moon faces of the Chinese delegation, nervous and sallow and chewing hard on American gum. All of us looking down as if trying desperately to memorize something we shall never see again. Up and over worn rocks and the black twists of pines and laboriously terraced paddies, and then the fringe of ochreous plains beyond the confluence of two ravined rivers.

It was there, just past a lean pagoda driven into a hilltop like a marking stake, that we saw them. An ant-horde of uncountable people disgorging from a central mat of human blackness that looked like a forest of some stunted growth, an immense and hardly believable spreading and scattering and trickling of Chinese moving on dubious destinies across a parched brown map. A million exiles setting out after nearly nine years of war to walk back to homes in distant provinces across a devastated land bigger again than my own country.

The crew-cropped navigator from Milwaukee pointed down and said, 'Some joe back in Chungking there, he figures it'll take most've these slopeys another nine years t'git home. I guess most've the poor bastards'll never make it.'

I tried to look back but a cloud scum had intervened and I could see nothing. I wanted to tell the navigator that on the previous morning, on the third day of peace, I had gone down from the steps below the Press Hostel to watch them setting out from their city of long exile. There had been an old woman in faded coolie blue with a treadle sewing-machine strapped to her back, and a wispily-bearded man with one trachoma-whitened eye who was bent double by the great weight of the sow he was carrying. I wanted to ease the weight of concern by telling the navigator that the Chinese, like their earth, had an infinite capacity for renewal. But he was making jokes now, and handing out sticks of Wrigley's to the Chinese passengers.

The world had rolled into a dry bruised dusk before we were clear of Szechwan, and in the early starless night over the velvet of Kwangsi the final battlefires still smouldered like the eyes of animals where a few months before I had gone with Conover in a slow jeep down from Kweilin through drought and death to Liuchow. And over Hong Kong all the lights of the island city came on quite suddenly as we were passing directly overhead: in the startling dazzle of these unanticipated jewels and brilliants, seen against a pewter sheen of island-studded ocean, the crew-chief gasped, '*Tracers!* Weren't they tracers?'

It was a funny little flutter of habituated panic in the man, for these were the lights of peace coming back to the world after years of darkness. This was, after all, an official flight into peace—China's delegation to accept surrender from the Japanese. He should have known that.

I knew it. The incident was valuable as a theme for copy, to be filed when the plane put down at Manila. Yet for all this it still seemed a little improbable, unreal. In a way, unwanted. Peace at press rates, filed Collect. They had even given it initials, VJ, like a serial-number or a code. It still seemed an unreliable source of confidence, not to be examined too stringently.

Afterwards, in the subjugated apathy of Yokohama, we had wooden blocks for pillows in the Bund Hotel and squat scared girls offered timidly to dance with us, and on the roads the Japs spat on our vehicles as we passed. There was a stink of putrid fish in the red and black shambles of Tokyo, and at Kawasaki, out of a tangled nightmare of steel girders rusted to the commonplace sanguine of blood, the prisoners crept from their holes, wild-eyed, skeletonic, timid as forest creatures, and watched the parcels of mercy raining down from an already weeping sky. They hadn't believed it either.

I have not been able to resolve this uncertainty about it all. I go everywhere I can seeking the texture of reality and proof, but everywhere it is elusive. It is not to be found in secluded Kyoto, where the sky weeps too, and they bring us *sake* and *geisha* to the empty hotel among the trees, and the robed priests walk apart from us in the temple gardens. Nor in Karuizawa, where we go to find the Butcher of Warsaw and find instead a little group of Russian collaborationists toasting the last Czar of All the Russias in Harbin vodka. I cannot find it in the face of the nervous little postal clerk in Tokyo who gives me, in the debris of the Ginza, the broken fragments of his pride—his treasured collection of overprinted stamps from the Asian and Pacific empire his country conquered and lost. What do I do with a thing like that?

At the surrender ceremony on the crowded decks of the *Missouri*, Shigemitsu limped, wearing a frock-coat and a black silk top-hat, and MacArthur used pen after souvenir pen to sign the documents that fix our futures.

But the sky kept on weeping in the melancholy of summer rain above the desecrated fused earth of Hiroshima, and in the hills twenty-five kilometres away, I sit with an exhausted Lutheran pastor beneath the softly dripping trees, bare-branched in summer above the sad carcases of birds tumbled on the earth and the smear of dead insects among the crimped dead leaves.

I find no glimpse of any reality for a future among any of these real things—if they are real—to which I have been a witness. There is no comfort yet in peace. There is hardly any triumph.

MELBOURNE, 1945

Gavin Turley was the shot. He would know. This was the conclusion I finally reached, after sleeping fitfully on the sofa, thinking in the wakeful times of all the things I might have said to Helen. About the brittle gaieties of her own war, her little court of brave Yankee colonels and gallant young majors. Yet there had really been nothing for which to forgive her. That was sad.

I left the flat early, without waking her or waiting for breakfast. After Peggy's death and with his war over, Gavin had never gone back to *Bangalore*, but I found him in a small flat above shops in Exhibition Street. A seedy building, fronting the street like a suppliant in cast-off rags, with two abashed and dismal shop-fronts, the one containing piles of secondhand books and an astronomical globe with a fist-size dent in it and what looked to be a coffee stain obliterating Orion and Eridanus; the other concealing rather than revealing a small jobbing printery. On buckled cardboard it exhibited faded, silver-printed wedding invitation cards beyond which one could vaguely make out an interior gloomy chiaroscuro of littered sheets and various prowling black machines with elongated limbs and wing-like flanges that gave them the appearance of pterodactyls foraging in primeval slime. Still clinging to the brick wall beside the window were the vestiges of a very old theatrical poster telling of Oscar Asche and *Chu Chin Chow*. On a sagging board above both shop-fronts it was still possible to decipher, through a mess of swallows' nests and birdlime, the grandiose legend ROYAL VENETIAN PALACE MART. The residential entrance was off a lane to one side, and up two narrow flights of scrappily linoleumed steps with most of the banisters missing. Above a landing a cracked plaster-cast of Beethoven's death-mask propped the broken bracket of a disused gas-mantle.

Yet the approach was deceptive, for the flat, although small and certainly in need of renovation, was sunny and pleasant and of good proportion. Gavin was in a faded dressing-gown and woollen football socks, making coffee. On a rack above the gas-stove an open book was propped, the pages held back by a clip clothes-peg.

The empty sleeve of his dressing-gown flapped excitement and pleasure as he bustled about to a crisp cannonade of talk.

'Bloody good to see you. You look fine, cock. Have some coffee. Thrice stewed, but fortifying. You must hate being back. In this shitty place. Sweep all that stuff off. Go on. Toss it on the floor. Anywhere. Only junk. I live in a midden of junk. Sugar there. No milk, I'm afraid. Biscuits in that tin if you want. Uneeda or Milk Arrowroot. Would have had Iced Baw Baws if I knew you were coming. Do ourselves well though, don't we? Bloody Australia! Land of rich resources. Home of the *bon vivant*, eh?'

Finally his great length subsided into a bulging armchair, the long legs folding in like the antennae of some probing insect. The black and red bands of the football socks aided the illusion. He showered himself with cigarette ash and grinned at me through big stained teeth.

I looked around and said, 'A bit different from *Bangalore*,' and he just nodded, waiting. 'Everybody here seems to be giving up their houses and taking little flats,' I said.

'That's right. The new nomadism. There's much restlessness in the air. Movement. Everything chopping and changing. Worming into little flats is a way of breaking us in. So we'll be used to it when we have to live in yurts. Or gunyahs.'

'We're in a little flat now. Helen, that is. Down in South Yarra.'

'I know it. Just a few blocks along from *Bangalore*. Used to drop in on Helen occasionally while you were away. Just casually, you know. She's been rather a lonely woman, David.'

'I had the impression she enjoyed any amount of company.'

'Nothing whatever to do with loneliness, surely?'

'We're splitting up,' I said. 'I'm leaving her.'

'Oh.' A blob of cigarette ash fell into his coffee, and he spooned it out and tapped it carefully into his saucer. Beyond the unruly dark mop of his hair a gust of cool wind flung powdery sprays of light through a bulging hessian curtain. 'That's a pity,' he said.

'Is it?'

'Nothing implied, cock. Just a general comment. The whole shitty situation. All personal relationships seem to be in a state of bloody chaos. Did you know the courts are sitting over the legal vacation to get through the backlog of divorce actions: they tell me three minutes is par for the course for an undefended action.'

'The war,' I said.

He looked at me carefully then. 'Yes, but you got a lot out of the war,' he said. 'It made you the big success. Our golden boy.' He kept looking at me. 'Perhaps that's the trouble,' he said. 'You could be still trapped in the double experience. Thus getting the perspective distorted. Part of the mystique of warring times. But we're done with the warring times, you see.'

'No, I don't see.'

'Remember Scott Fitzgerald thinking back, and hearing the Paris taxi-horns tootling out Debussy? What do the taxis tootle for you, Davy? *Warsaw Concerto*?'

I could see what he meant, and he was right in a way. The gusty breathing of the locomotives in the goods yard smelt of cities pulverized and far away. Ships still came and went in the river docks marked by numbers and alike in the anonymous grey of war. The bitter-sweet songs of the long years that had passed since that first explosive equinox of conflict, songs already nostalgic but not yet stale, jostled for position among the cadences of memory. My mind was stuffed with a war surplus of souvenired images—uniforms, army decorations, pin-up pictures clipped from magazines, coffee-grounds and khaki underwear, jeeps, flags, beards, clips on webbing, flight-bags, women's faces all wearing the same smile, smoke drift and gharri wheels, ricksha shafts and the black hollows in city alleys, oscillations on a radar screen, rubble heaps and white cement dust making plaster-casts of swollen corpses, and the charts of aircraft silhouettes pinned against bamboo slats. On the first night of my return I had hung up my uniform and put on the unfamiliar and oddly glamorous Donegal and grey flannels of earlier years, which Helen had thoughtfully preserved for me in a linen bag stuffed with moth-balls. But that had been my one gesture of exorcism, my only outward concession to change either in the times or in myself. I still felt that the long journey out from Szechwan had hardly even begun.

'And what do the taxi-horns play for you, Gavin?' I asked, looking at his empty sleeve and thinking of his dead wife.

'Oh, you don't *have* to hear them, cock. Like the wily Odysseus, one can always stuff one's ears with wax, you know. And then, since I'm being terribly literary this morning, we can always remember that aphorism of Kafka's—"and then he went back to his work as if nothing had happened".'

'How *can* you bloody well go back as if nothing had happened?'

'Why not, cock? And, anyway, what else? A lot of people will have to, won't they? I suppose I did all right out of it, really. Masses of gratuity and deferred pay and a cosy little pension as compensation for absent friends.' He flapped the empty sleeve at me. 'Do you know they even offered me a kind of hook thing, a sort of grapnel gadget instead of the old stump? Quite useful, I suppose, for holding a book while one's doing the cooking. In the end I decided for the rather more histrionic empty sleeve. Although I'll tell you something funny. The bloody thing doesn't look anywhere near as glamorous with a civvy jacket as it did with uniform. They should allow us as a special perk – the maimed, I mean – to go on prancing around in our panoply. Wouldn't you think? Even if only to stimulate the good old jingo spirit. As it is, we're simply handed to the pacifists on a plate.'

As I was leaving he said, 'Do you remember Cress Morley?'

'I do indeed,' I said.

'Ran into her the other day. We talked about you. She'd seen in the *Post* that you were back.'

'Is she still in the army?'

'Yes. A lieutenant now. About to be discharged, I gather.'

'I'd like to contact her,' I said, remembering her.

'Yes. Everybody would. You can get her at LHQ. Victoria Barracks switch will put you through. Ask for Publications. But do be careful, cock.'

'Careful?'

'I'm not thinking of you. Careful of her, I mean. She's rare. One of the rare ones. Don't spoil her. In fact, if you want my advice, and clearly you don't, I shouldn't get involved with her at all.'

'Why do you say that?'

'You two would destroy each other. You wouldn't last six months together.'

SYDNEY, 1966

Meredith had to try to piece it all together, seeking it where he could in the narrow tight slots of clarity lying between the great fields of pain flinging out of himself and away and back into a past where it no longer hurt. Oceans and continents and vast plains of pain that having been experienced and endured could not hurt any more, but still had to be flung away and back to make room for new experiences of pain. There were times when he felt the whole secret almost to be within his grasp.

There was neither night nor day in the windowless Recovery Room, only the cold noncommittal gleam of the tube lights and the white walls alive with the hiss and suck of oxygen, so that time existed only as an abstract in the endless flinging recession of the sheets of pain dropping into a past composed entirely of fragmented things he didn't have to go through any more. He felt elated at this discovery that all experience, even the most painful, turned into something that no longer had to be experienced.

He wished he could make this revelation known to Cress. He was aware of her from time to time standing beside the trolley—whether night- or day-visiting he never knew—sterile-capped and masked like the sisters and nurses who bent over him like wind-blown flowers with attentive, caring eyes. But then he could make nothing known to Cressida, apart from primitive soothings and encouragements through the pressure of their intertwined fingers, because there was a plastic thing in his throat and a tube running from it to the oxygen valve, so he had no voice and no way of communicating except through the fingers and the movement of his eyes under the sweat and tangle of hair and forehead. Sometimes they doused him with floods of cold water, then turned an electric fan on him.

He was sorry he could not communicate what he had discovered or at least begun to suspect, because the importance of it needed to be made clear, to Cressida in particular, but also to thoracic - part of body between neck and belly same as thorax.

those on the other trolleys. There were only three other trolleys in the Recovery Room, so he must have been in there for a good many days, because there had been quite a number of these other people who came and went from the operating-theatre. The faces of one or two he recognized from the thoracic ward below, but they had been poised then on vertical bodies being prepared for surgery, walking around in dressing-gowns and doing breathing exercises under the fingery manipulations of the girl physiotherapist in white. One of them, Petros the Greek, had not really been vertical because he had no legs and was only a strong, swarthy face and a thick torso with the powerful chest and strong arms of the legless, but Meredith had met him once or twice in his wheelchair in the toilets or waiting to use the ward telephone. He had never spoken to him, though, and he had not known he was a Greek until he had heard him groaning and raving away in the Recovery Room. Meredith would have liked to have spoken to him. Often when the white curtains were slid back on their ceiling runners they would look at each other across an expressionless plain of mutual pain, and Meredith would have liked to have said something encouraging, surprising him with the Greek words coming out of the Australian face – *Te kanete, Kyrie Petros* or *Then pirazi* or *Perastika sou* – but with this thing in his throat that made him mute there was no way of saying anything at all to Petros, who just lay there, strong and unexpectant and broken off, like part of a sea-worn old ship's figurehead washed up. At some stage he was not there any longer, and a long time after, when Meredith was recovering, he heard that Petros had gone in again for additional surgery and had died under the anaesthetic.

But there were others to take the place of Petros – a clownish vocal Russian migrant who was visited by a short, stout, Jewish woman who stood by him tongue-tied and scared, incongruous in the white medical mask below the black peasant's babushka, making queer little ritual gestures like forms of magic; a boy of fourteen who didn't seem frightened at all; a youth with a chest staved in by an automobile accident who stared all the time at the blazing white of the ceiling. And the social woman. Meredith thought of her as the social woman. She was a terrible mess of crushed bones beneath the sheet and she had a face that had once been very beautiful and was still comely. She was only flickeringly conscious. She looked to be about the same age as Cressida, only more tired, which was understandable. A number of different men visited her, all staring down without ever saying anything, their eyes above the white masks hurt and helpless. Meredith thought of them as the woman's lovers, although they could have been only business associates or relatives. In the circumstances who they really were didn't matter.

So Meredith lay for a long time in this timeless area that was concerned with pain yet lay beyond the reality of pain (only much later did he learn that for thirteen days he had existed very precariously on the razor-edge between living and dying), listening to the hiss and suck of the oxygen and the insectine clicking of the Bird's machine pumping a measured, plastic-tasting, rubber-smelling continuance in through his neck where sharp grits of pain were lodged, hearing the dislodged talk of the nurses and their inappropriate laughter, and wishing that he could convey to Cressida the exultation he felt about finally *knowing*.

When he had been a small boy in Melbourne there had been two little mechanical mannikins in the window of Cole's Book Arcade, dressed as Jack Tars, little dolls really, which worked at a kind of windlass thing which flung over, rhythmically but jerkily, oblong boards printed with statements like COMIC BOOKS, FICTION FOR ALL AGES, GAMES AND PUZZLES, NOVELTIES AND STATIONERY, THE GROTTO AND ACQUARIUM, GIFT BAZAAR. Meredith was reminded of this by the way the sheets of pain moved, as if there was a toy windlass inside him, moving it out of him in flinging, slapping jerks. At first, in the shadowy clefts and apertures between the jerks, the remembered ghosts had gathered, but later they had all vanished to make room for the clarity of the revelation. It was the clarity that was the special thing about it. (It was quite remarkable that after all those years he could still remember that Cole's Book Arcade had spelt AQUARIUM incorrectly.)

Later, as he gradually got better, the clear vision of his revelation slowly faded from his mind, and long before he could write it down, or talk about it, he had forgotten what it was.

ATHENS, 1959

He knew where the beginning of that part was, if anything could be said to have a beginning.

When he had come out again into Righillis Street he had found the day unexpectedly bigger and brighter, as if the circle of sage-mauve mountains with the singing names had made a big effort while he had been inside and had shouldered the clouds higher. The heavily handsome glass and iron door of the apartments where Dr Georgaikis had his practice whispered behind him, folding the centrally heated air in after his departure with a soft click like a furtive footstep. The apartments faced a sordid vacant lot with trodden ramps of clay and half completed excavations holding yellow rain from the night before, and the abandoned shafts of reinforced concrete with bent spines of steel crooked against Hymettos catching the morning light were the sad notations of Athens in transition. How it had all changed in just a few years. Was still changing. The parched tingling smell of cement dust came at him on the cold fitful wind, not from the vacant lot, where nothing was happening, but from the hideous new buildings all around where concrete-mixers were chattering and shovels stirring thickly at the grey muckheaps, and diminutive men in shabby clothes were climbing ladders behind rough palisades covered with chalky dust. On some buildings whole façades were hidden by vast ugly screens of sewn sacking darkened by wet patches. But the dust still drifted.

He could still see the particular expression on the doctor's face when he had been admitted from the waiting-room. A little flick as of something being withdrawn or concealed, like a drawer being closed or a hand laid across something written. Then the over-frowning, pretended absorption in the papers on the desk, that artificial trick of tapping at his pockets and testily pushing aside the piled-up trade bulletins and brochures from the drug houses.

'I shall want you to come back here this evening, Mr Meredith,' he had said, frowning again, as if some other thought had abstracted his concentration. 'Around eight, after surgery hours,' he said in his precise, unaccented English. 'We shall want to have a little talk. And by then I shall have seen the radiologist's report on the X-rays.'

A smile then, friendly and fleeting, although his pale eyes seemed still to be searching for something he had mislaid.

So there were nearly ten hours to be filled in before the verdict, Meredith thought, walking up past the Royal Palace to the thick green wall of the gardens where two Evzone guards in frilly skirts and white stockings and pompom shoes slow-marched and turned, balletic figures outside the toy props of the sentry-boxes. Their dark eyes as he passed, so much younger than his, slantingly watched him from beneath tasselled skullcaps.

He thought of Cressida four hours away . . . more, really, because the *Nereida* would have left Piraeus already on its scurrying daily Odyssey through the Saronic islands: by this time it would be coming up to Aegina, with *bouzouki* playing and old Dimitri raffling his big fish among the passengers and the boys selling pistachio nuts. He thought painfully of Cressida, and of blurred and brilliant white houses spilling down the rock amphitheatre to the crescent harbour and the dark dance of the Aegean seas, and Cressida in one of the white houses making coffee in the cool flagged kitchen. It was hard to imagine all this down there beyond the smear-fume of the Piraeus factories. Meredith wondered if *he* would be there, with her in the kitchen.

The thought came lunging at him, so unexpectedly that he stared at the people waiting on the corner as if they might be able to explain it to him, but they were watching the traffic policeman in the nickel helmet and the only one who seemed interested in him was a shabby lottery-seller with his long slotted stick of lucky tickets, but he was only interested in selling him a number. It was a quite definite feeling he had about Cressida, more than just a vague suspicion, more than drawing conclusions from what Calverton had said on the day of the picnic. Or did Calverton know more than he had let on?

The traffic policeman blew his whistle and flicked his gloved hand impatiently and Meredith, crossing with the crowd, set himself deliberately to think of something else.

So Meredith thought of the ten hours that would have to be filled in, of murder trials he had covered at the Old Bailey, before they had come to Greece, when he had been a newspaper correspondent in London. Sometimes the jury had been out ten hours or even longer before they filed back to the benches bearing gravity like some miraculous ikon, and the prisoner would be brought in and held there standing between two stiff, bulb-eyed constables while the jury foreman recited the verdict in a voice scratched by solemnity.

The plummeting traffic rush of Queen Sophia Street was a nervous tumult of hurry beneath the sedate, slow lift of the flags on the legations and the embassies, behind the sedate, slow posturings of the Evzones. On Syntagma, beyond the flower-vendors, the coffee-tables were laid out neatly like a rare collection of postage stamps hinged to the page of an album. The chill wind was tugging at the artificial-looking oranges in the trees and nobody was seated at the postage-stamp tables. Meredith chose a table exactly in the centre of the square, and arranged another set of thoughts.

When he had got up in the cheap little hole down near the Temple of the Winds and was dressing for the appointment with Dr Georgaikis he had made a point of pulling on his left sock first, which he remembered always having done as a child for the good luck of the day, and then, when he was lacing his shoes, he saw with pleasure that he had put both socks on inside-out. He left them that way. As he went out through the swing doors of the hotel the first thing he saw was a white horse drawing a shallow, decorated little cart laden with cut flowers and potted ferns to the flower stalls outside the church in the Plateia Agia Irini. He resisted the temptation to spit-wet his finger and mark a cross on the toecap of his shoe and mutter the incantation, 'First luck white horse!' Walking up Kolokotronis Street towards the old palace, he made a careful point of dodging around two step-ladders which straddled the pavement. Nearer the end of the street there was a third ladder and he thought of boldly walking beneath it, but when he came close to it he saw that four thin cords had been tied between the rungs and the iron grille of a shop window, so that nobody could pass beneath the ladder anyway, and he had to pick his way around it through a pile of cement rubble, a tangle of traffic, and a shrieking argument between a barrow pedlar and a taxi-driver.

And now at Syntagma, sipping Turkish coffee and cognac, he could afford to be amused at these childish superstitions. He knew very well what the medical diagnosis was going to be. He was the age for it, his chain-smoking and his nervous disposition gave it validity, and three of his best friends—all of them news-papermen—had died of it. This was why he had so stubbornly resisted all Cressida's worried pleas that he should come up to Athens and see a doctor, until he had lost so much weight it could be put off no longer. Although in the end it had really been Calverton who had persuaded him. It all went back, of course, to the affair with Jacques—had there been an affair? he had never really known, although Jacques had been emphatic enough—and all the anxiety and the drinking that winter, and then the pneumonia, and the dreadful precariousness of their position in Greece, and his fear of having to be forced back again into society. Now that the examination had become a *fait accompli* and he was aware what the verdict was going to be, he felt very calm about it all. As if a difficult problem finally had been resolved. Not relief so much as release.

He left Syntagma then and walked for hours through Plaka and the old section of Athens, taking a beer at a roadside stall and a *pita* with *souvlakia* from the barrow of a kerbside vendor. He still loved the old part of the city in spite of the new concrete monstrosities and the blowing cement dust, and on this day it seemed to assemble itself for him with a kind of limpid innocence:

cabalistic - (cabal) small group of intriguers; secret plot.

for the first time he seemed to see it with a child's unsullied eye—the subtle blending of colour wash over colour wash on crumbling stucco walls in shabby streets, white lace in dark cool windows, a spider's weave among the rank growth of nettles, a tarnished doorknocker in the form of a turbaned head, a charcoal fire kindled beside a pale chipped door, a knife-blade stirring sparks from spinning emery in dark Promethean caves that smelt of flux and solder. Meredith would stoop to rub a finger along a grooved edge of ancient marble surviving as a threshold, stop to pick a feather from a crevice in a wall, touch the nubbled skin of a *frappa* in passing a fruit stall. He watched children absorbed by devices in the dust or chalking their cabalistic *graffiti* on the ruined walls of a library that had once been Hadrian's. Along Pandrossu, where shoes hung like the fruits of strange trees, a tray-bearing vendor of spectacles shouted his enticement, 'Glasses for long sight and short sight!' And in Monasteraiki, amid the copper and the brass and the hot iron smells, and the dust and garlic, there were blue beads on the donkeys and the goats had the eyes of agates, and a cockerel of beaten gold strutted among the steam-pressed ducoed taxis. A woman was weaving chair-seats out of rushes. The carpet men were down from Macedonia.

It was not until late afternoon that he realized how weary he had become. He was coughing badly, so he found a table outside a coffee-house on a busy street, from where he could see past a jittery-bright Telefunken sign to the austere columns of the Parthenon standing theatrically on the rumpled grey-pink burlap of the Acropolis. He had once thought of writing two novels, one on Peisistratus and one on Pheidias. Up there the pale, fluted, saffron-washed marble had looked down on twenty-five centuries of mortal ambitions, the important ones and the trivial ones, and watched them all blow past like the cement dust in the air.

The panic hit him with the coming of Nitsa: her spiky heels castanet-rapping against the marble pavement squares seemed to rhythm the sudden quick beating of his heart.

He had known her less than well—a transient summer visitor to the island whom he had distantly admired for her beauty and

ebullience - exuberant, boiling
rotogravure

vaguely envied for her youthful ebullience – but he grasped at her coming now with a desperate familiarity, springing to his feet and greeting her as if they were the most intimate of friends. She remembered him and responded with a smile that was warm enough, but would not stay and have a drink with him.

'I have to make a plane. I'm on my way to the terminal now. Love to some other time. Some other flight, perhaps . . .'

He remembered now, she was an air hostess – stewardess? what did they call them? – on one of the Continental airlines. Which one? Olympic probably, since she was Greek. There had been a crash the day before in a storm over the Pindos, everyone killed. The newspapers had been full of it, and those sickening grey pictures of torn earth and litter. He would have to dodge any mention of that, find some other point of conversation that would hold her, bring her to his table, seat her beside him.

'Oh, come on, you must have a minute,' he pleaded.

'No. It was one of our planes that crashed yesterday,' Nitsa said brightly, smiling at him. 'So we all have to be very perky. Couldn't afford to be late, you see. But I'd love to some other time. I really would.'

She was gone with the same warm smile, and the prickling quick clatter of her heels on the marble rapped the cold little studs of fear into Meredith's heart. There could be no tactlessness for Nitsa in death or disaster. She had the onward rattling of those high spiky heels to guide her.

After she was gone Meredith felt cold and afraid and alone. The sky had turned the colour of curdled cream except in the west above the factory reek of Eleusis, where it was growing dark and yellowish like something putrescent. Reek and stench now when there had once been ancient mysteries. All the world was turning into something else.

He set out for the surgery, walking very slowly, taking the longest route: even so he was twenty minutes early for the appointment and had to wait alone in the dull waiting-room with the German rotogravure magazines.

'As I thought,' Dr Georgaikis was saying, carefully studying his own impacted fingers, 'pulmonary tuberculosis, certainly not serious, not these days. A shadow on the upper right lung, fairly trivial really, an area rather more extensive high on the left lung. Your traditional writers' disease, eh, Mr Meredith? The Brontës. Keats. Kafka. All the rest of them. But hardly to worry about these days. Drugs, rest, care, peace of mind, you will be right in no time. You've a good tough constitution. Nothing malignant, thank goodness. There will, of course, need to be some readjustment in your way of life. We shall have to do something about your smoking. *And* your drinking. Particularly, you must try not to worry about anything. Peace of mind is what we are after. Simply that, Mr Meredith. Simply that.'

When he came out the sky was a swinging glitter of stars like powdered ice, and the street was deserted beneath the dark banks of its pepper-trees, and he walked slowly across the road and down one of the clay ramps to the empty allotment. He had an appalling feeling that there was nowhere else for him to go. He sat on a heap of soil and shingle and stared down at a stagnant pool of water in which the star-sheen swam like tiny fishes.

Crossing the road, he must have grabbed at the hanging foliage of the pepper-trees because he could smell the crushed pink of the corns on his fingers. The smell brought back images of his childhood, and then the other, later images began to jostle in. Meredith sank his head into his hands and wished that he was dead.

SYDNEY, 1968

It will all come together, I am sure, like the pieces of a mosaic or the scattered chips in a kaleidoscope. At the moment it's a mess. Ruptured syntax. This wild leaping around through time and space. First person one minute, third person the next. It doesn't matter. I am not trying to write, just setting things down to get them straight. After all, none of us is first person all the time; we can be third person, too, and sometimes no person at all, only a space filled around by other people: we can no more claim a consistency of εγψ in the Greek sense than we can really believe we are a part of a sustained and forward-flowing chronology. I think I prefer the kaleidoscope image. The shaking of the fragmented chips, the patterns forming at random. This is easier than believing in a planned design.

MELBOURNE, 1945

Mr Brewster[1] leaned well back in his rosewood editorial chair, studied the ceiling intently, closed his eyes against whatever it was he saw there, and with something of an effort linked his fingers across the great globe of his paunch.

The thought crossed my mind that if his belly had been fashioned of something solid and durable, and not just guts and flesh and unhealthy living and flatulence, a Brunelleschi would have had to throw the dome.

'Let us deal,' he said, 'with the China articles first. I personally found them fascinating, David. Powerful. A most revealing series. I am quite genuinely sorry that we shan't be able to use them.'

'*Not* use them? Why?' I crouched forward in the deep leather armchair. Mr Brewster opened his eyes and peered keenly at the ceiling moulding. He twitched one nostril, as if he were taking snuff.

'Policy. Yes, my decision is to do with policy. By running them we should be playing into inimical hands.'

'But . . . but you asked me to write them, and—'

'I did.' He performed a ponderous forward tilting movement to meet my anxious inquiry: his eyes swivelled down from their high focus, his soft pudgy hands moved forward to touch the edges of his blotter, the swivel-chair canted to the horizontal, and his neat little feet, which had been dangling in the air, came to rest like points on the Persian carpet. 'I even instructed you to pull no punches. And you pulled no punches. The three articles therefore do present a most outspoken and forthright attack. An indictment, one might even say.'

'But I understood that was what you wanted.'

'An indictment,' he went on calmly, 'not only of the *Kuo-mintang*, but of the entire régime—Kung, the Soongs, even Chiang himself and Madame. *Especially* Madame.'

'That's right. It was intended as an indictment. Surely it's high time.'

'That there has been a lamentable record of political corruption in Nationalist China no intelligent person would be prepared to deny.' He took up a paper-knife, tapped the point gently into his palm, and cleared his throat. 'Unfortunately, however, we have to consider choosing the lesser of two evils. And I am afraid, David, that in the general tone of these articles of yours it is difficult not to detect a . . . well, let us say a sympathy for the Chinese Communists. Our readers certainly would interpret the pieces as being pro-Communist.'

'My sympathy, if you want to know, is for those millions of poor devils over there who've had the stuffing kicked out of them for generations by every Tom, Dick or Harry who comes along. I'm not interested in party lines. Communism, or any other Ism. What I am interested in is seeing that China gets a chance of looking at real democracy working for a change. They never have seen it.'

'You were in Yenan with the Chinese Reds?'

'I went up there, yes.'

'They impressed you?'

'Yes.'

'You met their leaders. You interviewed them. These are extremely astute people, David. Perhaps they have influenced you more than you realize.'

For a long moment I could only stare at him. 'But good God,' I protested, 'going up to visit them doesn't *ipso facto* turn *me* into one of them! I went into Tibet, but I didn't come out preaching Lamaism. Interviewing Gandhi didn't make me rush out and buy a spinning-wheel.'

'There's no need to get hot under the collar about this, boy,' Mr Brewster said soothingly.

'I am not getting hot under the collar. I'm only saying that China is something we ought to know the truth about. We've never been able to tell the truth. Not under *that* sort of censorship. Not until now.'

'I quite understand your professional enthusiasm. But we are a conservative newspaper and we take the conservative policy line. And the conservative view – and this, remember, has dictated the bulk of high-level policy in Europe since the collapse of the Nazis – is containment of international Communism. It *is* a threat, David. A very real threat. And we should be betraying all our best beliefs were we to disregard this fact.' He put the paper-knife to one side. 'Your articles, therefore, although quite admirable in every other respect, we feel to be dangerous from a policy point of view. And so, with a measure of regret, we have no alternative but to spike them.'

'You are the managing editor,' I said grudgingly.

'Just as a point of interest, I did not rely solely on my own judgment. I gave them to Harvey Tseng to look over. You know Tseng?'

I nodded, waiting.

'With the Consulate here. Great little chap. Most charming. He gives a monthly dinner-party at his house in South Yarra, with the most fabulous Chinese chow. Pamela and I have been going along there for years. We wouldn't miss one of Tseng's parties for – ' he chuckled – 'I was going to say for all the tea in China. Yes – well, Tseng read your articles and said he found them most interesting and stimulating. He disputed some of your conclusions, which I suppose is natural enough, but the point is he most strongly advised against publication. Rather on the grounds we have already discussed.'

'Harvey Tseng,' I said, really angry now, 'is the little bastard who kept cabling back to Chungking stuff from my dispatches, all out of their context, to try to get me black-listed and thrown out of the theatre! Tseng is nothing but a rotten little *Kuo-min-tang* pimp!'

Mr Brewster, obviously taken aback by this outburst, blinked several times, smacked his lips together noisily, crisply tapped the blotter with both hands, and became testy. 'Oh, come, come now, Meredith,' he said. 'You are being unnecessarily temperamental. And you are also being completely wrong about Tseng. *And* unfair. In point of fact, he is one of your most ardent admirers. Always most warm in his tributes to your work. I might add that he has been pressing me for some time to bring you along to one of his dinner-parties. He even—'

'You'll have to apologize for me. Tell him I don't use chopsticks.'

'You are taking a most curious attitude.'

'It wasn't worth it, was it?'

'What?'

'The war. It wasn't worth it, was it? I mean all those millions who are dead now. We haven't even begun to clean up the mess from it, and here we are busily trying to arrange the next one.'

'You are simply piqued by this decision about your articles, Meredith. And being absurdly emotional. Is it wiser, in your opinion, to offer aid and sympathy to those who are against us, than to forgive the shortcomings of those who are on our side?'

'Earlier this year in China, there was drought and famine in Kwangsi Province, and I drove a jeep down a road through a hundred thousand dead bodies.'

'Nobody is disputing that you have had remarkable experiences. Marvellous experiences.'

'Those hundred thousand were all dead, you might remember, because a clique of *Kuo-min-tang* bastards like Harvey Tseng were manipulating the currency market. They made the best part of eight million American dollars out of their little racket. What do a hundred thousand dead matter?'

He opened his mouth as if to say something, closed it again, and frowned at the wall-clock. 'I must be in the boardroom in precisely seven minutes,' he said impatiently. 'So it behoves us to move on to the next subject without delay.' He consulted his desk pad and said, 'The proposed South American assignment. Miss Pilkington's memorandum informs me that to date we have attempted to secure bookings for you on no fewer than seven ships. In each instance we have had to forfeit priority since all these vessels have been taken over to transport the wives of American servicemen. In the circumstances I have asked Miss Pilkington to discontinue these abortive approaches for the time being.'

'The assignment is off, you mean?'

'Not necessarily *off*. But certainly indefinitely postponed. Well, South America has been there for some considerable time, and will still be there, I trust, a year or so from now.' He paused, smiling, but I could only look at him bleakly. 'I dare say your wife will be pleased. I was talking to her last night on the telephone. She has been a very lonely woman, David. After all, she has had her share of the long absences. This change of plans will give you a chance to be together, to get back to normality.' He smiled even more, to indicate that he had forgiven me my outburst. 'However,' he continued expansively, 'I have something else in mind which I think might overcome your disappointment over South America, and even make you feel somewhat less contentious about your China pieces. In a nutshell, then – for this board meeting is pressing me – we have decided to cease publishing the old *Rural Record*. A mercy killing, really. It has been moribund for years, and the war, I am afraid, has been responsible for its quietus. This means we shall have machine time to devote to something else, and so we intend to launch an entirely new weekly magazine. A *popular* magazine. Something very modern and lively, with a progressive urban outlook. Young, vigorous, sophisticated. All rotogravure. Good splashes of colour. What we want is a magazine of general reader-interest, to get into the quiet of the suburbs as well as the bustle of the metropolis, with the emphasis on this new, dynamic, postwar world we are entering.'

He was tilted back in his chair again, eyes closed, hands clasped across his paunch, dreaming his dreams. 'This country of ours, boy, has hardly tapped its energies yet. And a country, remember, tempered and hardened in the forge of war. A land of immense, indeed of boundless opportunity. We are going places, David, and what we want to do is to give a lead toward this vision splendid.' He came forward again and opened his eyes. '*Vision.* That is what we plan to call the magazine. *Vision.*' His eyes creased into little pink pouches of benevolence. 'We have decided, David, to appoint you editor of this new project. The full board met yesterday afternoon and agreed unanimously to my recommendation.' He waited, with a side glance at the wall-clock, but I could only stare at him. 'Well?' he said. 'What do you have to say about it?'

'I don't know. It . . . it's hard to say anything. There have been rather too many shocks this morning.'

'Think about it, boy. We shall be talking much more anon. But I really must hurry off to this meeting now. By the way, those articles of yours are here on my table if you wish to preserve them. Dash it all, you can put the stuff in a book if it weighs on your conscience.'

He manoeuvred himself from the desk with a grunt, grasped a folder of papers, and made towards the door, furiously puffing. I closed the door behind him and walked back slowly and eased myself gently into his rosewood chair.

I could see the trap quite clearly. There was no escape to South America, no escape from Helen, no continuation of the improbable continuities. The offer, instead, of the chains of office and the sleazy little securities. Conformity. Safety. The sad suburban rectitudes. At Teng-yueh, during the plague epidemic, the Chinese had thought that the disease came in an invisible miasma rising from the ground, drowning and killing the small creatures first, and then the larger ones, and finally man himself. A miasma. That was what this was like, a miasma rising up out of the twisted hatefulness of the city, something unseen and unheard and even unsuspected, engulfing and destructive. One day perhaps it would spread everywhere, and engulf the whole country.

It was quite a long time before I reached over to the desk and picked up the stapled sheets of the three articles, and for a while I stared at the typescript without reading it, then I slowly tore excrescence- unnatural outgrowth; growing out of redundant.

the sheets this way and that way and dropped the pieces into Mr Brewster's waste-paper basket, and when this was done I lifted the receiver from one of Mr Brewster's four telephones.

'Miss Pilkington?' I said. 'I wonder could you get me LHQ, Victoria Barracks, please. I want to speak to Lieutenant Morley. Publications.'

MELBOURNE, 1945

There was an hotel in Elizabeth Street, next to the central post office, facing a shabby edifice which was very notorious in Melbourne at that time, a place known as the Tin Shed (for that was unabashedly what it was), some sort of surviving temporary postal annexe that was always being cartooned and maligned in the newspapers as a 'civic eye-sore'. (Melbourne people have always been great ones to take affront at anything smacking of a civic eyesore.) The hotel next to the shameful and offending shed was naturally known as the Tin Shed Hotel, although its correct name, the Post Office Hotel, was there in broken letters above the name of the licensee, one Aaron Riordan, a gentleman of considerable eccentricity, who encouraged the common misnomer since it gained for his establishment a good deal of free publicity. Riordan had a big board behind the saloon bar on which he pinned up all the printed diatribes, polemics, cartoons, and indignant editorials concerning the adjacent excrescence, sometimes adding pithy comments of his own.

I cannot remember how it was exactly that Cressida and I came to stay that first night at Riordan's hotel, which normally had a rather specialized clientele, Riordan having a soft heart for the more or less unsuccessful fringe people of Melbourne society—vaudeville and circus artistes in particular, but also seedy race-course tipsters, hucksters of one sort or another, side-show people, and battered punchy pugilists who had reached the stage where they would be lucky to get an occasional prelim bout at the Fitzroy Stadium.

I must have taken Cressida there after having shaken off the pestering English naval officer who had wanted to drive her home in his Bentley, knowing that Riordan would let us have a drink upstairs after hours.

For me, that was the last of the era that was coloured by the true and particular exuberance of what Gavin had called the warring times. There had been the meeting with Cressida Morley, still trim and upright in her khaki uniform, much grown up in the year since I had last seen her, much lovelier than I had remembered, with lieutenant's pips on her shoulders; the English officer's drunken insistence on joining us; the raffish bedlam of Riordan's after closing time; a drunken American corporal playing 'The Atcheson, Topeka and the Sante Fe' over and over on a battered juke-box; the continuing free-and-easy moralities of the earlier time; and the meeting upstairs with Archie Calverton[2] and Beazley. It was as if everything unconventional and wayward and unpredictable was being preserved for some strong and unspecified reason: there seemed to be a tacit guarantee that whatever relationship developed between Cressida and myself it would for ever remain a little out of true with the orthodox values. We stayed all night together, and the difference between getting home to Helen at two or three in the morning and not getting home to her at all filled me with the strongest sense of commitment.

Archie Calverton and Beazley were in the upstairs dining-room when Riordan took us there for some illicit drinks; they had both been newspapermen before the war, but now they were working as script-writers for a popular radio comedian and were down from Sydney working on a show. Beazley was past fifty and Calverton not yet thirty, but both men had similar oldish, pinched, weary faces, and they lived in a constant wise-cracking dialogue maintained solely for the purpose of accidentally stumbling on good gags. Each carried a reporter's notebook and a pocketful of pens and sharpened lead pencils with which to jot down anything promising that came out of their interminable repartee, which some people found hilariously funny and others considered very tiresome. They were always shoving

Benzedrine inhalers into their nostrils and sniffing.

We had some drinks with them, and Calverton, who dreamt of becoming an actor, explained that they had to stay up and work right through the night to complete a script which conviviality and a race meeting at Moonee Valley had interrupted, and indicated that it would be perfectly all right if Cressida and I cared to make use of their hotel bedroom. 'Contraceptives in my overnight bag if you need them,' Calverton said helpfully.

In the morning, having slept little and loved generously, we sat together entranced, while the sad, colourless, city light groped through grimy window-panes and outside a fat bored pigeon pecked at nothing on a granite cornice frosted with birdlime and drizzling rain gurgled in the downpipes. Cressida sat on the edge of the shabby rumpled bed and quoted *Preludes* all the way through—she seemed to know all of Eliot by heart—and I remembered that the very first time I had met her, when she had been the gamin corporal of the anti-aircraft gunpit, she had been reading *Tristram Shandy*. 'Oh my God you're beautiful!' I said, and reached for her and pulled her down into my arms again and the warm enchantment of the bed. Later, when she was dressing in her severe neat uniform and arranging the knot of her tie, I told her that I loved her and said, 'Will you come away with me?'

'Where?' she said.

'I don't know. Somewhere. Somewhere away from here.'

'That's very vague,' she said, and paused, thoughtfully looking at me with those incredible green eyes. 'But yes, I think I'll come with you. You probably don't remember, but the last time we met you'd been to Venezuela, and you promised to take me there.'

'Did I?' I laughed. 'Well, I don't think now that I'll be going back to Venezuela. But I'll take you somewhere. I'll take you to Rome. And London and Paris and Athens.'

'What about your wife?' she said quietly.

'That's finished,' I said. 'I've left her.'

'Then what about your job?'

'I'm quitting that too,' I said.

'Oh,' she said. 'You are being serious about this, then?'

'I've never been more serious in my life.'

'But why? What's the reason?'

'I don't think I know. Not yet. Not really. I just don't want to be trapped in this bloody place. I don't want to fall into these awful dull ruts. I don't want to end up living in some dreary bloody suburb growing antirrhinums.'

She laughed then, and after a moment said, 'But aren't you taking awful risks? It won't be easy, will it?'

'I don't know. It might be. It should be easier than trying to put up with what *they* offer.'

'It mightn't be easier with me. You don't really know anything about me.'

'I know everything I want to know. I know I love you.'

'I'll come with you, darling,' she said. 'I don't know what *I* can offer. Or what I can promise. Except . . .' She came then and lifted her face to me. 'Except no antirrhinums,' she said.

When we went down to breakfast the same cheerless light had invaded the scruffy, antiquated dining-room, which still had tatty antimacassars over faded plush chairbacks and dusty gas-lamps in crooked brass brackets and a framed faded photograph of Phar Lap winning the Melbourne Cup. Calverton and Beazley were in deep sleep over the ash-littered table, their heads down on their shirt-sleeves and an empty whisky bottle tumbled beside their Benzedrine inhalers.

It all kept turning on the ratchet of improbability, because almost at once the Five Faltinis, with the FF monograms printed on the fronts of their white cotton gym-shirts, came cart-wheeling in through the door, one after the other, in diminishing sizes, with grave faces and an immense professional *esprit*. The Faltinis were 'resting' at the time, midway between the end of a low-billing run with the Tivoli Circuit and the seasonal opening of Wirth's Circus ('The Greatest Show on Earth') and it seemed they offered this matutinal performance of their acrobatic skill as some substitute for the board and lodging they were unable to pay. Riordan seemed unmoved by their nimble somersaults. He was standing by the broken billiard-table he used for stacking dishes, looking at their antics with a hardened eye; then he went across to their table with five plates of fried eggs and bacon miraculously hooked within the fingers of one hand.

'Maybe you can't bloody well pay for your rooms,' he querulously admonished them, 'but at least you might try to kick in with a few bloody butter coupons!'

Cressida reached out across the table and took my hand. 'No antirrhinums, darling,' she whispered. I could feel myself sinking into the cloudy green swim of her eyes, giddily spinning away, random as a blown leaf, into times for ever perilous and precarious. The deep joy of the unforeseen stretched out ahead of us.

Riordan took us furtively through the locked empty bar, past the angry headlines saying TIN SHED IS CIVIC EYESORE, and outside the wet footpaths of Elizabeth Street were scurrying with girls and men pell-melling to shops and offices. I took her arm and pushed into their earnest onrush, and we battled to the tram stop against the steady tireless tide of their ordered hurry and conforming discipline. It never occurred to me then that there was safety in their numbers.

THE ISLAND, GREECE, 1963

It is not so much borrowed time as given time, the time that Calverton bought for us, and although I can see he was right in granting us this breathing-space, it is hard to get rid of the feeling that we are back here on a kind of moral sufferance, held in a state of suspension, waiting. But what, exactly, are we waiting for? The apocalypse? A way out? Some unexpected stroke of good fortune? I think actually we are waiting for a kind of prize to be awarded. A sort of accolade to mark with respect the years of our expatriation, the stubbornness of our struggle to maintain whatever it is we have been trying to maintain – or have been forced into trying to maintain – for so long; our doughty battle, if you want to impart a certain spurious flavour of the heroic, to uphold the principles of individuality. There should be a prize, surely, as some sort of compensation? (Of course one began to suspect, long ago and emptily, that there is no guarantee about prizes.)

Is it altogether unreasonable and illogical to expect something after thirteen years of expatriation? Thirteen if you count London, although ten is nearer the mark, because London the first time was more a state of suspended animation at the end of a long boom, ten thousand miles long, with a tube running through it from which we drew both sustenance and illusion, and wires connecting the extremities to be pulled so that our activities could be ordered. The illusion then was of distance, the tremendous length of the boom, although a flawed illusion of freedom. Because we were still safely within society, conforming to the rules more or less, still travelling in the bus. But freedom, of course, is something else altogether. To find that you have to jump off the bus and let it go on without you, even if all you want to do is walk around, as Calthrop said, and pick the daisies . . .

What worries me at the moment is that we do not seem to have really proved our point. I find myself far less enterprising than I used to be; one feels it increasingly hard to discipline oneself to work. I continue to take refuge behind little fences of evasion. Lately I have been spitting up blood, but I say nothing to anybody about this; there is no practical way of retracing one's steps in this direction, and I suppose one has finally to come to terms with it. To be sure, Cressida and I are probably both drinking more than is good for us, although we share a tacit agreement not to admit it, but after the nightmare of that second experience in London, we have a much deeper dependence upon each other's company, and a kind of harmony which at last seems to have broken down or surmounted the earlier barriers. I suppose we have come to terms with this, too. But at any rate we still have some reserves of tenderness to share, which is useful while we are waiting.

Take today for example. An early November day. Guy Fawkes Day to be exact, although this of course is not celebrated here. Elsewhere it would be described as perfect Indian Summer weather, although here they call it the *Gaitharaki kalokairi*, 'donkey's summer', nobody seems to know why. At midday we sat in the mild sunshine outside Evangeli's tavern, looking across a bland milky sea, and we sipped wine for several hours and talked – good talk – and came home in the afternoon, both a little fuddled, and lay on the bed for a while in our clothes, with the warmth of the sun streaming in the windows, and then we made love, which we had not done for a long time. The only trouble was that we were treating the day as if it were a Sunday, whereas yesterday was Sunday, and the day before we had asked people up to sit and drink around the fire and talk and read poetry (on an island like this there is not much else to do besides drink and talk, if one is not working; and there was a dead scarab beetle upside down in the carriage of my typewriter to prove that I had not been working lately), although that was not a Sunday either. Still, it was very agreeable. Perhaps all the foreigners who are living here are waiting for something. Special private apocalypses.

Getting on towards evening there was a chill dew falling and I got up from the rumpled bed and went down and made a fire with the last of the broken well-head. Some time back the village authorities put a new head on the deep public well which is the communal centrepiece of the cobbled square outside our front door, and tore off all the ancient thick balks of rotten wood which had been there for a couple of centuries. Foresightedly, because it was hot then, hardly past midsummer, I, who had been seeing many things with a more frugal eye, dragged all the old rejected timber into our woodshed against the contingency of winter fires. Through the generations when the wood had covered the well it had come to be carved all over with initials, dates, names, and even hearts pierced by arrows. Although mostly initials. Greek capitals, which always looked nice.

I was staring into the fire and a deeply scored Delta Gamma

burnt away as I watched, and then the red edges began stealthily to push a black stain of char all around a name, Fotini, carefully pricked in with awl holes. She would be the next to go, I reflected, and wondered who she was. Or, more probably, who she had been.

This prompted the somewhat disturbing reflection that the time would come inexorably when somebody quite strange to us would be wondering, as idly, about David and Cressida Meredith. What kind of people they were, what sort of lives they had lived, how they had come to be here. On this rocky little island in Greece, half a world away from home. (In the fashion of island nomenclature it would probably go on for a very long time being referred to as 'the Australian House', just as, until the novelty of us having bought it, it had always been called 'the House of the Cannons', because Pavlos Zaraphonitis, the brig captain who had built it way back in 1788 – the very year, oddly enough, when my country was first settled – had mounted two brass cannons on the roof terrace, so that his returns from blockade-running adventures could be signalled to the town.)

Fotini burnt up and turned into a powdering of grey ash as I watched, and that probably was the last of her for all time. But tomorrow I will take the ash and sprinkle it around the three surviving seedlings of the Australian passionfruit which we have grown from the packet of seeds my sister-in-law Sheila sent us from Melbourne. The instructions on the packet said that wood-ash in the early stages was good for the stimulation of growth; so this is a practical matter, really, nothing to do with ritual or sentiment or symbolism.

LEBANON BAY, 1946

The effect of writing the last entry in this journal or whatever it is has been twofold. In the first place it has filled me with a nostalgia which is almost painful; and in the second place it has made me realize that this business of waiting for the prize may have become very distorted. Why should we always think that the prize is given at the end? Perhaps often we are given the prize right at the beginning, or quite early in the piece, and then have to work for it, to justify the award.

The focal point of these reflections is here in Lebanon Bay,[3] on a cliffy coast of the Pacific a hundred-odd miles down from Sydney, by the mile-long sweep of lonely beach where Cressida was born and had her childhood. But first I must sketch in events as they led up to this: it can be done with reasonable brevity because the importance of many of the incidents has long since faded.

After Cressida's discharge from the army something of a scandal exploded in Melbourne when I left Helen and went to live with Cressida (interested participants in the scandal, in the manner peculiar to Melbourne, were still taking sides twenty years later), and quit my job with the *Morning Post*. Some of the things that happened I handled reasonably enough, but some I conducted with foolishness, with unnecessary angers, and with a good deal of emotional instability. Everything I did, I suppose, was dictated then by the wild and overwhelming love I had for Cressida Morley. She behaved much more calmly and reasonably than I did. I had wanted to send in a note saying, 'Get stuffed, Brewster!' but she made me see the gaucherie and the ingratitude of this, and so I tore it up and wrote a polite and formal letter of resignation. For weeks we drifted around more or less aimlessly, attending far too many parties which inevitably ended up with people taking sides either to attack or defend us, and when this began to get too much I decided to begin writing a book. I was still very angry at Brewster's attitude, but I could not make up my mind whether to write a novel or a kind of polemic against war called *It Wasn't Worth It*. I couldn't decide which to begin—had I deliberately given myself a choice as a way of evading the commitment?—even after we had gone down to stay together, away from everybody else, in a friend's beach cottage which had dead rats in the kitchen cupboards (which Cressida disposed of while I sat brooding at the typewriter) and extraordinary curtains featuring a printed pattern of Snugglepot and Cuddlepie the Gumnut Babies, and where a private detective kept us under observation for impending divorce litigation.

I had become obsessively jealous of Cressida, and in a bar along the coast from the cottage, where we had both been drinking, she bit my finger to the bone while I was wagging it at her in a quite unfounded accusation of her having flirted with Archie Calverton, who had come down to visit us and to talk more about his future acting plans. Calverton, in fact, had brought a girl with him, and they both got very drunk and stayed the night, the most of which they seemed to have spent with the terrified girl cringing in a corner of the living-room, trying to hide her nudity behind the Snugglepot and Cuddlepie curtains, and dodging the oranges which Calverton kept hurling at her, quite violently, from the far corner of the room.

After that we went back to stay at Riordan's hotel. By this time Riordan had leased the dining-room section to a Yugoslav named Ivan so that he could make of it a Continental restaurant: he was a superb cook with a jolly Italian wife, and the old dining-room now looked very smart with burgundy drapes and reticent lights in brass candelabra, and good silver and glass and gleaming napery. Phar Lap and the stained antimacassars had vanished. These great changes had all happened so quickly—this was my first encounter with that 'accelerating rate of change' which later was to have such a profound and disturbing effect on the whole country—but in a way they suited us, because all the old clientele had been driven away, and upstairs we were the only guests staying in the hotel, and Ivan used to bring up to our room, quite late at night after the restaurant had closed, wonderful leftovers or dishes he would make specially for us, and then he would sit on and drink with us and talk for hours about the world overseas, Belgrade and Prague and Paris and New York and the trans-Atlantic runs on the *Queen Mary* and *Mauretania*. He was very gay, Ivan, slim and graceful, with an illuminated clown's face, and we both grew to love him dearly. He was an incessant talker, witty and always optimistic. He never talked about Auschwitz, though, where he had spent some time. Ivan was the only reason for sadness when we decided to leave Melbourne: his final gesture was to insist on passing on to me one of his suits – he was very dapper in his dress and went to a good tailor – to supplement the grey flannels and by now rather rumpled Donegal jacket which was about all the wardrobe I had brought with me. While we were staying at Riordan's I did finish writing the book – it turned out to be the novel – but it wasn't very good.

It was an impulse, really, that took us to Lebanon Bay. There was a girl lieutenant named Janice who had been one of Cressida's special friends in the army, and she had been discharged and was returning to her home in Sydney, so we picked her up in my car and drove her to the station on a Sunday morning to catch a troop train, and then Cressida and I walked across Spencer Street to get some breakfast at an hotel that advertised MEALS AT ALL HOURS – RAILWAY TRAVELLERS SPECIALLY CATERED FOR. There is hardly anything in the world more desolate and deadening than Melbourne on a Sunday morning, unless it is Toronto, and a hot blustery north wind was driving leaves and scraps of old paper and dry chaff in eddies down the ugly street, and when we rang the hotel bell a fat surly thug in dirty shorts and a singlet came to the door and glowered at us. 'Who the hell d'you think you are, sport?' he snarled. 'It's Sunday mornin', ain't it? We don't serve Sunday mornin's.'

I indicated the sign by the door, and said, 'This place is called Batman's Hill, isn't it?' He scowled at me. 'And Batman founded this city, didn't he? And when he founded it he said, "This will be the place for a village." And how bloody right he was! Now let's have that breakfast.'

He admitted us grudgingly, and on a filthy tablecloth we were served a revolting mess of cold eggs and bacon in congealed grease, and Cressida grimaced at me and said, 'Janice is lucky, isn't she? Darling, why don't we get out of here and go to Sydney?'

'Why don't we?' I said, and we went back to Riordan's and

packed our meagre luggage and loaded it in the car and set off. It was to be nearly twenty years before I would see Melbourne again.

We didn't go straight to Sydney, though. We went first to Lebanon Bay, so that Cressida could see her parents. They lived in a small and shabby weatherboard cottage so close to the great surf beach beyond that the back fence, itself the bleached uncolour of driftwood, was tilted inward almost horizontally by the weight of blown sand and drifted kelp and the brittle dry gossamer of sea-lettuce, and there were mighty singing swathes of indigo Pacific holding together the sagging creepers and tormented garden trees, so that even the cottage's buckled corrugated iron and old paint and cracked trellises became integrated scraps of a prodigious natural majesty.

When I pulled up the car there were two diminutive white-haired women sitting at either end of the small narrow front porch, in identical cane chairs, one reading and the other knitting. They looked like well-matched bookends. These were Cressida's mother and grandmother. Her father at this time was still working in the adjacent blue-metal quarries, from where we could hear distantly the intermittent barking of dynamite explosions. The older of the two little women seemed to cock her head at me as she said, 'Bunger Bradley.' This cryptic observation mystified me, and I did not realize until later that her head was bent to catch the echoed detonations, and that Bunger Bradley was the man responsible for tamping in the charges and creating the explosions, which, to Cressida's grandmother, were important punctuations in her otherwise sterile days.

We stayed in Lebanon Bay for two months before going on to Sydney. If there is any particular area of one's life which nostalgically one would like to live through again without any change whatever—and there are very few that beckon back—I am pretty sure this would be it.

Cressida had not long turned twenty-one, but already she had that invincibly calm quality of a woman sure of her beauty, and with it—one saw this most vividly when she was away on the cliff rocks or the swept dunes of her mile-long beach—another quality that was wild and wanton and free. A kind of pagan quality, it was, and anything but calm. You were aware of it when the beads of sunlight slid along the high sharp ridge of her cheek, and the corners of her widc mouth seemed to tremble on an edge of incommunicable laughter; when she would stare away, quite withdrawn, as if listening to some music that was only for her ears; when she skipped lightly barefoot across glowing sea-wet rocks covered with tiny blue needle-sharp shells which made me totter after her in a hobbling agony; when she would march in, waterjets squishing around her, shouting like a delighted child, through the nobbly soft *cungevoi*; or rolled herself slim and naked and sand-encrusted down the night-cool cushioning flow of the pale dunes through the black calligraphy of the marram-grass, and the ache I would have for her was in the heart as well as in the loins, and I would follow her dumbly to the edge of the crisping sands. Sometimes she would stand there as if spellbound, staring out across the ocean's slow deep heart-beat to the black platform that supported the prodigality of southern stars, and on her rapt face there was an utter absence of dismay. She seemed to exist, then and there, in her own assured entitlement to freedom. And then she would turn and we would fall together, coupled in unrepeatable ecstasies, our bodies caught in the curl of foam and soft spume and the grunt and crunch of the surf-singing shore.

In this virginal childlike quality she possessed so remarkably one could still recapture the grubby urchin of the gunpits whom I had met more than two years earlier, but now she had grown into all her features, the full rich mouth and high cheek-bones, the astonishing eyes, the hands which I had remembered as being too big and square for her immature body now small and soft and capable, the broad brow that was deep honey-brown and no longer freckled and crowned by brown hair either pulled back into a severe sleek chignon or blowing wild in the sea-wind. Her legs were long and graceful, her breasts firm and high, her body glowed with youth and sun. Sometimes she would lie naked on the sands at midnight and tell me with childish solemnity, 'If you could only star-bake long enough you might turn silver.'

Often I found myself thinking back to Gavin Turley's drunken worship on that dim night of candlelit reunion at Mario's, from which I was dragged off again by the war. 'You have here a savage, David. An authentic savage. Born on a barren mile of Pacific beach. Not a soul goes there. Nothing but sand-dunes and sharks and kelp. Oh, a log or two of driftwood perhaps. And our Cress. Never wore a pair of shoes until she was thirteen. Like Christopher Robin, she still has sand between the toes. Important to remember this, cock. *Very* important. Bless you for your sandy toes, Cress . . .' And I still see the Cressida of then, in her army uniform, with the candlelight in her eyes—those eyes of ocean shallows, marsh grasses, reef seas, shoalwater—and behind her the bomb-burst of chrysanthemums, the litmus of the hydrangeas, glass and silver glimmering, coloured bottles in a bar mirror beside the comic caricatures of Mussolini and Hitler and Graziani and Tojo: I still remember that infinitely disturbing impression she gave of only awaiting some cue or some encouragement—perhaps even only some other unquestioning human alliance—to release all the forces she was holding in check and reach a pure, rapturous intensity of living that seemed as alien to me then as some far-off foreign land.

Yet for a while, I think, we have found this unquestioning human alliance; at least during this time in Lebanon Bay we have been given our own small vision of Paradise, and this share of Paradise has been contained and complete in itself. There has been no other world around us, no intrusion from past or future, everything has been held in a long pause within the sea and the sand and the winds and the high sky, held in the sweet heat of the clovered coastal fields, the lantana, the cool-shaded fig-trees, the sorghum sweeps. Should we ask for more than this? It will mark both of our futures indelibly, but we are not to know it yet.

Before it ends there is a day to remember.

One of what Cressida's mother calls the Blue and Gold Days, or the Illawarra Days, which would always incite her to intone Tennyson, beating at her pots, looking out from her kitchen window into the mild north-easter across scalloped bay and quarried cliffs.

There was nobody but us on the long stretch of beach, no tidemark or footprint. No solitary rod fisherman challenged the careless measured dignity of the surf. The swollen hot breasts of the dunes hid us from the road and the rackety railway.

We swam in the toss and turbulence of a deep gut between the rocks, enjoying the delicate perils of the suck and seethe and undertow, diving into dark light-splintered caverns of rock and rolling weed to find oysters and crayfish and the grapey fruit of bladder-wrack, and we came naked from the tingling water to the shallow rock pools in the sand where we had peaches waiting in a brown paper bag and a bottle of Moselle plunged neck downward into the firm and tensy grit, cooling in the fanning flow of the sea-rim.

Cressida floated on her back in the rock pool while I uncorked the bottle, floated in a dreamy abandon, arms flung and legs wide apart and eyes closed against the sharp blue radiance, and I was a long time over my trivial task because I could not take my eyes from the stupefying loveliness she presented. I could live a thousand years and never again know such loveliness—the honeyed domes of her small sharp breasts, rose-whorled and dark-pinnacled, floating above the gentle water lap, and there was a golden glint of down, wet and metallic, brushing her thighs across curves of umber flesh, where water-drops dewed like tiny pearls, and fading on the pale cool silk-soft slopes within, and the pink hint of cloven mysteries below the flat gold plane of her belly where the neat mounded triangle of her hair, tangled and sun-spangled, crimped and flowed and curled into tiny ringlets, moving with the water.

She sat up and we ate the peaches and drank half the bottle of wine, and caressed one another, and then I corked the bottle suddenly and thrust it back forcibly, deep into the sand. We made love in the cool water of the pool, with Cressida's hair feathered about her in the rock crevices and trailing and drifting across green weed and the star-patterned limpets, and a crimson crab as miniature as a brooch sidled off, and there was a pink sea-anemone pulsing beside us a steady roseate fleshy breathing rhythm, a metronomic measure that could have been useful if one had been detached enough.

It lasted a long time. The frills of surf sucked and licked and whispered around the neck of the wine-bottle and the hissing and the kissing of the sea seemed a part of our union, and the rhythm of our love was keyed exactly to the ocean rhythm that came deep and booming through the sand and echoed up through rock and water beneath the tender violence in the amalgam of our bodies. And as my own life moved inside her tight enclosing warmth, throbbing, thrusting, sliding—each thrust a crash of surf, each sliding retreat the sighing of the downward-sliding sea—we seemed an inextricable part of some absolute congress of nature, as if sand and sun and sea were all sentient and conjoined with our own conjunction.

And still it went on for a long slow time, and then we came together in a hot interior flooding, a boiling sea-rush that seemed scalding beside the sea-cooled impact of our limbs.

She floated away and back, drifting and blissful, a frail ribbon of some viridian weed caught upon one breast.

'We must always remember this,' I whispered.

But for a long time we forgot about it.

And soon there was almost no money left and it was time to leave Lebanon Bay and find the world again.

CENTRAL AUSTRALIA, 1965

This is a curious place for the three of us to be sitting and talking about Paradise.

One scraggy dun dwarf of a tree with leaves hung vertically like sharp knives gives no illusion of shade or cool, but it is friendlier than the rest of the bare, fissured, gigantic tor, almost as old as the world itself, up which we have struggled. We are ringed by other bizarre domes of eroded rock, and beyond is the dry ocean of desert and the violet hump of Ayers Rock dreaming in mirage above the light-play of mulga and spinifex and hot red sand. When we are silent there is silence everywhere. The birds fly below us, shoaling like minnows, and make no sound in the soundless air. This is as it should be: the rocks were here, wearing away, before life came to the earth or the sounds of life: our talk, being intrusive, is blocked by long pensive silences. Our fingers move, striking, among the hot flints and jagged little spikes and limp rock-growth. Cressida remarked earlier that it looked like an English herb garden, but it does not feel like one.

A while back Tom said, 'You know, there is a kind of feeling of Paradise about it, something Promethean; beginnings and endings running together. You get it up in some of these places, being quiet, this immortality feeling. I mean, we haven't lost Paradise, it's still the terms in which we work and live on this earth. It's this other thing you sense here, that these always were the terms; that's how we came out of the swamps, and that's how the birds got wings. When the birds fly they fly as if they're in Paradise, don't they?'

We are really here retracing Tom Kiernan,[4] because Tom is back in Australia again after all the years away, back for the national retrospective show of his paintings, and this has brought the three of us together again, gathering up old threads to see what changes time has made.

Tom is a big success now, but this, besides making him fairly wealthy after all the years of battling, has made him wiser and gentler. He has got over the bitterness. He still has the old drive and energy, and a ruthless devotion to his paintings, but in the pauses now he is more contemplative than he used to be. It seems that a kind of intense humility keeps driving him back over the old ground.

I imagine the retrospective shattered him a bit. Walking around by himself in the midnight-empty gallery through thirty years of his own work, thirty years of his life. Perhaps the rest of us don't have his sort of humility because not many of us get a chance like this to look at ourselves and what we've done. Although not many of us would have said what Tom said (being so notable a man suddenly), looking at his remarkable paintings very thoughtfully and shaking his head and saying:

'It's a succession of failures, really, isn't it? That's what we are concerned with, I suppose, trying to overcome the sequence of failures to keep trying for what we're after, and developing a kind of stoicism about it.' He thought about that for a bit, then went on, 'And then the speeding up. This business of getting farther away from birth and closer to death. And you find everything speeding up because you've got to get it down, get it done.'

The heat across the desert is like a curtain blowing and in all the vast miraging ocean there is no evidence of human presence. Desolate. Arid. Empty. Heedless. The dead heart of this extraordinary land of ours. Yet earlier we had been talking about the delicate fragility of it all, its gentle poetry, a very real sensuousness within the lonely impassive hugeness, the needle-sharp twigs and burrs and bindies that grabbed at you, the leafage soft as flannel. This is what started them off about Paradise.

'If I had to paint it again now,' Tom said, 'I'd paint it quite differently: I'd build it around this delicate embroidery, this tapestry, this herb garden. It's as if all these years have been useful only so you can learn to see things differently. As if we have to turn ourselves into somebody else before it can make sense. Well, maybe we do, maybe we do.'

When he said this I found myself thinking what a very strange thing it was for me to have grown to love this country, after having hated it so much. To love some of it, anyway. And then I thought of Tom's first one-man show in Melbourne just before the war and of how they had flung pots of green house-paint all over his pictures and driven him out with their philistine rantings and screamings. Driven him finally to the ends of the earth. They kow-towed now, of course, because he was famous in London and New York. And wealthy. One man in Melbourne the other day had said to him, 'Always sign your paintings, Mr Kiernan . . . er . . . Tom. May I call you Tom?' 'Why not?' said Tom. 'That's my name.' 'Always sign your paintings, Tom,' the man insisted, 'because that's just the same as signing your name on a cheque.'

He is talking to Cressida mostly, so I just let the tape-recorder run, and perhaps later I'll transcribe it down just the way he talks, because it's different on a tape-recorder from the way we imagine we're talking, or the way writers write down talk the way they think it comes out. It would be silly not to take advantage of material aids in these very material times.

But after a while he turns to me and laughs and says, 'Nothing much else changes, only us, I suppose. Do you remember what we were like twenty years ago? God!' he exclaimed and laughed again. 'Do you remember Sydney, those years just after the war? No room for Paradise or poetry then, eh?'

SYDNEY, 1946

When Cressida came back she said, 'Have you been along to the bathroom yet?' and I said no, I'd been waiting for her to clean up, and asked her why. 'Oh, it's interesting,' she said.

The bathroom—there was only one to each floor of the Princeton Apartments—was at the far end of a corridor angled around a euphemistic light-well from which came weird clankings and groanings and the catarrhal cleansings of other residents. The corridor was all gloomy tones of brown, and the excremental colour and smell of this dingy byway went with the bathroom, which had stains on the walls like old maps and blotches more repellent in the toilet-bowl where something seemed to have happened with Condy's Crystals. The cracked wash-basin was a mess of squeezed-out toothpaste tubes and rusted bobby-pins, and the final sordid touch was a framed printed sign screwed above the ringmarked bathtub which said GUESTS ARE POLITELY REQUESTED PLEASE NOT TO SHIT IN THE BATH. 'Politely' was the bit I liked. It was hard to believe that this had been set up in type, in Bodoni Bold, and printed.

When I went back to the musty bedroom I said hopelessly, 'We should have looked around more. We should have tried for something better than this dreadful bloody dump.'

'It's cheap,' she said, not pointing out that the Princeton had been my choice. 'It will do for a few days while we sort out. When you get a job we can look around for something else.'

'Someone said it was used as a kind of leave place for the troops, GI's mostly, a brothel, I suppose, more than a residential,' I said as if this was a mitigation. 'Put toilet-paper down on the seat first,' I warned.

Cressida went to a window so opaque with city grime that it seemed as if a wartime black-out screen was still pasted over the glass. 'Well, at least it's in the Cross,' she said, as if she could see out. 'It's a pretty street. There's a flower-stall over there. And we don't have to sit up here. We can always go out.'

She turned away and sat on the edge of the bed and wiggled her toes. 'I think I'd better tell you now,' she said evenly. 'I'm going to have a baby.' The expression on my face made her laugh. 'It's hardly surprising, darling,' she said. 'I suspected it a while back. Now I'm sure.'

'But are you sure?' I said stupidly, hardly hearing what she said.

She laughed again. 'I'm a very regular girl. Yes, darling, I am quite sure.' She came across and put her arms around me. 'It's all right,' she said. 'It's not anything to worry about.'

'It is something to worry about.' I tried to fight down a flurry of panic. 'I'm not divorced. We can't get married.'

'Who said anything about getting married? I haven't said anything about it. We love each other, don't we?'

'Yes, but . . . You see . . . Well, listen, this is serious. I mean, do you want to . . .'

'Get rid of it? Oh no, I don't want to get rid of it. It'll be our baby. I want to have it.' She didn't seem frightened or worried or excited, just serene and calm.

'Well, that fixes it,' I said. 'We're going to get out of this bloody terrible dump! You're not going to have it here.'

'Crikey, I hope not,' she said, and flung herself back on the bed, hugging her laughter into herself. 'Nor am I going to have it for quite a long time, darling,' she added after a while, her mouth twitching. 'So while we're waiting why don't we get dressed and go down and have some coffee at the Arabian?'

Coffee in cramped dim cellar lounges and the soft play of branch- and leaf-shadow in the autumn streets, as much as the emotional and physical raptures of a love still sublime even in the sleazy room of the Princeton, have been the palliatives of this uneasy arrival time of the last few weeks. There really are flower-stalls in Kings Cross and the one run by old fat Maggie has become *our* flower-stall, and we now have *our* tobacco kiosk where Cressida has charmed an old dragon of a woman into letting her have under-the-counter cigarettes, so we no longer have to save the tobacco from our used butts to be rolled up in airmail paper or smoke those terrible South African things that smell as if they are made from wildebeeste dung. And we have our own coffee-lounge where we can hear *our* songs on the juke-box, 'Laura' and 'It Might As Well Be Spring' and 'The Breeze and I' and 'Deep Purple' and 'Night and Day'. And in the evenings we can walk through light-dazzle and cacophony under the bronzing leaves, and nobody takes any notice of us or cares who we are, although heads turn wherever Cressida walks.

Kings Cross is a little spurious and more than a little self-conscious, and its air of cosmopolitanism is an awkward masquerade, but there are misfitting foreigners about and odd eccentrics, and a raffishness has persisted, and it is better than

Melbourne, and better than the rest of Sydney, which is even more war-scarred from its self-inflicted injuries. A coarser, tougher city, poised on an edge of violence. A cocky, callous place. Amid the merciless tensions of the town these past weeks have been a time of abeyance, of putting things off.

But that all came to an end this morning.

I think in spite of everything we have both become very depressed by the Princeton and the furtive faces we see in odorous corridors and the sounds we hear from behind closed doors and the sneaky hoverings around the institutional entrance hall, but I have been moody about making a change, and hardly able to afford one anyway.

This morning over coffee, Cressida said, 'It's time you thought about a job, darling. Or I did. We keep putting it off.'

'They know I'm here,' I said.

'But do they? You haven't even tried to contact Mr Tomlinson.'

'He knows,' I said impatiently. 'It's nearly five months since I quit the *Post*. Christ, he knows. Why should I go cap in hand, pleading for favours?'

'A job, darling, isn't necessarily a favour. The phone's there in the corner. Why don't you ring him?'

'All right, I will,' I said. And when I got through to Tomlinson he said, 'Where the devil have you been, Meredith? Been waiting weeks for you to contact me. Where are you speaking from? Yes, well grab a cab and come straight in. And make it snappy. I've an editorial conference at eleven.'

In the event it was he who made it snappy. He seemed petulant about something and was brusque and caustic with his secretary, but he greeted me warmly enough and made a point of recalling a wartime meeting we had had in Washington and indulged himself with a brief tonic scatter of dropped names, then came to the point crisply:

'Right. We could use a good feature writer. We do have Brian Jefferson but he's getting very unreliable. Turned into a parlour pink. Can't be trusted any longer. So, yes, there's a place on the *Globe* for you, Meredith, if you want it. You can have a senior grading, a flat thousand a year, and no bargaining.'

His secretary, still sulking, took me through the clamorous big reporters' room, which was in the frenzy of edition time, and down newspaper-smelling labyrinths to the small cluttered cubby the feature writers used. Jefferson was there, looking uncertain, a thin gaunt man with a pale, twitching face. He was polite and helpful but not effusive. We went across to the Long Bar of the Australia for a drink. Although quite early in the day, the huge bar was crowded: with most of the city's bottled beer running to the black market, all the bars were doing boom business and the swill began early. Jefferson drank Australian whisky, doubles, with beer chasers. His drinking hand had the shakes and he kept the other hand in his trouser-pocket jingling keys and coins. He told me he had been a colonel in Intelligence during the war, right through from the Middle East (he was one of the few in the bar, though, not wearing a returned serviceman's badge), and when he mentioned that we had a mutual friend in Archie Calverton, the penny dropped and I remembered some very passable war poems Jefferson had written. Calverton, he said, had come back to Sydney and was acting with a new Little Theatre group – 'a bit leftish' he said – doing Ben Jonson's *The Alchemist*. Calverton, he said, was a bloody promising actor. I ought to go along.

'What does Tomlinson want you to do exactly?' he asked, trying to sound casual but with his uneasiness showing through.

'I don't know,' I said evasively. 'He's going to work something out.'

'They might give you a column,' Jefferson suggested hopefully. 'The gen around the office is they're planning to run a daily column.' He thought about this, jingling his pocket frantically, then said rather timidly, 'You'll like the *Globe*. It's not a bad paper to work for. Tomlinson's a pretty good bloke really.'

I was anxious to tell Cressida the news, and I suggested walking back to the office with him, but he said no, he'd stick on there for a bit, so we shook hands and he went over and joined a big bunch of other early drinkers around Freda, the popular one among the Long Bar barmaids. His left hand kept fumbling away in his pocket.

Walking up to Elizabeth Street for a tram, I kept on hearing that jingling rhythm from Jefferson's pocket, and this brought back a few suddenly recaptured lines from one of his poems about the retreat to Crete. A good poem, as I remembered. As the words went through my mind they moved to the jingling sound of the coins and keys in his pocket.

There was a big crowd on the safety-zone and the trams, as usual, were banked up halfway along the street. Near me stood a nervous little European refugee—the odd round shape of the hat and the long coat and briefcase and thick-soled shoes testified his origins—and as the line of trams began to move again he turned to the man next to him, a tall rawboned type with a trap mouth and jutting chin, and asked in a heavy, thick accent. 'Iss zhis, z' next one, for z' Bellyview 'Ill?' The rawboned man looked at him with sidelong contempt and snarled, 'Why don't you reffo bastards learn t' talk English!'

I still don't know what made me react the way I did, but I had him by the shoulder almost before I realized what I was doing, and I threw a wild punch at him and began snarling myself, 'You wait till *you're* in Prague, you rotten uncouth bastard, and you're asking directions in *your* impeccable bloody Czech!' And then we had bumped through the crowd and were lurching across to the gutter, flailing at one another and brawling and swearing, knocking over the newspaper billboards, and the little refugee scuttled aboard the first tram that came along, whether it was for Bellevue Hill or not, but by this time a red-faced policeman had us both by our jackets and he was snarling too, 'You break it up, you two bastards, or you'll both be in *real* trouble!'

Coming back to the Cross, I smarted with humiliation and anger—anger with myself, mostly, that I had allowed myself to become trapped in the snarling violence and vulgarity of the place.

But tonight Cressida dug into almost the last of her army deferred pay so we could settle the account at the Princeton and have a celebration dinner in candlelight at Gleneagles. I drank too much of the wine, but it helped to make it gay. I said nothing about Jefferson or the incident at the safety-zone. Although Jefferson was much in my mind, with the words of his damned poem going round and round: it would have been easier to tell her, I have just realized, if I really knew what is going to happen here.

SYDNEY, 1948

I need to hold some continuity here, so I had better get this bit over with and try to deal with the last couple of years the way they have built up to this obsession we have to get out of the country: the trouble is that so much seems to have happened since we moved up from Melbourne. (We aren't the only ones, by the way, because all the Melbourne crowd appear to be coming here, some only in panic flight from that constrictive city, others evidently considering Sydney the better springboard for the jump to somewhere else.)

The divorce came through – I didn't defend the action and it actually did take only three minutes, which confirmed Gavin Turley's 'par for the course': funny to think how much of life can be dissolved so quickly, the hopes and failures, the struggles and betrayals, all blown away with no more ado than a draught through a dusty courtroom – and the final papers arrived while we were living in a poky bed-sitter in Manly, sharing a kitchenette with two lesbians and a wharfie, and we were married that same week in the local Registry Office where a churlish young man, training himself in the regimen of bureaucracy, went to a lot of trouble to keep us waiting while he made out dog-licences. Cressida spent the wedding morning sitting on the beach darning and cobbling the secondhand suit Ivan had handed on to me at Riordan's pub in Melbourne, and when we got back to our unromantic little room that night I went to the open window – at least the night and the moon and the stars and the black tracery of the Norfolk Island pines were beautiful – and I gave a great stretching yawn of exhaustion and relief and the whole arse fell out of my trousers with a wonderful rending sigh.

Cressida had the baby three months later. She only just made anathema- anything detested, hateful

it to the hospital because of an altercation with a taxi-driver who didn't want to take us because it was time for his lunch. When I threatened to call the police he grudgingly capitulated, driving at mad breakneck speed and cursing and muttering all the way.

Still, with all these unpropitious omens, the baby was a fine boy, and the fact that we still couldn't find a place to live made us forlorn only when we were separated and even this added to our joy and excitement when we could be together. Before the baby came Cressida and I used to stay up half the night writing appealing, desperate letters, and then we would walk miles around the dark deserted streets putting them in the letter-boxes of houses that looked as if the owners might be kindly, sympathetic people. Remembering the traditional warm-heartedness of Australians it seemed little enough to ask, just a reasonable place for the two of us to bring the baby back to, but something had happened to Australian hearts, and 'baby' and 'children' had become words of anathema in the community, at least among the propertied and the ensconced, and although we wrote hundreds and hundreds of letters we never got a single reply.

So Cressida went back to Lebanon Bay after she came out of hospital and I moved to a verandah room over a cheap restaurant kept by 'Pop' Charlton, an old American who had come out here years before to mine copper. However conventional and orthodox I was obliged to keep my professional activities at the *Globe*, I still insisted on my private life being different and even a little quirky because this was where, in the long night hours after working all day in the office, I had to try to hammer out my own freedoms. I had begun another novel, taking it this time slower and more carefully, and there was something romantic and fitting about writing in the small hours of night in this shabby makeshift little den built on to the end of the wide verandah, with the rain roaring on the corrugated iron overhead and dribbling down through the sorry foliage of the oleanders and the surf pounding away this side of the sandhills where Captain Cook had found Australia: it was a world quite removed from the abrasive claptrap of the city.

The room was an entomologist's paradise. Its regular

inhabitants were fleas, bugs, ants and spiders—they, as it were, *occupied* the place, whereas I only visited there to work or sleep—and there were regular visitations of mosquitoes, flies, sandflies, ladybugs, grasshoppers and praying mantises, and even odder intruders would get there like Emperor gum moths and stick insects and caterpillars, or an occasional great hairy tarantula. One night when a chapter had bogged down I made an inventory and among the more normal denizens I found four separate species of flies and six of ants. There were also many mice, an occasional rat, and once a very large warty toad palpitating in the darkest corner of the room.

The food served by the old American was plentiful but execrable, but in a way I enjoyed staying there because he was a kindly soul and a useful reminder that compassion did exist here and there within the callous disinterest of the city. The place had a septic tank which leaked and overflowed, and sometimes Pop would call me down at dead of night and together we would surreptitiously pump it out over a vacant allotment near by, taking care that the wind was in the right quarter. The old man was also a skilled and whimsical raconteur, and he vitiated much of my loneliness with his garrulous Munchausen stories of his travelling life in a lilting, slow, Mississippian drawl. According to his account, he had come to Australia before the First World War and struck it rich with a mine east of Alice Springs (he had made and lost several fortunes, he claimed) and although he was now in his middle seventies he was still obsessed by all manner of wonderful get-rich-quick ideas, and he would go on very excitedly and then he would begin to blink and his eyes, tired old questing eyes, would grow dull suddenly and you would realize that really he was defeated and knew it, defeated not by his own years so much as by his awareness that Australia had turned into something else and stopped being the kind of country that provided his sort of chance. Still, while he had me there he could talk about it and have his brief dreams, so what he did to help me was surprising in a way.

What happened was that I heard of a flat that was going, but they were asking key money of five hundred pounds. Key money was the iniquitous system prevailing between the 'haves' and the 'have-nots'; it had become so commonplace among the many rapacities of the city that it hardly warranted identification with the more majestic grafts which had established the new social patterns and given an almost religious significance to the gospel of 'the quick quid'. 'Well,' they would say, 'at least you can make a quick quid out of it, and if *you* don't someone else will.'

The trouble was that I didn't have five hundred pounds: I had three hundred left, all that remained from having sold some books and pictures and cashed in a life-insurance policy. (I had also sold to a dealer the collection of over-printed Japanese war stamps given to me by the poor little Japanese postal clerk at that moment of obsequious fragmentation on the Ginza, but the dealer only gave me three pounds for it.) I told the story that night to Pop Charlton and next morning at breakfast there was a bundle of banknotes on the plate beside my rehashed dish of bubble-and-squeak. 'Well, you gotta get out of here, don't you?' the old man mumbled, and hurried off to his kitchen. I was able to pay him back the two hundred pounds a few months later with the money I got from a publisher's advance on the novel I had finished, and only then did I discover that that had been all he had left from the many fortunes he had made.

The five hundred pounds went partly in the key money and partly as the cost of the 'effects' which had to go with the flat—one worm-eaten carpet, two broken chairs, and a warped deal table—and then I had to bribe the garbage man to take this away as junk. The extortionist from whom I got the flat was a nervous returned serviceman who was having wife trouble and mistress trouble and seemed desperately unsettled. 'I don't like doing this,' he said defensively, 'but I got to have the money to get away.' You knew the way he spoke that he was running out on both women. 'I think I'll push up north somewhere,' he said.

It was an unattractive flat on the ground floor of a hideous big block in liverish brick, enclosing the garbage area and communal incinerator, and set in a wasteland of tiled red roofs pressing down on dwellings all the same, all jostling for treeless foothold, part of an enormous monotonous sprawl that crowded all the way to the very edge of the awesome coastal cliffs, and no doubt would have crowded half the way to New Zealand except that the Pacific Ocean got in the way. A huge brick sewerage stink-pole dominated this repellent vista like a monument to bad taste and the sea beyond it was evilly curdled by the city's effluent. Sydney is a city of light and wind more than of architecture, and in the pale shimmer of summer heat under the pulsing fierce light refracted from the vast harbour in the centre, or when smoke and dust drifted like Pompeiian ash before the gasping hot breath of the westerlies, the surroundings were like some gigantic incurable wound still weeping through the spread gauze between the ugly dryness of the scar tissue. The majesties of nature and the monstrosities of man have a cheek by jowl evidence in Sydney more insistent, I think, than in any other city in the world, but few seem to perceive, or at any rate to be worried about, the enormity of our offences.

But Cressida was able to come back from Lebanon Bay and we moved into the flat and bought a few cheap pieces of second-hand furniture and made some other things from padded butter-boxes covered over with gingham, and with a few pictures up and some books around it began after a while to look all right. We were happy again, and together. There was nothing to be seen from the windows save other brick walls so what was outside didn't matter all that much. Since then it has become our small enclave jealously preserved within the surrounding hostile wilderness. Not only ours, either. It has grown to be a kind of temporary haven for quite a few people who cannot, or will not, fit in with what is happening.

'It's beginning to be,' Cressida said some time back, 'a sort of home for the bewildered.'

What *is* happening is not easy to define. It isn't only the greed and the selfishness, or the savagery of the disenchantment. It isn't even simply that the chaotic disintegration of the country makes victory seem like a dirty word. Oh, the old cant is going on just the same, the comfortable complacencies of the secure and the undisturbed, the babbittries and hypocrisies, the cocky self-assurance of the superficial, the jingoistic platitudes of the badge-wearers, the clichés and venalities of the politicians: yet dissatisfaction hangs in the air like a fog. It is surprising how quick people are to take affront; on the least provocation they will flare into anger or resentment or a vicious kind of xenophobia – Continental Jews and the dispossessed from Europe are the popular targets; when anything goes wrong, if it can't be blamed on the trade unions or the Commos it's always attributed to the machinations of the 'bloody reffos' (the trade unionists and the Commos are just as bad about this as anyone else) – and the prevalent attitude is a kind of baffled belligerence. 'Up you, Jack, I'm all right!' But a lot of people seem to slump just as quickly into despair and frustration and depression, as if it's all too much for them: these are basically decent, warm-hearted people who seem to be aware that something is spoiling them even though they don't want to be spoiled; they cannot identify the poison that is seeping in, so there is no way of finding an antidote.

I feel sometimes that we must have thrown away something we once possessed – an illusion, maybe, or a delusion – something that was able to shield us like an old coat that was familiar and still handy at times, and not until we had discarded it did we realize that it could still come in handy, so that we have been trapped in a sudden sharp change, as when an unexpected south-easterly begins cutting open a warm day, and we are left naked and unprotected against the raw buffeting. There is no indication up to date that we are to be given any time, or even the material, to fashion a new coat.

The ones with the chip on the shoulder don't need a coat, of course. Just the other day I was at the Long Bar drinking with a chap who had stayed off at Honolulu on his way back from the States and he happened to mention a fine Hawaiian surf beach he had discovered. Quick as a flash one of his friends turned on him. 'If you liked the bloody place so much,' he said angrily, 'why did you bother coming back here?'

The edginess of people is understandable in one way. The

southern cities writhe in an agony of power failures and blackouts and strikes and shortages—there is hardly a day when the newspaper billboards aren't blacklettering the streets with MORE POWER CUTS or BLACKOUTS PARALYSE CITY or GENERAL STRIKE IMMINENT or INDUSTRY AT STANDSTILL—and Cressida bathes the baby while I hold a candle or tries to cook a meal over a fire in a kerosene tin in the back yard.

So when a plague of fleas came in from the humid beaches recently I couldn't help thinking of that passage in *All Quiet On The Western Front* where the army of rats, during the big bombardment, tried to invade the dugout; this led on to a kind of science-fiction jolt of feeling that some new evolutionary thing was taking over from a failed experiment; Tomlinson even got me to write a feature for the *Globe*, pointing out that fleas proportionately were far stronger and tougher creatures than we were, and that it was only our superior brains and size that saved us. The superiority of our brains seemed a pretty debatable point, but at least the flea plague had its funny side in the way everybody, even the most genteel, abandoned their inhibitions and scratched away in public or vied with each other in claiming the number of bites they had sustained or turned into great pundits about fleas, advocating infallible solutions to the problem, like sleeping with leaves of mint scattered between the sheets. (Our genteel inhibitions are very fragile coverings when circumstances become raw: I was reminded again of *All Quiet On The Western Front* and the warm and somehow beautiful social communion of the men sitting round in the sun just behind the front lines, bogging together on their open box latrines.) Cressida and I settled for a system where tumblers and cans of water were kept all around the bedroom, but this meant we had to spend hours in pouncing every night, trying to protect the baby. Between us we could usually account, once we became expert, for a hundred or more fleas a night. Often it would become so exhausting that we would give up and collapse on the stripped bed and make love in a kind of joyful masochistic delirium, with the fleas jumping all over us and the baby sleeping in his cot underneath the netting.

During that season of the plague we did scratch a lot.

Of those who came to the flat Jefferson has been the most troublesome (Calverton is a bit troublesome too, but in a quite different way), especially on Saturday nights, when the place has become, tacitly, open house. Cressida cooks a big spaghetti or minestrone and people bring bottles, usually a cheap and potent red wine put up by an Italian migrant. They are noisy parties, with everyone launching into harangues or shouting one another down to cover their own doubts and frustrations, and often end with a flotsam of drunks sleeping on the floor or still mumbling owlishly into bilious dawns: occasionally, for no apparent reason, a party wearily takes up again and continues on into Sunday night. At some time or other in the course of these events Jefferson always becomes too obstreperous and has to be forcibly evicted, but he takes no umbrage at this and is invariably the first to appear the next Saturday evening, frequently bearing some secondhand book he has picked up as a kind of peace offering.

I tend to find the parties rather a strain, and this for a number of reasons. I suppose I am not, strictly, a true devotee of the wild Australian 'rort' and always remorseful in my hangovers, but it goes deeper than this. There are guilts at work – the lurking, not quite explicit guilt I have about Jefferson, which refuses to respond to logical examination; an even more tenuous guilt involved with my vaguely disturbing suspicions of Calverton; and the much more definite guilt of having a far better job than any of my visitors, a solid standing in the community, and, if I choose to accept them, very assured 'prospects'. I have the least validity as a rebel. I am also uneasy about the court of admiration which Cressida inspires. She obviously loves the maverick company. She is always calm and gay and warm and pleasant to everybody and a stayer to the end, and she is lovelier than ever since the child was born, and now that she is pregnant again there is a serenity about her beauty that is breathtaking. I cannot rid myself of the feeling that most of the men are drawn to the flat simply by Cressida; with Calverton I am quite sure of it. (There are times when I wonder what sort of person Julian, the baby, is likely to grow into, sleeping imperturbably in his cot through the crashing decibels of uproar, the wild political arguments, frenzied polemics, the gabble of splintering rhetoric and the crash of breaking glass, through the full-volume battering of 'Symphonic Variations' and 'Ebony Concerto' and Beethoven's Ninth, the uninhibited sexual contests. All this, besides the flea plague!)

If there is one thing common to the people who come it is a sense of displacement. They incline to be dogmatic about this, although they are a pretty disparate crew and there is not much else that seems to unite them. They are mostly young, or youngish: they have all been involved in some capacity or other in the war and have not found subsequently any satisfying substitute for that involvement. Yet they are not really quite the dispossessed or the outcasts they like to insist they are. Certainly they are disillusioned and dissatisfied—the Bomb symbolizes the former and is endlessly discussed; the sad state of this country is more than enough for dissatisfaction—and although they are entitled to feel let down they seem resentful rather than rebellious. Even when they are in the full swing of drunken conviviality, frustration will release little jets of anger at the way society is constituted against them. But what they think of as society is, of course, in just as big a mess as they are. As we all are.

I sometimes think Cressida is right and 'bewildered' is the best word for them.

It is this country that they blame. It is something they see as rotten in the fabric of Australia that has soured them. One night a while back when Jefferson was building up to one of his diatribes he began glaring around and thumping his fist on his thigh. 'What the hell has gone wrong with this bloody country?' he furiously wanted to know. 'What's happened in just a couple of years to the blokes you knew? We've turned into a race of pimps and bludgers and philistines and racketeers! But, Jesus, we weren't like *that* in the war. Over in the Middle East or up there in New Guinea you couldn't have met a better bunch of blokes. They thought about things. They *believed* in things. They had ideals. They *were* going to make this a better bloody world. And look at the bastards now!'

Well, Jefferson had reasons enough for bitterness: and there is this feeling of suffocation, of smothering under some soggy heavy blanket of timid conformity and dullness and worthwhile values twisted awry, and a kind of belief, or hope, that no other climate can be quite so stifling as this. This feeds the native sense of isolation, that torturing affliction of feeling too far away from where anything important is happening, lost on the hidden undercurve of the world. So there is much talk of striking off overseas. But would they like it better there, in the grim grey anticlimax, with victory-fingered Churchill casting a dark huge shadow over Europe's gangrenous corpse, and the lethal ash adrift in Asian skies, and the sad tides lapping and lapping at the beached hulks of man's spirit, and lapping all the way out even to this hidden undercurve?

Few of them, at any rate, actively seem to be doing anything about it. Jefferson has settled for his own waters of Lethe between peddling dreary handouts for a dull Government department. Calverton is an exception. He takes phenobarb to get to sleep and Benzedrine to stay awake and acts interminably in appalling radio soap operas and runs his own mobile little theatre to take Molière to the factories, and when he can he saves to try to get away to London.

With the same Mecca in mind little Janice, Cress's friend from the women's army, spent her deferred pay on a travelling suburban library and trundles books around the streets in a home-made hand-barrow. She is only a wisp of a thing, so she has a lot of guts. And there are two other girls like her who were in the army with Cressida who have teamed up with a native crew and bought a lugger and gone pearl-fishing out of Thursday Island. It's funny that in this country so firmly entrenched in the belief of audacious masculinity the girls often seem to display the real audacity. With the others it's mostly talk and argument. In the Long Bar of the Australia every day is somebody's Gethsemane. Or a Golgotha built on bottle-tops.

Jefferson's case is different.

It would have been about four months after I joined the paper

STILL?

when they sacked him. By that time I was writing most of the main features, but perhaps that had nothing to do with his dismissal. He was still supposed to be doing the critical stuff, theatre and books mostly. But he was drinking more and more heavily. There was an occasion when several of us had to front for him for two whole weeks. We would take it in turns, some of us to write his copy and others to go searching for him – and lying like troopers to keep Tomlinson and the news editor from realizing what was going on – and eventually he was found in a revolting back slum room in Surry Hills with a half-caste Aboriginal woman, and he had not washed or shaved in a week or more and was covered in filth and not very coherent. Calverton took him home to his flat and nursed him through the DTs, and one night when I went to see him he was whimpering out his own poems in between fits of screaming or sobbing. Two days later he was back in the office, beautifully tailored and wearing a new bow tie.

LONDON, 1950

It has not been real until now, this feeling that we have finally got away. Escaped. Tilbury is a curious Rubicon, pewter-grey in the drizzle, a dull shine, more a gleam than a shine, hardly a shine at all. The people on the dockside are startlingly small in size, gloved and muffled, their breath steaming, stamping their feet and punching their hands together, looking up without interest at our beige leviathan warping in under flag-flutter and smokedrift and the soft alloy of the damp low sky. A greasy light edges the wharf sheds but does not reach the marshy flats beyond. The dwarfs on the dockside show no excitement. Why should they? The men stand miserable and squat in their flat cloth caps, the women huddle under black umbrellas in winter boots and pixie hoods and gruel-coloured clothes.

The twelve hundred people who for a month and for thirteen thousand miles have been contained in the metal belly of the leviathan wait in their queues, divided into alphabetical groups. Not sheep-like, though; most of them are irritable and shrill, importunate and querulous with the stewards and ship's officers, all of whom have also become cranky with landfall. Some of the passengers appear to have rejected the homecoming; they don't seem to realize this is England or want to go ashore; they have turned their backs on it and lean morosely along the port railing like dejected birds, the massive purring ramparts of the ship's weight between them and the dockside. They stare across the sluggish tide at barges and tugs and lighters sliding in sea-snot on drab enterprises not remotely concerned with us: a white plume of steam farts from a tug's funnel and at once vanishes in the heavy dun air, and no sound follows it; this is their and Tilbury's indifference to anything momentous in our arrival. The many birds wheeling lethargically above the estuary are crows, not seagulls.

Most of the passengers who shun the homecoming side of the ship surprise me by this attitude, for they are almost all from the English group and one would think would be excited by this moment of return: well over half the passengers from Australia have been English, disgruntled migrants who went out there and hated it and are coming back home again. All through the voyage they have been telling us how much they hated it out there, but none of them seems very happy now.

The only really happy person on the deck that I can see is a middle-aged Australian named Bert Bloxham and he weeps copiously as he tugs his beret down over his cold ears and blinks across at the dreary prospect. He has been saving for years for his trip Home (the word is always given a capital in his letters, which he invariably asks us to read). He wept when we raised the Lizard and saw the green Cornish folds beyond, and wept again for the Isle of Wight and the Dover cliffs, and he has much weeping yet to do—for St Paul's and Westminster Abbey and Buckingham Palace and the King and the jewels in the Tower and Shakespeare and the Cheshire Cheese and the Lord Mayor's coach and Whitehall and the Changing of the Guard. Bloxham's beret is looking stained and tatty. The size of the ship confused him, and although he suffers from chronic catarrh and is always hawking and spitting he never could learn to spit to leeward so that he was always getting the stuff back in his face or over his beret.

Flannery, the rich professional globe-trotter who made his quid in wartime profiteering and who admits to being a 'first-class lurk merchant' and who has bored us rigid all the way from Sydney, wears a black bowler for his London landfall and swings a furled umbrella; in Colombo he wore a solar topee, in Suez a red fez, in Marseilles a beret, in Gibraltar a tweedy English cloth cap. He has the wrong shape of bowler for London – they will take him for a plumber – and, anyway, his accoutrement is marred by the large ugly kangaroo badge in his coat lapel, and at the moment the effect is ruined by his possessive protectiveness for a leather bag and pouffe which feature multicoloured camels, sphinxes, palms, and pyramids. The anticlimax of arrival is almost dispelled for me by the comforting thought that I shall never again have to listen to Flannery's interminable stories of his vulgar vapid voyagings. He wears an expression of petulance, no doubt seeing ahead of him the arid little stretch of transience he must get through before he can board another ship and seize his next captive audience. Flannery carries in his baggage – his 'ports', as he calls them – a full swagman's outfit complete with blanket-roll, billy, and cork-hung sundowner's hat which he brings out for shipboard fancy-dress occasions; his wife has a rubber mask in the form of a dog's head and a kind of black-and-white spotted shift with a tail sewn on, and a 'tucker-box' to sit on, and at the grand parade Flannery leads her, barking, on all-fours around the floor while the ship's orchestra (rehearsed and bribed in advance by Flannery) strikes up a snatch or two of *The Road to Gundagai*. In each of Flannery's trip books he lists the number of prizes they have won as 'Waltzing Matilda'; the total has reached sixty-three. He has confided to me that they hate London really – 'can't ever wait to get out of the dreary bloody place!' – and they spend most of their time at Australia House, checking the Boomerang Club notice-board for 'current functions' and reading 'all the good old local dirt in the Aussie papers'.

Farquharson, the British Council man, is still in the bar, drinking last-minute gins and stocking up with duty-free tins of Player's. He is an amusing and agreeable fellow, tall and stooped and untidy and very like Gavin Turley (he has the same sort of big soiled teeth), and he is on a special leave to settle some family matters, legacies and estates, occasioned by the death of his father. He is not happy about returning to England because he has fallen passionately in love with Australia, doting on its climate and what to him is its absence of class distinctions, and during the voyage he has endured, albeit encouraged, much enmity from his disillusioned returning countrymen, for whom he has undisguised contempt. Farquharson is a Balliol man and there is some quality about him that I envy very much; he has a kind of gentle assurance about himself and all that surrounds him, and a wonderful lucidity of thought and expression – he is very intelligent – that makes one think he was formed immutably, just as he is now, all those years ago before he came down from Oxford. Whenever I talk to Farquharson I always feel that the rest of us were taken out of the oven too soon. He plans to clean up his affairs with the utmost dispatch and hare off back to his beloved Australia, but he intends returning intrepidly, for he plans to ride a motor-scooter back, and on the voyage I have been giving him some background about the Near East and Iraq and Iran and Baluchistan and India. He promises post-cards from Isfahan and Dizful and Karachi. He has, incidentally, a tremendous thing about Cressida. I imagine this is why he is hidden in the bar, avoiding the awfulness of goodbyes.

The office has sent a black hire-car with a uniformed chauffeur. The East End is unspeakably squalid and wretched, the bomb damage voracious, London itself all charcoal-black and white with the Portland stone stained and weeping in the rain, the red omnibuses flower in the gloom like incandescent blossoms, and the trees are bare and blurred. It is the way we expected it and we are excited and happy. However, the office flat is not ready, the hotel is appalling, and the children have suspected whooping-cough. We look across to the misty dankness of Kensington Gardens, and while Cressida wonders whether she should risk taking the children across to see the Peter Pan statue I read the letters that were delivered at Tilbury.

Calverton is already here and has been lucky enough, I learn, to fluke a part in a play running at a theatre in the Charing Cross Road. Tom Kiernan, who left earlier, is painting somewhere in Spain. Jefferson, back in Sydney, has been carted off to a home for inebriates, and is not expected to come out. Jefferson didn't get away in time.

It is alarming to wonder whether we did.

SYDNEY, 1949

No, no, Meredith, you can't get away like that. This is the old 'With one bound Jack was free!' formula. And, besides, you are not free: you may never in your life be free—this is one of the little things we have to work out—but certainly you are not free at this stage. It is ridiculous, in terms of the arrival at Tilbury, to talk of your having 'escaped'. Why, you have not even *tried* for freedom yet. Calverton escaped, and Kiernan, and, going in the other direction, so did Farquharson, I suppose. But not you . . .

It is highly debatable whether David Meredith could at any stage have saved Jefferson, although his guilt about this persisted for a long time: it was far more likely that the poor devil was an example of the born victim, the murderee, carrying inside himself the germinating seeds of his own doom. But what is not in the least debatable is that Meredith, for all his inner desire to cling to instability, has kept a pretty tight grip on the world where 'the office has sent a black hire-car with a uniformed chauffeur'. He has removed himself, but he has not escaped.

There was a chance to escape—admittedly risky—when the novel which he had written after work on Pop Charlton's verandah was published, for while it had no particular *succès d'estime* it was favourably enough reviewed, and, by Australian standards, it made a respectable amount of money. Meredith at this time cultivated a bohemian kind of life outside his office hours, selecting as his friends and acquaintances struggling painters and poets and would-be novelists and composers and actors, who behaved rather blatantly in protest against the inadequacies and unappreciativeness of the hostile materialistic society: the rays of success seldom illuminated – except for the actors supported by commercial radio – this shadowy self-created fringe-world in which they bleakly revelled. Meredith's modest success as a creative writer made him, therefore, an envied novelty with an obligation to continue the struggle (which had nothing to do with his success as a journalist), and Cressida tried hard to urge him into committing to the gamble. The creative urge really did gnaw at him, and for a week or two he wavered, torn by the conflict in his ambitions. In the end he stuck to the safety of his position with the *Globe*, on the ground that he was not justified in jeopardizing to such a hazardous and precarious prospect the future of the children, a daughter, Miranda, having by this time been added to his responsibilities. He was now writing the daily column which Jefferson had much earlier predicted and was not oblivious of the prestige in the community which his byline gave him. He was much sought after by people courting publicity, he delighted in making social appearances – receptions, cocktail-parties, art openings, first nights – in the company of his beautiful wife. He enjoyed the fun of being a columnist. There was even an amusing flirtation (quite harmless because of his obsessive passion for Cressida) with a dancer whom he was able to build, through favourable publicity, into a cabaret star with the unlikely professional name of Jelly Crystal. During this time he seemed content with both worlds.

When he could he would run a paragraph in his column from one of Jefferson's departmental handouts, because Jefferson was finding it not at all easy to adapt either his alcoholism or his literary style to the dull demands of a Government bureaucracy, especially while still under a cloud politically.

Jefferson had been an early victim of the witch-hunt. The waves of strikes and stoppages and the general restless tumult in the land were attributed by a great many Australians, seeking the simplest solution to dilemmas altogether too baffling, to the evil threat of Communism. In Europe the Cold War was developing in bitterness and intensity. In China the tiger was stirring. In Australia it was a time of prevalent suspicion, and almost any nonconformity was suspect; these were a people disillusioned and disturbed and somebody had to be blamed for what was going wrong: it was a time of irresponsible accusations and superficial examinations on the part of some, and on the part of more a weary ostrich-wish just to bury the head in the sand. It was not an atmosphere likely to heal Jefferson's already bruised idealism: indeed it provoked him, with the help of liquor, into even wilder furies of anger and contempt. 'They won't even *think*, they won't even try to think!' he would rage in his cups. 'They want to level everybody down to their own dreary bloody mediocrity and apathy.'

'Well, they're fed up too,' Meredith would try to reason with him. 'They can see everything becoming a bigger and bigger mess, and what can they do about it? Out here, what say have *we* got, for God's sake?'

'We can try, can't we?'

'Try? I tried for two years to talk about China, to write about it. Nobody was interested. Nobody cared. Then everybody is shocked because the Chinese Communists begin to take over, and it's the Yellow Peril all over again, and it's suddenly the Near North instead of the Far East, and there are Commo agents and Commo spies lurking under every desk and table.'

'Isn't that exactly what I'm saying?'

'Berlin. The Bomb. China. What can *we* do about things like that?'

'We could bloody well try to think. We could do more than just sit on our fat arses talking about beer and sport and race-horses and the SP.'

That was the way it always went, little verbal vortex discussions swirling around furiously, then draining down the plughole. In the event Jefferson was toppled by something trivial and undramatic, nothing nation-shaking. He had done no more than write favourable reviews of the performance by a Little Theatre group of a proletarian play and of an art exhibition by a contemporary society which included in its mixed membership some painters of known leftish sympathies. The exhibition, it should be added, was held in the gallery of a great city emporium, enshrined one might say in the very cathedral of capitalism's profit system, the high priesthood of which was not at all averse to collecting gallery rental and a thirty-three-and-a-third per cent commission from pictures sold, quite regardless of any political affiliations the exhibitors might have had. The same impartiality was not extended to Jefferson.

Although not even remotely a Communist he was already suspect for the extreme liberalism of his political views, and he had disturbed many people by outspoken articles he had written against war (like Siegfried Sassoon in an earlier war he had to win a Military Cross before feeling himself entitled to become a pacifist). His writing was good enough to excite envy, and he also wrote poetry, which in itself was, in Australia, a pretty dubious activity unless the poetry was balladic, chauvinistic or sentimental, and Jefferson's troubled verse certainly fitted into none of these categories. After the publication of the contentious reviews a few angry letters to the editor were received from irate readers and published, and two anonymous informers telephoned Tomlinson with quite fictional accounts of Jefferson's furtive undercover activities on behalf of the Communist Party. In the same week a certain columnist writing under the pseudonym of 'Palamedes' in a fortnightly journal of the extreme right made oblique references to a 'parlour pink' and 'fellow-traveller' writing in the dailies who was 'deliberately fomenting anarchy and undermining all the decent values of the community'.

It so happened that Meredith had earlier gathered certain interesting and accurate figures concerning 'Palamedes's' tax evasions and thought of running a paragraph about it in his column but Tomlinson ruled it 'highly dangerous' and refused to print it: no doubt he was glad enough of a lever with which to dislodge the troublesome Jefferson. Meredith took a proof of the rejected story and showed it to 'Palamedes', deceiving him into thinking he intended to run it: this ruse produced a very abject apology to Jefferson, but by then it was too late: Jefferson had his notice. In the long and terrible drinking bout that followed Jefferson's spirit drained away, so that when he finally got the job writing Government handouts he felt enormously grateful and steadied up for a while. After Jefferson's dismissal Tomlinson gave Meredith a raise in salary. The column developed an urbane and witty character and was not much concerned with controversial matters.

Such was the climate of the time.

It was during this period that Graham Crossley appeared. He called at the *Globe* office one morning, with the dark flannel suit, brown porkpie hat, gaberdine trenchcoat, and air of quiet friendliness which he would continue to wear like a uniform. He carried with him the briefcase which he would in future seldom be seen without, the sort of briefcase one might expect to find chained to the wrist of a King's Messenger. He was a calm, handsome man in his early thirties, a pipe-smoker who drank only black coffee or dry sherry, and Meredith was pleased to see him again. They had not met since the final year of war in China, where Crossley had served as a major in British military intelligence; he was now, it seemed, representing certain English export firms in Australia.

After this first reunion he became a fairly regular caller on Meredith, always dropping in around edition time, just after Meredith's column had gone to press, and they would go to a café next door for coffee and to talk about this and that, mostly reminiscences of China and discussions of what was happening over there, with Crossley puffing away at his pipe and doing most of the listening. One morning Cressida was there while in town for shopping and she invited him to the flat for dinner.

From this point he began to call on Cressida with the same casual regularity as he continued to do with David—he was occupying a small bachelor apartment in the same suburb as the Merediths—these suburban calls almost invariably being made while David was still in the city. Cressida at first found him agreeable company; he never spoke about anything in particular, would sometimes help her with the babies or the dishes, usually brought along a bottle and would take a dry sherry or two with her, and gave the impression that he had a deep affection and admiration for her husband. But after a time she became uneasy at the regularity of these visits and some curious and intriguing quality in his demeanour. He would often prop himself in the doorway, puffing away at his pipe, watching Cressida at work in the kitchen or attending to the babies, and for twenty minutes at a stretch he would never take his eyes off her and never speak a word. She began to wonder now about his intentions, although he never gave even the hint of making an overture, and finally she confided her perplexities to her husband.

'For God's sake, how long has this been going on?' he wanted to know. He had come home late from the office, and he was edgy because he had been drinking with Jefferson.

'Oh, months and months,' Cressida said.

'And you only tell me now.'

'What do you mean, darling? It hasn't really begun to worry me until now.'

'You said it's been going on for months.'

'I've often told you Graham has been here. He only lives three blocks away. He drives past the flat almost every day.'

'Apparently he doesn't drive past. He pops in.'

'Quite often. I've usually told you.'

'Not lately you haven't.'

'No, I don't suppose I have. But, darling, it's only that I haven't known how to put it . . . I don't even know what it *is* about him that worries me . . .'

'What does he do when he's here?'

'Nothing. That's the point. He doesn't do anything. He just

sort of . . . watches. He might have a drink or two. Sometimes he helps with the children. Or the washing up. Or just talks. No, he doesn't do anything really. That's it.'

'You mean you'd be quite happy if he made a pass at you?'

Cressida looked at him a moment and then said evenly, 'Well, at least I'd understand that, wouldn't I? I needn't necessarily be happy about it but I would understand it.'

'I'll bet. You have another male caller, don't you?'

'Who?'

'Archie Calverton. He drops in too, doesn't he?'

'Archie? Of course he does. You know that. He's our friend.'

'When I'm not here, I mean.'

'David, what are you trying to get at?'

'Does he pop in every second day like this other bloke?'

'Neither of them pops in every second day. I think you are being —'

'Wait a minute. It's only *now* I learn about Crossley, isn't it? Although you admit it's been going on for months and months. So I simply wonder about Calverton, that's all. I'm only asking if he's another of the regulars.'

'He comes every so often,' she said patiently. 'If he isn't recording or hasn't got a show.'

'When I'm not here.'

'You know very well that he's usually working when you're not. And vice versa. Anyway, he doesn't come all that much. He likes swimming at Bondi, he drops by occasionally to see if I'd like to drive down with him and take the children. Darling, what *is* this all about? What are you getting at? You know about Archie as well as I do.'

'Do I? I'm beginning to wonder. If you want the truth I'm beginning to wonder about a lot of things.'

She was dismayed and she loved him and she knew he had been drinking with Jefferson, which always upset him, and she tried to reason with him, but he went on goading her and it ended in a blazing row.

The problem, of course, was that Meredith was obsessively

jealous and Cressida obsessively honest. He loved her so totally that he had to possess all of her, even when the totality of that possession hurt excruciatingly. There were times when he would have been happy to be lied to, placated, soothed, so long as he was endorsed in his ownership, and reassured, for he was haunted always by an abiding fear that he could not hold her, that she would slip away from him into some other man's possession. He had never been able to forget Gavin Turley's warning that they would not last six months together, that she would destroy him. (It was significant that he remembered it this way and not, as Turley had said, that they would destroy *each other*.) To arm himself against this threat he had to try to know, even if the knowledge was a form of masochism, everything about her. He would question her about her life before he had come to her, screwing the sick tension of his stomach into a grinding knot. Cressida, on her part, with a love that was far less demanding, was perfectly willing to concede him his ownership, for her loyalty to him was an unqualified as her fidelity, but her honesty forbade her to grant to him a retrospective possession, and perhaps this was what rankled with him. And so she answered him, not happily, though, and with a reluctance that had nothing to do with deception. She admitted a casual intimacy with Turley, that there had been other men equally casual, the fleeting ephemeral liaisons of wartime, and one or two deeper involvements which had also been fractured by the fluxes and exigencies of war. (It was the confession of Turley as a lover that wounded him most grievously even though it was the slightest of her youthful affairs; Turley he knew, Turley was his friend, Turley he could visualize, the other men in her past were only shadows, not even shapes or names.) These amorous adventures had been no different, really, than Meredith's own wartime experiences and had quite ended by the time they came together in Riordan's scruffy hotel; he would try to see this and understand it, but there was no consolation in it. Once, knuckling at his self-inflicted wounds, he had tried to insist that she tell him how many lovers she had had, and she had looked at him for a long time, as if she wanted to say nothing and simply take him into her arms, before she said, 'I don't know, darling, I never kept a score.' Try as he might he could not get her to lie to him so that he might find a different sort of comfort in disbelieving her.

Two days later Crossley, in his usual way, called on Meredith at the office, and later, over the customary coffee, Meredith brought the matter to a head quite bluntly.

'Listen, there's something I've got to ask you,' he said, and Crossley puffed at his pipe and nodded, his neatly manicured fingers tapping on the ground Three Nuns tobacco tin. 'I want to know why you're always dropping in at the flat when I'm not there, hanging around Cress.'

Crossley looked at him through a slow plume of blue smoke, then rubbed his chin and chuckled softly. 'Not to worry, old boy,' he said calmly. 'No ulterior motive, I mean. I can explain. At least I hope I can. I'm awfully fond of Cressida, as you know, but that isn't . . . er . . .' He stopped for a moment, then smiled and said, 'Look, I had planned to take this thing up with you today, anyway. I think it will explain it.' He reached down and picked up the briefcase from which he was almost inseparable and for the first time in Meredith's presence opened it. He rummaged carefully, extracted a foolscap-size dossier file tied with pink ribbon and tossed it on the table between the coffee cups. 'I'd like you to take a look through that,' he said, and put his pipe back in his mouth.

'What is it?' Meredith asked, untying the ribbon. Neatly printed on the folder was a name, *Blackwell, James Douglas*, and *WTZb*/47/1329.

'Dossier.' Meredith looked up at him sharply, but Crossley smiled and went on imperturbably. 'You remember Blackwell. Correspondent. China, Burma, India, Malaya.'

'I remember Blackwell.'

'That's his dossier. I don't want you to read it all. Just riffle through.'

Meredith didn't read it all, although he was tempted. It was a fascinating and alarming document. Leafing through it, he completely forgot about Cressida and what he had wanted to talk to Crossley about. Once he looked up and said, 'Jesus, apparently the poor bastard wasn't even allowed to go to the john for a bog without somebody watching him!' The entry which prompted this read, in part: 'Kunming-Dibrugah 21/6/43, ATC, auth. Gen. Cheves, transient billets, no association. 22/6/43 Dibrugah-Dum Dum RAF Transport, proceeded Calcutta, billeted Bristol Hotel, dined alone, then drank at cocktail-bar until retired to room 2235 hours. Twice visited bar toilet but no contact or conversation.'

The dossier, with many entries of this nature, covered Blackwell's professional and private peregrinations over a period of nearly three years. The final entry dealt with Singapore and Blackwell's departure from there on a day of May, 1946, on a RAF Transport flight. Below this final entry was a hardly legible rubber stamp imprint across which somebody in red ink had written in a crabbed hand that had a curious look of being perfunctory, 'No further action. This man now clean.'

Meredith closed the folder and tied the pink ribbon in a neat bow, pulling at it until both loops were evenly matched. 'There,' he said, and looked intently at Crossley. 'Interesting,' he said. '*Bloody* interesting! But what the hell has it got to do with me? Or Cressida?' he added, remembering.

'Blackwell was late on the scene, and he didn't get around all that much,' said Crossley. 'Nowhere near as much as you. He never got up to Yenan, for instance, as you did. Nor Lanchow and Urumchi. He never did the Red River area. Mengtsze. Wenshan. Those places. Actually if you go through that dossier carefully you will find that he was never in touch with the Communist areas or elements.'

'So what?' Meredith said guardedly.

'Well, I mean there's *his* dossier. Can you imagine what *yours* is like?' Again he chuckled softly. 'Yours is quite interesting. And three times as fat as that one.'

'What's all this about?' Meredith had that same feeling of sick, inexplicable guilt that so frequently overcomes an innocent traveller in front of a Customs officer.

'I'll be frank with you, David. I still work for the Foreign

Office. I was working for them when I knew you in China. I still am. The import agency is a cover. For some months now I've been checking on you, and—'

'Checking on me! For God's sake! Why the hell should *you* be checking on *me*?' He stopped and looked hard at his companion. 'Is that why you've been hanging around Cressida?' he asked.

Crossley, unruffled, nodded over his pipe. 'Well, we have our various little ways of finding out about the people we're interested in. I mean, Cressida's ideas about you, and the whole relationship generally, actually these are relevant angles in the overall design.'

'The overall design, no doubt, being a State secret,' Meredith said sarcastically.

'Not at all, old boy. Not now. We've completed our checking and we're perfectly satisfied about you.' He took Blackwell's dossier up and returned it to the briefcase, which he then closed and locked. 'Four chaps,' he said, 'are to be dropped in to North China, using the term in a broad geographical sense. I mean it could be Mongolia, or Manchuria, but the object of the exercise is to penetrate the Communist-dominated areas for the purpose of obtaining certain information. I shall be one of the four, and we'd rather like you to be one of the others.'

Meredith looked at him in astonishment. 'Are you out of your twit?' he said at last. 'Drop *me* into China! You must be completely barmy! How do you know what I really feel politically? What chance—'

'Oh, we're able to cope with any problems you're likely to raise, old boy. You'll have to go abroad and undergo a two-year course anyway. Indoctrination, briefing, language and so on. And naturally there'll have to be some work on your physical appearance. But we really are quite expert in these matters. The point about you, David, is that you have an adventurous spirit, you're physically tough, you have had a couple of years in China—you know the country and the people and you already have a smattering of the language—you have an intelligent appreciation of the basic problems, you've actually spent some time with the Communists, which gives you an unusual intimacy about their habits and methods, and you are a trained professional observer. So we naturally became interested in you as a possible candidate.' He knocked his pipe out very carefully, and as carefully began to refill it.

'As a candidate for what? For getting in early to stir up a Third World War?'

'Or to prevent it,' Crossley said between puffs of smoke.

'Listen, Graham,' Meredith said to him seriously, 'I had one marriage buggered up by the war. I've married again. I have two small children. I'm very much in love with my wife and family. I've no intention of buggering that up too, not for any of this cloak-and-dagger bullshit.'

'Your wife and family will be taken care of very handsomely, David. In the event of anything untoward happening they would be looked after for the rest of their lives—better perhaps than you could look after them.'

'I don't know how to thank you.'

Crossley disregarded the sarcasm and said, 'You'll naturally want time to chew this over, to talk with Cressida, so I would suggest——'

'You needn't suggest anything. I'm not interested. Not even remotely interested. I've got to the stage when I'm too old and too tired to keep on chasing fire-engines.'

'Nothing more to be said, then?' said Crossley equably.

'Nothing.'

Crossley smiled and nodded and reached for the slip of paper underneath the sugar-bowl. 'My turn to pay the bill today, I think,' he said.

'There is one other thing,' Meredith said.

'Yes?'

'What happens to that big fat dossier of mine?'

'I'm not really sure. We shall probably hand it over to your Commonwealth Security people. They might find odds and ends of interest in it.'

'I see. Am I allowed to talk about this business?'

'Why not? Nobody will believe you.'

Outside the café Crossley shook hands and left him, but stopped at the kerb and called back, 'Love to Cressida.'

Neither David nor Cressida ever saw Graham Crossley again, although they heard indirectly about him some years later.

Not long after this the big party was held to send Archie Calverton overseas. A visiting English producer had seen him acting in Shakespeare and had indicated a willingness, indeed an eagerness, to help him if he could get himself to London. It was a big party in a sprawling old beach house at Avalon, with gallons of cheap claret and a bathtub full of home-brew, and everybody from the fringe world was there, the actors and writers and poets and painters and general misfits, and a silk top-hat was put down on the carpet in the centre of the room and everybody was invited to kick in with what they could spare—a quid or a fiver or a tenner—towards the Calverton General Transportation Fund. The top-hat was propped against a sign somebody had painted which paraphrased the old convict ballad: TRUE PATRIOT HE, FOR BE IT UNDERSTOOD—HE LEAVES HIS COUNTRY FOR HIS COUNTRY'S GOOD. The money that went into the hat was enough to pay for Calverton's steamer fare to London with a bit over for drinking money. After the party Calverton was too drunk and too emotional to drive, so Meredith drove him home with Cressida in the back seat holding him up, his head on her shoulder. She had to prop him up twice so he could throw up through the open window as the car rushed southward through the spangled humid blackness of the night, but for most of the time he and Cressida quoted poetry to each other, Shakespeare and Donne and Herrick and Marvell and Eliot, and every now and then Calverton would drunkenly protest his deep love for both of them, but particularly for Cressida, and David, solitary in the front seat and driving down the sprayed bright fan of the headlights, felt alone and desolate, not knowing the poems or not being able to remember the words, and having nothing intimately to share.

It was a few weeks after Calverton sailed when Meredith was

offered a second chance of freedom. He had been sent on a special assignment to the Snowy Mountains in the Australian Alps to write about the opening stages of a gigantic new hydro-electric and irrigation scheme that was designed to drill great tunnels through the rocky hearts of mountains and to reverse the courses of five rivers, and the work force for this vast and challenging project was composed almost entirely of foreign migrants. There were men there from almost every country in Europe, and from Canada and the United States, and Russian engineers from the great Siberian dams, and a Cambridge graduate was in the cookhouse in a soiled chef's hat chanting Virgil against the scream and shudder of the blizzard outside.

The yellow tractors against the glaring drifts of snow, the beards and mackinaws, the polyglot babble of smoke-hazed mess huts, the tingling atmosphere of a collective excitement; these as much as the sheer audacity of the concept had a profound effect upon Meredith: he returned from the assignment burning with a new ambition. It was four in the morning when he got back to the flat, but he wakened Cressida at once to tell her about it, and they drank interminable cups of coffee while he talked until long after the winter dawn had broken.

'It's like coming to an oasis in a desert, when you've been thirsting for something of promise, something to believe in. It's magnificent, darling! It's exciting! It's the only *visionary* thing I've seen since I've been back in this bloody country. Anyway,' he said firmly, 'it's made up my mind for me. I'm going to chuck in the job on the *Globe*. I'll put in my resignation today. Because I'm going down *there* to work. I'm going to find out all about it. *Live* with it. And then write it as a novel. It could be the greatest bloody novel ever. It *could*, Cress. It's the most fabulous theme. It's got everything. *Everything*!'

He saw then that she was crying, and for a moment he was startled until he saw that she was crying with happiness.

But nothing came of it. For that very same day Tomlinson called Meredith into his office and talked for a time about the deteriorating situation in Berlin, and in Europe generally.

'So we propose,' he said, 'to send you to the London office for a few years as our European correspondent. Miss Fielden—' he glanced at his secretary—'has a copy of the terms of agreement, which I think you will find quite satisfactory. She has also pencilled passages for you and your wife and family on the *Orcades*. That will give you three weeks to get packed and to clean up your affairs. All right?'

Meredith said nothing about resigning and never spoke about the visions he had seen in the Snowy Mountains.

SYDNEY, 1968

Today it is quite an odd feeling to be rushing forward to now, whizzing through the last eighteen years as if they had never happened, although something must have happened because the now seems to be so different from the then. Different, that is, until you think about it, because in the crucial and basic things it might not be so different after all. Perhaps nothing really changes that much.

These reflections were sparked by Julian bringing round some of his undergraduate friends from the university. I have kept pretty much to my room because Cressida is due back today and I want to be as fit as possible, but I could hear them in the next room being sure of everything in between playing Bob Dylan records on the pick-up. Dylan, being young, gets considerable homage from them: he is not a god, because all their gods are dead; he seems, rather, to be a kind of high priest of their ideas and rituals. Not just the rituals of protest and dissent and rebellion, which are normal enough with the young, but their ideas of loneliness and aloneness and of being alienated altogether from us of another generation. They talk and listen together as if we would not be able to understand it. As if loneliness and alienation are things they have just discovered for the first time. One of the girl students is Jefferson's daughter Anne: her stepfather, unlike the traditional stepfather of novels, dotes on her and spoils her and is putting her through university, and I found myself wondering whether she could ever realize the awful depths of loneliness and alienation her father suffered before his final collapse. Still, he has been dead now for twelve years, so it doesn't really matter.

There is one of Bob Dylan's songs they keep playing and replaying, a kind of esoteric diatribe against a certain 'Mister Jones' who seems to symbolize the 'oldies' and 'squares' of my generation and the hoarsely reiterated refrain is a taunting, 'Something is happening here, and you don't know what it is – do you, Mr Jones?'

But neither do you, Mr Dylan. Nor they. Not yet.

The early budding is deceptive; these dark, night-flowering hybrids, loneliness and aloneness, take a long time in the growing. Yeats was seventy-two and only two years away from the grave when he said, 'Talk to me of originality and I will turn on you with rage. I am a crowd, I am a lonely man, I am nothing.'

FROM AN EXPATRIATE'S JOURNAL[5]

London, 1950. These people are quite different from us. We like to think of ourselves as 97 per cent British, but they are not like us at all and we feel alien. This morning at the Round Pond in Kensington Gardens two well-dressed elderly gentlemen were sailing model yachts and one wet his finger and lifted it to the cold drizzling air and said, 'A shade westerly I think, old boy,' in a cultured accent, and there was another man birdwatching on a wet bench with binoculars focused on the bare branches of the elms, and not far away a fourth man, bareheaded in the rain, slowly paced the paths, an open book in his hand, reading poetry aloud to himself. Later, in the city, a bearded fellow in a long, shabby, flapping raincoat came charging down the Strand shaking his fists in the air and shouting, 'Will it never be warm! Will it never be warm! Will it never be warm!' Nobody turned to follow his tumultuous course.

The sun is far to the south, trundling along the chimney-pots like a squashed persimmon. This is a leaden grey place, and the faces in the queues are grey and docile: there are queues for buses, for ration-books, for cod-liver oil and orange juice, they even queue sometimes because there is a queue and they wonder hopefully what is at the end of it. They queue patiently to take their turn to watch men cleaning away the bomb debris. In Fleet Street the varicosed charladies are down on their hands and knees soon after dawn scrubbing at steps and footpaths in the cheerless chill and if you ask them how they are they twist up a jocular kind of grimace and say, 'Ar well, mustn't grumble, sir.'

Behind the gay fashionable streets and the bright façades of tradition the heavy grey wilderness is gigantic and brooding: the Thames slides through it like a mystical poem, shot with Turner's light. A brash young Australian painter was in the Codgers yesterday drunkenly asserting that he had come to set the Thames on fire. He, like others before him, will find this river non-inflammable.

The grey houses are crushed together in grey geometries, in dismal flat recessions, pressed against each other for warmth, crowded by strangers wearing experienced or secondhand faces. All things are different. In this city there are about the same number of people as in the whole continent of Australia: this is disturbing but I am not sure that it is the real reason for our feeling insignificant; rather it is a sense of the omnipresence of some long historical process—something we do not have yet—and an awareness of the painful accretion of the slow centuries, of all the blood and triumph and struggle.

Sometimes when I think about it I am afflicted by a dull dense pain for these grey people in their grey queues, for only ten years ago they were the indomitable ones who became victors and conquerors. In the grey queues nobody wears laurel. Is all human triumph as bitter and sad as this?

France, 1951. There is a marvellous dilapidation about French farm buildings. Everything is either dust-coloured and peeled off or a splendid faded blue, the blue Chinese coolies wear. Whole families in the fields all wear the same blue and they work with white horses, heroic and great-rumped, like the chargers in mediæval jousts. One was pulling a plough right up to the edge of a ruined fort of the Maginot Line, which was quite overgrown with weeds and grass and brambles. The sheared furrowed waves of the moist tan earth swept all around its futility. Here and there yellow flowers clung to the blind embrasures, and there was a cherry-tree in blossom.

We shall have to do this every year, get away for a few weeks on the Continent, just the two of us, sharing things again. Both of us have an insatiable curiosity. There is so much here to learn. During the day we have given up eating in restaurants. We stop in some little town or village and buy a long loaf of bread and pâté and soft country cheeses and a bottle of the local wine and eat blissfully along the roadside in the sweet cool grass beneath the plane-trees or the poplars.

The roads of Picardy are long and straight and the tall poplars meet at a point miles away. The sky is enormous with big lazy whoofs of cloud and on either side of the road there are buttercups and forget-me-nots glittering in the verge, and behind the hedges are the endless rows of tidy little white crosses, sometimes disappearing perspectively over a rise in the ground. The ploughing by the heroic white horses sweeps the earth into dark banks around these fields too. The names of these places of battle and death are not in the least outlandish; they go back for centuries to Froissart and before, and they are very familiar to me from the silk postcards my father sent home from the First World War. The graves take up a tremendous area of the arable land, but there are the sturdy workhorses and the labour in the fields and the flowers and the trees grown and in blossom again and the crops springing from the ever-lasting earth.

There is an old woman picking dandelions by the side of the road. She gathers them into a basket. She is dressed in black with a blue apron, and black thick stockings and boots, and when she bends over you can see how her stockings are rolled just above the knee. 'I can do them that way,' says Cressida. 'You have to roll the stocking tightly, then gather up the slack and twist it round a coin or a button, then tuck it firmly under the roll. It doesn't work very well with nylons,' she says.

It is exciting when Cressida says this, knowing the flesh of her thighs, but this old woman's bare legs above the stockings are skinny and knotted into ropes of sinew and she stoops very slowly as if they hurt. But she has collected a great many dandelions. Is she really so old? Do peasant women work until they drop, or is it the unremitting work that makes them look so old? Questions like this intrigue us, coming from a land that has nothing even remotely comparable to the peasantry of Europe, a land where it is not easy to starve and which has never known such continuity of suffering. These are some of the things we must try to learn about and understand.

The old women are scattered along every road, gathering things, usually faggots, which are roped to their bent backs when they have sufficient for a burden. They all move patiently and tiredly – solitary figures mostly, for they seldom keep company with one another – and they never look up as the car goes past. The men do, leaning on their hoes. If you wave, sometimes they wave back. But not often.

Germany, 1951. Cress is excited because this is her first foreign frontier-post; not counting Luxembourg, but I don't suppose anyone really counts Luxembourg. Germany is different. 'But the uniforms look exactly like the ones in the movies,' Cressida says in some surprise. The Germans are most polite and make a little joke or two, and are gallant with Cressida; a very handsome young officer retrieves from the Customs post the pair of sunglasses she has forgotten and bows as he presents them to her. They do not look at the car or our baggage.

This is an oddity too. Australia is the only continent that has no frontiers, no confused agglomeration of cultures and customs and races and languages, so crossing a frontier can be as novel to an Australian as snow seen for the first time by a desert dweller.

(It was on the ship coming over here that Cressida for the first time in her life saw snow—the wintry flanks of Etna flushed rose-pink in the dawn as the ship headed for the Straits of Messina: that very same day her first volcano was kind to her, too, for Stromboli was in mild eruption; Marseilles in a soft and pearly rain completed the magical enchantment and she was captive to Europe.) The German war memorials and war cemeteries have the same place-names on them, the same battles remembered as the memorials and cemeteries in France. Yet the fields from the roads look exactly like the French fields, with the same crops growing, although creamy German cows pull the ploughs here and the heavy waggons instead of the splendid French horses.

Something else different is the great number of mutilated young men one sees; the plastic surgery somehow is startlingly obvious with the peasant work clothes.

We have the distinct impression that the Germans are more implacably industrious than the French. Or the English, for that matter. There is hardly an inch of land left untended. Even on the roadsides the crops are planted to the edge of the bitumen.

The Alsatian villages are often very primitive, with the cows stabled on the ground floor of the houses, and the places stink of dung and squalor and hardship. The more primitive the village, the more ornate the shrines and crosses. But almost every village, however poor, has a beautiful communal fountain and the women with their buckets and jugs are always composed in these places with a wonderful instinctive grace. They wear simple traditional clothes, a kerchief round their hair and the long full skirt with the fitted bodice—that basic womanly fashion that Dior had the wit to give to the sophisticated world.

Along the Moselle there is a calm dreaming beauty, a serene loveliness that one has never seen before. The terraced vines are still only gnarled sticks, precisely looped, reflected in the broad, shallow, slow river with all the other reflections, apple orchards and clusters of cottages grouped around sweetly baroque churches and castles and clouds. On the grass along the river banks the women spread their washing, and one woman with rolled sleeves and bare feet sprinkles the spread linen with a huge watering-can, treading the wild flowers underfoot. In the woods an early cuckoo says 'cuckoo' in impeccable English. At night little fires burning beneath the vines to ward off frost twinkle like fireflies.

At Coblenz we strike the shattered heart of Germany, and a fury of rebuilding out of rubble and ashes, and outside Freiburg in the rain we find an inn where Goethe stayed.

Heidelberg. American Headquarters are here in this ancient and lovely university city and long before you reach it you sense that the union of learning and militarism is bound to be an uneasy one: all along the road from Mannheim you pass the half-jesting road signs that say LOS ANGELES CITY LIMITS and 12 MILES TO REAL STATESIDE COFFEE. There is a pervasive discontent in the city itself and nightmare confusion of military trucks and cars in the narrow streets.

We came to visit a young couple we had met in London, both students at the university, and we had plum cake and sweet liqueur with their gentle, kindly parents in a stifling, over-furnished parlour, and at night we were taken by the young couple to a students' wine-cellar.

Again the company was courteous and friendly and eager to talk with us and it was a gay and happy evening until around midnight, when a beautiful tigerish redheaded girl wearing a white trenchcoat and nothing beneath it arrived with an escort of three arrogantly handsome young men, one with a heavily scarred face (we were informed that he was leading a movement to revive the illegal practice of duelling). The girl and her companions were obviously of some particular consequence for they were greeted with eager enthusiasm and within a very short time they were the dominant personalities of the gathering. The girl in the trenchcoat was encouraged to dance on the table – this was when we realized she was naked beneath the one garment – which she did frenziedly to a wild accompaniment of shouting, singing, handclapping and the pounding of tankards on the trestles.

Only the possessed frenzy of the girl can account for the

sudden change in the atmosphere. She was writhing and whirling above us, with the distorted sweating faces of her companions behind her, and all of them, I realized, were ranting and gibing at Cressida and me. Instantly we were surrounded by other faces, all the other faces, all violent and hating, even our friends, the young couple we had come to visit. Everyone had suddenly turned demented, shouting, screaming, threatening, deriding. They yelled Nazi catchcries, spat at us a verse of the Horst Wessel Song, howled for the lost Hitler, taunted and goaded. They hated us and wanted to kill us and would have done so, I knew, without compunction.

But when I grabbed Cressida around the shoulders and began to push through them towards the door only a few of them jostled at us; the rest stood back to let us pass, contemptuous and smiling. I looked back from the doorway through the blue reek of smoke, but I could no longer see the young couple who had been our hosts. The girl in the trenchcoat and her three friends had gone to an end table where they sat huddled together over their wine, chins on their fists, their backs turned uninterestedly to us.

At sunrise we drove out of Heidelberg, but all through the day a sense of evil and ugliness clung to us like a contamination or a bad dream that cannot be dispelled.

So much of Europe is a bad dream. Or worse. Occasionally one sees how thin the crust is above the pit. Can we, coming new and brash and inexperienced from the distant undercurve of the earth, ever hope to understand these things? We shall have to try, if we are to stay here.

Lerici. The clock on the tower in the market-place showed seven minutes past nine, but the big bell tolled twice, boomingly, swinging its big brass mouth so heavily away from the little tilted weed-grown tower that one expected the architectural absurdity, already leaning dangerously, to tire finally of the impossible burden of the giant bell and collapse into a mound of old thin dust. While the big bell tolled the little one set up a frantic unrelated clamour, so fast that the sounds tripped over each other irritably. These sudden mad cacophonies occur at the oddest intervals and bear no relationship to the hour shown by the clock.

At any rate the evening promenade in the square below had thinned out to a few gossiping fishermen, reluctant to move indoors out of the soft Italian spring night, and a group of children already fed and now permitted a final freedom, gravely twirling their skirts until they collapsed from giddiness. The gathering of soft-talking earnest men in black who earlier were standing in front of the *Communisti* posters like punctuation marks in the black type have all gone, although in the Communist Party office above the plastered posters the man in shirt-sleeves at the lighted window is still picking out something with one finger on a typewriter. Men are assembling for some sort of party below the window of our room where twelve tables have been pushed together and decorated with open carafes of red wine and baskets of bread and mounds of fruit. A prodigious orange moon rises on the jangling echoes of the demented bells: it is four times as big as the squashy London sun and so tango-jazzy in colour and precise in shape that it surely must have been clipped from a parchment lampshade of the nineteen-twenties.

The party seems to be some sort of reunion, with the ribaldries and self-conscious laughter of such events, and the practical jokes and speechmaking, but as the carafes circle the laughter becomes more raucous and the jokes less inhibited. Cressida and I, in our cool tiled room above the restaurant, look out across the dark gulf where Shelley drowned, but after a time we close the shutters against the mounting racket and go to bed.

But we are not to sleep. The high leaps of laughter rocket through the shutters, but now with a new sound woven between, a thin, high, haunting music that soon silences the laughter. We open the shutters again and look down upon a square white with moonlight, upon broken bread and spilt wine and congealed food on oily plates, upon dark heads attentive to the lively trio at the head of the tables. They are three very old men in round-crowned hats and long shabby coats, bending bobbing shoulders over pipe and strings, jigging out a measure to their tune. Their thin legs bend, fragile and brittle as twigs beneath their flapping rags, as they shuffle out a sprightly parody of youth, and their heads are tilted each to the other in listening attitudes, and the pipe trembles so faint and far away that it hovers on the very threshold of sound, and the faint thrumming of the strings rises and falls above the reedy whisper like the beating of innumerable tiny wings over a summer pond. We cannot see the faces of the musicians. The Communist at the typewriter patiently labours on in his oblong of light.

We go back to our bed, but the music plays through us, a gay young persistent tune, endlessly repetitive yet constantly refreshing, with bells somehow mixed up in it, pealing with discordant laughter at the ironical pipe, ever higher, ever clearer, leading them on with such joyful absurdities that we cling to each other on the soft sheet, laughing in delight at such exquisite nonsense.

Afterwards we sleep a little, then rise together, quite awake, to hear the music fading, lightly, lightly, with the strings thrumming again and the pipe dancing on six notes that are the distillation of spring and youth and the Mediterranean and crushed flowers and spilt wine, and when we go hand in hand to the window, creeping there without a sound, the table below is quite empty and the Communist gone from his window and there is nothing in the moonlit square but the three musicians slowly going away. Still we do not see their faces. A very tall and thin old man is in the centre, and his two companions are very little old men, strange stick figures under the funny round-crowned hats, and as they play they bend their knees and shuffle from side to side, keeping an exact rhythm on their infirm old men's legs. They shuffle on past the *Communisti* posters, on into the dark shadows of the clock tower, and quite suddenly they are gone from us. Still we stand, listening, until we can no longer be sure whether we really hear the vibration of that thin, high, magical note. Pan in the moonlight, and youth, and beauty . . . So much of Europe is a beautiful dream, too. But are good dreams any easier to understand than nightmares? I think perhaps Cressida understands. She is awake beside me for a long time, quite still, staring up into the cool play of shadow and moonlight in the high dim room. Her cheeks are wet and she says nothing. It is a long time since I have seen that secret rapt expression on her face, not since Lebanon Bay, when she would stand at night on the ocean's edge and look out across the dark heartbeat of the Pacific.

I would like to talk to her, but I feel awkward, and to talk would be a kind of intrusion, and I do not, in any case, know what to say.

Siena. Within sight of Siena we were held up for hours by the cars racing in the Mille Miglia—there is always some *grande spettacolo* on the Italian roads; coming down from Venice we were hours trailing at a walking pace behind a huge Communist political demonstration marching with bands and banners; in Bologna there were election riots; near Florence a circus festival of some sort, later a religious procession carrying an enthroned painted Madonna—but a policeman finally took pity on us and opened a way through the crowds and guided us across the road between the powerful rushing snarlings of Ferraris and Maseratis. So although it was then late afternoon we were able to get in through the gate of the lovely walled city before the holidaying townspeople had returned from the *spettacolo* down on the road. The narrow streets walled by mellow stone were empty of people but echoing with the beating of kettledrums and then we came to a pageant of young men in mediæval costumes marching behind drums, and they were tossing and twirling huge and gorgeous silken banners, practising for the ancient Palio. We drove into the heart of the town behind the slow tapping beat of the drums and the flaunt and flight of the vivid whirling flags and the cloaks and doublets and plumed hats, and an urchin later found us a charming room in a wonderful old house of apricot stone overlooking the tilted dish of the piazza. In one of the other rooms someone was playing Scarlatti on the harpsichord. In the arpeggio passages and the leaping skips there was something of that same elfin quality that had been in the music of the three old men of Lerici.

One must come to Europe to find out how much of life, and

the flavours and colours and melodies of life, we have lacked out here.

Orvieto. There is something pervasively grim and sinister here, the harsh jagged outcrop above the plain, the dark tiers of stone rising above the overgrown dank tombs of the Etruscans. The custodian of the tombs is a toothless old peasant woman named Amenia; she has thin hair and is shrewd and sly and coarse and indestructible, yet she searches among the weeds and gathers for Cressida an armful of *petit angelo* and wild roses and pink clover and mint.

The cathedral still sits in the Dark Ages, in a square where thick weeds grow between the cobblestones, facing mediæval houses that are crumbling and sagging and appear not to be inhabited any longer. There is a dirty restaurant and a sweets and postcards and pottery shop with unidentifiable flyblown objects only vaguely discernible through the filthy glass.

Weeds grow right up to the door of the cathedral and the vast and intricate marble façade. Inside everything is bare and gaunt and bleakly intimidating and there is an intangible essence of disuse and decay: it has been here six centuries so perhaps this is only the accretion of time. A skeleton rests in a glass-fronted case set into the wall below the faded frescoes, it is draped with stained netting stuck about with stained and spotted paper flowers, and before the grisly relic two women pray with a passionate intensity. One is old and grim, the other young and slatternly. A small boy who is with them keeps edging away, his eyes wide with terror and bewilderment, his bottom lip quivering. The old woman snaps at him harshly and drags him back, then punches him between the shoulder-blades until he is forced down upon his grimy little knees before the decorated bones. Watching the terrified child, it is hard for us to concentrate on the Signorellis or the Fra Angelicos. As we take our leave the boy is being forced down on his knees again, this time before the silver shrine that contains a bloodstained cloth.

We sit at a pavement table on the Via Garibaldi thinking of Dante's words, *La città di Orvieto e alta e strana.* Orvieto is high and it is strange. Here there are more Communist posters than ever. Every building in sight is plastered with them from paving stones to roof eaves; they seem to be all that is holding some of the buildings together. We drink the famous sweet white wine of Orvieto until our heads are aching, and go to our dingy room depressed. We are the only guests in the hotel.

Rome. One marvels at the healing qualities of man and the recuperative power of the earth. It is hardly credible that only six years have passed since I was here, when the men and boys were clustered whispering around the Piazza Barberini, husbands offering their wives or daughters, boys offering their mothers or their sisters for cigarettes or a few cans of army rations. The very shop is there at the bottom of the Via Sistina where I bought the bracelet of Roman mosaic to send to Helen and then went, carrying a musette-bag of rations over my shoulder, with a girl who was sad and desperate and beautiful, to a dismal bare room in a black waste somewhere behind the Corso Umberto. I did nothing, though, except leave the rations with her, and cigarettes and a handful of lire, and on the way back to the billets in the Hotel de la Ville I stood on top of the Spanish Steps and flung the mosaic bracelet into the darkness. I wonder how the girl has survived these six years, or whether she has.

Six years ago, coming up from Anzio to the last hill girdling Rome, the devastation was total; it was difficult to walk between the bomb-craters and the shell-holes, and one could survey an entire visible landscape and see no building standing. Yet man has gone back and re-established himself, and the earth is cured and gives its yield again.

The Hotel de la Ville is booked out so we have taken a top floor room in a Swiss *pensione* across from it: this is a retrospective journey for me and I am anxious to recapture things. Which is not easy. The Rome of now, vibrant and gay and alive again, seems an utterly different place from the Rome of 1944. I get lost trying to find the route out to the Appian Way, and lost again, towards dusk, trying to locate the Pantheon. So that it is quite by accident that we stumble across the wonderful absurdity of the Trevi Fountain, and fully night by the time I rediscover the little *trattoria* looking across the narrow square to the Pantheon, which is as I remember it, huge, unrepentant, still sullenly pagan despite the spindly cross planted on top of the great dome. The children who play in front of it shun the gloomy columns of the portico. The cats of Rome are more at home, the scavenging cats of Rome, howling and fighting in the pits below street level on either side of the church. This is their territory. A foul stench rises from it.

While Cressida and I are eating, two fire-engines rush clanging through the square and off down a narrow side street, and the square at once explodes with shrill life and excitement, and what seems to be half the population of Rome floods through the square, trotting in pursuit of the delicious impromptu treat. They are screaming, jostling, gesticulating, laughing as they run towards the ringing echo of the fire bells; some, in linked groups, make the pell-mell a kind of dance, children jump and skip, one fat fellow wearing a waiter's apron tootles on a cornet as he jogs along. Cressida, intoxicated by this tide of human warmth and joy and natural ebullience, turns to me, her eyes shining. 'Come on, let's go with them,' she pleads. 'Let's run too and see what's happening.' But I hold her by the hand and say, laughing, 'Remember what we said, we don't chase fire-engines any more.'

This has been a happy night.

Yet one goes on being teased by the time before. Along the Appian Way we lay warm in the soft sunshine in the high yellow grass, and I thought of that freezing night in the Palace of Caserta when I had looked into a dim old spotted mirror and for the first time became aware of the changes in my own face, and for the first time realized that I was turning, that I wanted to turn, away from my own country and my own people. I had thought of myself then, six years before, as already an expatriate. But was I even yet an expatriate? Would I ever be?

In the Forum we stood on the grooved step where Julius Caesar bled and died, and in my mind was that scene of six years earlier when the Italian Socialists had been allowed their first political meeting, here among the ancient ruins, and the crowd was here, quiet and earnest, and all around it the cordon of embittered, war-weary Texas infantrymen, with loaded tommy-guns and orders to shoot at the first sign of violence in the demonstration. We hardly saw, then, the new shapes the world was taking.

The bust of Hadrian was still in the bar of the Hotel de la Ville when we went there for a cocktail, and I remembered that this was where I had received the last letter from my brother Jack, the saddest letter I had ever read, but with the news in it of the birth of his son, and a casual postcript mentioning Cressida Morley. Bombardier Morley then, and now my wife, beside me in a pink linen dress drinking vermouth. She reached for my hand and held it tightly. I told her, that first night we spent together in Riordan's pub, I would take her to Rome . . .

I had to leave Cressida alone at a café table under a plane-tree in Via Veneto for a few minutes while I made a telephone-call. When I returned she was surrounded by an admiring and competitive court of seven men, two of them priests, those very secular Roman priests with their flapping black gowns, round schoolgirl hats and inevitable briefcases, who scurry about everywhere, frantically busy on affairs that cannot all be to do with the Vicar of Christ. The other five were the typical handsome, well-tailored predators of the Veneto; they grinned unashamedly when I returned to claim Cressida, and swaggered off in search of other quarry. These days, says Cressida, Lupus the Roman Wolf is male and biped, wears a fob and a gloss of brilliantine on his hair and that look in his eye.

Yet what electric charges flicker in these great streets of Europe, what surging tides of life swirl around the café tables and shop-fronts. It is hard to remember the drab and lifeless streets of a Melbourne Sunday without a little shudder.

The Loire Valley, France. Almost every château improbable as a fairy-tale. The sky and river pearl-pale with heat and light, the willows grey more than green, the sandbanks soft and gleaming like a woman's flesh. The Loire is done in washed water-colour as Italy is done in oils, in colour it is as delicate as Italy is strong. Orange lichen on dark slate roofs. The enchanted silvery towns.

Round haystacks with a slice cut out of them, like a cake. What implements do they use to cut them so neatly?

Port St Quay, Brittany. It is like a little fishing-town run up by Christopher Wood. There are bright blue nylon fishing-nets drying on the walls with the brown ones. The fishing basin is about half a mile square and the ebb of the tide leaves the boats leaning at odd angles on the green carpet of weed. The pattern of masts, anchors biting into sand, crabs scuttling. The boats are coloured extravagantly and always settle down as if arranged very precisely on the green weed by an expert set designer.

I am determined never to try to speak French again. I had been chagrined in the south when a waiter, from whom I had ordered, clearly I thought, *croissants et café noir* for breakfast, brought me two hard boiled eggs. Last night at a fisherman's *estaminet* overlooking the harbour, I made some comment in French and one of the fishermen left at once, cycled a mile to his house and back, returning with a catalogue of roses. Nobody, as far as I know, had mentioned roses. Later I ordered *cognac* and the waiter brought me Coca-Cola.

Do the French do this deliberately? Or is it simply that Australians, having no frontiers or foreign neighbours or need for languages, and being lazy talkers anyway, have no gift whatever for other tongues?

London. Our English friend listened attentively to all we had to say, replenishing his gin-and-tonic from time to time, and when we had done smiled at us most charmingly and said, with a little unbelieving shake of his head, 'You mean you actually covered all that distance and then missed the Mantegnas altogether!'

THE ISLAND, GREECE, 1956

There is something about the occasion which, for this place, is curiously formal. The kind of formality that fixes it, as it were, back in time, or even outside time altogether. It began formally, with a neat handwritten note from Little Grace asking would we care to come up in the late afternoon to hear the clavichord. (She is Little Grace because there is another American woman of the same name, taller and older, who is distinguished as Big Grace.) She has only just had the clavichord shipped down from Athens and unpacked.

Little Grace looks as if she has stepped straight out of a Cranach painting. She is slight and has long straight pale hair and a face that is shy and innocent and haunted. She lives with her small daughter Becky in a simple, tiny, white-washed cottage which she rents from Pepika, who teaches us Greek and is headmistress of the school which our two children attend. She was a student of music in America but married while still in college and came to Europe with her husband, who has now left her. This happened about a year ago, since when she has been drifting around Athens, and she has come to the island because living is simpler and cheaper here.

The room is limewashed in peacock colours, darkish blues that don't quite match where they have been repainted, and iridescent greens, and the colours devour even the brilliance of the Greek light, so that the room is already dim, although the little crescent harbour seen down the tumbled amphitheatre of the houses and the sun-gilded russet of the roofs is vivid yet and sparkling with daylight.

In the room there is an antiquated double bed in curly black iron surmounted by brass acorns, a huge chest of drawers and a lovely small round table in walnut intricately inlaid around the Greek initials of some people long dead – the initials on the table are different from those on the chest – four spidery black chairs with cane seats, a woven peasant rug on the floor, striped in Braque colours and faded tints, and, of course, the clavichord, a Dolmetsch, upon which burns an ornate Venetian oil-lamp of blue glass. The house has neither electricity nor water. On the shuttered window-ledge, dark against the sparkle of the harbour, are a terracotta water-jug plugged by a lemon and a graceful earthenware pitcher. Little Grace lights two other cheap brass kerosene lamps before she begins.

The room darkens while she plays. Little Becky crouches on the bed, quite still, all huge black eyes and a tousle of sun-bleached hair. The rest of us are quiet, too, only occasionally murmuring an appreciation – Stephanos, the charming stout banker from Athens, and his wife Katina, who wears long false eyelashes and a large and costly ruby-studded Byzantine cross on a chain around her neck (she is deeply pious and concerned about her shortcomings as a Christian); Virginia, the distinguished visiting young lady author from London who is here to write her Greek island book, and her tough, handsome Australian husband Barry, who is developing as an intellectual since he gave up smuggling between Spain and Tangier to marry her; and Morgan the homosexual painter from New York; and Cressida and me.

She plays Couperin and Mozart and Scarlatti and Bach, and the fragile notes, spun with a delicacy that is almost feeble, hardly stir the quiet in the dark quiet room. It is intensely beautiful and moving, and there is something intensely moving and beautiful, too, about Little Grace, absorbed and concentrated under the blue gleam of radiance and her little daughter behind her crouched silent upon the bed.

When she is done Virginia asks if she might try the instrument. She plays Bach with great force and assurance, but it is not the same at all. The ineffable moment is gone, the magic fades.

Little Grace has to stay with Becky, the others move in a sinuous file down the winding steps to our house, where I make up a charcoal fire in the old hooded stove—we have no other method of cooking—and Cressida grills shish kebabs, which we eat in the walled garden with bread and wine. The mood of quietness affects us all, for it is very peaceful here, the flame of the candles hardly wavers in the air, hardly illuminates the swelling pale curves of the two big whitewashed water-jars, hardly touches our shadowed thoughtful faces or the vines hanging from the trellis above. It is as if we are all still listening to the fragile music.

'I suppose,' says Morgan at length, 'this is why we stay on and on here. This sort of thing. Evenings like this one. We're caught in the web.'

'But you don't stay on and on,' Virginia points out to him. 'You keep rushing about, backwards and forwards, all over the place. You don't belong *here*. You don't belong anywhere.'

Morgan nods, looking down into his glass of wine.

'Well?' says Virginia, impatient for his reply.

'I was just trying to figure out whether to get plastered straight away or stretch it out for an hour or so. Sure, you're right. I don't belong any place.' Morgan, who has been drifting around Europe for the last eleven years, is one of the standard nomads who keep dropping in here, one of that ever-growing army of expatriates, mostly American, who have lost themselves in the flux of Europe, following patterns of movement as rhythmic and as rigid as the flight of migratory birds, eternally seeking some truth and reassurance, or some escape, they are never able to find. His pattern runs through Spain and the Balearics, parts of France, the dissolute German seaports, Naples and Venice and Brindisi, Athens, the Greek islands. He is endlessly in trouble. Police. Alien permit authorities. For drunkenness mostly, or the perversity of his sexual morals, more recently drugs have come into it. Sometimes he is robbed when drunk, or beaten up, and that creates trouble too. Three times since the war ended he has gone back to the United States, and has always been repelled and has fled again to Europe, where he can lose himself in the flux. The last time he went back to volunteer himself into a psychiatric clinic, then escaped from the place by jumping from a first-floor window.

He still limps as a result of this. He is, unlike many of his nomadic confrères, a painter of talent, but he has no confidence in himself, nor in anything much except the validity of his death-wish. Dissipation has prematurely aged him, yet there is a great charm in his long sad Byzantine face; he is degraded and failed and lost, yet he has an almost saintly gentleness about him. When he is sober, that is.

'You won't settle anywhere, that's your trouble.' Virginia's persistence will break this tranquillity as surely as her Bach broke the spell at Little Grace's place. 'You must always be rushing from what? And *to* what? You're running away from yourself, that's all. But then you get somewhere else and the first thing you do is unpack your bag and take yourself out.'

'Check,' says Morgan.

'So you don't belong anywhere.'

'Check,' again, smiling into his wine.

'You two belong here,' says Virginia, looking across at Cressida and me. 'You don't go rushing about. You've settled for something.'

'They're integrated people,' says Morgan.

'Can you really settle and belong, as an alien?' Stephanos asks quietly. 'Don't you ever feel you want to go back to your own country and your own people?'

'Never,' says Cressida.

'If you're asking *me* Virginia's answered for me.' Morgan smiles. 'I don't have a country or a people. I just have a bag with me inside it.'

'And you, David?' asks Stephanos.

'Oh, occasionally.' I hedge a little. 'Vaguely.'

'Never!' Cressida doesn't hedge.

'I think it would worry me,' says Stephanos thoughtfully. 'I have travelled about a good deal, and there are places other than Greece that I like very much. If I find myself liking them too much I pack at once and hurry home.'

'Perhaps we could feel that way too,' Cressida suggests. 'About Greece, I mean.'

'Could you? I wonder . . . Up there this evening at Little Grace's, I was thinking about all you people. Why you are here. What it is doing, what it *must* do to you. Grace is here because she is lost and rejected and lonely, but if she goes on being here it will be fatal for her. It is not an answer.'

'But is there an answer?' asks Barry. 'For anyone?'

'To living, you mean?' Stephanos nods. 'Oh, I think so. Life itself. To contend.'

'With what?' I say. 'The bloody rat-race?'

'Even with that. The alternatives to contending might, you know, just possibly be worse.' He pinches thoughtfully at his lower lip. 'I was reading Hawthorne the other day, his memoirs and notes. I was interested in what he wrote while he was in Rome and could feel himself falling into the thrall of the place. He was wise enough to see that by staying on in a foreign place he would have to exchange reality for emptiness. The realities of living would always be deferred, pending the return to one's native air. A future moment. But gradually there would be no future moments, because of the fear that the native air would no longer be sufficiently satisfying. So a substitute reality would have to be transferred to the temporary alien shore. And one would end up by having not a choice between two countries but no country at all, or, as he put it, only that few feet of either in which one finally would rest one's discontented bones.'

'Well, that's okay by me,' says Morgan. His intonation suddenly is thicker. Evidently he has decided to speed up the process of withdrawal.

'The trouble with some of you people is you're like the lemmings,' Virginia begins but falters then and does not go on. Nor does Stephanos, and after a time they all leave.

Cressida and I stay on in the silent garden.

For quite a time we have nothing to say to each other, sitting under the dark dip and plunge of vines listening to the silence, into which, every now and then, Athena's little owl plunges a tinkling liquid drop of sound. There is a special quality about the Greek silence: it is soothing and healing but not soporific; it hones the senses while it tranquillizes. Perhaps we are still infected by the mood of the evening. Or perhaps it is another of the tacit little truces of silence which, since London, and more frequently lately, tend to develop when just the two of us are left together.

'Stephanos,' she says at last, stating the name almost absently. 'What he said. Do you think he's right?'

'I don't know. I suppose he could be. I mean, living this sort of life . . . I imagine after a time it could unfit you for the other sort of life. If you allowed it to.'

'Are we allowing it to?'

'I don't think we're incurable cases yet, one way or the other. After all, we've only been here two years.'

'Did you mean that, about sometimes wanting to go back to Australia?'

'Not really. I hardly ever think about Australia. It's all so bloody far away. And so unimportant. Besides, we haven't got the fare.'

'London, then?'

'Bugger London! Go through all that to escape, you mean, and then shamble back holding your wrists out for the manacles again. Oh no!'

'But Virginia isn't right either, is she? Saying that we two belong here. We don't really.'

I think about this and say, 'No. No, we don't belong here.'

During the morning there had been another disputatious scene at the police office. Again all foreigners resident on the island, including children, had been summoned down peremptorily to listen to a threatening harangue concerning residence permits delivered by Lieutenant Manolis, the fussy little senior police official on the island. He stages these dramas at regular intervals, whenever he gets his bowels in a tangle about something. A foreign girl's bikini. The scolding of his own shrewish wife. This time his normal irritability and pomposity had been lacerated into rage and suspicion by yet another Cyprus crisis. He has a basic dislike of foreigners, especially the English, and he is highly emotional about Cyprus and *Enosis*: whenever he gets upset or his patriotism is inflamed he will go on wild rampages of frantic xenophobia, suspecting all of us of being spies for the hated English, and threatening to revoke all alien residence permits regardless of nationality. There are, in fact, no English residents left on the island (Virginia is only visiting on a tourist's visa), for he had already cancelled the permits of a timid and inoffensive young water-colour painter and a hardworking, dull, middle-aged potter from the Midlands and had them both thrown out of Greece. But this had not made him any more reasonable. 'No, we don't really belong,' I say to Cressida. 'We're still aliens. They could boot us out tomorrow if they wanted to.'

LONDON, 1954

It was just on four in the morning when the ringing of the door-bell jabbed into my disquieting reverie. I thought that the car I had ordered the day before to take us to London Airport must have come half an hour too early.

Cressida had already dressed the two sleepy children in their jerseys and duffel-coats, and was in the bedroom packing the last of their things – the frayed teddy bears and golliwogs that could not be left behind, and Julian's toy soldiers – and I had been sitting in the living-room, my guts in a knot of apprehension, staring at the sepia marks in Mondrian patterns on the wall behind the emptied bookcases and the darker printed rectangles on the wall-paper where our pictures had hung. There were two or three hooks and nails still in the walls, and from these and from the curtain rods above the windows swung little greasy filaments like rubbed spiderwebs. Mementoes of the last unpleasant smog. The place had a dreadful air of melancholy, as if life had already passed out of it, gone with the baggage I had already lugged down to the front hallway. On one of the barren bookcases was an empty Rémy Martin bottle and two champagne corks in their twists of wire, sad vestigial reminders of the party of two nights before, when our friends had come around and we had given away our books and pictures and phonograph records and ornaments and toys and surplus clothes and things, and in a fine euphoria of exuberant adventure we had stripped our lives of all but the few necessary possessions we would take with us to Greece. We had felt gay and splendid, and even brave.

But now in the empty desolation of the flat it was a very different matter. No gaiety. No exuberance. Only the awful silence and emptiness and the soilings of a dead inhabitation, and this racking apprehension in my guts about what we were committing ourselves to. And the knowledge that it was too late now to do anything about it. Whatever the doubt or fear or despair, there was no turning back. We were committed. Irrevocably.

Earlier, two months earlier, after I had cabled my resignation to Tomlinson, there had been a chance of turning back; I had had disturbing second thoughts about the gravity of my decision and had hurried home from the office in the evening to tell Cressida that I had reconsidered it and had decided against the venture. She had been very calm but not to be dissuaded and settled it all by saying, 'We can't back out of it now, David. It's too late. I've already cancelled the order for the winter coal.'

The doorbell rang again, and I went down and Calverton was there, dishevelled and fairly drunk and without an overcoat or hat although the air was icy and dank in the moist mustard of November fog. He seemed to be cringing, cowering there forlorn and shivering against the murky blots of the Bayswater Road trees, and his left hand was half extended with the fist clenched.

'Holy Christ!' I exclaimed. 'What are *you* doing here?'

'Just came to see you off.' He sounded defensive. 'Say goodbye.'

'At this hour! You're a masochist.'

'Give it a go,' he said with a surprising vehemence. 'Give it a real bloody go.'

'Yes, I'll try,' I said.

'No. Give it a go. You'll be tempted to come running back, but—'

'Look, come in out of the cold. We're not pushing off for

another half-hour or so, and Cressida will—'

'No,' he said fiercely. 'No. I've only come to give you this. Bring you good luck. Put it on. Wear it. I've always worn it.' He shoved the clenched fist at me and forced something into my hand. I knew what it was without looking at it. The thin gold chain and the gold St Christopher medallion he always wore around his neck as a charm. I tried to say something but couldn't.

'Look, I'm off now,' he said. 'Got a girl up in Soho, she's waiting.'

'But you've got to come up and say goodbye to Cress.'

'No,' he said. 'God no!' He turned then and trotted off across the area into the fog. The street lights were gibbous and sickly and by some trick of refraction his figure, lumpy, misshapen, jerky, grew bigger and bigger as he retreated, loomed huge and faint for a moment like some spectre of the Brocken, then vanished into the greasy swirl.

SYDNEY, 1966

In a hospital ward, Meredith realized, there was no such thing as silence; there was always someone stirring, groaning, coughing, muttering, moving, the starchy stiff whisper of the night nurses' uniforms behind the jabbing flashlight beams, the metallic click of equipment, the soft slow hiss of oxygen. From outside, too. The muted moan of the city's night traffic, more stridently punctuated along the road beside the hospital, nocturnal shuntings in the adjacent railway yards, the running clangour of buffers, soft pantings of locomotives interspersed with quick shuddering snorts like animals in pain, and from a point far away, always the same point and at the same time, the nostalgic faint mournful cry of train whistles fading north towards Newcastle. And overhead the undulating drone of freight planes taking out the country editions of city newspapers; a sound different from the jets and very familiar to him; the final utilitarian missions of the old DC3s. Once the admirable workhorse of war.

It was by these things that Meredith timed and fixed his wakeful nights. It was mostly during the nights that he became aware of himself again, that he could feel the mists thinning and dissipating in his brain, that he could will the emaciated and motionless hands on his sheet into grasping, at least figuratively, back at life again. It was by the sounds studded in the dark blanket of night that he could mark out the way back. By the sounds and by his own fits of coughing. They encouraged the coughing because there was still a lot of blood to be coughed up. They had removed the tube from his throat, but the hole was still there, healing well they said, covered by a kind of flap of gauze. Sometimes he would cough so violently that his breath would jet out through the hole in his throat and blow the gauze off, and he would have to ring the night bell and summon a nurse, who would gently clean up the mess on his neck and fix another flap across and bring him a cup of tea. Often, of course, the nurse would be busy with other patients and he would just have to lie there for a while in the darkness, listening to the air whistling and bubbling through the hole in his neck; he even experimented with trying to make the whistle into a proper tune (Freud no doubt could have explained why he chose 'The Whistler and his Dog', which he remembered from earliest childhood as being his father's favourite air) but he never succeeded. If the nurse was not busy she would sometimes sit for a time and talk with him. The nurses and sisters, and even the normally uncommunicative surgeon who had sliced his lung out, seemed pleased now with his progress, although all of them a month before had not given him much of a chance.

Even so, Meredith never thought at all of anything in the future, his mind quested endlessly back into the past, picking up the threads, which, although familiar enough, never seemed precisely the same as before the operation, as if their colour and texture had changed subtly during the time of blankness. It was from midnight to dawn that the trains and the newspaper planes were active and between listening for them he would often find himself thinking of the peculiar therapeutic quality of the silence back on the island in Greece. There had been no traffic on the island because it had been all precipitous steps and no roads at all, not a single wheeled vehicle in fact, so that the everyday sounds at the most were confined to the soft pit-pit-pit-pitting of the donkeys trotting past or their strangled braying or the wasps humming in the vines or the pure notes of the little owl. He remembered the time of Calverton's crack-up, when he had come out to stay with them; he had been a trembling mess of nerves and alcoholism, but he had cured himself by staying in the walled garden listening to the quietness; he would just sit there as if entranced and after a week or so the smoke from the cigarette in his fingers would rise in a thin ruled line and the glass of wine on the table beside him remain untasted for hours on end.

Such memories did not slide easily back into clear focus: often his mind was still woolly and thick with pain, and it took him many nights of thinking and remembering to assemble laboriously two particular vignettes.

The first was of tramping with Cressida across the mountains to a shepherd village known as Piso. They had set off before dawn and when they reached the first spur, smelling of limestone and sage and wild thyme, they could see the sea on both sides of the island, with the moon setting behind one rim as the sun rose above the other. A little later a pale veil of mist rose from the Mediterranean, lit from outside by the sun, so that all the island seemed to be fixed in absolute shining silence within a pale, dome-like, airy cloche. As if nothing existed elsewhere. It reminded Meredith of the glass dome on his mother's old piano where his father's First World War army biscuit was preserved and the mementoes of forgotten weddings and christenings and twenty-firsts.

They had walked on through the dome of this silence, not daring to talk until they stopped at a peasant's white cottage to drink cold well water and to eat figs from the tree, damp and cool with dew, and it was several hours later before the curious intrusion came from that outer world which since sunrise had been banished. It came in the form of an aeroplane, a fighter, which flew in out of the opalescent curtain and circled above, round and round again, as if watching them.

Cressida had stared up at it, her face darkening, and said, 'I don't like it. It's scary.'

'Why, what's the matter?' he asked.

'It will probably happen like this one of these days,' she said.

'What will probably happen?' The plane went on banking and circling, with hardly any sound.

'It's the way the world will come to an end for people,' she said. 'I expect it already has for some people. Like this. Out of peace and quietness. Something strange and unexpected comes in from the sea, and hovers up there like a hawk circling, and then strikes.' She lowered her eyes and looked around among the boulders and flints and prickles and flary spikes of asphodel. 'There is no place to hide, is there?' she said. 'Nowhere at all.'

Meredith related this incident to the second vignette, which actually occurred years later, after the tourists had discovered the island, and they used to go to their own quiet ledge of sea-rocks in a hidden bay where they could still swim naked and in peace. They would go in late afternoon after Meredith had done his writing for the day, and always at a specific point in time, just as the blue of the sky began to deepen into its dusky violet, they would sit together pensive in the silence watching the jet's condensation trail ruling its impeccable Euclidean angle upwards from south to north, higher and higher in the magical luminescence above the clipped silhouettes of a hundred scattered islands. Sometimes they could detect the plane itself as a pinprick of light, but usually they could see only the vapour trail. They knew it to be the giant American bomber from the NATO base in Crete carrying its H-bombs on its vigilant daily patrol around the Balkans, and it was this knowledge that made them pensive. In their pattern of living at this time the sinister ruled line of vapour in the sky was frequently the only intimation they had of another world beyond the island.

Meredith found it disturbing that when he tried to fix his thoughts on peace and quietness, as a form of therapy, it always turned into something else. Perhaps Cressida had been right in the first place. There was no place to hide. No shield of peace or quietness, no sheltering bell of luminous air. Still nowhere to hide. Nowhere at all.

LONDON, 1954

Meredith had read somewhere that the *pastness* of the past was really a clarity of vision about it, the ability to make judgments of it of general moral significance, but when he sought back he always found the Greek experience to be much more vivid and more clearly defined than the years in London. This was not merely that Greece had come later than London—usually it worked out that the further you went back the clearer the evocation—nor that Greece had scarred him more deeply, but rather that London, except in brief disconnected flashes, was not to the same degree that 'palpable, imaginable, *visitable* past' that could delight such a writer as Henry James.

Yet clearly it had been in London that the seeds of pain were sown, that the breach in their personal relationship, never at that time expressed nor even hinted at, began insidiously to encroach upon their love.

He had not observed then that their lives together had begun to take different separate courses, perhaps because of the circumstances, either imposed or self-created, in which they now found themselves. They were, in fact, virtually trying to absorb into the duality of marriage three differing lives, each one of which often hardly seemed to be connected to the others.

During the day Meredith was very much occupied with his work and interests in Fleet Street. Usually at night, after the supper dishes had been cleared away and the children put to bed, he would sit on at the end of the dining-table, pounding away at his typewriter until long after midnight, working furiously on a novel. London stimulated him in a way Australia never had. He no longer had to be concerned about the smothering blanket of Australian indifference; contention now was with a much more formidable barrier, a London indifference which could be either amused or bored by colonialism but never impressed. Australians were good cricketers and confidence men, swashbuckling soldiers, inveterate sportsmen and gamblers, but not to be taken seriously in other fields, although of some interest for their crude gaucheries and astonishing diction. But in the brooding black wen of the gigantic metropolis, in the spawning, seething, hardly communicable anthill, especially in the labyrinthine warrens around Fleet Street, smelling of ink, where every court and alley seemed impregnated with the centuries of writing, he found his own creative nourishment and excitement. It filled and overflowed his available hours. He was, for the most part, happy.

It was a different matter for Cressida, whose activities were both constricted and restricted. She was bound in by climate, by propinquity with too many anonymous people, by the demands of her two small children, walking them to the Round Pond or the band rotunda in Hyde Park, to the London Museum or through to the other museums in South Kensington, to the Montessori school, driving them to Richmond Park to see the deer, to stiff little afternoon tea-parties with stuffy dull parents and spoilt sallow children. Often she must have contrasted this shielded, artificial, supervised life with the huge freedoms of her own childhood in Lebanon Bay. She had been sternly admonished by an attendant in Kensington Gardens for allowing Miranda to paddle her bare feet in the Round Pond; Julian had collected and classified the leaves of oak, elm, yew, beech, lime, birch, poplar, willow, hawthorn and chestnut, but had never climbed a tree.

The flat itself was pleasant enough, one floor of a converted Georgian house on the Bayswater Road, but often lonely: it was the better part of a year before the other tenants in the building acknowledged her good mornings by other than a noncommittal grunt. When her husband was home he was more often than not engrossed in his writing. Occasionally of an evening they would have a few beers at a near-by pub, but beyond this they seldom went out. During their first few months in London there had been heady excitement about the plethora of theatre and music and all the things to be seen and to be done, but after a while their going to plays and concerts or making excursions to places of historic or atmospheric interest became more and more infrequent. (Yet Meredith was inordinately proud, and possessive, on these rare occasions when he did take her out, to a first night, or a cocktail-party at Claridge's, a concert at the Albert Hall, a ballet at Covent Garden; it was surprising, for the delight they shared in these experiences, that he did not do it more often.)

Cressida looked forward to the two days of the week when Mildred Dapp, the elderly Cockney charlady, came to 'do' for them. Mrs Dapp, a stout and indestructible widow who wore extraordinary garments and a fantastic hat with rabbit ears, had an abiding detestation of the Royal Family but was the staunchest of Tory voters. On the days she came, Cressida always got up very early and had the flat spick and span by the time Mrs Dapp arrived; she would then make tea and toast for the old woman and listen to her interminable fascinating stories of her years in aristocratic service. Never having had anything to do with servants, Cressida was rather intimidated by Mrs Dapp – she could never feel other than sensitive to the injustice of a young woman in her twenties delegating all the hard work to a woman old enough to be her grandmother – so she went to some pains to spoil her and to wait on her hand and foot.

They had not many real friends. David was able to satisfy his gregariousness in his professional work and his circle of Fleet Street acquaintances, but he seldom brought any of this world into his domestic sphere, for fear of invasion into the precious hours he allowed himself for his creative writing. They both found the English not particularly disposed to be over-friendly – this reticence (or was it indifference?) that allowed people their private worlds in which to live their private lives appealed to Cressida in a way, for as time went on she had a strengthening concern to hold herself within her own privacies, however sombre they sometimes were – and for no explicit reason they inclined to avoid social contact with their fellow-Australians living in London. They saw something of Tom Kiernan, the painter, between his energetic painting forays on the Continent, and quite a lot of Calverton; and Janice, Cressida's friend from the army, who had earned her fare to London out of her labours with her wheel-barrow library in Sydney, stayed with them for a few months until she got a job with a Bloomsbury print-dealer and her own little flat in St John's Wood. At intervals there were business contacts or visitors from Australia who had to be socially entertained. They came and they went, seeming as time passed more and more outlandish in their short bumfreezer jackets and funny hats and curious clothes and the fixity of their ideas, excitedly dispensing gobbets of news which to the Merediths seemed dull or distant or monumentally unimportant, or like information of as dubious a veracity as the sketchy outlines of old maps. Indeed, under the grey enveloping atmosphere of London their own country came more and more to seem like some infinitely remote *Terra Incognita*: there were times when Cressida would not have been notably surprised had the next batch of Australian visitors walked straight out of Sir John Mandeville, with their heads set under their shoulder-blades or their feet kept in warming pouches. (Admittedly she could not quite reconcile this image with the reality of one such transient visitor who had deplored the nature of the English climate with a scornful, 'They call this bloody stuff sunshine! Jesus! Wouldn't you give it all away just to be back there now, sitting on Bondi Beach with a bottle of good Aussie beer and a pound o' prawns?')

To Cressida, Australia, and Lebanon Bay with its bare beach a mile long, and the natural entitlements to freedom which to her younger self had been so unassailable only five or six years before, seemed now to be things beyond time as well as beyond space. She had no longing for Australia, no nostalgias. What she yearned for she presently did not know. There were times when it ached for recognition, but she could not place it; it was not, she knew, for anything in the past. In the meantime she had to live by habits, not by yearnings or by spontaneous impulse, as in her younger years: like Emma Bovary she saw that happiness must flourish better in some special places than elsewhere, just as certain plants flourish better in certain types of soil, yet she must still strive to keep up the appearance of happiness so that David could continue to believe in its reality. This she did well, both publicly and privately.

Meredith, watching her, occasionally sensed something troubling in her introspection. She would sit thoughtful and still on the edge of her bed in the darkened bedroom looking from the window across the black blockade of rooftops and the threatening army of the chimney-pots. (Cressida saw them differently; the only time he remembered her speaking out of her nocturnal reveries was once when she said, apropos the chimney-pots, 'They look like the charred stumps of a dead forest.') At other times she would have an open book in her hands but be staring away at something inside her own thoughts, with that expression in her green eyes that Janice had called 'Cressida's dripping-tap look'. As if she thought she could hear a tap dripping somewhere. But whatever she heard, Meredith suspected, it was not the particular music that played for her. It was not the look in her eyes he had seen on the sea's edge at Lebanon Bay, or at Lerici after the three comical old men had piped their fragile haunting little melody away. He never spoke to her about it.

As time went on the annual few weeks they could allow themselves for travelling on the Continent became more and more important to both of them.

For Cressida it was spiritually like some pagan vegetation rite of regeneration and renewal. In the sunburnt pepper-and-salt of Provençal landscape, in the sunny blue light of the Mediterranean, amid rocks and olives, in the carefree, slower, winy, singing zest of the Latin south, she seemed reborn; she responded to it all like a string plucked on an instrument. She was still beautiful, more beautiful in her late twenties than ever she had been, but repolished now by a recapturing of the earlier joy and vivacity. Yet when the time came to turn north again she always went ungrudgingly, drawn now by a hunger and anxiety for her children, who during these holidays stayed at a pleasant farm-school in Hertfordshire, because, as she would say, 'They must be getting sick to death of the food up there; I know the poor things loathe the fish they get.'

For David these European vacations were essential in a different way—for tonic and therapeutic rather than for spiritual values. By the end of a second year in London the strain of attempting to do two demanding and highly concentrated jobs was beginning seriously to tell on him, and he was being mauled also by the division in his interests. He had by this time had two novels published by a Bloomsbury firm highly distinguished in the more rarefied levels of poetry, *belles-lettres*, drama, criticism, fine arts, and scholarship, but just feeling its way, not entirely successfully, into the more hurly-burly world of fiction. So that while Meredith could raise eyebrows (being Australian) at literary cocktail-parties by saying who his publishers were, his advances on royalties were very small and his sales so inconsiderable as never to justify expectation of any further sum beyond the initial royalty payment. On the other hand, both books, possibly because of the publisher's imprint, had received passing commendation of a sort in a number of the better literary columns. While far from being hailed as a 'discovery' there were little measures of praise for some aspects of his writing and two critics even saw indications of 'some considerable promise', this apprehension, of course, being substantially qualified by what the critics then went on to say. Meredith, none the less, was immensely encouraged, and feverishly went to work on his 'big' novel, a very ambitious historical reconstruction of the passing of the Ming Dynasty. Writing this in spare hours at night after the pressures of a full day's newspaper work, he pushed himself very close to a breakdown—he was also drinking pretty heavily as a stimulant between the two tasks—and Cressida forced him finally to consult Carl Kronfeld, her doctor, who obligingly prescribed drugs for three weeks to enable Meredith to complete the novel, but was impelled to utter a warning.

'All that is actually wrong with you is that you are trying to do the impossible,' he said. 'You are attempting, most unwisely in my opinion, to fill two full-time jobs at once. You have just turned forty, remember, and you do not have all the old elasticity any longer. So you had better make a choice, had you not? I really,

Mr Meredith, do suggest this most seriously. I am offering you only a very temporary postponement, by no means a cure. You *must* make a choice. There is no other way out, Mr Meredith. So it is really up to you, is it not?'

It was an outside endorsement of a dilemma that now continually confronted him. Increasingly his passion and mental energies were being diverted to his creative writing; with his newspaper work he was still conscientious, but he was aware that with it he was developing a destructive cynicism concerning its worthwhileness. It was a curious reversal of the earlier situation in Sydney, where he had felt creatively frustrated but secure and satisfied in his newspaper work; here it was the journalism that filled him with an empty hopelessness; only from his private writing could he derive stimulus and comfort and belief.

Strict in the division of the two sections of his life, he rarely brought home to Cressida the journalistic problems that tormented him (there were times when desperately she wished he would, but having her own reticences she was cautious about his, so she did not tell him this), but not very long after the consultation with Dr Kronfeld he came home one evening tense, depressed, exhausted, and a little drunk from having had too many brandies with the boys in the Old Bell at Ludgate Circus, and confessed to her his dissatisfactions.

'All they bloody well want now is meretricious muck,' he said irritably. 'Here's Europe being torn to pieces. The bomb hanging over everybody's head like a great black evil cloud. The mess left in Korea. England going down the plughole. The Yanks and the Russians at each other's throats, to work out who's going to run the poor bloody brave new world. Witch-hunts everywhere. And Berlin likely to blow the whole damned lot of us sky-high any minute. So you try to write anything about it, and they sub it down to pap or spike it altogether.'

'You've got to keep trying, darling,' she said.

'Trying? What's the bloody point in trying?'

'If you believe in something you've got to keep trying.'

'The bastards are only interested in circulation. Build

circulation. That's all they're interested in. And you don't build circulation on jeremiads. Besides, the advertisers don't like it.'

'You're tired, darling.'

'I'm bloody tired. And bloody fed up.' He poured himself a stiff brandy and went to the window and brooded over the Bayswater Road traffic jam, bottlenecked at Notting Hill Gate, interlocked and motionless in the brown halated gloom all the way back to Queensway.

'We're letting them turn the world into a rat-race and a jungle and nobody gives a bugger!' He turned suddenly and said to her savagely, 'You try to write anything intelligent and important and they won't wear it. Too gloomy. They won't use it. They don't *want* it. They want cheap sex and titillation, another Princess Margaret surprise, what's new about Lady Docker's gold-plated Daimler. There are millions of people homeless in Europe who don't rate a paragraph, but they'll give the whole front page to some trashy little film starlet's views on men. Or the latest sex-change. Or some dreary suburban clergyman's fun with his choirboys. Or the latest sleazy Mayfair scandal. The only thing there's any room for these days is shit. Pure unadulterated shit! Do you know what they cabled for today?'

She shook her head, wanting him to get it all off his chest.

'They cabled for a Sunday story on who has the biggest tits – Lollobrigida or Diana Dors. The size of a film star's tits, you must understand, my dear, is far more important to our readers – and to the Great God Circulation – than the imminence of a nuclear war or the fact that three-quarters of the world is starving. The bastards even asked me to beam radio-pictures to illustrate the story. Do you know what I did?'

'What did you do?'

'I got an agency to photograph two big grapefruit side by side on a plate, and I sent that out by radio, and a caption saying that on the wide screen, in her dancing scene, Lollobrigida was a metre in circumference, thirty feet apart, *and swinging*!'

Cressida repressed a smile, and said seriously, 'Golly, what will they say about that?'

'I don't give a bugger what they say. They wouldn't know the difference anyway. I'm just chock of it, darling.'

'David, why don't you get out of it then? You don't have to stay. Not if it tears at you like this. Not if it's all so . . . so worthless. You don't *have* to put up with it, do you?'

'No?' He seemed a little taken aback, and looked at her carefully, then around the room just as carefully. 'What about all this?' he said. 'This flat? The car? The big salary, the expense account, the living allowance?'

'Well, what about them?' she said quietly.

'The nice school for the kids? All these books? Your clothes? Mine? Holidays on the Continent?'

'But we don't own these things, darling. They're not ours. They own us, really, don't they?'

'Well . . . yes, I suppose they do.' He nodded slowly. 'But the fact remains that if you have to be a prostitute you might as well be a high-priced one.'

'You don't have to be a prostitute. I mean, that's up to you really, isn't it?'

'That's right,' he said, and turned back to the window. He was silent for a long time, then, 'That's right,' he repeated more softly, looking at the static traffic. 'That's dead right, darling. It's up to me.'

They said nothing more about it, and in the event two factors, at that time unforeseen, forced the decision. One was the modest success of the novel on the Ming Dynasty, which was widely reviewed and received generally good notices, ran to a second impression, and to the surprise of everybody, including the publishers, earned several hundred pounds above the royalty advance.

The second was a fortuitous meeting with an elderly Australian woman[6] in a crummy little flat in Pimlico, who had for years been quietly exploring off the beaten track in Europe. Tom Kiernan took them to meet her – she had once been an art dealer in Melbourne and an enlightened early patron of his work – because he had just returned from a painting trip to Calabria, and he wanted to give her as a Christmas gift a picture he had done of the little coastal village where the old lady had placidly lived for several years.

'Italy, alas, is spoiling,' she said ruefully. 'Even in the south. So I am glad, Tom, that you caught it before it was too late. It is sad about Italy. Now one must go farther afield, I am afraid. Greece is the place, I think. Yes, Greece is still possible, I feel. You know Greece, Mr Meredith?'

'Not really,' he said. 'I was there twice during the war, but not for very long. Cress has never been there.'

'But you liked it?'

'I loved what I saw of it. It wasn't the best time, you know, a war the first time and a revolution the second. I loved the people.'

'I was back there only six months ago,' she said, and went on to tell them of her discovery of an unfrequented little island in the Aegean, crumbling into picturesque ruin, where the most wonderful old houses could be bought for twenty or thirty pounds and stately mansions for a hundred, where life was sublimely leisurely and peaceful, and living very cheap.

'You should find a place like that, Mr Meredith,' she advised, out of an old and kindly wisdom. 'You should find a place like that where you can get away from all this and try to write something worthwhile.'

They used the money which the novel had earned to take their next holiday in Greece. They travelled by the Orient Express and in Greece in the spring they found the scarlet poppies blooming in the fields at Epidaurus, and the white horses on the plain of Argos, and they found Delphi and Delos and Athens and Corinth (where Cressida remembered the quotation from Horace in *Tristram Shandy*: 'It is not every one that can get to Corinth,') and they found Mycenae and Crete and Rhodes and Patmos, and they found, on a blue bright blowing day, the island the old woman had told them about, and the proprietor of a crumbling waterfront hotel appropriately called the Poseidon delighted them both by demanding to see their passports before admitting them—

suspecting them to be illicit lovers and not man and wife—then showed them to a room the shabbiness of which was glorified by a whole ceiling flamboyantly painted with Phoebus Apollo driving a mad chariot through a golden aura of crude pigment, and from their window they looked below to a vivid rocking tangle of fat-bellied *caïques* unloading lemons and loquats and quinces and goats and earthenware water-jars.

GREECE, 1961

If we could leave now, at least it might be a way out of this trap into which we have fallen.

People are being helpful. Some of them. Well, most of them, really; only the few are malicious, hoping for the destruction to be total. These are the ones who, going down the drain themselves, would relish our company in the final plunge, if only to prove the fallacy of our earlier integration. The others, the rest of them, I suspect, are simply getting tired of seeing us clawing at each other.

'It is perfectly understandable,' Miriam said the other night with, I think, genuine sympathy. She can be haughty and at times stuffy, with her 'country' airs and superiorities, but there is often a warmth in her honey-coloured eyes that belies the beaky arrogance of the patrician nose, and the thin cold disapproving mouth. 'You simply cannot cut yourselves off on a little island, as you have done, for all these years. Not without reckoning the cost. Life becomes altogether too claustrophobic. Even incestuous. In the long run fatally destructive. And it *has* been a long run, hasn't it?'

'Yes, a long run,' said Cressida quietly. 'Nearly eight years.' She met my eyes for a moment, and tried to smile, but looked away.

'Then accept Beatrice's offer. You simply *must* have a change. You should both get back to the other kind of life for a while. Whether it is a better kind of life or worse is beside the point.

It is *different*. It will be a change. It will help straighten you both out.'

'Do you think we need straightening out?' I asked.

'Certainly. Staying on here, you are not really doing each other very much good, are you?'

For a long moment neither of us answered, then, 'We still survive,' I said.

'Yes. I am sorry. That is none of my business.' She would be tactful now and skirt around the real issue, I thought, and her next words proved me correct. 'You do have the children to consider, don't you?' she said with an edge of reprimand.

'We've always had the children to consider,' Cressida said. 'I don't think this has done them any harm. It might have done them a great deal of good.'

'Up to the present, very likely. But what of their future, my dears? Julian is a brilliant boy, a very brilliant boy. This I am the first to admit, but what about his education? Is it to be nothing beyond a primitive little Greek island school?'

'He probably gets a damned sight better old-fashioned classical education here than he'd get most other places,' I said. 'He learns the three Rs the hard way. And he keeps up his English. We get the books sent out. He's doing all right, you know. After all, he's only fifteen.'

'Precisely. You know perfectly well what Sir Terence thinks about him, about his going on to Oxford. The child should be given his chance, and—'

'Oh, for Christ's sake, Miriam, let's be practical!' I cut in irritably. 'What bloody chance have I got of sending him to Oxford? The only spare cash we've got – *when* we've got any spare cash – goes on getting a few books out for him from Foyle's. If he really *wants* to go to Oxford, and he's good enough, he'll do it in his own time and on his own terms. In any case, that's all years ahead. We have more immediate problems.'

'For which Beatrice has offered what seems to be a very reasonable solution,' said Miriam, assembling her features into a mask of patience. 'A simple exchange of houses for six months or a year. Beatrice and her family take over this house, they have their Greek sabbatical, and she can get on with her painting. You take over her house in England, and get back in touch with the real world.'

'You think it's a good solution?' I said.

'Admirable. The house is divine. An early Tudor farm-house and nothing in the village later than Jacobean. The most charming part of the Cotswolds, and the Vale of Evesham right below you. And some awfully pleasant people whom you will get to know. Moreover, if you wish to escape from Gloucestershire, there is a perfectly good train service to London, where you can stay with me, if you wish. I repeat, I consider the solution excellent. I wonder you hesitate.'

'I think,' I said carefully, 'that going back is a kind of confession of failure. That's all.'

'For heaven's sake, David, I suggest it is you who should be practical,' she said severely. 'You've lived on this island for eight years. If not entirely, at any rate largely on your own terms. You have had eight long years in which to do what you have wanted to do, which is considerably more than most people are ever able to achieve in a lifetime. Do you honestly feel that it has come off?'

'Some of it has, I suppose.'

'I am talking of the primary objectives. You have tried, I agree. You have worked hard, quite hard really. You have had a number of novels published, yet none of them, you must admit, has been particularly successful.'

'But perhaps the one I am just finishing will be,' I suggested.

'I hope so. I do hope so, David. But please hear me out. You are now forty-nine years of age and you are still struggling to become established. You have grown more and more out of touch with trends and people and social patterns. If you don't mind my saying so, I suspect you are falling behind.'

'I've been thinking that myself,' I admitted.

'Moreover, you have been very seriously ill, and your health remains in considerable jeopardy. That is another thing,' she said tartly. 'You need proper medical care and attention, not this casual intermittent Greek quackery. And poor Cressida having to poke needles into you! And rushing off all the time to look up the home doctor section in *Pears Cyclopædia*! I've never heard such arrant irresponsibility!'

'What else can we do?' asked Cressida. 'There's no doctor on the island. Besides, I'm very good with a needle. Half the island comes to me now for their shots.'

'Cress is marvellous,' I said. 'Do you know she practised for days on a raw potato before she started jabbing me in the bum?' It was time for the full evasive action, I felt, forcing a lighter tone, but Miriam was not altogether to be diverted.

'Just look at you now,' she said reprovingly. 'You are supposed not to be smoking, aren't you? Or drinking. You drink far too much. Both of you do. Your children are running wild, especially Miranda. She is like some wild little pagan creature who—'

'I don't think there's anything wrong with being wild and pagan,' Cressida said, a little wistfully. 'She'll only be young once . . . maybe she'll only have this chance once. At least she is free. She's happy and she's free.'

'But are *you* free?' Miriam asked quizzically. 'You two?'

'I was thinking of the children, of Miranda. Not of us.'

'But you must, my dear. And surely you cannot think that *you* are free. You live this detached, isolated . . . yes, this *inbred* existence—yet you are totally dependent for this existence, for its continuance, on an outside world which you have rejected. Do you honestly consider this to be freedom?'

Cressida shook her head slowly, staring away. 'Oh no,' she said. 'No, I don't consider we are free. Miranda is, though,' she said, turning to the older woman with a smile. 'For a little while. I suppose it will have to come to an end for her one day, too.'

Miriam shrugged, spread her gaunt beringed hands, and dropped the subject. So the real issue was safely circumvented again. Miriam had been right, of course, as far as she had gone; she had been right about the drinking, too, even while tactfully avoiding specific instances; it was only when we drank too much that the constraints of habit and mutual decency and consideration dropped away and we abandoned evasions with each other, only then that the complicated façade so painstakingly erected and preserved over so many years crumbled into dusty desolate ruin.

But looking back on it there is no clear black or white about anything. It is all a hopeless tangle of the good and the bad, the serene and the savage, the brutal and the beautiful, of love and hate and loyalty and betrayal. It is hope and despair, and magical experiences that become soiled and smutty, and delicacies that jar, and murderous attacks delivered with the gentlest of touches. The priceless things are all mixed up with the cheap trash and junk. It is a trap from which there is no escape, a thicket in which we can find no path. Sometimes when I look back to see the way we have come it is all overgrown again, and even the memory of what we have passed through is blurred and distorted. The clear pure spring we drank at long ago is tainted, and I can no longer separate the gayest and happiest of festivals from the bitterness of quarrels.

Is it the island that has done this to us? Or only ourselves?

If we could find some way out of the thicket, the tangle, the clashing rocks. Some way out. One is almost desperate enough to ask for *any* way out. I don't think we can find redemption here. It must be elsewhere.

GREECE, 1959

The day begins joyously, as such days seem to. The naval band, pomp-pomping on its brass and rattling and thumping its drums, tattoos through the twisting lanes of the white-washed town in the first gleams of dawn, exuberantly waking everyone for the day of festival and the honouring of the Hero.

The monastery of the Virgin is wreathed in victors' laurel, and all through the day the bells crash and call, frenetic above the whip and dance of a thousand little flags, blue and white like the sea and the tumbling wavecrests, like the white houses against the shine of the enamelled sky. The flags tug out in the singing wind from the tower of the monastery and link every post along the quay and snap at every masthead. The little cannons on the headland fort defy the bells, barking like terriers while vainly attempting thunderous greetings to the warships arriving and the crowded island steamers and the brisk pinnaces skittering in to deposit white uniforms and brass and gold and epaulettes and tasselled lanyards and swords and cocked hats and sashes and decorations. The Hero is the Navy's hero.

Getting on towards sundown the priests in their Byzantine robes pace their solemn smoulder to the little museum to take the Hero's heart in its casket of gold from where, the year round, it rests among the old portraits and guns and relics and the crude water-colours of square-rigged ships; they take it and carry it held high for all to see through narrow streets and lanes where dusk has begun to seep and a thick and magic silence after the summoning bells. The altar-boys go first with the great gold ecclesiastical banners and young girls with braided hair under lace kerchiefs, strewing flowers on the cobbles, and rosemary and upland thyme and the sweet spiced *faskómmila* from the mountains, advancing slowly, slowly, slowly through the prescient padded dusk, trailing the heavy taffeta skirts of their ancestral costumes. They approach to the muffled, steady beat of drums, not loud but echoing with a curious smothering resonance from high pale walls and overhanging balconies—the same walls, the same delicately wrought balconies overlooking the same lanes where once the Hero strode, powerful among his peers, a short nuggety man in a red skull-cap and a wide sash thrust through with pistols . . .

The slow ceremonial tide flows past the house, shot with dull gleams of gold and silver and crimson, strewn with flowers, followed by all the townspeople in hushed shuffling procession. And the shrouded twilight beats to the steady, muffled, powerful beat of the Hero's heart held high in its golden casket.

This is how it begins, and then it is time for the gaiety, and everyone is down at the waterfront, and the band is striking up beneath the flags and the strings of little coloured lights. Not 'Colonel Bogey' any more, but Greek dances—first a bubbling effervescent *hassápiko*, then the *tsámiko* and the *kalamatianó*—and suddenly everyone is dancing. Chairs and tables are pushed away. Sent spinning. Glasses crash. In every pocket-handkerchief of space thus wrested from confusion there are matrons and shop-keepers and girls and artisans and shepherds and labourers all kicking up their Sunday-best heels and slapping at shoe-leather and not a whit concerned about dignity or decorum or the splitting seams of their new festival clothes. Panting waiters are trotting in cheerful agitation with trays of sweets and honeycakes and glasses of *ouzo* and cherry brandy and copper pots of retsina, and the band blares louder, and the girls whirl and whirl with snaking braids. Some of the tourists and the foreigners are joining in. Calverton, in a sweat of rapture and excitement and alcohol, has found Miranda as a partner, Saxon-blonde among her Mediterranean-dark school-fellows, wearing the exquisite old island gown of grey taffeta as if she were born to the right of it. The mayor, already giddier with *ouzo* than with the *tsámiko*, stops at our table to compliment us on our daughter's dancing. Even Lieutenant Manolis, the police chief, salutes us with a raised glass and forces the suggestion of a smile.

'These folk sure have the greatest feel for *joie de vivre*,' an American at a near-by table calls across to us. He is by himself at the table beating the rhythm of the dance upon it with his empty glass. He is a tall, handsome, strong-built man with amused cocoa-coloured eyes that harbour a kind of eager submission to gaiety; the eyes are young, but a neat full beard, reddish-brown, makes it difficult to guess his age. He wears espadrilles and light-blue Mediterranean pants and a faded French workman's jacket. 'Man! will you look at that dancing!' He shakes his head and laughs infectiously. 'I guess we've all got a whole lot to learn about the meaning of zest.'

Cressida laughs with him and calls across, 'Just you wait a few minutes. It's almost time for the fireworks.'

She has hardly spoken when one of the island steamers shoots in around the headland in a carnival of lights, and above her the aubergine summer sky bursts into a thousand coloured flowers. A great concerted sigh of wonder floats along the waterfront. The long mole explodes into fountains of fire, flamefalls and cataracts, wheels of whirling light, huge brilliant incandescent blossoms unfolding, orange and magenta and poison green. From the high sky descends, slowly, a dreamlike fall of Dufy stars. There are set-pieces as big as houses all around the harbour, and the black silhouettes of scampering pygmies running beneath sulphurous Niagaras. Scuttling figures out of Bosch. But the people who laugh and point are calling attention not to hellfire but to the magic of a dream.

A boat on the harbour is suddenly afire, opening up on the purple water like a Japanese paper flower, yellow and pink and with crinkled edges to the flaming petals. There is a stampede to the water's edge, a black flurry of men and boats against the glare of spectacle. The fire is conquered, the charred and waterlogged wreck towed soggily to the crowded quay. The fisherman who owns the boat crosses himself with Job-like acceptance and bows to the will of God. '*O Theós*,' he says, smiling into the pyrotechnic glow. Everyone is dropping money into a cap, banknotes and silver and nickel, and Stephanos finds a golden sovereign in the old-fashioned coin-case he always carries, and the fisherman is laughing louder than anybody else. '*O Theós*,' he says. '*O Theós*.' He repeats it with a kind of awed exultation.

The band strikes up again with *Yerrakina* and handkerchiefs are fluttering and circles forming beneath the explosive shower and dazzle of the continuing rockets, and the bearded American has brought his chair across to our table, and with it his glass and cigarettes and a carafe of retsina and a half-empty bottle of bourbon. For a long time he sits without talking, happy and smiling, a child's delight in his dark warm eyes as he watches the joyous frenzy, sometimes looking across at Cressida and shaking his head as if he must unwillingly awaken himself from a dream.

On the black mountainflank that overhangs the town like the

petrified wave of Hokusai, lights begin to prick, and gradually the dancing stops and people turn to watch. The prickling, twinkling pinpoints appear slowly and erratically, random dart-holes in the wall of night, but coherence grows and it is all but complete as a droning buzz of admiration and wonder comes from the watching people, and there, high in the night, stretched against the mountains and the stars beyond the smokedrift, stretched across the visible world, a thousand winking lights spell out the Hero's name.

'The boys from the high school here,' Cressida explains to the mystified American. 'Our son is up there with them. It's their contribution to the festival. We've been months saving all our empty Nescafé tins, and then stuffing them with cotton-waste soaked in kerosene, and the boys have been climbing up and down for days putting them into position on the mountain. Look, they're coming down now.'

A twisting snake of torches slides down the great rock and the whole waterfront bursts into ovation as the boys come trotting along the quay, blue shorts and starched white shirts, flushed and sweating faces, but holding their blazing pine-brands high, and running an extra circuit of the little town, either just for the good measure of exuberance or to prove that they are not really exhausted at all. Above them sparkles the fiery symbol of the Hero.

The American says with an inflection of wonder, 'But this must be the last really *innocent* festival left in the whole darned world.' His teeth as he smiles are very white. 'Boy, am I glad I decided to quit Athens and see something of the islands. I figure I'll stay awhile.'

'Oh, it isn't always like this,' says Cressida. 'This is the big night for this island. It only happens once a year.'

'Sure. But I guess I'll still stay.'

Calverton has returned to the table, gasping and laughing, and, in the necessity for introductions, the bearded stranger identifies himself as Jim Galloway, an architect from Connecticut 'doing the statutory pilgrimage to the shrines of the old gods'. It is still hard to pick his age. His body is young-looking and firm, and there is something boyish and almost naïve in the quick infection of his smile, but his hair is streaked with grey and the thick mat of his chest is almost white where it thrusts out from the faded French jacket to form a nest for a tiny thin medallion on a thin gold chain. When he is serious his eyes seem older. He could be forty or so.

'Say, why don't you two get up and dance?' he suggests to us, but I shake my head and say, 'I don't dance. I'm afraid I'm a bit short in the breath for it. And I don't know the steps. Cress here is the dancer.'

'How about you then, Mr Calverton? You can't tell me you're no dancer. I was watching you earlier.'

Calverton laughs. 'If you were watching me earlier you'll know I've done *my* bloody dash. Their daughter has danced me right into the ground. I'm completely bloody well whacked. For the rest of the night I intend to stay with the devil I know.' He brims his glass of wine, lifts it in a quick toast, and drains it in one long gulp. 'Why don't you dance with her yourself?' he suggests to the American. 'She'll instruct you. You'll pick it up in no time.'

'How do *you* feel about that, Mrs Meredith?' he asks, smiling, and Cressida, smiling back at him, has already risen and is holding out her hands to him. 'Hey, great!' he cries.

He does pick it up quickly. His movements are lithe and graceful and he seems to have an instinct for the sprung rhythms of the beating tune. He is even taller than I had realized, head and shoulders taller than Cressida, whose face is tilted back laughing up at his laughter. They swirl away in a serpentine line of spinning partners and fluttering handkerchiefs, are lost in the swirling crowd. A table somewhere is overturned. Glass splinters and crunches beneath stamping feet. The charred fag-ends of fire-works smoke and splutter on the mole. On the black mountain the Hero's name is guttering out into random flares and tiny flickerings like the eyes of animals. Everyone is singing.

'Costas!' Calverton shouts for the drink waiter, thundering the empty carafe on the deal table. 'Let's get stuck into it,' he says thickly and happily. 'Let's tackle the problem very seriously, sport. Let's you and me get properly pissed!'

I don't know how much we drink but the wine hardly affects me, although Calverton gets so drunk that I have to take him back to the house when Julian and Miranda go, and he passes out as I roll him on the day-bed. By the time I get back to the waterfront the festival has run its course. A few waiters and yawning boys are sweeping around the weary legs of a dozen or so of the hardier revellers. Tables and chairs are stacked in untidy tiers outside the taverns and coffee-houses. The charred hulk of the burnt boat has been hauled up on the mole between the bollards. The masts of *caïques* move soothingly against impassive stars. A drunken fisherman sleeps on the marble statue, one arm around the laurelled neck of the Hero, the other firmly clasping the marble lion which has human ears and the face of Bertrand Russell.

I sit there for a long time, dreaming and thinking and dozing and wondering. I am perhaps a little drunk after all, drunk enough to have a kind of detachment, or at least a submission to abeyance. I have no wish to confuse myself by having to face possible issues. Mine is the only chair and the only table still implanted squarely and emptily on the long silent sweep of the abandoned waterfront. The moon has risen above the black lip of the mountain and a dark sheen of damp has settled on the flagstones and the surface of the table feels greasy beneath my elbows. They have all gone now, the late revellers and the aproned waiters and the tired boys, and there is hardly a lighted window in the whole town, ghost-pale and still and pearly under the moon. There is only me at the lonely table and the fisherman curled up on the ridiculous statue and the beacons flashing red and green at the harbour entrance. It is very quiet. Now and then an owl calls and there is the faintest tinkling drift of bells from the high sheepfolds and goat pastures or the distant strangling paroxysm of a donkey, and the sea sucks and whispers at the sternposts of the moored boats. Where Cressida is, and the bearded American, I do not know. Perhaps we have crossed each other, and she is already home.

But it is long after I get back before she returns. She walks into the kitchen slowly, her face rapt and dazed, as if she is sleep-walking. But she does not seem surprised to find me sitting there, and smiles affectionately.

'Where have you been?' I ask.

'We danced and danced,' she says.

'But the dancing's been over for hours.'

'Oh, and then we walked. I walked him round the rocks and past the cave, almost to Piso. I wanted to show him the end of the gulf and the islands in the moonlight. It was so beautiful.' She is looking out through the door at the fall of vines, heavy now with fruit. There is dew in the air and the smell of jasmine. 'He is very sweet,' she says softly. 'He really is a very sweet man.' She is still staring into the moonlit courtyard, but I dare not look at her except furtively; I am too tired and also too wary to try to trap any expression in her eyes.

She turns suddenly and shakes her head in that quick way she has, as she does when swimming, shaking water from her eyes, and jumps up and embraces me fiercely. 'Darling, hasn't it been heavenly?' she whispers, her cool face pressed against mine. 'Hasn't it been the most heavenly night?'

GREECE, 1959

When the cable came from Archie Calverton I had not seen him for five years—not since that foggy November morning when he had thrust on me his St Christopher medallion and rushed off down the Bayswater Road—but his name was always cropping up in newspapers and the illustrated magazines, so his message did not come as any particular surprise. It read:

> COMPLETING CURRENT FILM WHICH REAL STINKER WITH THREE WEEKS SHOOTING ATHENS AND OTHER GREEK LOCATIONS BY WHICH TIME WILL HAVE HAD GUTFUL STOP AM GETTING NEAR END OF TETHER STOP ALTERNATIVE TO NUTHOUSE OR JOINING ALCOHOLICS ANONYMOUS MIGHT BE

RECUPERATIVE SPELL ON QUIET GREEK ISLAND WITH OLD MATES STOP CAN YOU COPE WITH DRUNKEN DERELICT WHO OTHERWISE HAS END OF ROAD IN SIGHT STOP IF OFFERED WELCOME WILL PROMISE NOT TO OUTSTAY.

'I suppose it's really for you to decide, David,' Cressida said. Her eyes were anxious as she folded the cable form carefully and handed it back to me. 'You're really not well, you know that. And you still won't see a doctor. You *are* trying to get on with your book. So Archie would be another distraction, perhaps a lot of strain you can't afford.'

'But we can't turn him down if he *is* in a spot,' I said. 'We can't, can we?'

'It depends, I suppose, on whether he'll be troublesome or not.'

'He wouldn't be the only one. We ought to be accustomed to people being troublesome.' I thought about it and said, 'There was that business in London, of course. Which might make it a bit awkward.'

'Yes. That's why I said it's really for you to say.'

'Although that's a hell of a long time ago. Obviously he *wants* to come. He might have changed, of course. I mean, since we last saw him he has really become a big shot. He is the only one of us who's pulled it off, isn't he? Really made a success of it, I mean.'

'Does that worry you?'

'I don't know. No, I don't think so. Half his luck.'

'You can't honestly mean that, David. Not after having read that cable.'

'I wasn't thinking of that. Just the sweet smell of success. At least he has had a decent whiff of it. Which is a bloody sight more than I have.'

'It does worry you, then.'

'All right, it might,' I admitted. 'I'm not sure. I imagine these things depend on how much you have to pay for what you get. If we have him out here perhaps I can find out how I really do feel about it all. At least he'll be someone different to talk to. What about you? Would *you* like him to come?'

'Yes, I would. I've always been terribly fond of Archie. He would be someone different for me to talk to, too.'

'Well, let's go down to the port and shoot him off a cable.'

It was not possible, of course, for either of us to realize then the devious little ways in which fate shapes the critical tangents of one's life.

LONDON, 1954

What is difficult to achieve in these notes and jottings and reassembled memories is a proper balance in the tensions, because there has to be a place for the cool, detached observer and there has to be a place for the one who, being totally involved, is both the sufferer and the inflicter of suffering. If these are one and the same person it is not the easiest thing in the world to find a complete honesty of understanding.

It is easy enough, on the surface of it, at least *now* it is easy enough, to see the rot developing from within, in both of us to different degrees, but certainly in *both* of us, and it is equally easy to find such comparatively clearcut reasons as my possessive jealousies and Cressida's own possessiveness of that silent uncommunicated private world in which her own myth was harboured, creating dreams which became, at times, more powerful than realities. Such a myth, I suppose, is possessed in the first place as a protective talisman against forces unspecified but inimical, perhaps as a kind of compass needle for direction, but if the myth comes to possess rather than to be possessed it can turn into a dangerous form of sorcery. It can create a kind of self-hypnosis and blind us to the fact that realities are more powerful than dreams; those who think otherwise must suffer and die, because they are the victims of what someone has called the 'romantic malady'.

Perhaps this is a man's point of view: I sometimes suspect that man, basically, is much more fragile than woman, and it is possible that a great measure of strength is needed to hold to the protean substance of the dream. Men do seem to be better when dealing with realities.

Still, for a long time, in London, I believe that neither of us really understood what was wrong, or going wrong. There was nobody to tell us, and we were careful not to try to tell each other.

None of us can ever overcome the wish to shape ourselves in the image other people have of us; not entirely, at any rate. The reflection we instinctively value most is projected not from mirrors but from other people's eyes.

I remember Archie Calverton calling at the flat one evening—this was during the first year we were in London—with the manuscript of a play his agent had asked him to read. He was anxious for our opinion because while he was in two minds about the part offered him and more than half inclined to reject it, he had reached a critical stage in the London theatrical scene and could hardly afford a mistake. He had been fortunate enough to get a part in a play very soon after his arrival in London, and good notices for his performance, but the play, although a modest *succès d'estime*, ran for only nine weeks, and for a good many months afterwards Calverton suffered the chill blast of English indifference. The fact of his not being homosexual closed the doors of some producers against him, the fact of his being a 'colonial' closed others (and sent him to a speech expert to deal with his Australian accent), and the English producer who, in Sydney, had encouraged him to come to London and chance his arm in the big leagues seemed never to be in when Calverton tried to contact him. He was a little disheartened and disillusioned by the time he came to the flat with the manuscript, having in the intervening months lived precariously on the proceeds of two small roles in radio plays and a few bits of casual crowd work in films and a cautious incursion into his meagre savings as the result of a vague half-promise of 'something quite good for you which might be coming up in the next Shakespeare season'.

Still, he was cheerful enough on this night—he always did have a marvellous rapport with Cressida—and became very gay and affectionate. I remember thinking that, except for a better complexion and a more polished urbanity – I saw that he no longer sniffed at a Benzedrine inhaler, nor kept up any repartee of wise-cracks – he was remarkably little changed in appearance from the night, four or five years earlier, at Riordan's pub in Melbourne. Handsomer, I thought, and more assured, certainly better dressed, but the same young-old face, although interestingly tired now rather than pinched and weary. He had taken to cheroots, black Burma cheroots, instead of cigarettes and drank only dry Martinis, which he insisted on mixing himself, very strong.

'What I want to know,' he said, settling down in an armchair with his drink and the typescript of the play open on his lap, 'is this. In a marriage is it an immutable, inescapable fact that one or other of the two partners must be submissive? The wife to the husband or the husband to the wife?'

'I suppose,' said Cressida, 'it depends on the marriage. On the extent of understanding and tolerance between them.'

'The theme of this play,' said Calverton – 'I'll give it very broadly; I'll read you some bits later – is that modern man stubbornly refuses to acknowledge his changing state, which is being brought about by woman's refusal, or disinclination anyway, to be submissive any longer.'

'But isn't that rather sweeping?' said Cressida. 'Is this just dealing with the moralities, sexual moralities? The double standard? I mean, surely this isn't something *new*? A woman can be submissive to her husband for any number of reasons. Always has been, and probably always will be. Because she wants to. She's that sort of person. Because it suits her, makes her life easier. It could be pure animal cunning, so she can get more out of him.'

'Basically the play is concerned with the sexual angle. The present-day change in attitudes and patterns.'

'Oh come on now,' I protested. 'Women have always played it whatever way it suited them. Writers have been wrestling with that one for centuries. What about Anna Karenina? Hedda Gabler? Moll Flanders? Emma Bovary? They were submissive only for as long as it suited them.'

'Anyway, how can you do anything except generalize?' said

Cressida. 'A woman might also be submissive because of loyalty, or a love big enough to forgive shortcomings, or simply because of a wish not to hurt. Or, if she has children, because of her family. Or even finding herself caught in a trap, with no way out, and making the best of it. Or simply just not having any alternative.' She paused. 'Or all of them bundled together,' she added thoughtfully.

'But not necessarily because it's a woman's *job* to be submissive? Her conjugal duty?'

'No, not that. That's just the Victorian hangover. It's changing. It should, too.'

'In the play,' said Calverton, 'the husband has a line in the second act, where the relationship has begun to curdle, and he says to his wife, "We don't seem to be able to coincide any longer".'

'Golly!' Cressida laughed. 'Surely he's not suggesting that marriage has to be a permanent amalgam! Two-in-one, eternally fused! A gold ring on a finger doesn't create a chemical change. It doesn't turn people into something else. They're still people, two distinct people. Everyone finally is a private human being, and everyone finally has to live with himself. Or *herself*.' She laughed again. 'Archie,' she said, 'I'm beginning to think this is neither a very original play nor a very good one.'

'I'm inclined to agree with you,' he said ruefully. 'Unluckily, they have not offered me the part of the husband. I could play *that* for laughs.'

'Non-husbands always can,' I said in mock reproof. 'It's time we all had another drink.'

'I have a final question for *you*,' he said. He tapped his finger against the manuscript. 'This bloke says a man's objections to his wife's frailty is not so much a question of possessiveness as one of injured human pride. Which is much more difficult to deal with. What do you say about that?'

'Nothing. How can I? I have the ideal marriage and the perfect wife. She has no frailty.'

We all laughed, and I took his jug of Martini over to him and he tossed the manuscript on the floor.

The play never did come off. Which was not surprising. The interesting thing now, looking back, is that in that trivial discussion, ostensibly innocent and largely academic, there was the first hint of Cressida's secret and deeply buried feelings, the first fugitive glimpse, like an image hardly formed in a clairvoyant's crystal, of futures not yet shaped for us.

The months that followed were, for Calverton, difficult ones. Apart from a brief season in provincial repertory he spent most of the time 'resting'—which meant a good deal of pretty solid drinking with the fringe-bohemians who frequented the Antelope at Sloane Square and the King's Head on Cheyne Walk, hating the superficiality of it yet needing its brittle sophisticated veneer to gloss over the hollowness of frustration and despair. He was haunted, I think, by the awesome sense of loneliness which the very weight and tone and scale of London can impose upon a man. He had his mysterious girl in Soho—she was, I gathered from drunken admissions, a mulatto and a prostitute with whom he had some curiously gentle and necessary relationship—and he would go, very late at night and usually drunk, to her for comfort, or flee from her in rage and guilt and remorse. He came often to visit Cressida, especially when he was feeling low or contrite or in need of encouragement or some different form of comfort and reassurance. He was astute and sensitive enough to see that Cressida was also lonely, and he would call usually during the day, when I was working in Fleet Street—just as he had done in Sydney, when I was working with the *Globe*—and sometimes would take her walking in Hyde Park or to the little flea-house cinema at Notting Hill Gate where they ran revivals of old movies for a shilling a seat. Sometimes, not often, he would be there in the flat when I returned from the office in the evening, and Cressida would always seem gayer and freer than normally she was at the end of a day pegged to the inexorable routines of the children. He would usually only stay to have one drink with me 'for the road', and then take himself off—to wherever he spent his lonely nights.

It was, in fact, quite a long time before I was aware of a

recrudescence of that earlier faint, troubling suspicion of him—hardly even jealousy then—that had worried me in Sydney. It came slyly at first; I would catch myself watching from behind a cultivated air of casual bonhomie for meaningful gestures or expressions or situations; and it came uneasily, for it also frightened me that I might find, actually have *revealed*, evidence of something ulterior in their seemingly innocent but certainly mutually pleasurable companionship. I see now that this disturbance of my own mind was closely related to my growing dissatisfaction with myself.

Jealousy is one of the more corrosive of the passions, and they say that all passions have their roots in something insecure within us, something of ourselves that we shrink away from. The trouble is that disappointment with ourselves never moderates our expectations from others; on the contrary, it raises them; but then, having been thwarted in our own hopes or expectations, we are inclined towards a secret wish to be disappointed also in our expectations from others. This is a pretty vicious form of sadomasochism, but I have been reading up a bit lately on the elements of jealousy, and there seems no doubt that we are always prone to torture and sacrifice others when we torture and sacrifice ourselves.

It was, in fact, quite some time before London itself grew to be disappointing, which was not the fault of the great metropolis itself but a dawning realization that I had been blundering around in circles for more than six years, ever since coming back from the war and leaving Helen. I was still trapped in the squirrel cage, spinning an interminable meaningless treadmill, still torn by conflicting ambitions and desires, unwilling to commit either to one thing or the other—the precariousness of belief or the safeness of conformity.

Cressida, in this situation, and whatever my own doubts, was the keystone of reassurance. She was always there to fall back on. At least I had *this*. This possession beyond price, this unflawed perfection, this prize among women. I would tacitly demand and undemurringly she would give all that could be desired of a wife and a mother. She would be there with laughter and gaiety when a mood was frolicsome, with solicitude and gentleness when I was tired or depressed, with encouragement in the bleak hours, with love—and generously—when only love was needed. She was a good and intelligent talker, a charming hostess, a warm and sensible mother. When one was afflicted, as one frequently was in London, by feelings of inferiority, one had only to take her out to the theatre or a party to have one's ego inflated to the *n*th degree by the extraordinary admiration she would evoke by her striking beauty and the sheer charm of her personality. She seemed, on her part, to have no demands. It took me a long time to realize that she deliberately geared her own moods to mine, to what I expected of her. I am sure she realized long before I did how tottery and jerry-built was the edifice I had created around myself, and she would have known that she was the cementing strength, any weakening of which might bring it all down in ruin. Her compliance was sedulous, yet never seemed like compliance or submissiveness; she tried, and perhaps genuinely wanted to be, as I expected her to be.

The English climate did not suit her—being a sun-worshipper she missed the sun, and although she loved the bare physical beauty of London's winter chiaroscuro, the long grey months of a shadowless world were inclined to make her melancholy—and possibly the inaction of her proscribed life was an equally depressive factor: I do remember that one of her peaks of ebullience was when she drove Janice to Stratford to see Calverton playing in *Othello* in a dangerous blizzard behind snow-ploughs and through wrecked and derelict cars; and she would sparkle, too, in the wilder freedoms of the Land's End peninsula when she took the children to Cornwall for their school holidays.

The climate, at any rate, did affect her health, and after the first winter she became a patient of an Austrian doctor who had a practice in South Kensington. The doctor, Carl Kronfeld, being from Vienna, was by way of being something of a psychiatrist as well as a GP, and his practice was rapidly growing fashionable, particularly with a group of very attractive young married women, several of whom Cressida got to know and to invite to the flat. Kronfeld seemed to think (rightly as it eventually turned out) that there were deeper psychological reasons than mere climate to account for Cressida's indifferent health, and Cressida, who liked and admired him, became a regular patient.

I made no particular objections to this, although for obscure reasons I disapproved secretly of Cressida being ill and I have always harboured qualified suspicions of European psychiatrists, but I did become a little uneasy one evening when I returned from the office earlier than usual and found Cressida drinking sherries with three of Kronfeld's other patients, all exceedingly beautiful young women. Later, half-jokingly, I said to her, 'That doctor of yours has certainly got an eye for a pretty woman. He's getting himself quite a stable of beauties, isn't he?' Cressida smiled and said nothing.

Some weeks after this I met Kronfeld—he had to be called in for one of the children—and found him younger than I had expected; not particularly handsome, but an interesting personality, polished, highly intelligent, and full of a warm Continental charm, and although his conduct was punctiliously professional I was very conscious of Cressida's deep and, it seemed to me, personally *involved* attention to whatever he said, and I was sure I detected in his otherwise professional eye some hint of warmth and admiration for her that had little to do with doctor-patient relationships.

I am sure I never said anything directly to Cressida about this, but she discontinued the regular consultations and for the rest of the time we were in London only visited his surgery when she was really ill or the children had to be taken.

One sees now, of course, that the incident with Dr Kronfeld was, in effect, a rehearsal largely in mime for the more vociferous drama with Calverton. Both keyed to the same theme—suspicion.

The suspicious mind believes more than it doubts. Being guarded and defensive, it is a sign of weakness, and it is always sure that a powerful and ineradicable weakness, usually evil in intent, lurks in every other person. And the weak like to destroy weakness whenever they come across it. I read a line somewhere, I have forgotten where, which said, 'Woe to the weak when they are preyed upon by the weak!' It was not so much that I detected, or even suspected, weakness in Cressida, but that I mistrusted life itself. At heart most men, I suspected, even good men, were predatory animals, and a beautiful woman was always vulnerable to their sly importunities, their calculated flatteries, to even fortuitous moments of emotional compatibility. Then there was this quiet, withdrawn, secret area of Cressida to which I could never quite reach, at which I hesitated even to grope, a part of her which, for all my possessiveness, I could not possess. Supposing then that another man, working on some totally different level of understanding and companionship, came to find the key and stirred these buried longings at which I could not even guess? Could any man then *not* covet what legally was mine? A man such as Archie Calverton?[7] A friend? But why not? Perhaps by its very nature it *would have to be* a friend! There was no precedent against it. And the two of them did share a peculiar personal harmony of their own: I remembered Calverton's farewell party in Sydney and the drunken poetry in the back of the car going home. Moreover, Cressida knew, had known from the beginning, of my suspicions of Calverton; might this not, with womanly caprice, invite thoughts which otherwise need never have been aroused? Force the two of them into a sharing of an imposed culpability, which was to say a sharing of a part of Cressida denied to me? A private propinquity all their own?

The poison, once taken, began insidiously to spread.

Yet it was a subtle poison. It would remain atoxic for long weeks and even months on end, then, for no explicable reason, eat at me corrosively, day after day and wakeful night after wakeful night, then turn inactive again and leave me overwhelmingly relieved that I had triumphed over my baser impulses and not committed the irremediable error of misjudging or unjustly condemning the woman whom I loved and trusted. During the long period when Calverton and Cressida were seeing most of each other I was completely successful, I think, in concealing my suspicions.

Then, for a year or so, we saw very little of Calverton, for a sharp change came in his fortunes. He did get the half-promised Shakespearian role, which led to a Stratford season in which he played a virile Mercutio and a memorable Iago; he at once became much sought after and signed a lucrative film contract. Luck had worked for him in that his reach towards eminence coincided almost precisely with one of those changes in Thespian fashions that occur from time to time, in this case the supplanting of the classically handsome matinée-idol type of male lead by craggier, uglier, more interesting-looking men. It was not very long before Calverton's young-old eroded face with the sharp deep-set eyes and gaunt cheekbones, the big sensual mouth and the spiky tangle of hair, became a regular presence on the news-stands, looking out from the covers of the picture magazines and the front pages of the Sunday tabloids. It must be added, of course, that he had by this time proved himself a remarkably good actor.

He took a luxurious maisonette apartment on the Thames at Chiswick Mall, bought himself an expensive and powerful sports car, gave up Burma cheroots for snuff and dry Martinis for champagne cocktails, but evidently retained the solace of his mulatto girl in Soho, and in the intervals between film shooting resumed his dropping in on Cressida.

Around this time I was obliged to spend two weeks in West Germany and Berlin, a nervy and dispiriting assignment, covering NATO exercises, interviewing devious politicians, and trying to sort some sense out of the steadily deteriorating Cold War scene. Towards the end, in a mood of bitter despondency and frustration, I gave up the struggle against censorship and falsehood and misrepresentation, against the dangerous deceits and blind delusions of the military-political machine at its worst, and cut the assignment short. I was able to get back on a returning RAF transport flight. We landed at dusk on an Essex airfield, and I stayed on drinking in the flight mess until they could arrange transport for me down to London. So by the time I got home, stale and tired, it was close to midnight. My feelings of disillusionment and anticlimax were not alleviated by my finding

Cressida out and Mildred Dapp, as baby-sitter, asleep in the guest-room.

When I wakened the old woman she told me that my wife had gone to a party, and insisted on getting up and shuffling out in furry slippers with her wispy grey hair in curlers and crocheted wool shawl wrapped around her voluminous flannelette nightgown. 'No, madam expected t'be back rather late, sir, so thought it'd save everyone trouble and bother if I stayed the night,' she explained. 'Now I'll make you a nice cuppa tea, sir, and fix a tray,' she said fussily. 'There's where she's at, sir, on that pad there. Address is writ down, sir, and telephone number. Just in case, she said, there's any trouble with the kiddies. Lord love us, sir, as if there would be! Been perfick little treats they have. Not a mite of trouble. Now I'll get you your pot o' tea right away, sir, and—'

'No, don't you worry, Mrs Dapp. Thank you. I'd honestly rather have a whisky. I want to 'phone this number anyway, so why don't you just pop off back to bed?' I dialled the number and waited but there was no answer. The old woman was still there, fussing and frowning, so I hung up and said, 'Do you know whether my wife took the car when she went out?'

'Oh no, sir, no, she didn't. That friend of yours called for her, that nice Australian actor man Mr Calverton. He's been here quite regular this last week or so. My, he's getting very famous, they say, sir. Did you know he's acting in a picture with that Ursula Deems they're making at Pinewood and—'

'Look, do pop off back to bed, Mrs Dapp,' I said. 'It's after midnight. I really don't need anything. And I'm going out again as soon as I've had this drink.'

'If you're sure you will be all right, sir.'

'Quite sure, Mrs Dapp. Good night. And thank you.'

I went down to the square and got into the car and sat there irresolutely for some time before switching on the ignition, but then I decided to drive to Chiswick anyway, where at least I could wait in the car until one or both of them returned, but when I got to the Mall the maisonette was a blaze of lights, and after a little delay Calverton himself opened the door in answer to my knock. He started as if he had expected someone else, and blinked once or twice and then stared at me in blank astonishment. He was a bit drunk and unsteady on his feet, but motioned me to enter, and called over his shoulder, 'Three guesses who's here!' (Was this called, I wondered, as a warning?)

The sitting-room was a chaos of glasses and bottles and overflowing ash-trays and party litter, and there was a haze of stale fug that prickled my throat and eyes.

'David!' Cressida gasped, jumping up from the rumpled divan on which she had been sitting. 'Darling!' she cried, her eyes shining. 'Oh *darling*!' and flung herself at me with open arms, and clung to me. (You really are a marvellous bloody actress, I told myself.) 'But . . . but what in heaven's name are you . . . I mean, how did — ?'

'Conned a ride back,' I said brusquely. 'RAF flight,' I said, holding her stiffly and speaking across the top of her head. The tortoiseshell comb was dislodged and loose in her hair. 'I thought I'd surprise you.'

'Well, you've certainly done that, darling!' she laughed happily. 'Hasn't he, Archie?'

'You can say that again. Caught red-handed. Wallowing. Soul-baring. True confessions and party post-mortems.'

'I see.' I spoke stiffly as I glanced around. 'And quite a party by the look of it,' I said. There was a spill of red wine and cigarette ash on one corner of the carpet, and a dozen empty Heidsieck bottles on the floor, and a couple of the pictures were knocked askew. Cressida's hair had loosened from its chignon: she looked flushed and vaguely dishevelled and radiantly happy, and although she was not drunk you could never doubt that she had been drinking. 'Well, *quite* a party!' I repeated.

'You can also say that again.' Calverton pulled a wry face. 'Supposed to be cocktails. From five-thirty. Most of the bloody guests were still grogging on at eleven-thirty.'

'It's now after one,' I pointed out.

'Jesus, is it *that* already?'

'Funny idea, if it was only to be cocktails,' I said to Cressida, 'arranging for Mrs Dapp to stay the night. She said you told her you expected to be late.'

'Well, you know how these things are.' The implication of my remark seemed to mean nothing to Cressida, and it was Calverton who answered. 'They tend to get out of hand. We thought the old duck would be more comfortable in bed at your flat than turfing her out in the cold night air. Apart from trying to wedge *her* backside into my bucket-seat to drive her home! And then the party just dragged on and on.'

'So I see.'

'We had that dreary bastard Rory Kenway, and he just wouldn't bloody go! Spent the whole night making terrible clumsy passes at poor Cress here . . .' He began to laugh and Cressida moved back to the divan, laughing too. 'Down on bended knees he was at one time, spouting Yeats at her . . . insisting that Cress was *his* Maud Gonne.'

'Oh, I thought that was your particular ploy,' I said, and the tone I used stopped them laughing. Calverton looked hard at me.

'What?' he said.

'I thought *you* were the one who had the peculiar poetic affinity with Cress.'

'Come again, sport. I'm dull. Thick in the head. I don't get you.'

'I always had the impression you were her private troubadour.' My temper flared suddenly and I said, 'Look, let's all stop bull-shitting about. When I got home tonight I 'phoned you. Around midnight. Nobody answered. You were too busy, I take it.'

'Well, for Christ's sake!' Calverton rubbed his fingers into his hair. 'It was *you* who 'phoned!'

'So you *were* too busy to answer then.'

'Look, just hold on a sec, sport,' Calverton measured his words carefully. 'It's what I've been telling you. About this bastard Kenway. He stayed on to the death but we finally got rid of him, but then he stopped off at a 'phone-box at Chiswick High Street, and he kept calling us to ask if he could come back, because there was something important he'd forgotten to tell Cress. So when the 'phone rang again we decided this time not to answer it. That's all. I mean, for Christ's sake how could we know it was *you*? I am bloody sorry, sport, but after all you were supposed to be in Germany, weren't you? You could hardly expect us to know it would be *you* calling up at midnight.'

'Well, that's fairly bloody obvious, isn't it?' I said coldly.

'Go on,' said Calverton.

'I mean if it's a case of when the cat's away . . .'

'What are you getting at?' Calverton said softly.

'Christ Almighty, what do *you* think? I'm not getting *at*, I'm getting *out*! And you two can go back to your intimate little *tête-à-tête*. Or you can both get stuffed as far as I'm concerned. I'll take a rain-check on my homecoming. I mightn't be as good at acting as you two, but I'll practise up a bit and give a repeat performance when the conditions are more propitious.'

I walked out then in an awful silence, feeling sick. Driving east out of Hammersmith through the empty black streets I could still see them both – Calverton's twisted face, frozen in an expression I had never seen on the magazine covers or in the tabloids, and Cressida crouched rigid on the divan, her cheeks ashen, her eyes wide and emptied of everything but pain. They were consummate actors, the both of them, I kept telling myself fiercely. They had to be. *They had to be!*

I left the car in Salisbury Court and spent the night in the Press Club, staring out across the empty derelict shell of St Bride's to where the black dome of St Paul's was fixed against the dingy sky like a moon seen from the side where no light shines, and I spent all the next day trying to recover from my hangover.

In the evening I went back to the flat. Cressida greeted me quietly but affectionately, and the children noisily and affectionately. Neither then nor later did either of us say anything about the incident of the night before. If Calverton ever called on Cressida again I never knew of it; in any case, soon after this he played the lead in a quite important film that took him off to East Africa and thence to Hollywood: I met him again only briefly on that morning we set out for Greece, and then neither of us was to see him until five years had passed and he came to stay with us.

GREECE, 1959

Nowadays we get down to the port about eleven-thirty to wait for the Athens steamer to arrive, because if it gets in on time they clear the mail before the *Taxydroméion* closes for the luncheon break and the long siesta. Mail has become a vital link with the outside world, the linch-pin of our survival in a way. We live *poste-restante* now, like the rest of the foreigners who crowd the tables at this hour outside Evangeli's corner shop. From here we can watch the grey mailbags being carried up the steps of the post-office, while drinking retsina or kokkinelli and wondering what the bags contain. Something for us? Money or the promise of it? More bills? Acceptance or rejection? Success or failure? Hope or despair? Another chance? The canvas bags stencilled with the posthorn and the Greek symbols are bulky and misshapen by such possibilities. (Evangeli and his wife Sofia attend to our drinks with great civility and friendliness. They are aware of our dilemma and solicitous for us; Evangeli keeps extending our credit so that we owe him now for more than six months' groceries, but you would never suspect this from his attitude; only last week he wanted to lend me some money to tide me over—'you must also have cash in your pocket,' he said, 'to buy the other things, the cigarettes, the fruit, the little things for the children.' Often, with a shy little flourish, he will bring to our table a *katastári* of wine on his own account.)

Money or the promise of it is what all of us really crave, what we are down there hoping and waiting for. But for this hungry and acquisitive air that marks our casual, convivial vigilance we might resemble some curiously mixed pack of animals drawn to a drinking pool, although animals, of course, would look more noble, less decrepit-looking, and would be watching in a different way.

While we await the clearing of the mail we study the passengers landing from the longboats which are rowed out beyond the harbour entrance to meet the trim white steamer. We have a practised vigilance in this, too. We can pick the foreigners who are likely to stay and these we scrutinize carefully for their possibilities of interest or disruption. We are less concerned by the day or overnight tourists, who saunter with studied speculation around our tables, sometimes approaching us with diffident or bumptious inquiries: we are an established and recognized 'foreign colony' now, bohemians to them, and artists and existentialists, outlandish oddities, rejectionists, dropouts from their own social systems, mavericks, even decadents, a genuine tourist attraction of the island at least as convincing as, and more bizarre than, the Shrine of the Hero's Heart, or the Venetian marble campanile of the monastery, which has been restored since the earthquake, or the Byzantine frescoes in the church of Agios Ioannis. (Actually there are sights more bizarre on the island—a good example is the library of skulls of dead nuns which are kept in immaculate rows on clean white shelves decked with fine feminine lace in the convent which looks down on the harbour from a forbidding crag—but the tourists never have time to find them.)

It is extraordinary to realize, now we are a genuine foreign colony growing more numerous every week, now tourists pour in by every boat, now even the Government travel brochures feature the place as a 'colourful haunt of bohemian artists and writers from all parts of the world', that when Cressida and I and the children came to settle just five years ago we were the only foreigners here and the island was shunned by tourists.

(The mail today is disappointing again. Two more stories rejected . . . the still unpaid account from Foyle's . . . a dull letter from Australia containing a clipping from an article about us from a women's magazine written by a girl journalist who galloped through here a year or so ago. The article is headed *Australian Family Finds Peaceful Idyll on Greek Island.* It has colour rotogravure pictures that look as unreal as tinted postcards. Nothing else in the mail. No money and no promise of it.)

When one considers how quickly and how alarmingly change

has come to this remote pinpoint on the surface of the earth, one cannot help thinking of what it has done to us also. Everything has changed, is changing, around us; we have changed, too, and keep changing. Just as dramatically, perhaps even more alarmingly. Today I might succumb to the ironic impulse to examine the cost to us of the peaceful idyll we have found in this brightly-tinted rotogravure world we inhabit. Do I dare? Why not? It might, in fact, be useful to draw up a kind of profit-and-loss account before Calverton arrives next week out of his bright prestigious world of fame and money and success. Then we shall all know where we stand.

Yet it is not altogether easy to do this. From what stand-point does one weigh it all up? The material? The physical? The spiritual? Certainly on the material side – and probably this is the basis on which a person like Calverton would tend to judge it – I seem to have turned out a flop. I no longer have too many illusions about this; the dreamy time, which lasted for the first year or so we were here, when everything seemed bathed in the romantic effulgence of the Greek light, ended a long time ago – and with it the modest capital we had brought from London – and there was no great novel, and no best-seller, and no fame, only harder and more desperate work to get something published, *anything* published that might enable us to get by on publishers' advances. (I still do get my books published, though, and the more intellectual of the foreigners here seem to find this unforgivable; they, being avant-garde and unpublished, consider me a 'commercial' writer and therefore contemptible.)

There is no way of setting all this out in a properly audited manner because I grew too disheartened to keep up the neat book-keeping ledger I bought and in which I began, hopefully, to enter earnings and accounts. Still, a general summary of the last five years, presentable to Calverton, would run something like this:

First Year: Arrived in Greece. Capital after arrival slightly less than £1,000. Lost in Paradise for first six months, getting established, searching around, lotus-eating. Refused, on principle, Volos earthquake assignment. Finished new novel. Very confident.

Second Year: Influx of foreigners begins. Many distractions but working hard. Original capital exhausted but two books completed and one published. Moderate reviews and poor sales. Getting by on publishers' advances. Confidence now very shaky.

Third Year: Began badly. Seriously ill with double pneumonia. Brought on by what? Overwork? Financial anxiety? Worrying about Cressida? Probably all three. Six months' working time virtually lost. Two more novels published but neither cleared advances. Situation saved by sale of two short stories in New York.

Fourth Year: Foreign colony now becoming increasingly disturbing problem. Too many diversions, involvements, parties. Physical health poor as result of earlier pneumonia. Concentrating on short stories, but none so far accepted. Completed novel (potboiler). Drinking too much. Understandable? Situation precarious. May follow agent's suggestion and try writing thrillers also under pseudonym.

Fifth Year: Must repeat *must* stick to planned programme for year. One serious novel, one thriller, at least four short stories. Should be able to cope if drink less, work harder, avoid distractions. Would like to tackle journalism, but now out of touch. Problem is no work permit available here and every penny must be earned outside Greece. Difficult situation. Wish we were somewhere else, but how do we get the fare out? Health continues to deteriorate. Just skin and bones. No energy. Should go to Athens for check-up . . .

Well now, that really would be something to show Calverton when he comes! I wonder what he would think? Not to worry. It could have its interesting side; seeing somebody, I mean, jaded by a surfeit of success.

On the other hand, it would be unreasonable to suggest that everything has been in debit. There have been transcendental moments too, magical experiences that cannot be entered in any ledger. They have to be included in the reckoning. The warmth and kindliness of simple people like Evangeli, the lessons we have learnt of the true values of living, of the run of seasons and the poetries of rock and water and rain and sun and light and fire. The calmness we can find if we seek for it. There is no rush here where no wheel turns and everything moves to the gentler pace of the plodding mule or pattering donkey, where hours rest easily on the couch of peace, and the calendar is a slow ratchet of unfretful customs and sanctified days and innocent festivals. There are no other time-tables. Save those of life and death—the kerchiefed midwife squeezes lemon juice into the eyes of the wailing newborn and superstitiously spits three times into its face for good fortune, the passing bell tolls resonant messages of peace in the placid day. Sometimes a whole year has gone by without us seeing a newspaper or hearing a radio; when finally we do the news from the outer world seems much as it was before the silence. There is nothing in particular that we have missed. No peace has settled out there. The mutilation continues. The place-names and the people's names change from time to time or wax and wane like sickly moons, but the madnesses persist, and the miseries endure. Now the Middle East is in travail and Cyprus torn and bleeding and a Europe under threat and duress writhes still in its long agony, yet even these, our neighbours, seem as remote from us, as meaningless to our present existence, as these new strange satellites which roll above us on unearthly orbits through constellations named for older and more enduring mythologies.

We are still out, all of us, on the various stages of the long journey from Szechwan. Yet here we still have time to watch things grow. The children thrive in an environment that is rich and full and free. Cressida, who has found her own juvenescence in this world, yearns for no other. There is a great beneficence here if one looks for it.

Weighing it all up, perhaps I shall be able to tell Calverton when he comes that we are still in credit.

SYDNEY, 1966

The men have been here all morning planting the new trees. I have been sitting since breakfast watching them. There is to me a kind of ritual importance about this, and a comfort in a way, now that one will have time again to watch things grow, but besides this it has become imperative that one should have something to believe in and look forward to. The trees are all what the nurseryman calls 'natives'—acacia and seven different kinds of eucalyptus, bottlebrush and grevillea—and the workmen were amused at the extent of the 'forest', for this is what they kept calling it, we plan to grow around ourselves. They laughed, too, about my insistence to have a sugar-gum planted right in the centre of it all.

But it is there because of the old sugar-gum which I planted before the war in Beverley Grove, smack in the middle of the front lawn, in defiance of Helen. Although that particular tree had had a different ritual significance. It had been my banner of revolt, my symbolic rejection of Australian suburbanism, my taunting, in a way, of Helen herself. (Later I had to dig it up.)

And here we are, not only back in Australia but undeniably back in suburbia, and planting trees again. The city is a hidden thing and four miles away from us but its savage heartbeat comes to us in the stillness, dull and throaty and threatening, like the distant growling of some dangerous beast.

It is interesting to think of all this in the terms of the circling movement we have made—or if one chooses to be more nationalistic a kind of boomeranging out and back again—and what it has meant. And all that has happened in the sixteen years since we set out from here. Last night there was a curiously ambiguous scrap of dialogue during a talk Cressida and I were having on this very subject, and it still sticks in my mind.

'But we have shared so much,' Cressida said.

'Have we shared it?' I asked.

'We should have,' she said.

Then we got on to discussing plans for the garden, and Cressida laughed and said, 'I'm all for trees, yes. No antirrhinums, though. That still goes, doesn't it?'

'God forbid!' I said, and I was suddenly taken back to the night in Riordan's pub—nearly twenty-three years ago!—the night after Gavin Turley had told me we could never last six months together . . .

The trees we were planting now, of course, are no longer a symbol of active revolt; they are more in the nature of protection, a windbreak, a palisade, if you like. Cressida had dreams of a walled courtyard like the one we had in Greece, but this is not possible, no more possible than us having a house here like the one we had on the island—although this house is pleasant enough and reasonably old and it has a feel of being solid and protective and reliable. With it we should be able to refute Stephanos, our banker friend in Athens, who thought we might end up belonging nowhere.

Not that we can yet be entirely confident about this place.

Both of us still feel alien here, even after having been back a year or more, but I am beginning to think that every one of us in this rushing crowded nervous society which has finally trapped us is alienated these days, even in surroundings innately familiar. All of us, wherever we are, seem to live in little sheltered enclaves thrust into foreign territories which we mistrust, and cannot help suspecting to be subtly hostile and menacing. I do not understand or know anything, really, of the customs of the people, my own compatriots, who live across the harbour in the western suburbs, or those to the north or the east or the south; they are far stranger to me, infinitely less comprehensible, than the Greeks were. I am sure we do not really *want* to know each other, but who is to blame for this? Have I lost my sense of curiosity? do I find them simply not interesting enough? is it that I just resent their possession of a comfortable complacency that I have failed to find? or scorn them for their conforming, unthinking anonymity? Perhaps they are the lucky people after all, the unthinking ones, taking it as it comes and not questioning it. They are, after all, basically decent people, most of them. They live their own lives. They don't interfere. They don't demand very much. Why then do I pity rather than envy them?

A couple of years ago, in Athens, we talked about this. It was the night that Papandreou called the first big political rally of the centre and leftish groups and there were thousands of people packed in the big square outside the university, but the machine-guns were set up in all the surrounding streets, and for a square mile around battalions of steel-helmeted troops stood watchful with sub-machine-guns in army trucks, and there were scores of tanks, black-bulking and squatly menacing as primeval monsters, crouched across the wide thoroughfare, their sinister long gun-barrels levelled down at the thronging human tumult that filled Panepistimiou. Cressida and I, chilled by the atmosphere of violence and brutality that hung over the city, retreated to Zonar's bar, which was crowded by foreigners—the politically incurious, I suppose, as well as those others, like us, who had come in out of the black, threatening storm of ferocity. A fat American tourist in seersucker was arguing about the price of Kentucky rye whisky.

We sat silent over our drinks for quite some time, and then Cressida said, 'Do you know, this is the first time I've been anxious to go back home. To Australia. I'm glad *you're* going. I hope it works out for all of us.' She moved her glass like a chess piece and said, 'There's nothing out there like this, is there? I mean in Australia we don't live on this brink of terror and savagery do we? Never knowing when the edge will fall away, the crust break . . . it reminds me of that day of the earthquake, feeling the ground beneath your feet suddenly turned to jelly, wobbling around like one of those old-fashioned weighing machines . . . and suddenly you can't any longer believe in something you've *always* believed in and taken for granted.'

I remember the day very well. On our island it had been

classified only as a 'severe tremor'—the real disaster had been on the mainland at Volos, to the north, where hundreds were killed and thousands made homeless—but it had been severe enough, all the same, to level scores of houses and to bring down the marble bell-tower of the monastery. It happened at mid-morning on a spring day when the market boats were in from the Peloponnesean farms and Cressida had gone down with the children to buy fresh fruit and vegetables, and I was alone in the house writing when the earth growled and shuddered and lamps and crockery crashed and all the books were hurled from the shelves, and I found myself running down to the water-front in a sweat of fear for Cressida and the children. I found them walking calmly through the still-drifting dust and the debris, none of them even scratched or bruised although Cressida told me that the dislodged blocks of marble, falling from the monastery, some weighing ten tons and more, had crashed all around them, and she had thought that the great bronze bells, clanging as they fell, were ringing the warning of earthquake when they were, in fact, already the toll of earthquake. All the people of the island slept that night on the beach because old *Kyria* Calliope, the ancient crone said to have the gift of prophecy, had talked of a vision in which the Virgin had warned her that two more, greater shocks were to come, and Cressida told me that the moment of real fear was that terrible instant of realization that the solidity and security of the earth beneath one's feet, in which one had always trusted without thinking, was not true at all. (It has taken us a lot longer, of course, to come to understand that we all live perpetually on the edge of this earthquake.)

This had happened not many months after we went to Greece, and that was when I received the urgent cable from a Sunday newspaper in London offering me a very lucrative fee to cover the Volos disaster for them, but I was wise enough—or rather, at the time I thought myself wise enough—to see the bait in the trap, so I turned the assignment down. It had taken me long enough to free myself from the insidious blandishments of journalism, to stuff my ears with wax against the beguiling siren song of money and self-importance and excitement. I knew that if I defected so early on my purer beliefs, if I ran back so soon I would for ever keep running back; since the journey at last had begun, I, like the craftier Odysseus, would have to keep the wax in my ears and go on with it . . .

But I am wandering this morning, sitting here, watching the new trees being planted. The trouble is that thoughts are inclined to drift when one is just sitting and watching and not moving any more. We are not told what happened to Odysseus after he got back to his Ithaca and ridded himself of the suitors . . . did he plant trees, I wonder, olive and quince, and pistachio and resinous pine, and retreat into reverie behind them?

The trouble is that once one becomes used to quietness and immobility there exists the danger that withdrawal will continue. First to within the forest and the palisade, and within this again behind the sheltering fence or wall, then back to the more confined security of the house, and finally to the tight shelter of a single room, from which one might still look out through the branches and foliage of the trees to watch the people coming and going along the suburban street, the people with dry and empty faces, the drought faces that have never grown a crop. It is what Kafka said: Keep narrowing your circle, but make sure you don't leave yourself outside.

Last week we attended one of the little theatres here, the first night of a new satirical-political revue produced by students of one of the universities. The invitations called for 'formal dress', but this turned out to be part of the satire, since the audience had to enter the theatre through a sheep-race and looked the silliest damned fools shuffling like sheep between the fences in dinner suits and long gowns, and the very young players could then be supercilious and patronizing and tremendously knowledgeable about the mass stupidities and hypocrisies of the older generation. As usual, they savaged the stale old mythologies and were very cutting about the conventional sacred cows of the land which we are supposed to worship, but it all ended up as one huge, awful, hollow, aching cliché. They were only beating at the same shadows we were beating at before they were born, and just as ineffectually; they raged at us with the unreasoning impotence of teething babies, so it ended up being very funny, although not in the way they thought.

One begins to wonder how long the safe and spurious iconoclasms are to continue. The second year we were on the island, which was when the big drift of foreigners began, was the great time for the existentialists. They were a mixed bunch, French and Swiss and German and American (and almost as mixed in their sexual proclivities), but their unofficial leader and spokesman was Jacques, a Parisian painter aged about thirty who still moved within the aura of having actually sat with Sartre at the Flore and the Deux Magots. His demeanour, except when drunk, was quiet and reflective, and he had a quick, handsome, faun-like animality that imparted a curious quality of assured but controlled arrogance. He wore his corn-pale hair in a Roman cut and a small gold ear-ring in his right ear and the scantiest scraps of clothing over his lithe brown body. His physical appeal to women was almost irresistible, but Cressida's captivation was much more, I am sure, an admiration for the complete freedom with which he lived his self-chosen days and nights.

'You are your own life and nothing else,' he would say to us. 'You lose this life, you lose everything. There must be nobody else, no involvement.'

'This is a very selfish philosophy, surely,' I would protest.

'It is a very selfish world, my friend.'

'You make no allowance for other people. For love. You don't try to make any communication with the rest of humanity.'

''Umanity? *Pooof*! What do I care for 'umanity? It is what they punish us with for not living our own lives. 'Eaven is what we find inside us in the fullness of our own existence, and 'Ell is other people. If we communicate we destroy each other, if we love we murder each other. Maybe we cannot save ourselves, but nobody can 'elp another to save 'imself either. To be free, it is all there is.'

Certainly he believed in it himself, for his behaviour was as careless and unquestioning and as natural as it is possible to imagine, and he was genuinely quite indifferent to what anybody thought about him. His effect on Cressida, who had already found the indolent simple freedoms of the island life an intoxicating draft after the restrictive life of London, and who had opened in the sun like a tropic flower, was profound. They shared a particular affinity of attitude which made them respect and like each other in a special sort of way. Cressida would often walk around the cliffs to the little cottage he had rented, to see his paintings or to swim with him—he was strong and unstylish in the water and she taught him diving and the Australian crawl—while I would stay in the house at my typewriter, churning out words, words, words, and trying to stifle the agonizing suspicions that gnawed at me like some insatiable grey rat. But whatever I suspected I had to bury it away; I could say nothing to either of them; after the incident in London with Calverton I could not afford any repetition of the fiasco, because another mistake like that could topple it all, and the commitment now was too deep and built too painfully and laboriously to have it brought down in meaningless ruin.

So I held my tongue and worked all the harder and tried to smother suspicion and joined the interminable round of drinkings and dancings and parties that threaded a mad neurotic pattern of frolic through nights and days and sunsets and dawns, from cottage to cottage and tavern to tavern, shouting our freedoms at each other.

One sees now, looking back over the intervening years, how treacherous were these freedoms, for even then we were all filing through the sheep-race, rushing away from one oblivion towards another. But, whether sure or unsure, we were individuals, or so we assured ourselves. We had escaped our societies. Nobody was watching us. We could be free, we could behave as we liked. We had found the meaning of existence. The real meaning of existence was there all the time, of course, in the simple pattern of the island which we had annexed as our own primitive milieu, but after a time we could not see it for the mired footprints of our own excesses.

The departure of Jacques from the island was interesting. He must have known of my suspicions even though I had never voiced them. He called on me to say goodbye an hour before his steamer left for Athens. 'I 'ave made the private goodbye to Cressida,' he said. 'I 'ope you do not mind. I say now goodbye to you, but before this there is something also I must say. Cressida and I, we 'ave never been lovers. I 'ave loved Cressida but we 'ave never been lovers. You understand?' He held out his hand then and said, 'I think you are very lucky man, my friend.'

We heard of him years later. He was living in Paris and was married and had three children and a steady safe job in a Government drafting office.

But soon after he left the island the combination of worry and overwork and the hysterical saturnalia of the foreign colony, and the whole messy muddle of my own neuroses, took its toll. I became ill at a Christmas party, developed double pneumonia, and didn't leave the house for six months. This led to the tuberculosis a few years later, and that by the same unbroken thread to the men here in the garden this morning planting the trees. So in the end we are all of us vulnerable to some tiny wog or bacillus or virus we can't even see.

Well, these musings anyway have passed away the morning, and the last of the trees is in and the watering completed. I gave the workmen cold beer and we sat on the timber deck looking down on the new tender leafage, such a delicacy of filigree and coloured light, and one of the men said, 'You know what'll happen, them trees'll bring the birds back. In a couple of years they'll be that tall, and all the birds'll come back.'

ATHENS, 1964

Meredith never could work out exactly when, or even how, it was that he first began to think of returning to Australia, and now, sitting in the air terminal at Phaleron, with Cressida and Tom Kiernan there to see him off, he wanted to be jocular about it to cover the real trepidation he felt. It would never do to confess this trepidation; they had been too painstaking in their attentive encouragement to let them down: if it was to be an untriumphal return he would have to make the best of it.

Through the rippled wetness of the glass he watched the explosive halations of light as the Air-France Caravelle taxied past through the lash of wind and sleet; there had even been a light flurry of actual snow driving out past the temple of Olympian Zeus. With the fog at London Airport there was another hour to be filled in before the Sydney-bound jet was expected. Cressida's hand still clung tightly to his, and his wrist and fingers ached a little.

'What I really feel,' he said, smiling to make a joke of it, 'is it's all rather like that final journey back to the elephants' graveyard.'

'Oh come on,' Kiernan protested. 'Not as bad as that. You'll find a lot of it's pretty good, you know. Not all of it by a long chalk, but quite a lot of it.'

'You've been back four times. You've never been tempted to stay.'

'You mightn't want to stay either,' Cressida said. 'You won't know until you get out there, will you?'

'No. But I don't want to come back here. That's for sure. Nor England. So what does one do?'

'Find out,' she said. 'And let us know. We'll follow you out if you think we should.'

'Mind you,' Kiernan warned, 'they'll try to take your kidney fat. They'll be waiting to have a go at you. They always are. But you've got the precious vial of sacred earth, haven't you? Just use that. And you'll be right.'

Meredith grinned and took from his pocket the little aspirin bottle and held it up. A few days before, down on the island, Kiernan had produced the empty bottle and taken it into the courtyard and filled it with earth from beneath the mandarin-tree, and screwed the cap on tightly and handed it to Meredith and said, 'Now, follow my instructions. When you get off the plane at

Sydney the press will be there to interview you. So what you do is make this ritual gesture. You must take the vial out of your pocket—make sure they're watching—and empty out the dirt. Do it very solemnly. They'll want to know what you're up to. Then you tell 'em you've been carrying this little scrap of Australian soil with you as a kind of talisman for all the fourteen years you've been away, but now you've come back to God's own country again, so you don't need it any more. That's the sort of thing they love.'

But this was Greek earth, Cressida had protested, and Kiernan frowned with mock solemnity and said, 'Oh, but he mustn't tell 'em that. They wouldn't like that at all!' Then he had laughed and said, 'Last time I went back I came off the plane and went straight down on my hands and knees and kissed the tarmac. I got the best press I've had since I left the bloody place. You see, out there you've got to do this sort of thing or they'll kick you to pieces. They've got to have your kidney fat. They don't *like* us going away, you see. They can never understand why we *had* to go away, why we *stay* away. So when we do go back, we've got to go back repentant, and singing there's no place like home.'

Meredith, waiting to go back, felt neither repentant nor obdurate; he felt sick, old, tired, and fearful, and he had no song of any sort upon his lips. Waiting in the wintry bluster of the night at Phaleron Airport, Meredith found himself remembering the time on the island a few years before when the Australian Dried Fruits Convention had landed on his doorstep. He had been up in his room wrestling with a book that was going badly when the door-knocker thumped and he had gone down swearing to find the lane choked with staring Australians, sixty-eight of them! They were members of a convention organized by the Australian Dried Fruits Board to study the currant-growing around Corinth and the raisin and sultana industry in Crete and the Peloponnesos, and when they had come off the morning steamer someone had told them that an Australian family was living on the island and they had enlisted a guide to bring them to the house *en masse* so they could check on this.

Since there were too many to be invited into the house Meredith had to go with them back to the waterfront, where they interrogated him closely, particularly one man who seemed to be a self-elected spokesman. He was a small man with a big chin and a thin stern mouth. His eyes seemed short-sighted behind rimless bifocals, and each question he asked was accompanied by a suspicious squint, as if he was well aware that he would be answered by a lie or an exaggeration or at best an evasion. He, and most of the rest of the party, clearly disapproved of the irresponsible way of life which Meredith, a fellow-Australian, had chosen to follow. 'But how do you get on living with these bloody Wogs?' the spokesman wanted to know. 'Don't they drive you up the wall? And the kids, what about their education? You mean to say they're at school with the Greek kids, not even talking their own language? Jesus, you're taking a risk, aren't you? You ought to get back to good old Aussie, you know.' He became proud and expansive then. 'You'd never know the old place now. You've never seen progress like it. You'd see a lot of changes. Everything out there's going ahead like a house on fire. I tell you, you don't know, you just couldn't believe, what you're missing. Isn't that right, you blokes?' The rest of the delegation nodded vigorously and vehemently mumbled assent. 'You're mad to stick on in a primitive backward little dump like this, when you've got it all made for you out there in your own country. After all, you owe it to your kiddies, don't you? I mean they're entitled to the best, aren't they? It's *their* future you've got to think of.'

They went away on the early afternoon steamer, some of them the worse for the *ouzo* and retsina they had insisted on drinking because Meredith had told them that the astringency of the Greek liquor helped compensate for the oiliness of the Greek food, which gave their spokesman opportunity for another homily on 'people who live on greasy tucker and always pong of garlic'. Meredith quietly pointed out that every Greek in sight had good skin, splendid teeth, and his own hair (which, he added to himself, was a damned sight more than could be said for most of the Dried Fruits emissaries) but nobody paid much attention. Rowing off in the longboats some of the party drunkenly tried to sing 'Waltzing Matilda' and 'Advance, Australia Fair', and old Babayannis, the one-eyed muleteer, who was standing on the quayside next to Meredith, beamed approvingly and said, with real admiration, 'They are good people, the Australians, fine people. We remember them from the war. Larissa. Nauplia. Crete. They were our friends. And brave. Very brave fighters. Fine people. The best.'

'Yes.' Meredith nodded, remembering, and wondered whatever had happened. Their spokesman was right; you *could* see a lot of changes. They seemed so narrow and insulated now, and yet so sure of themselves, so complacent about their small channelled certainties. You could only respond to them by using the instant litmus. Turn pink . . . Turn blue . . .

Until then he thought he had forgotten what Australians were like, but this visitation proved to be only a beginning. A new Greek shipping service began between Australia and Piraeus, and troubles with Nasser in Egypt established Athens as a stopover for the QANTAS planes in place of Cairo, and off-season cruise liners from Australia began to call in at Greek ports. So it was not long before Meredith's compatriots were regular arrivals on the daily steamers. Meredith, waiting outside Evangeli's for the mail to be sorted, found he could pick from a hundred yards away an Australian coming ashore, not by their clothing so much, although this was often an indication, as by a way they had of standing and walking and their manner of holding their heads in relationship to their shoulders. There were some who carried identification with them much as their forefathers had carried trade union banners; they would wear Digger-type slouch hats and carry knapsacks sewn all over with the blatant symbols of an aggressive chauvinism, Australian flags and kangaroos and Southern Crosses and boomerangs, or just the simple word AUSTRALIA, although more usually a maroon QANTAS overnight bag with its kangaroo insignia would be deemed identification enough.

What kind of defensive mechanism operated? What were they so anxious to prove?

To these transient visitors the novelty of finding an Australian family actually *living* a foreign life with foreigners in a primitive alien community proved both intriguing and disturbing. Most of them would try to seek out the Merediths, as if they were rare denizens of some exotic zoo. A few of the more sensitive seemed genuinely to envy the—to them—simple enchantments and leisurely pace and undeniable beauties of the island life; the majority, however, were never able to leave without offering some friendly and well-intentioned castigation. The substance of this was always much the same. In actually choosing to live with foreigners, the Merediths were being un-Australian, were missing out materially on the best the world had to offer, were foolishly cutting themselves off from prospects of infinite promise, were precariously enduring discomfort when they were entitled to enjoy surfeits of comfort in the world's highest standard of living, and were being wilfully wayward parents in denying their children their birthright of life in God's own country.

Meredith was never able to find any effective way of countering these charges, for they seldom seemed interested in, or even able to understand, what he had to say about the richer human values and firmer traditions of European culture, the prevalence of historic continuities, the deeper intellectual challenge, the consciousness of being in a mainstream of human conflict and aspiration, not in a backwater or stranded on some remote dry billabong. He thought at one time that he would have a mimeographed circular made, setting out his own manifesto and his answers to the standard questions he was always asked, a copy of which could be handed to each newcomer as a way of saving time; in a still more resentful mood he also thought of printing a sign and nailing it to the front door of his house: BUBONIC PLAGUE—KEEP OUT!

Yet in spite of the shallowness of their attitudes, the naïve chauvinisms, the absurdly blinkered prejudice and intolerance, he found himself unable, finally, to dismiss them. Whatever the irritation and impatience and resentment he might feel, he could not keep away from them. There were even aspects of them he found himself approving, admiring, defending—their natural eagerness to be friendly, their simple civilities, their lack of affectations, the rough honesty with which they would look at a matter, as they put it, 'without bullshit'. And there was something genuinely refreshing in their uncomplicated optimistic vitality after the tired, blasé, *Angst*-ridden attitudes of the world-weary cosmopolitans who had become Meredith's more usual social contacts on the island. Yet the tug of the fascination seemed more profound than this: at times Meredith could feel it stirring him deep down and troublingly, too subtle a feeling to be identifiable, a vague womb-yearning, the dimly sensed wash of foetal tides, or something atavistic and even darker. Not nostalgia. Nor homesickness. But something . . .

It was only to Tom Kiernan now that he ever talked about these matters.

Kiernan's years of expatriation had served him well. While he had not achieved Calverton's measure of material success or public reputation, he had attained success and reputation enough, and creatively and artistically his stature was a good deal larger than Calverton's; by any count he had travelled much farther on his journey than Meredith. But he was an unattached man—an asexual man, too, Meredith sometimes thought—who drove himself with a ruthless purpose and single-mindedness, endlessly exploring Europe in search of food for his imagination and subjects for his canvases, haunting the galleries, and painting, painting, painting. He seemed to live for only two things—his work and the few friends to whom he clung with almost obsessive loyalty, perhaps because he allowed himself so little of social relaxation, and needed his few friends for the desperate moments of human loneliness. He painted as he lived, with the energy of a titan, the dedication of a martyr, the passion of a lover. He took prodigious risks, and usually got away with them. He never spared himself, nor anyone around him. 'You would have to be his friend,' Cressida once said of him. 'If you were an enemy, or even only an acquaintance, he would dip you in pitch and put a match to you if he needed a torch to paint by.' He detested any sort of compromise, in himself or in others. 'I fly with Icarus, not with Daedalus,' he said in a moment of rare boastfulness. This was at a time when Meredith was feeling dispirited about a novel he was writing, and he had confessed to Kiernan his defeatism.

'It won't come out at the end of my fingers,' he said, 'the way I see it in my head. The reason is simple, of course. The theme is too big and my talents aren't big enough. I've just overreached, that's all.'

'I fly with Icarus, not with Daedalus,' said Kiernan.

'That's all very well for you. But I'm me, not you.'

'Balls! If you *want* to fly, if you think you *can* fly, then all you've got to do is jump off the twig and bloody well *fly*!'

Yet clearly even Kiernan was not sufficient unto himself. The powerful and passionate mystique that drove him seemed centred far away from the trampled arena of his activities; the true wellspring of his inspiration was still located, illogically, in the distant land that had driven him out, so that every few years he would be compelled to return to Australia to, as he put it, 'fill up the jug again'. He was usually involved in controversy when he got back to his native land and seldom stayed there long, but he would always send off to Meredith a terse report on a post-card, messages like *Europe still has better ossuaries but not bigger ones* or *Something might be cooking here but too soon yet to open the oven and see.* He would always return to Europe renewed and reinvigorated, and go into another furious spell of painting, although anything specifically Australian seldom appeared in his work. He would invariably come back by way of Greece and stay for a few days with the Merediths, and he would tell them amusing or startling tales of life 'out there' in the remote southern continent, but seemed more interested in finding out whether there was anything he had missed out on in Europe during his absence. It was taken for granted that nothing would be missed by being absent from Australia.

Once he played the conventional old joke and brought back with him a handful of Australian gum-leaves and threw them on the fire in front of Meredith, and said, 'Just sniff that up, man, and you'll be out there like a shot!'

'That'll be the day,' said Meredith, laughing. But the odd thing was that the moment the aromatic pungency of the burning leaves struck his nostrils he experienced for an instant a real pang of hunger for something experienced and lost far back in time, and staring into the fire at the darkening curl and shrivel of the scimitar leaves he saw again the blue hazes of hot big distances and brown leaves in a tangle of fallen bark.

GREECE, 1959

'What do we do it *for*, that's the question,' Calverton said and rolled lazily over on the other elbow. 'It's a sort of truculence we have, I suppose.'

Eyes narrowed against the shimmer of the summer light, he looked out beyond the turquoise and amethyst of the shallows to the scatter of islands in the gulf. The islands, running all the way to the heat-misted hills of the mainland, had a contrived quality, a theatrical unreality, as if placed there for effect by a too exuberant designer. They were far too numerous, and improbably shaped. Some were flat and bare, hardly more than shoals, others rose high and thin and sharp like rock needles, some were peaky and darkly timbered, others gnarled and bare and cliffy, there was one that formed a perfect equilateral triangle, its base lifted above the sea-rim upon a thin band of transparent light, and another, squat and crouching, that looked like a petrified toad. All were waterless and none inhabited; only a few had names.

The children squatted on the pebbles at the water's edge, absorbed in collecting the pastel-tinted shells of sea-urchins, and the others swam or snorkelled around the small red *caïque*  mirrored at its anchorage in the secluded little bay, its inverted image in the water as precise against rock and weed and sand as its higher half against sky and islands. In the *caïque* Petros the boatman slept shadily beneath a ragged awning of canvas. The brown, huge, bearded figure of Jim Galloway, also sleeping, drifted in blueness on an inflatable rubber mattress. It floated slowly into and through the reflection of the boat, making no ripple or disturbance, not even affecting the upside-down, looking-glassed letters of the *caïque*'s name, *Metamorphosis*.

'This is all right,' said Calverton, peering out, relaxed and at peace and thoughtful. 'Well, it's more than that, of course. It's bloody wonderful. But it isn't *us* really, is it? It's turning one's back on it. Dodging. A kind of evasion of what it's all about.'

'I wouldn't know,' I said. 'I've never been able to find out what it is all about.'

'I think it's to do with this truculence we have, like I said. Something aggressive. A chip on the shoulder. That's why we have to get away. To prove something. To prove it to ourselves, I mean . . . not to the place we have to get away from.'

'Why can't we just stay in our own country and be truculent there?' I watched the drift of Galloway's mattress. Cressida was far out on the other side of the bay, breaststroking slowly, the mask on the top of her head, searching among the grey and yellow rocks that formed one of the ox-horn tips of the cove. On the other tip that faced it there was a whitewashed shrine to St Nicholas, hardly bigger than a privy, shaped and glistening like a frosted cake. Where Cressida swam the submerged rocks seen through the glassy water were just as detailed as the rocks above baking in the sun; there was the illusion of levitation; she floated in clear blue air. I brought the focus of my eyes back to the ants busy on the crusty bark of the pine-tree that shaded us. The trunk was being tapped for resin, and the long scar in the bark, shiny and red-glazed, ran like a seeping wound to the conical tin cup where several ants were trapped in the gluey overflow of the juices.

'Oh, some do,' said Calverton. 'The real Aus' who's never left home can be the most truculent know-all bastard in the world. But that's not the same. It's not what I'm getting at. I mean what makes us different from Galloway there.' He squinted towards the floating figure. The mattress had bumped against the rocks, and was slowly pivoting. 'He's a Yank. He's got it different, easier

I think.' He chewed for a while on a pine-needle, then spat it out. 'Different, yes . . . it's the *different* quality of this truculence of ours,' he resumed musingly. 'We do have to prove something, but it's to ourselves, not to someone else. And I think out there in Australia we can't really get *at* it. We're always punching at shadows, or clouds. In one way the fight's too equal. In another way it's hopelessly uneven.'

'Why do you think he has it easier?' I asked, watching Galloway.

'The Yanks only have to prove it to others now. They proved it to themselves long ago. They've always had the fights promoted, properly arranged, the rules all fixed, the records intact, so that it's all there for easy reference. Revolution, civil war, frontiers to subjugate, mountains to climb, rivers to ford, plains to cross, the Redman as the perfect adversary, the right sort of issues like slavery or liberty. They could get it all straight and fixed and settled. Get it all worked out on their own terms in their own country. The revolution succeeds, the frontier is subdued, the mountains climbed, rivers forded, plains crossed, the Redman gets licked, the slaves are freed. More or less. So then they can dream up their own mythologies out of what they've done. Cowboys and Indians, if you like, and violence, and rugged individualism, and success, and Mum, and automobiles, and money, but it's still a viable mythology that they can get their teeth into. They're *intact*, you see, they've got a shape, they come out of the oven properly baked, with a nice golden-brown crust.'

'Galloway'll have a nice golden-brown crust if he sleeps on that Li-lo much longer,' I said. 'Go on.'

'Well, out there in Australia it's different from that. We're always trying to spar around with a great shape . . . no, not even a shape, an amorphous something that won't settle into a shape . . . not even into an idea. A bloody great drifting cloud. An enigma. When you punch at it it just gives and fades away, then there it is again, but behind you now, the same thing, impassive and indifferent. It can't be beaten because you can't ever peg it down to what it is. So that's why we have to go away to punch at something else to get this truculence out of us, not necessarily because it's easier – well, you know it might be a damned sight harder – but because at least you can see what you're hitting at. At least it's understandable.'

'How does that explain Tom Kiernan? Why does he have to keep going back?'

'I don't think you can explain Tom. Maybe you don't have to. He just burns himself up on what he's doing. Or maybe he's just burning himself up on this enigma I'm talking about, trying to resolve it, to get the answer to it out through his paints. Perhaps that's why he has to keep going back, just to look into the eyes of the Sphinx again, trying to find the answer to the riddle.'

'You're no different. You accuse him of burning himself up, but what about you? When you came here a month ago you weren't just burning yourself up, you were bloody near burnt out.'

'I chase a different carrot. I'm not interested in guessing games. All I want is to have it my way, man, and in big lights. I just want to fuck the other bastards because it's me that's fucking them. I believe in the Twentieth Century Fairytale. The PR Fairy Godmother who waves the big wand around and gets me everything I want. Big fast expensive cars, amiable women with long straight legs, champagne breakfasts, autograph books, cameras, lights, homage, fancy apartments, genuflecting headwaiters, the right clothes.' He grinned. 'Mediterranean holidays like this.'

'With the poor relations.'

'That's right. Slumming in the Aegean with the poor relations. Basking in warm sunshine and cold envy. Success is all bullshit. You know that, sport.'

'I can hardly remember. What are you envious about?'

'You.'

'You must be joking.'

'Do you remember Riordan's? I remember thinking, all that long ago, that you and I were going to move out one day and go somewhere. I didn't know where, or how, or much about either of us, but I never dreamt it might end up on a Greek island with the two of us sitting on a beach envying each other. You do envy me, don't you? Because I'm what you think is successful.'

'Oh yes, I suppose I do in a way. I don't begrudge you, though. You did it the hard way.'

'That's right. And then settled for the easy way. You started off the easy way, and then settled for the hard way. That's one reason I envy you. I should have stuck with the people I used to believe in, Shakespeare and Molière and Shaw and Chekhov and that bunch; I could have been a bloody good classical actor, you know, and not just another glossy prick in the sixpenny magazines.'

'You could still. Nothing to stop you. Surely now, with your reputation, you could write your own ticket.'

He shook his head slowly. 'Not really. It's where the field of force is. My drive comes from behind. The demon's behind me, pushing, kicking me in the arse, urging me after the great big juicy carrot. But Kiernan, you see, is *pulled* by his field of force. It's something that keeps out there in front of him, pulling at him, drawing him on . . . his Holy Grail, a will-o'-the-wisp maybe. But always out there in front of him. He has to keep reaching for it. That's the whole bloody difference. I don't reach any longer.'

'You used to.'

'Sure, I used to. I used to play Molière in the factories with ten bob's worth of props. Now I just get pushed around and pushed along. There's a big difference.'

'But you're glad you got away from Australia?'

'Why not? There's nothing out there for me. There never was, except being young and cocky and truculent, and wanting to have a go. When you get rid of that there's nothing left. There's no provision for later, after the cocky phase has worn off. You've seen it, for Christ's sake. The brave young adventurous Digger turns into an RSL slob, the heroic fighter-pilot becomes a nong, the lithe young athlete gets a beer-belly and fallen arches, the dedicated young actor who takes Molière around the factories settles for the advertising business. I'd rather do it over here in the big leagues. The opponents might be tougher, but at least the purse is bigger. Why not? It'll all be the same in a hundred years' time.'

'And where do I stand in all this?'

'If you want it straight, mate, you hardly stand at all,' he said, picking at the pine-needles. 'You're practically flat on your arse. Not because you're burning yourself up. Because you're eating yourself away. You're beginning to look like a bloody Belsen victim. You're mad, you know, not to go and see a doctor.'

'All right, I will, I will. One of these days.'

'Well, take my advice. Don't leave it too long.' He rolled over on his back and put his hands behind his head and closed his eyes. 'It's funny, you know,' he mused, 'but there are probably blokes out there in Australia who envy the three of us, three of the bloody expatriates. Kiernan with his shows in Paris and London and New York. Pictures in the Tate. Me getting leads in Hollywood movies. Having Sunday-newspaper affairs with glamorous floosies. You living on your Greek island and writing your books. Jesus, if the bastards only knew! Kiernan turned into a kind of animated anchorite and burning himself to a cinder trying to toss Turner or Rembrandt or Signorelli. Me drinking myself fatuous and keeping one jump ahead of the funny farm. You down to your last few quid and looking like something the cat's dragged in and acting out the death-wish. What do you weigh?'

'Weigh? Oh I don't know. Around nine stone, I guess.'

'Liar. Not that it matters. I still envy a lot of things you've got. *I* do it too, you see.'

'Such as what?'

He opened his eyes and blinked up at the silver slivers of light pricking the dusty dark green of the pine. 'I envy you Cressida,' he said quietly, 'but that's not new, I always have. I envy you the kids, because that's a kind of continuation I don't have. It's a discipline, too, and maybe that sort of discipline is what I've been lacking. I envy you the books. I think writing a book, any sort of book, is something worth doing. Something satisfying. I envy you the fact that you still *believe* in something, even if it's only yourself you believe in . . . no, not "even", maybe *because* it's yourself you believe in. And I envy you this. This kind of life. Out of the rat-race. Whatever it costs it's still enviable, I think. Still worth persevering with. Still worth looking after yourself for.' He rolled over quickly, propped himself on his elbows and squinted out across the bay.

The two children were coming back from the rocks underneath the little white St Nicholas shrine. Cressida was swimming in towards the shingle, back-stroking, towing along the mattress on which Galloway still slept. Petros was bent over the gunwale of the *caïque*, lowering into the dinghy the wicker flagons of wine and the discs of bread and the melons and grapes and baskets of picnic food, and two of the others, dripping from the sea, were arranging the stuff between the thwarts.

'I think I know why you won't go up to Athens and see a doctor,' Calverton said.

'Do you?' I could think of several reasons.

'I think you're scared of leaving Cress here on the island,' he said. 'With him.'

'Him?'

'That's right,' he said, knowing he did not have to elaborate. 'That's one of the things wrong with you,' he said. 'You eat yourself up too much over Cressida. You don't have to, you know.' He pressed himself up from the soft prickly bed of the pine-needles. 'They're bringing the stuff ashore,' he said. 'We'd better start getting organized.' As he was flapping the twigs out of his towel he said, 'I have to go up to Athens for a few days next week to see Ackermann. I'll take you with me if you like. Time you went to a quack, sport.'

'We'll see,' I said.

'The death-knell of childish hopes,' said young Julian, appearing from nowhere with a conch shell and a mask full of sea-urchins.

'What's that?' Calverton grinned down at him.

'Whenever Dad says "We'll see" it's called the death-knell of childish hopes,' the boy told him.

'It better not be this time,' Calverton said. But Julian was already running off to show his trophies to his mother, who was in the shallows now, gay and laughing as she tipped the protesting Galloway off the mattress into the water.

'There's nothing to stop you coming to Athens with me,' Calverton said. 'Nothing at all.'

'I know. I said we'll see.'

ATHENS, 1959

It was Big Grace, the American spinster, who gave him sanctuary when Dr Georgaikis insisted that he should stay on in Athens for a month or two so that he could begin his treatment and get his daily shots of streptomycin at the clinic.

Big Grace was from the Middle West, from Iowa, a quiet, gentle, warm-hearted woman almost as tall as Meredith and of about his age. She was not in the conventional sense beautiful, but there was some quality of the plains about her, and something calm and Gothic and enduring, that gave her splendour. She had doctorates in both divinity and philosophy and had been at one time a Congregational minister, but had left the church and, with a small research fellowship, gone to the Middle East to study Old Testament history; there, late in life for such an experience, she had become involved in her first love-affair, with a Jewish professor of archaeology, which meant a great deal to her but was terminated by an air crash outside Gaza. Big Grace sold up the family properties in Cedar Rapids which she had inherited, invested her money wisely, and was able to live on these investments in Athens, where she bought a charming old Ottonian house behind the cemetery at Metz. From her windows and balcony she could look over a green sea of trees to the slender columns of the temple of Olympian Zeus and the perfection of the Parthenon perched on the Acropolis rock. She made her annual journeys across to the Levant and continued her research and writing – she had by this time published two important monographs and was engaged on a book dealing with the religious significance of the cult of violence and war in the Old Testament.

The experience of her Jewish professor had left her with a controlled melancholy which she assuaged by many acts of kindliness and by abandoning herself wholeheartedly to the simple good-natured exuberance of the Greek way of life; her feeling had become pagan, her philosophy Stoic. She had been a good friend of the Merediths for some years, making gift-bearing visits to their island home from time to time, and was devoted to David. So much so, indeed, that she almost welcomed the illness which had forced his stay in Athens; it provided companionship in her loneliness and a man to care for, and perhaps some sort of compensation for what had been lost in fire and wreckage in the arid hills beyond Gaza.

Meredith, too, was grateful for the arrangement, and, after the first few days of worry and wondering about Cressida, he grew increasingly content with it.

Twice a day, after he had been given his needles, he could walk back to the house from Georgaikis's clinic through the trees and lawns and shrubberies of the Zappeion, taking it slowly and stopping luxuriously to rest on walls and benches, where he would sit and watch the children with their spinning hoops and swooping kites, and the chattering Greek nannies with spoilt fat babies who sat bloated and gurgling in big English perambulators, their bibs hung with blue beads and other amulets against the Evil Eye, or anglophilic Greeks from the social groups of Kolonaiki playing tennis on the courts of an exclusive club. They invariably called to each other in English, Meredith noted, and always in the correct sporting vernacular, 'Jolly good shot, sir!' and 'Oh bad luck, old girl, just out!' The foreign inflection always made their cheery robust calls sound odd to Meredith, as if their voices were being dubbed for quite different people altogether. A few years earlier they would have been calling to each other in French; a few years hence, he reflected, they probably would be imitating the Americans.

In the house at Metz life was pleasant, tranquil, and uncomplicated. The walls were lined with books, there was a record-player and a fine library of music, he had a workroom of his own, with a real desk and worklight—Dr Georgaikis had permitted, indeed encouraged, Meredith to spend two hours each morning writing—and he had begun, at last, to write the novel about China which he had thought of starting fourteen years before, after he had submitted his resignation to Mr Brewster. Big Grace, like some devoted and dutiful wife, was solicitous for his least wish, and from this solicitude seemed to derive considerable pleasure. Often it was enough for the two of them merely to sit on the balcony, whether talking or silent seemed of no account, sipping their drinks and looking across at the glitter of Athens spread like a magic carpet between the dark timbered peak of Lycabettus and the bare nobility of the Acropolis and the Hill of the Muses beyond. By the laziest movement of their heads they could take in all the pepper-and-salt sprinkle of the plain as far as Piraeus and the luminous shimmer of the Saronic seas beyond; in the golden clarity of early morning and sometimes at evening, just before the violet dusk settled, he could see way past Salamis and Aegina and thought he could make out, a dim shape lifted above the sea-rim, another more distant island.

It was for a few weeks a period of curious euphoria for Meredith. For the first time in years all matters had been taken out of his hands. There was now a commitment to healing, and he could do nothing but accept it. Dr Georgaikis had brought in his verdict, and Meredith was prepared to heed the voices of prudence. He hardly smoked and drank almost nothing, he worked a little, idled, dozed, slept a lot. Within the comfortable, friendly sanctuary which Big Grace had given him there was nothing to divert or distract; he was a docile and scrupulous patient. He allowed himself to relax, to drift. It was out of his hands.

Another patient under Georgaikis's treatment at this time was the American painter, Morgan; sometimes they would meet in the doctor's waiting-room and later walk together in the Zappeion Gardens. Three years had passed since the night of Little Grace's clavichord recital, and Meredith was shocked at the appalling degradation of Morgan's condition. (Had he, too, he wondered with a clutch of panic, deteriorated as noticeably?)

'I don't go there for this vitamin therapy he's promoting,' Morgan told him one morning, as they sat together under the orange-trees watching the children on the swings. 'I've settled now for liquor, liquor and my kind of sex, when I can get 'em. Not food. I never eat food, so he figures I got to have this vitamin therapy before he can do anything with me.'

'You do look as if you need something,' Meredith said.

Morgan glanced at him quizzically and said, 'You're no Mister Universe yourself. But sure . . . sure, I'm in bad shape. Okay, I don't go there looking for body build-up. I go there to talk, to confess, to chuck up. Georgaikis listens. He sits there with his fingertips stuck together and he listens and he writes things down on those little pads of his. Nobody else in the world listens to me any more. Only Georgaikis. Do you know, he never bills me for the consultations. He just listens.'

'I'll listen to you.'

'You?'

'Yes. What do you want to say?'

'Nothing. I don't have anything to say.'

'What do you say to Georgaikis?'

'Not a thing. I don't have a thing to say. Talk with me is like vomit, it doesn't mean anything, it just spills out. What is there to talk about?'

'You.'

'Look, I'm a blank space between monthly remittances. That's all. Tell me about Big Grace.'

'She's fine. She's a splendid person. You know she's very fond of you.'

'Sure.'

'She's concerned about you too.'

'Sure. She's a great woman. She's helped me through some tough times. That's why I don't see her, why I never visit any more.'

'You should. She asks about you.'

'She does? And what do you say to her? No, don't tell me.

You want to know why I don't visit any longer? I'll tell you why. I can't look at her eyes unless I'm plastered. She's got the kind of eyes I can't look into unless I'm really stoned. And I don't want Big Grace to see me when I'm really stoned. Not now. Not any more.' He ran his fingers from the widow's peak of his greying hair slowly down his ravaged ikonic profile to the collar of his shirt, exploringly, like a blind man fingering Braille. 'They make it harder for us, don't they?' he said.

'Who?'

'The healers. Big Grace, wanting to save people. Georgaikis with his therapies. And listening. Vitamins. Needles in the ass. Why don't they just turn their backs on us? Leave us alone. To work it out. What the hell does it matter?'

'I suppose it matters to them. They're concerned.'

'Sure they're concerned. But why? Well, look at you. They've taken you over. Like a goddam salvage operation. You're not adrift and foundering any longer. You're in good hands. You're being looked after. So now, you're respectable, see, you're not dramatic any more. Hell, TB isn't dramatic any more, is it? They've made *it* respectable too. They should have left it the way it was. Galloping consumption. The way it was. Chopin spitting blood all over the keyboard.'

It was a week after this conversation that Morgan came to the house at Metz. Meredith was there alone, waiting for Big Grace to return from her shopping at the American delicatessen in Kolonaiki, where she would go once a week to buy special delicacies for the two of them, and looking down from the window of his workroom he could follow Morgan's approach along the crowded roadway at the bottom of the steps. He could see him for a long time, because Morgan was very drunk and progressed only with difficulty. When he stopped from reeling or staggering or prancing a few yards at a time in a stiff-legged, jerky, limping trot, he would stand swaying, breathing heavily with his head lowered and shaking from side to side, a circle of open-mouthed Greek children around him, and then he would push through them and blunder on, his arms thrown out for balance like a ropewalker's. Once he missed his footing on the kerb and fell headlong across the road, and a battered old tourer stopped with a surprised scream of brakes and two stocky Greek workmen helped him to his feet and brushed the dust and chaff from his jacket. Morgan dumbly accepted these ministrations with stiff arms like a puppet, then pushed the men gently aside and lurched on. The two Greeks shook their heads and laughed a little. It took Morgan a long time to negotiate the steps, and then he disappeared and there was another protracted interval before the doorbell began to peal.

Meredith made no attempt to answer it. He was shocked by Morgan's condition, and sorry for him, but he felt a responsibility for the house in the absence of its owner; Big Grace would hardly welcome such a visitation, he told himself: better to pretend that nobody was at home, then Morgan would go away. He hoped he would go away before Big Grace returned. So he remained where he was, keeping quite still, waiting and listening. For ten minutes, intermittently, the ringing continued, punctuated with the heavy thuds of a fist pounding on the door—the man certainly was importunate!—and after this a long silence and Morgan reappeared at the top of the steps and stood there swaying and blinking and irresolute, but his body began to sag and he sat down on the low sandstone wall of the garden. He stared around as if surprised to find himself there, and turned his head quickly and vomited into the shrubbery. It seemed to exhaust him, because when he had finished being sick he sat crouched forward with his head buried in his hands, and five little Greek girls in black school smocks with white buttons approached timidly and sat on the ground in a half-circle around him and played five-stones with their sets of knucklebones. The white bones flew and fell above the turning, darting, plunging little hands, and between each toss the shy dark eyes of the children would look up at the bent, inattentive figure on the wall.

Meredith began to feel intensely concerned for the American. Surely he should go down and do something . . . what did it matter about the state he was in? He was, after all, a friend. He needed looking after . . . clearly he was in no condition to look after himself. Yet he was still gripped by a powerful reluctance to commit, to become involved; and while he hesitated he saw, to his relief, Morgan straighten himself and struggle to his feet and begin to move off slowly and cautiously down the steps, clinging to the stone coping of the wall as he went. His limp was much more noticeable going down. The five little girls followed a few paces behind him, preserving their rearguard distance behind his laborious descent by hopping and skipping on the stones, one step down and two back and up, and three more down, in a kind of impromptu little dance. At the bottom of the steps the children ran off to the right squealing and laughing, and Morgan blundered away in the opposite direction, past the cigarette kiosk, and the Fix Beer and Papastratos signs, until he was lost to sight in the agitation of people and traffic.

But Meredith kept staring down, sick and disturbed; the overwhelming sense of relief had been only fleeting, now he felt remorseful and guilty of a betrayal. *Why* had Morgan called? He must have been in trouble, needing help. There would have to be some imperative reason to force him there in that condition, against his scruples, to meet Big Grace's eyes. He must have needed help, to come there at all; his long and fruitless wait at the door indicated an urgency.

It would have been quite some time before the sound drifted into Meredith's cognition—the pulsing wail of ambulance or police sirens along the street to the left. There was a sudden flurry of people around the cigarette kiosk, a few men and boys were running. *Morgan!* He was running himself before he realized, through the house and out the door, and down the steps two or three at a time, in desperate bounds. The traffic was heavy in the street—decrepit buses and heavy lorries carrying marble blocks for the stonemasons' yards and overladen market vans taking the detour to skirt the city and the usual swarm of motor-tricycles with junk and ironmongery—and like all Greek traffic it moved at reckless speed and in wild disorder in a bedlam of tyres in shrill protest, brakes squealing, shouted imprecations, the imperious discord of demanding horns. Meredith, trotting and jostling and gasping for breath, could imagine the mangled, bleeding, drink-sodden body of Morgan lying broken in the dust and filth and ferment.

But as he frantically pushed through past the Papastratos sign he stopped suddenly. For there was Morgan, not twenty feet ahead of him, quite calmly sitting at a wobbly iron table on the pavement outside a little *kafenéion* drinking *ouzo* from a tall thin glass. Meredith, pale and trembling, the breath wheezing in his diseased lungs, could still hear the sirens but now from very far away, with a lilt of mockery, fading into silence. Morgan saw him and made a drunken gesture of invitation. Meredith went to the table slowly, trying to fight back his anger.

Morgan executed a florid wave towards a vacant chair. 'So there y'are,' he said thickly. 'C'mon. Drink. Been waiting one of you t' come back. Wen' t' house. Nob'y home. Hammered goddam place down. Nob'y there. Figured best I wait here have li'l drink.'

'You don't need a little drink,' Meredith said coldly. His rage now was a threat to his self-control. 'You're drunk already. Look at the state you're in. You're full as a boot!'

'Oh brother!' said Morgan, beaming. 'But gotta see Grace. Big Grace. Gotta see her ver' important.'

'You're not seeing anybody. You're getting the hell out of here. Come on.'

'Gotta see Grace, man. You don't un'erstand. Gotta see her. 'Simportan'.'

'Come on. Get up. On your feet. I'll take you down to the end of the street and get you a taxi.'

Morgan tried to protest, but Meredith took him roughly by the shoulder and dragged him to his feet, and tossed some loose drachmas on the table and led him lurching away. At first the American struggled feebly, mumbling that it was important for him to wait there for Big Grace, but Meredith, in no mood to argue with him, marched him to the end of the street in furious silence. He found a cab waiting beneath a dusty clump of oleanders and bundled him into it without ceremony and slammed the door on him, and gave the grinning driver money and directions. He did not even wait to see the cab move off from the kerb, but turned his back and walked across to the corner coffee-house to order himself a double cognac, which he drank sitting in a dark corner at a marble-topped table beneath an old lithograph of the hero Kolokotronis.

He never saw Morgan again. Two nights later the American was severely injured in a brawl at a sailors' tavern in Piraeus, and was kept all night at the police-station before being moved into the hospital, so it was too late by then to do much about him. His death was variously attributed to the head and internal injuries suffered in the fracas, to malnutrition, and to alcoholic poisoning. In all likelihood it was a combination of all three. There was difficulty about identification, because he had no money or papers in his pockets—and there was a lot of additional confusion in Piraeus at the time because road excavations for a sewer near the police-station had dug up an archaic bronze Apollo and other ancient statuary—and it was some time before the United States Consulate was informed, so it was ten days after Morgan's death before any of his friends knew of it, and Big Grace spent another whole week of frustration and fury amid the interminable dusty corridors of Greek bureaucracy before she was able to locate his grave, an unmarked scar of ochreous clay in an unconsecrated section of the Piraeus cemetery otherwise overgrown with weeds. The scar of wet orange earth into which Morgan had vanished did not look all that dissimilar from the cloddy muck from which the bronze Apollo had been resurrected. Grace had a headstone cut at a stonemason's yard in Metz, possibly from one of the very blocks of marble which were being trucked past in the raucous street while Morgan, drunk, waited to talk to her about something. But what it was he had had on his mind that day she was never to know.

So poor Morgan finally left his suitcase and found at last, as Stephanos had predicted, his few feet of place in a particular country, his sad and sordid expatriated belonging.

And Meredith for the rest of his life would never be able to forget the picture of an American degenerate sitting crouched and lonely on a garden wall with five little girls on the ground around him, little girls with quick dark hands and slow dark eyes tossing knucklebones in the air.

But these things came later, because it was during the interval between that day and its sequels that Big Grace gave her party, and Meredith had other things to think about.

ATHENS, 1959

It was a party, Meredith reflected, that could, because of his separateness, go on having many surprises for him, unless he was prepared to inure himself against the capacity for surprise. Although he did not particularly want to do this. There was something estimable in his separateness from all the others – a detachment, even an aloofness, that arose out of his not drinking while everyone else was; out of the special nature of his illness which inspired a peculiar quality of consideration, even respect, that was never entirely artificial; out of his position, because of his tenure of Big Grace's house, as a kind of surrogate host, even – he smiled inwardly at the whimsicality of the thought – in a vague way as a kind of surrogate husband. It really did put one in an odd position to know where the ash-trays and spare glasses were kept, and swizzlesticks and coasters, to be aware of the name of the cat and to be singled out by it, to be informed precisely as to what was in the refrigerator and where the garbage was disposed, to be able to talk about the histories of the books on the shelves and the pictures on the walls and pieces of furniture and rugs. He was no longer, as each of the others was, merely a guest.

There were surprising qualities, too, in the very nature of the party. Seeing the foreigners from the island in suits and ties and socks and shoes, wearing party dresses and stockings and jewellery, and sophisticated make-up and elaborate coiffures – people so long familiar as raffish and careless in garments of casual shabbiness, with sandals and bare feet and salty hair . . .

the white-jacketed waiters hired from Zonar's for the night, delivered in a van with the expensive catering, quite different from the crop-headed aproned urchins slopping wine on the tavern tables of the island . . . the drinks he had almost forgotten—Campari and Dubonnet and daiquiries and whisky sours and old-fashioneds and gimlets and Manhattans and vodka. It was a scene dislodged in time and space, a happening elsewhere, anywhere but here, anachronistic, a race memory of the tribal gatherings of long ago. Yet nobody had forgotten the rites. Not these, the chameleon people. They fitted in exactly, punctiliously, as if nothing had intervened, the mannerisms, laughter, wisecracks, conversations, coquetries, affectations and avoidances, ingratiations and innuendoes, all were the same.

Yet not quite the same to Meredith, detached from them. Onlooking. Able to discern and weigh and judge. Able to be surprised.

It was intriguing, for instance, to realize that the party could have been taking place in California or Chicago or New York; its very essence was its Americanism—one of the celebrants tinkled ice-cubes in the thick glass of his old-fashioned and said to Meredith, admiringly, 'Boy, this sure is a real Stateside clam-bake!'—and it started him reflecting on how subtly and unsuspectingly he and Cressida had transferred their associations over the past few years. Of the sixty or seventy people at the party only they and Calverton were Australians—and they could hardly be classified as Australian any longer—and there was no more than a token handful of Britishers and Continentals, and the only Greeks present apart from the hired waiters were Stephanos the banker and his wife. Meredith found it odd that the party was so flagrantly American, because Big Grace herself had for years deliberately removed herself from her country and its way of life and virtually all the guests who were her compatriots were even more vehement rejectionists. Yet whenever the tocsin of the cocktail-shaker was sounded they came together like iron filings drawn to the poles of a magnet, as if by the reassembling of their scattered particles into a pattern of reassuring nationalism, they could endorse both the nationalism itself and their reasons for having rejected it, as if proof of their own rugged individualism could be found only in a compulsive ritual attendance at the hearth – even when an expatriated hearth – of rugged individualism. They depended a great deal, really, on the mythologies they professed to have discarded; one saw this very clearly whenever they came together; they were all fugitives who were finally never able to make the last desperate break to achieve the final freedom, escapees who never quite escaped. (Meredith was, at this time, not aware of the exception to this, for the night of the party was, in fact, the very first of the five nights that Morgan lay cold and unclaimed, three miles away, on a mortuary slab in a dingy room smelling of formaldehyde and urine and raw cement.)

Meredith found it curious to consider how many of their friends and acquaintances now were Americans. Although was this so surprising? America's was the sickest and the most nerve-shattering of the Western societies and consequently America's expatriates far outnumbered all others on the Continent – but he and Cressida had come to accept this and although they tried not to model themselves on the Americans they did feel more at ease with them than with most of their own Australians, more able to identify and to understand. Identify? But how *could* they identify with this specific pattern into which, in the final analysis, they could never properly fit; was it not, rather, that he and his wife had reached a point where they had lost, or were losing, their own identity, and were ready to accept any substitution for the loss, however superficial?

The very weight of Americanism, powerful enough to crush its own rejectionists, or to draw them back and destroy them more insidiously – he thought of the famous expatriates, the Ernest Hemingways and Scott Fitzgeralds and Nathanael Wests and Ezra Pounds – to ruin or befoul what it wanted to love and revere and admire: surely it would have no respect for the isolated alien stranger who happened to get in the way.

A kind of Americanism was already taking over the rocky little island which an old lady in Pimlico, only five years before, had recommended to him as a place simple and unspoiled, where he could get away from the pressures of modern society; but already the Americans were transferring to it those aspects of their own nature that they never seemed able entirely to eradicate. Eventually they would have to try to turn the island into something else, into a kind of preserved facsimile, a reminder of their own renunciations. The time would come, Meredith suspected, even there, when there would be waiters in white jackets hired from Athens, and copies of *Life* and *The New Yorker* tossed around, and imported food and drinks bearing the correct labels, and gay men and women vying in smart clothes and brittle chatter, and there would be an expatriate there too, an expatriate who from three thousand miles away had blissfully gone back home, who would tinkle the ice-cubes in a thick old-fashioned glass and admiringly comment, 'Boy, this sure is a real Stateside clambake!'

And then the new expatriates coming—and they would still be coming, for every society kept on creating its rebels and misfits and fugitives and protestants—would have to turn away and find some other island. Perhaps one day there would be no more islands left . . .

In his mood of separateness, Meredith felt quite dispassionate and detached about this. About everything, in fact. The night was bound to have its problems. A difficult test for him. But he felt pleased with his demeanour; he was perfectly calm and composed as he waited for Jim Galloway's arrival.

He knew that Cressida was involved with Galloway, had known it since the day before yesterday, when she had stepped off the island steamer escorted on the one side by her lover and on the other by Archie Calverton, an admirer of much older standing.

She had worn a grey suit and looked very beautiful, and she had done her hair the way Meredith liked it and on her wrist was the heavy silver bracelet he had given her in Rome years before. He knew that she loved him very much, and they had all walked together along the crowded pandemonious quayside. The circle of her love and the circle of her admiration—the pattern, as it were, of her ability to excite love and admiration—were concentric and complete. He was quite certain of the validity of his intuition, but here tonight at the party he would be able to confirm it, from the glances of the others, the social diplomacies, Calverton's protectiveness, the things left unsaid. It was accordingly most important that he should preserve his coolness and detachment.

It was important, for instance, to appreciate the significance of Calverton having arrived early while Galloway had not yet come, although they were staying at the same hotel. This would be a deliberate move on the part of the American: he would have an obligation to be present because to stay away altogether might be open to a misinterpretation, but he would make a point of arriving late and would find some excuse to get away early.

'How about I get you a proper drink?' It was Calverton, at his elbow.

'Thanks. I'll ride along on this tomato juice. Anyway I'm the one should be doing the honours. What about you?'

'I'm all right. I intend to go easy. You are looking bloody well, mate,' he said.

Meredith nodded. 'Why not? Living on the fat of the land. Even putting on weight. Nine pounds so far.'

'That's good. You certainly seem a hell of a lot better.'

'What's happened to Galloway? He hasn't turned up.'

'Oh, he'll be along,' said Calverton casually. 'He said he'd be late. There was some character at the Grande Bretagne he had to see on the way here.'

'How's everything down on the island?'

'Oh fine. Fine. Nothing very new, you know. Same old roundelay. The kids are in good form. Cress copes very well. Misses you, of course. All this week she's been like a pup with two tails, knowing she was coming up to see you. She looks marvellous, doesn't she?'

'She always does. Younger tonight, though. Happier . . . somehow.'

'That's being up here. Seeing you. Seeing how much better you look.' He said off-handedly, 'Jim's here. Must've missed him coming in. He's over there.'

Meredith, calm, turned slowly and looked across the crowded room. He could see the brown, bearded face above the other faces in the sitting-room, could hear his laughter through the buzz and crackle of talk. Meredith's eyes searched for Cressida. She was with another group on the balcony. 'Go and get him a drink,' he said.

'He's all right,' said Calverton. 'Big Grace is looking after him. Not to worry, he's in good hands.'

'When do you plan going back to the island?' Meredith asked.

'Tomorrow. Have to. Ackermann wants to go down and look the place over before he flies back to Rome. They've bought an option on that Woodward novel, and they think the island might possibly be a good location.'

'God, that's all we need! That'd be the stone end of the place. Galloway going back with you?'

'Yes. Well, he really only came up for the party.'

'You can have another party on the ship. Lots of company. Cressida's going back tomorrow.'

'So she told me. I thought she might have stayed on a bit longer.'

'She's worried about the kids. Anxious to get back.'

'The kids are no problem. I can look after them. Why doesn't she stay here with you and Grace for a few more days? Do you both the world of good. She needs a break from down there . . . a break from the kids, if it comes to that. And they're no bloody problem. Look, I'll go and have a talk with her and—'

'No. No, don't say anything. She wants to go back.'

Calverton shrugged. 'Whatever you say, mate. Hang on while I go and freshen up this drink.' He went off and was seized by a talkative, statuesque blonde from Kansas City named Clarissa and did not come back.

Meredith, detached and cool, was able to examine the subtleties of this conversation and to continue making his careful observations. He observed the studied way in which Galloway kept away from Cressida. He seemed to make a point of always being where Cressida was not, invariably offering the bounty of his gaiety and charm to some other woman; whenever avoidance was impossible and the fluctuation of social movement brought them together they impinged with a kind of casual nonchalance. There would be a brief exchange of smiles, a sentence or two superficially exchanged, then both would turn away and talk to someone else more animatedly and with louder laughter.

Galloway grinned and waved across to Meredith several times and once called something to him, incomprehensible in the hubbub, but it was some little time before he joined him on the balcony, Cressida having moved elsewhere, and for ten minutes his talk was warm and friendly and solicitous. He never mentioned Cressida, Meredith noted. Then he shook hands and said, 'I plan to beat it now, so I'll say goodnight. And good luck. I'll have a word with Big Grace and get on my way. Brother, am I pooped! Do I need sleep! Ran into a crazy crowd from the Embassy last night at the Seventeen Club, then we all ended up in some dive in Piraeus with a bunch of junior-grade lieutenants from the Sixth Fleet. Brother, did we hang one on! So it's a goddam early night tonight for James Galbraith Galloway. Be seeing you, David.' He held a hand up with his fingers crossed and winked encouragingly. 'Good luck with the cure,' he said. 'You get better.'

As predicted, thought Meredith, watching the big strong figure pushing towards the door through smoke haze and persiflage.

Once he had gone it was easier for Meredith to concentrate on the other subtleties, the way Cressida would keep coming to him with her attentions, the meaningful glances he would sometimes intercept from other guests who had come up from the island, and the quick, embarrassed way they would avert their gaze when they saw him looking. Occasionally he would trap Big Grace watching him with a concern in her eyes that was more than her normal solicitude.

When the last of the guests had gone he and Cressida and Big Grace sat out on the balcony looking across to the moonwashed columns of the Parthenon, sipping at nightcaps and yawning and talking desultorily while the men from Zonar's finished their work in the kitchen.

'Terrific party, Grace,' Meredith said. 'They all enjoyed it enormously. I know I did.'

'Me too,' said Cressida, patting back a yawn. 'I'd forgotten people had parties like that.'

'Jim Galloway was the only one,' Meredith said. 'I don't know if he enjoyed it. He didn't stay long.'

'I hardly saw him,' said Cressida.

'Oh, he was here. Came late, went early. Put in an appearance, anyway. That's why I wondered if he enjoyed it. It isn't like him, cutting out early like that.'

Big Grace glanced at him quickly, then bent her head over her glass. 'He told me he was out all night last night,' she explained, without looking up. 'He said he had a terrible hangover.'

'Was that it?' Meredith nodded. 'I thought something was bothering him. Didn't seem himself. Although we did have quite a chat together.' Big Grace did not look up. She twisted at the stem of her goblet, moving the circle of the glass around the table. 'You're going to have stacks of company on the ship tomorrow,' he said to Cressida. 'He's going back too, with Archie. They're taking Ackermann down with them.'

'That will be nice,' said Cressida. 'I wish it was you, though, who was coming. I wish you were better, darling, and coming back with me. We all miss you, you know.'

'Do you? Well—one day . . . It won't be long. Not the way things are going. Not the way Grace looks after me. Eh, Grace?'

Big Grace nodded, still with her face downcast, still making careful circles on the table with the bottom of her glass.

After Cressida left Athens, Meredith's detachment and composure drained away, at first gradually and then swiftly. He began to be irritated and impatient with the therapeutic routine of his treatment, found it more and more difficult to concentrate, even for an hour or two, on his writing, and begrudged the imposed hours of rest, although he was no longer sleeping well at night. He had gone back to smoking again, heavily, and in consequence had little appetite for food, even though Big Grace, worried by the change in his attitude, would go to special trouble to prepare dishes that he particularly enjoyed. He had taken to drinking in the evenings, cautiously at first but with increasing intemperance. When he found that the alcohol mixed unhappily with the drugs he was taking—the PAS churned at his stomach and the streptomycin produced unpleasant numbing sensations around his mouth and lips—he began by reducing the dosage and finally stopped taking the tablets altogether in the evenings. At his next weigh-in at Georgaikis's clinic he found that his weight had not increased, indeed he had dropped back a kilogram-and-a-half; that evening he lied to Big Grace for the first time, reporting to her that he had put on another two pounds. 'So obviously a bit of grog and smoking, in moderation, doesn't do any real harm,' he said, lying to himself as well. She smiled at him, but there was anxiety in her face as she watched him go to the sideboard to pour himself another whisky. They continued to sit together on the balcony after dinner, but where before there had been good music to enjoy and good talk or good silences to share, the silences now were long and strained, as if private and particular fears barricaded each of them off from the other.

Towards the end of the week after the party the situation was brought to a head by Clarissa, the blonde from Kansas City, who had visited the island at Calverton's invitation, had returned by that afternoon's steamer and dropped around to bring reports and to deliver to Meredith an affectionate note from Cressida scrawled hurriedly on the back of a shopping-list. Clarissa, the pampered only child of a real estate tycoon, was beautiful, rich, and indolent; when people asked her what she did she always said, with a brevity unusual in one so gifted in loquacity, 'Why, I just sit and watch things grow.' In this she under-rated herself, because she was in serious practice as a nymphomaniac. Men were the inflexible purpose of her life; she drifted around the Continent at her ease and leisure, taking a town that caught her fancy, or a village or a city or an island, and moving into it and staying there until she had exhausted the supply of available men. In the peregrinations of her erotic pillage she had come more and more to consider the

Mediterranean littoral her hunting ground. Sin, she believed, was more enjoyable where there was sunshine in shabby streets. (Stockholm was the only northern city she exempted from this judgment, but London she avoided as if it had never recovered from the Plague Year, and although she was not averse to interesting dalliance if it was offered in Paris she went there really only to buy dresses and scent and negligees.)

'I certainly must get right back to that fantastic island of yours,' she said to Meredith. 'And fast! It's so *cute*, the place, I mean, and there's more fun to the square foot of mattress than any place I've been since Ibiza out of season. Oh my, they sure do live it up down there! I mean honestly. They're leaping around from bed to bed like fleas on a blanket. Tell me, honey, however does that darling wife of yours stay the way she is? I mean honestly. So sweet and wonderful . . . well, she's just *grand*, and there she is with all that gorgeous manpower available, and she's so goddam attractive and everyone . . . Well, I mean honestly. I mean you have to admire her, don't you, the way she keeps herself intact, I mean, well, she's not *aloof*, anything but aloof, she can be the swingingest doll, but she does have this *separate* thing, she never seems to be mixed up, well, *fluid*, like the rest of the crowd. I guess it's kind of rare this thing she has. To be involved, I mean, and yet not to get caught up, to stay like she does, separate and intact. I can't understand it. I mean honestly. Lordy me, I couldn't handle it the way she handles it, not in a month of Sundays. Well, I guess that figures, I mean I *look* for involvement, it's a kind of hobby with me, but how does she manage to preserve this . . . well, it's a kind of quaint word to use, but this kind of virginal impregnability. I mean down there, I mean honestly, where anything, *but anything* goes . . . down there in Kamasutra Land with all that unleashed libido and those stunning men . . . all those bare brown chests and tight jeans. And all, goddam it, *available*! All ready and willing and able. Hmmmm-mmmmm!' She stretched seductively and closed her eyes in dreamy rapture. She pushed her legs out wide and opened her eyes and studied him. 'I mean honestly, David,' she said contentedly, 'does it worry you any, having a wife so disgustingly attractive, with so many admirers?'

'She's always had plenty of admirers,' he replied calmly. 'Ever since I've known her. And no doubt before.'

'It figures. Man, she sure is crazy for you, though.'

'Is she? I hope so.' Her teasing prattle made him embarrassed and uncomfortable, but he forced a smile. 'I can't imagine why. Not after all these years.'

'Archie is in love with her, of course. I mean honestly. You knew that? I mean Archie's been carrying a torch since for ever. The poor sweet bastard. A torch bigger than the one our Statue of Liberty carries. Can you imagine? My guess is that's why he's never gotten married. Isn't that scary? Honestly, I mean. Real scary. Dear Archie. Sweet Archie. The poor drunken lugubrious bum. Archie, you know, would be a real nice husband, a swell husband . . . well, for someone interested in husbands.'

'Archie's a family friend, that's all. We've both known him for donkey's years.'

'Sure. Oh sure. I'm only kidding. I have news for you, though. Jimmy Galloway's got a torch too. Did you know that?'

Meredith closed his eyes and tried to allow the rattle of the voice to pass over him, over the afflicting numbness. 'Now there's a guy I could fall for, Jimmy Galloway, I mean honestly, he's just my *type*, but for pete's sake what's a girl to do when he just mopes around after your Cressida, I mean honestly he's just crazy about her. Now that I *do* resent, I honestly do, because I could fall for that guy in the biggest way. So if you're answering that note I brought up will you just do me a whale of a favour and ask that selfish, devoted, bewitching, damned dame of yours to unlock the leg-irons and let the poor bastard loose before I get back down that way again. Well, I've got a claim, haven't I? He's one of *us*, a fellow-American, we *are* entitled to keep it in the family.' She looked at Meredith and burst into laughter. 'Oh, David, look at you, you're taking all this *seriously* . . . oh, come on now, you are a dope, I mean honestly . . .'

'It's not that,' he said hurriedly. 'I'm afraid I was hardly listening . . . I'd remembered I've some pills I have to take. I'd clean forgotten. So if you'll excuse me . . .'

'Why sure. But you listen to me, man. Just forget all this boloney of mine. It's my low-comedy line. I play it for laughs. Ha-ha! Big deal! Sometimes I get so excruciatingly funny I can make myself retch. That Clarissa Perkins, they say, she's as funny as a dead baby's doll. Listen, honey, your wife is a one-man woman, and don't you ever forget it. And for heaven's sake *you* don't have to lose any sleep over all those virile extras down there. I mean honestly. They're not men. They fill in gaps. You can leave *them* to *me*. I mean honestly . . .'

After he had taken his drugs he sat on the edge of the bed, looking at the note she had brought up to him. It was a scribble, tossed off, he would guess, on a table outside Evangeli's, a word or two blurred and blotted by a stain of slopped wine, a note that said nothing more than the little clichés of endearment and absence. He turned it over to the shopping-list, less scrawlily written than the note: *Fasolia. 2 kilos Bitam margarine. Lentils. 2 loaves psomi. Tomatoes. Olives. Cheese (feta? Edam?). Oil. Krakeraikia. Order charcoal and paraffin. Cigarettes. Pay Sorellis . . .*

He was acutely conscious of its reference to another life; it was an index to a different world – so different from the ordered, comfortable world of Big Grace's shopping-lists: he found it odd that communication with Cressida was closer through this curious personal and mundane cryptography than the clichés of endearment. Could you love a wife through a shopping-list?

By the time he returned from his afternoon visit to Georgaikis's surgery he had made the commitment and he told Big Grace he intended returning to the island by the Monday morning steamer.

She looked at him in astonishment. 'But you have to stay at least another month,' she protested. 'What about your treatment? What are you going to do?'

'It can be done just as easily down there.'

'You've asked Dr Georgaikis about this?'

'I didn't ask him. I told him.'

'And he *agreed*?'

'What else could he do? Oh, well, he wasn't madly happy about it. But he had to admit there was no *reason* I had to stay on in Athens.'

'Except this is the logical place for you to be treated. And obviously the best place. You can live quietly here, to a reasonable routine.'

'I can continue the same regimen down there.'

'With no doctor on the island?'

'Cress can give the needles. It's no different really.'

'You gave Dr Georgaikis no choice, did you? You just obstinately told him you were going, so what could he say?'

'Look, I'm sorry, Grace. I know how you must feel . . . I mean, after all you've done, and I can't begin to tell you how grateful I—'

'I'm not thinking of me. I'm thinking of you. You've been going so well, and now you're prepared to jeopardize the whole business.'

'Listen to me, Grace, it's not working out. It just *isn't* working out! I can't seem to get settled. I can't work. My brain keeps churning, churning, churning . . . I'm not sleeping very well . . . I just seem so appallingly bloody restless. I can't get any peace of mind any more.'

'I'm sorry about that.'

'For God's sake, it's not *you*, Grace. It's nothing to do with you. I owe more to you than I can ever—'

'I guess I know what's brought this up. It's what *she* was saying last night, isn't it?' There was an edge of bitterness in her voice. 'That bitch Clarissa! David, you're stupid to let her influence you. She's a crazy woman, she's got this obsession about men, about sex. I felt like slapping her across the face when she was rattling on with all that malicious, double-edged nonsense about Cressida. But that's just her way of trying to—'

'Now, come on, Grace.' He made the interruption gently, his hand upraised, as if to ward something off. 'We're two grown-up people. We don't have to kid each other. You know as well as I do what this is all about. You were perfectly well aware of the innuendoes at the party, you saw the way they looked.' She tried to meet his eye but glanced away. 'Clarissa and her mad chatter don't mean a damned thing,' he said.

'Well, you were happy enough here until she called, weren't you?' she said stubbornly.

'She didn't comfort me, if that's what you mean. I'll admit that. But I haven't been happy since the party. Not really. I was happy before that. Very happy. If you like, you can put it down to the fact that seeing Cress again upset me a little. I'm a bit lost without her, you see.'

'You have been working very well on your book.' She pointed this out with a touch of desperation.

'Yes, pretty well,' he conceded.

'The bits you read me out were grand, just grand. And you said yourself—'

'Oh, don't worry, I'll keep pushing on with it. Grace, listen, I really am terribly sorry about all this, about having to bring it to an end like this. But I do have to go. And you know why I have to go.'

'I think you're taking an awful risk. You're far from cured. I think you're deliberately seeking out more pain for yourself when you don't have to.'

'Maybe. Perhaps it's a human weakness to want pain, perhaps we have to have it, to live with it, because it dulls the other deficiencies.'

'But you could stay here until you're better, until you're strong enough to cope with it. Your going down now, in this condition, feeling the way you do, it's terribly foolish, David, dangerous . . . it's . . . it's like some sort of emotional death-wish.'

He laughed at that, but without much amusement. 'I don't know about death-wish. But dangerous, yes. It could be dangerous. And stupid. And irrational. But I have to go, Grace. I have to go because it's the only way I can find out. It's the only way I can get that peace of mind that Georgaikis is always going on about.'

She remained silent for a long time, staring down at her thin capable hands. 'David?' she said at last without turning to him.

'Yes?'

'I do want you to know that I have been very happy having you stay here. Happier than I've been for a very long time. Your being here has meant a lot to me.' She rose abruptly and moved to the railing of the balcony, and stood with her back to him, tall and stiff and straight.

The night had settled into its deep black-purple, with a prodigal scatter of stars above the blurred effulgence of the city's clustered diadems. They were testing for the *Son et Lumière*. Poked above the trees near Hadrian's Arch a Corinthian cap on a slender column stood in eerie blue light, the Parthenon and the crusty scarp of the Acropolis above it in ruddy luminescence, candy sticks on painted theatrical canvas artificially rumpled; they changed to green, like Prospero's palace, turned red as the breath of war, disappeared altogether while shoals of low-swinging stars rushed forward to dance for a moment in their icy glintings before vanishing again behind a cascade of gold. In the middle foreground below, less credible, were the turquoise and malachite shapes of a lighted swimming-pool and a floodlit tennis court, lozenged mosaics in a different darkness, and mannikin boys trotted on a cinder track around an emerald sportsfield where a regiment of Lilliputian girls moved to eurythmic dance as if the night breeze blew at them.

He went over and stood behind her, his hands resting lightly on the stiff shoulders.

'What I really want to tell you,' she said, 'is that this set-up is always here. For you, I mean when you get back, if you find that you can't . . . I mean if it doesn't work out you can always come back here, can't you? I want you to feel that you'll always be very welcome. You can always find a place here. With me.'

Only the Parthenon now was floodlit. In the blue light it stood against the darkness like a half-remembered dream imprinted on the night, a cry from elsewhere in some forgotten language.

LONDON, 1962

The big room is pale and cool and the daffodils are everywhere, the first of the crop, the daffodils I brought up two days ago from Gloucestershire. Miriam, affected as she always is by the seasonal harbingers, has massed them in bowls on the side tables and bookshelves, below the pedestal of the Giacometti figure, on the ledges of the windows where the curtains are flung wide and where they have become quite incandescent against the dingy darkness of mid-afternoon in Kensington. They remind me of Athens and the lighting of the Parthenon for the *Son et Lumière*.

Yes, they do remind me of that, with a genuine sadness of feeling and recall, but with that unembittered kind of melancholy one associates with autumns and certain times of dusk; they remind me of dead Morgan, of Big Grace, of opportunities that have slipped away. Whatever happens to opportunities when they have slipped away? Are there racks somewhere where secondhand opportunities are kept? Foreclosed opportunities? Reject opportunities? A council pound for stray and unwanted opportunities?

Absurd thoughts. But while I am waiting for Miriam to return it is probably wiser to consider absurdities than to start brooding over things again. The disaster of today, for example. The whole ghastly disaster of this return to England. These matters are just too depressing, and, besides, I can hardly communicate them to Miriam, because it was really at her insistence that we exchanged houses and came back to England. Another consideration is that if I confide in her the totality of the disaster it would be tantamount to, at best, a plea for charity and at worst a kind of moral blackmail. She would take it that I was asking for help, and would feel an obligation about it because she would consider herself responsible for having landed us in this situation.

Miriam is stately, but by no means rich. She gives a very distinct impression of wealth and position—it is as much a part of her as the short-cropped grey hair, her pearls, the stick she carries, the faint fragrance of cleanliness that goes with her—but she has to do a lot of scraping to preserve this impression. She has the house, of course, which is very lovely, and this room in particular is the epitome of wealth and good taste—the pale rubbed lime of the panelling, the Adam fireplace, the Stubbs horse and the Constable landscape, the Chagall above the sideboard, the little Samuel Palmer etching, the Giacometti and the old chandelier with some of the pendant drops missing—but all this is the inherited shape around her, no more to be dispensed with than a tortoise its shell. Anyway, she has been kind and helpful, and she can do no more for us than she has already done.

Today, moving back from Fleet Street to the Strand, I really did feel suicidal. The smog was heavy and foul-smelling and acrid—the red-glowing buses at eleven in the morning had their lights on—and I found breathing so difficult that at each lamp-post I had to rest, holding on to the fluted iron standards. Once a news-vendor rebuked me because I was standing right in front of the propped-up billboard that said DOCKERS NEW THREAT. 'Eh, c'mon, guvnor, d'you mind, let the customers 'ave a bleedin' *look* at fings!' I suppose part of the difficulty in breathing would have been psychosomatic, too, because I was still simmering about the two interviews; well, the one with Calthrop especially, because it was I, nine years ago, who had pulled the necessary strings to get him on the paper: then he had been all sycophancy and gratitude, now it was a different picture altogether. 'So it's actually a cock-up of several factors, isn't it, old boy?' he had postulated gravely, rubbing with his finger at some invisible mark on the top of his enormous desk. 'I mean, heaven forbid that I of all people should seem unsympathetic, but getting down to tintacks, and this we have to do, alas, there are these overriding factors of age, health, and out-of-touchness.'

'Nothing doing then?' I said, trying to seem careless. 'No job?'

'Not at the moment, I fear, dear chap. I really am frightfully sorry, you know; I mean I have been your most solid supporter for years, your going off to Greece and all that, this very estimable stand you've made for individualism—dashed plucky, you know . . . I mean the chaps at the Press Club all used to say you'd be trotting back here inside twelve months and all that, but by Jove you showed them, didn't you? And then . . . well, the years pass, don't they? . . . we naturally assumed . . . I mean, I was absolutely stunned when you told me that . . . er, well, that —'

'That it had turned out a flop. But that was the risk one took, wasn't it? The calculated risk. Calthrop, you've said you have nothing offering at the moment. Foreseeably nothing either, I take it.'

''Fraid not, dear chap. Frightfully sorry about this. But I mean, let's face it, in your condition of health the staff medical officer wouldn't wear it for a start. And the board is implacable about all staff appointments being subject to the statutory clean bill of health. Then, quite aside from that, you *are* forty-nine, which you must admit is rather long in the tooth to hope for a really successful comeback in this ruddy jungle. Not against the young bright up-and-comings. Absolutely ruthless they are, quite without compunction in this sort of situation. Which they rather relish. My dear chap, they would simply cut you to bloody shreds. It's a different world, Meredith, from the one you remember. Tough, vicious, and total. Papers folding. Mergers. The battle for circulation.'

'Fleet Street never was a Sunday School,' I said.

'Agreed. How right you are. The final point I am coming to, though, if you will forgive me, dear boy, is that your problem is not unlike that of a patient suffering from amnesia. Now look at it this way, you have been eight years out of circulation and —'

'I've never stopped writing.'

'Oh quite, quite. But your world of fiction, my dear fellow, this creative obsession, however admirable, however enviable, has no earthly connection with day-by-day journalism. Nor—' he laughed lightly—'nor, one might even suggest, with the harsh realities of daily living, the hurly-burly, the contemporary scene. Your idyllic Greek island, demi-paradise as I have no doubt it is, has very little bearing on the facts of life at Ealing Broadway. Whereas our world here pivots around Ealing Broadway, depends on Ealing Broadway, exists *for* Ealing Broadway. Now with this world you are obviously quite out of touch, you—'

'Possibly I am, but a ride in the tube would fix it, wouldn't it?'

'Oh, come on, do you really think so? In any case, I use Ealing Broadway symbolically. Look here, old chap, I'd be willing to wager you wouldn't even be *au fait* with the names of people, of places, the sequence of events, the significance of political changes that have occurred while you've been basking in the glorious Greek light, supping on the old poetic lotus. You wouldn't know the contacts any longer. The names. The attitudes. I mean, it's been all very well for you, taking life into your own hands, but these days, old boy, you just can't jump off the bus when it suits and pick it up again simply at your own convenience. I mean, all of us would jolly well love to hop off and saunter around and pick the daisies, but someone has to *drive* the ruddy bus, after all!'

'I could write you some Rip Van Winkle pieces,' I suggested drily, but he seemed to take it seriously, or perhaps it was just a way out for him.

'That isn't all that bad an idea, you know,' he said. 'Not necessarily *pieces*, but one feature might be jolly good. By Jove, yes! You coming back to the old stamping grounds, rubbing your eyes, stretching, looking around, marvelling at all the remarkable changes that have taken place while you have been out there blissfully dreaming in the sun. I'd certainly be happy to consider one good feature along those lines. Indeed I'd even consider a second piece, more the tourist angle, on your personal life out there on a Greek island. Bohemianism in the hot Mediterranean sun. The hedonists in flight from modern society. That kind of thing.'

'The usual contributors' rates?'

He laughed, but not very convincingly. 'Oh, in your case I imagine we could stretch a point for something a little better,' he said urbanely.

'I didn't really come here to try to flog the odd article,' I said. 'The problem I'm faced with is trying to get myself re-established.'

'Yes, well we *have* gone into that, haven't we? I mean you'll simply have to shop around, won't you? But I have warned you of the difficulties and I have been perfectly frank about my own position. If you like to have a stab at these features I've suggested I promise to give them my own very personal consideration . . . and, well, it would be *something* to go on with, after all, if we do accept them. I am sure you do appreciate, dear boy, that this *pro tem* is about all I can suggest. So why don't you have a good scout round, and then later perhaps we could have another little get-together. I am quite snowed under today—well, all this week in fact . . . but possibly some time soon we might have a bite at the old Press Club—the Dover sole is as excellent as ever, and the potted shrimps . . . I remember you and your potted shrimps—and then we—'

'I'm in London only occasionally,' I reminded him. 'I'm actually living down in Gloucestershire.'

'Of course. So you are. A lovely part, don't you think? Well, do give me a buzz any time, won't you? Something just might crop up. You never know, do you? Well now . . .' He was already rising, his hand extending to me its polite dismissal. 'My dear chap, it's been most exciting seeing you again. It really takes one back to the good old pleasanter days, eh? And do give my best regards to your wife. How is she? Likes being back? Adjusting?'

'Oh yes, we're all doing that,' I said. 'I'll pass on to her your good wishes.'

'Do that, dear boy,' he said and smiled me out.

After this I went in to drink a beer at the Old Bell, and then to The Codgers and on to El Vino's, but the faces were all different, and the interview with Basinghurst was even more chilling than the one with Calthrop, because he was much more brusque and offered no encouragement and only flung his final crust as I was going out of the door. 'Give me a ring next Tuesday week, if you like,' he called off-handedly. 'If you've landed nothing in the interim.'

Give me a ring next Tuesday week . . . the voice of Fleet Street. I looked in at the Cock but there were no familiar faces there either, so I went along to Old Mitre Court and slipped in to the Temple and walked around for a while under the leafless ghosts of trees in the damp gloom, looking at the fuzzy glow of lights in the legal offices, which, against the old brown brick, gave the most extraordinary sense of safety and security. You could hardly imagine a risk being taken here, or anybody jumping off the bus and just rushing off. Along King's Bench Walk the four rows of lights in the old buildings gave the curious illusion of being luminous traffic studs pegged along a wet four-lane highway, but the perspective led nowhere, only into a kind of grubby cotton-wool thing of mist and shadows. *Give me a ring next Tuesday week . . .*

I finally found myself on the Embankment, drawn to the river, so I walked slowly along almost as far as Waterloo Bridge to a damp and uncomfortable seat absurdly supported on crouching camels of cast-iron. The bridge was shiny with moisture and pale in the noonday darkness, and there was a lighted trailer-truck near me, from which two bright-faced cheery women from some charity were dispensing hot drinks, or maybe it was soup, to an aimless drift of idlers and derelicts in shabby overcoats. The cheery bright women were framed in the cheery brightness of the red cans and shiny bottles and gay labels and scrubbed paintwork of their bright dispensary, so they looked to be clipped out and pasted on the grey mount of their surroundings, more like highly-coloured reproductions of Vermeer or Van Eyck than real people.

The tide was just off the slack, the first of the ebb drawing hairlines of movement at the piles and stakes, and the rest of the river appeared to have a thick greasy skin on it, ruffled here and there like the mangy pelt of an animal where the soft seepage from a leaden overcast was more a drizzle than smog. In fact it was beginning to turn into real rain, because if I looked down quite close, near my feet, there was the faintest nervous stippling on the puddles. Southwark and Lambeth on the far side were only a bad blurry wash, a kind of long smudge, resembling a distant line of scrub more than the edge of a city, and the tugs and barges and lighters flowing down to Blackfriars Bridge were all taking the far bank and were only darker slices out of the damp dun day. *Give me a ring next Tuesday week* . . . The tugboat men and the bargees and the lightermen would all be W. W. Jacobs characters, loving the river, and you couldn't imagine any of them warping in to some dock and jumping off and rushing away. *Someone has to drive the ruddy bus . . . give me a ring next Tuesday week. If you've landed nothing in the interim . . .*

From where I was sitting I could look along to where Scott's old ship *Discovery* was lying (this, of course, was why I had chosen the seat), and she stood quite clear in the diffused gloom, her hull black and bulky like the carcase of a beached whale. It was quite a funny feeling sitting there and remembering the old ship, remembering climbing all over her more than thirty years before, when Mawson had had her, when she was lying at Station Pier, at Port Melbourne, and I was not much more than a kid and mad about ships, and just beginning to write for the old *Morning Post*. But she had been set there against sunshine and a blue sea and the gulls white and whirling out towards Gellibrand, and she had carried with her the indefinable aura of grinding pack-ice and lonely white continent and explorers' adventures and the great names and excitements, and the memory of it as I sat now in the London drizzle was tinged, too, with the innocence and wonder of my own youth, the *then* of infinite possibilities, the golden summers of childhood. Here the little ship was as lonely and lost in this cheerless, unpromising setting as the seedy derelicts adrift around the lighted trailer . . . as all of us. *Give me a ring next Tuesday week . . .*

Perhaps this was how adventurous journeys so often had to end. Perhaps the excited boy feverishly clambering around the sturdy decks back there in a lost and forgotten Melbourne had already reached the end of his journey, here in Mother London on a dismal day on Victoria Embankment, with the other scruffy deadbeats who shuffled around with no intent of aim or purpose. Certainly none of us had any intention of ringing anyone next Tuesday week. What would be the point? And in what way was I any different from them? My clothes were better, not cast-offs from earlier anonymities, but then I had dressed in my best for the interviews. Normally I wouldn't have to try that hard to look just about as scruffy as they did. I could see them all the way along the Embankment until the sequence of their hopelessness dwindled into mists, all sitting one to a bench on ridiculous florid seats identical with mine, all staring blankly at the river sliding sluggish and slow, the river which none of us could set on fire, the river which swallowed us all up and flowed on to the sea, eternal and impassive and indifferent. The river took reality and passed it along into dead time; the *Discovery* was only a forlorn memento of lost adventure, no longer the reality of adventure; the eager boy in Melbourne writing his 'Stunsail' articles about *The Glory That Was* on an old secondhand Remington had turned into a middle-aged man, tired and sick and flung on Victoria Embankment with the rest of the scarecrow jetsam.

I am no different from any of them. My cough is as bad, my breathing worse. I am a failure, and I am broke, and I have nowhere to go except cap in hand. *Someone has to drive the ruddy bus, after all!* The bastard! The contemptible bastard! He hated me really, hated me because I had escaped, because I had done what he might have done—he couldn't forgive me for that—and if he had done it *he* wouldn't have failed. He hated me because I had no right to jump off the bus and saunter round and pick the daisies. So it was all bullshit what he was saying. Nothing but bloody bullshit! He would have got me for it anyway, put the knife in, murdered me just for having done it when he hadn't . . . Oh, you resentful conventional bastard, you safe little man of straw, with your bland smile and your tight little cruel mouth and your hypocritical eyes and your whetted knives, and your careful footprints treading your circumspect little path. To where, you poor silly bastard? *To where?* The perspectives are the same, always the same. The luminous little studs on the four-lane highway, the cosy legal lights, the bus run through the daisy fields, the barges going down to Blackfriars, the sequence of dead-beats on Victoria Embankment, they all vanish into the same blurred confusion of mists and shadows.

Yet it is sad about the *Discovery* . . .

It will not be easy going back to the Cotswolds and telling all this to Cressida. And what now about the children? I fear there is another nasty time ahead. This time we shall have to face up to it, squarely, without evasion. The odd thing is that having lived for so long with the fear of its happening, it comes as a definite shock now that it *has* happened; one had been aware of the trap for a long time, but there had always been that obstinate conviction that the trap would not, after all, be sprung, that at the eleventh hour there would be reprieve, salvation, that the luck would change, that something would turn up. But now the feeling is of being pushed against the blank wall at the end of the *cul-de-sac*, unable to retrace one's steps and with nowhere else to go. Up Shit Creek was the way my brother Jack would have expressed it when we were kids together, with that grin of audacity with which, being young, he would welcome adversity, then laughingly embellish it: 'Up Shit Creek,' he would say, 'without a paddle!' Well, it has taken a long time to get there, but that's where I am all right. And no paddle. And nothing to laugh about. Maybe Morgan was the lucky one after all, getting out of it. Maybe even poor old Jefferson. Maybe the wise choice should have been made years ago when Graham Crossley had offered me the drop into Red China. That was thirteen years ago . . . and that thirteen years could be written off as a dead loss because here I was merely thirteen years older and farther than ever behind the carrot; what Calthrop justifiably called a 'cock-up', which was just his way of writing me off as a physical and professional failure—and even he didn't know about the emotional failure as well—and it made me wonder about the emissaries who'd come to the island from the Australian Dried Fruits Board, and then I was back again to thinking about Crossley and his offer, and I remembered his saying that if anything happened to me Cressida and the children would be looked after for the rest of their lives better than I could hope to look after them. Which would not be all that difficult, and would, let's face it, be pretty bloody handy right now! Especially as it is obvious that something *did* happen, because there had been a chap from Whitehall staying on the island who had told us that Crossley actually had been put into North China about ten years before and not a whisper had been heard of him since. I wonder did his briefcase vanish with him? And how was he able to get on without that pipe of his? I envy him, though . . . I imagine I have got to the stage where from the impasse any way out seems enviable. Even the river sometimes, the always flowing river, taking everything away into dead time . . .

Miriam has come in, briskly pulling at gloves and prodding up the fire and gabbling about her afternoon at St John's Wood where she goes each Monday to visit her titled but very old and impoverished great-aunt, who I understand had been a lady-in-waiting to Queen Alexandra but who now lives with five corgis, a deformed cat born with only three legs and named Tripod, and a Brazilian macaw which, Miriam asserts, swears in Portuguese. The account of the afternoon's dialogue, which sounds like something being read from the pages of Jane Austen, being terminated at last, Miriam nibbles at a biscuit, pauses over her sherry, and says, 'And now tell me, David, how was *your* day?'

I am tempted to tell her. But what would be the use? 'Not bad,' I say. 'Nothing very definite yet.'

'These things do take such a time in London. People in business nowadays are so slipshod. And irresponsible. Everything is put off.'

'Until next Tuesday week, as a rule,' I say lightly. 'Although I did see a couple of chaps.'

'Were you taken to luncheon?'

'No.'

'Then you were fortunate in that respect. Those endless pointless luncheons, my dear, they take up half the day. Where nothing, but absolutely *nothing*, is ever accomplished. They are such a nuisance. Such a complete waste of time. Still, if you can be patient with the insufferable procrastinations of such people, I am sure everything will work out splendidly. In your case, of course, there may be some delay. There is bound to be a certain diffidence.'

'What do you mean?'

'Well, they will have to offer you something rather special, won't they? You being an author, I mean. You would be much sought after, and coming from Greece and—'

'I don't think those things really make very much difference. In fact, I imagine—'

'Oh, come now, David! You surely are not suggesting that you be put on a par with people from those dreadful morning papers who keep pestering the Royal Family! No, you must just be patient. Let *them* make the approaches. After all, it's not for you to go courting them. Soliciting their favours. Is it, my dear?'

'Certainly not,' I agree. Miriam never jumped off buses, and I suppose her aged aunt never did either, for the simple reason that they had never had to ride on them. Probably they suffered and endured, like anyone else, worried, got sick, went without, improvised, pretended; yet there was something remarkable about this kind of integrity they preserved, like a cocoon of invulnerability; they could be ruined but they could not be humiliated; in relation to society they occupied a position immutably fixed, and inviolate to those mundane circumstances which should have, one would have thought, brought their outmoded artificialities crashing down. Yet Miriam traversed the Continent as if it was still the Grand Tour, knowing the right, little, and very old hotels with names like d'Angleterre or Thorp's, and staying with friends in Venice or Rapallo or Amalfi, always travelling off-season, always sending postcards, never lacking for companionship—immune, in a way, from the world's vulgarities and excesses. When she came to Greece she would travel by muleback to Bassae, before the tourist road was built, burdened by a dressing-case but staying overnight in peasants' huts in snowstorms: once she came with an elderly Anglican canon on an expedition in search of an ancient porphyry mine to which they had found obscure reference in some half-forgotten classical commentary. Miriam intrigues me by the paradox she represents: she establishes and preserves her individuality by an unswerving adherence to what, to her, are quite orthodox and conventional patterns. (We who are not indomitable and not impervious can only try to do it by rejecting what is orthodox and conventional; we turn our backs to our own society; Miriam doesn't have to because she only recognizes those elements within it that matter to her.) To Miriam, society has responsibilities and obligations to people of certain situations—not all to do with breeding or education, and not even very much with race or colour—and so she simply took it for granted that being a published author, and coming from an island in Greece, I would be, as she put it, 'much sought after'.

This quite erroneous belief had earlier led her into something of a débâcle, though it did have its funny side. (At the moment one is inclined to cherish desperately anything that has any sort of a funny side.) Soon after we came back from Greece she arranged a rather lavish dinner-party here in her house, to which she summoned a number of London's more eminent literary critics, with whom she had unspecified but obviously powerful connections. The object and purpose of her hospitality was for these critics to have the privilege of meeting me in the flesh and of becoming favourably disposed towards the novel I was about to publish.

The critics, in the event, betrayed little or no interest, either in me or the book (only one of those present at the dinner ever wrote anything about it, and then only to the extent of a few dismissive lines) and spent the bulk of the evening showing off to or scoring off each other. This so angered Miriam that she indulged herself in a kind of revenge, which still makes me laugh when I think about it, and this is certainly a day to remember laughter.

Miriam was a Bloomsbury habitué and spent quite a lot of time reading at the British Museum (it was probably here that she and the canon discovered about the porphyry mine), and during these leisure pursuits she had come across the merkin. During the night of the unfortunate dinner-party in my honour she realized that none of the assembled critics had ever heard of a merkin or knew what it was, so she deliberately embarked on a long discussion concerned with her researches, which greatly infuriated and mortified them because they did not know what she was talking about: in the end she galled them by having to explain, with punishing patience, that a merkin was a false wig of pubic hair worn by certain ladies of fashion in the eighteenth century. She teased them for their ignorance and quoted several anecdotes and an amusing lost-and-found advertisement which had appeared in a London journal giving notice of the finding, after a Garrick performance, of a used merkin in an aisle between the pit-boxes at Drury Lane. Although the critics then tried to show off to each other again in a good-humoured, bawdy theorizing about the purposes of the merkin and how it was held in place, they could not really overcome their chagrin at their ignorance, and they left early. Miriam was hugely amused and thought it would 'pay them out' for their having cold-shouldered me and my book, but by this time, of course, they had quite forgotten all about me and my book.

These thoughts passed through my mind, not altogether displeasing because related again to a childhood recollection of my brother's philosophy—'You can't win, nipper, you'll always find you're pissing into the wind!'—but the amusement, if that is what it was, lasted only briefly. Beyond the cheery glow and crackle of Miriam's fire and the incandescence of the daffodils, on the other side of the thin skin of pale panelling, was the outside world, dark and cold and depressing. Waiting.

'There doesn't seem much point,' I said, 'in my hanging around. There are a couple of chaps I might have to contact, but later, not immediately. So I might as well pop off tomorrow back to Cressida. You don't mind?'

'Not at all, my dear. She will be anxious for your news. David, winkle her out. Make her come up to town for a week or so. I quite fail to understand why she must bury herself away down there all the time. She has seen nothing of London. And I've not seen hide nor hair of her since she arrived.'

'I'll try. Can't make any promises, though. I'm not sure that she wants to come up.'

'The children, I dare say. They can be a bind. Shall you take a morning train?'

I nodded. 'The ten-ten, I thought.'

'Splendid. Then I shall drive you to Paddington Station. It will be on my way. I have the Leggatts tomorrow, at Maida Vale. Well, I suppose we should have a celebratory tipple. I am so delighted, David, that everything is working out so well after all.'

THE COTSWOLDS, 1962

Out of Evesham the wind changed and the sleet turned into snow and the higher ground along the Stanton road was already white, and at the farm the daffodils looked as if someone had begun packing them in tufts of soiled cotton-wool for transport to the flower market at Chipping Camden. Walking up from the village I could see the smoke pluming from the crooked Tudor chimney and there were beckonings of light in the narrow windows, little splinters of transparent colour like party decorations. The house was at the very edge of the village so that beyond there were no lights, and no stars either, only the heave and blackness of the high woods roaring in the wind like an ocean in tumult. Even puffing uphill against the wild cold buffeting, and with my thin city shoes soaked and squelching in the slush, I began to feel comforted. It occurred to me that this might have been one of the things one had learned by living on the island; the ability to appreciate things like this—the simpler and yet so infinitely more complex continuities of darkness and wind and storm and cold and the comfort of light and fire and warmth and the sharing of loneliness and travail. And Cressida had a great blaze of logs burning in the gratifying cavern of the hearth. Mau-Mau the cat and Harry the old big golden labrador were sleeping on the rug, twitching when a log cracked or a spark flew, with the children sprawled behind them playing Chinese Checkers. It was a good scene. I felt happy being back.

On the rickety table behind the door Cressida had savouries set out and an impressive display of drinks—whisky, gin, rum, cognac, ginger wine, sherry, soda, bitters, tonic, and half a dozen of a Saint-Emilion claret, and when I picked up a bottle to look at the label and saw it was Auzone I raised my eyebrows and whistled softly.

'What's the big celebration?' I said.

'Just you,' she said. 'You coming back. I thought it might be nice. I mean for us to celebrate. Just for once. A kind of welcome home.'

'Then it *is* nice. Well, I have a surprise, too. I bought a present for you. Over there. Unwrap it and try it on.'

'What is it?'

'It's a coat. I saw it in Harrods. It looked like you. It was there in the window and I said "That's Cress," and so I went in and bought it.'

She opened the parcel cautiously, and seemed startled, and said, 'It's suede! Darling, for heaven's sake, we can't afford a coat like this!'

'I know we can't. But I bought it anyway. Go on, put it on.'

She did and she looked beautiful in it, and she rubbed her hands slowly down the nap and said in a careful low voice as if untrusting of her words, 'It's gorgeous. It's simply gorgeous. But *why*? Why did you buy me a coat like this?'

'It's a kind of bribery,' I said lightly. 'It's for you to wear to London.'

'London?' She seemed alarmed.

'That's right. I have instructions, you see. Instructions to winkle you out. You've buried yourself down here for far too long. Now you've got to be winkled out. Miriam insists. She says it's time you had a bash at the bright lights.'

Cressida seemed about to say something, but thought better of it, and went to the window and gazed out. Soft snowflakes pressed and vanished on the glass, rhythmic impressions rather than impacts, as if the window-panes were breathing. The coat really did look marvellously becoming. So that was all right, anyway.

What did she see, looking into the blurring black of this endless winter that would not turn into spring, in spite of freakish daffodils? Did she see the shine and glitter of the Mediterranean?

The rocks and olives and prickly pear and asphodel? The peppery scatter of sage and sea and limestone, the sun on white cubistic houses, that enchanting spectrum of violets and blues and blending greens in the fluid Greek light, the dolphin-slice and phosphorescence of dark waters? The lost paradise? The faded dream? Did she listen to another music? In another room, with another person?

My heart ached as I studied her, as I saw her across that gap of past occurrence which we could no longer bridge, which we would never bridge now: having at such pains and labours fashioned the detour there was, thankfully, only its upkeep to worry about. I realize that we cannot relinquish the past, I sometimes think that secretly our longing is always to return to it, but in any case it always lurks there in its cunning ambuscades, ready to surprise us by jumping out, as fresh as ever, when we think we have forgotten. If it were not for this I suppose we should be able to dispense with the detour as well as with the bridge back, and even pretend, with a show of conviction, that nothing at all had happened.

Standing at the window in the brown suede coat one realizes what an immensely attractive woman she still is, even now when she is thirty-seven and the mother of children and harried hard by doubt and insecurity and misgiving. She is different, of course, from that young, wild, free, pagan creature of Lebanon Bay, of that earlier paradisal time of sixteen years ago. Great differences have gradually and subtly been built upon the structure of her bones (yet how lucky she was with her bones! . . . time's modellings are well suited by their armature), although one might need reference to some earlier snapshot to appreciate the extent of change and I suspect that many men would assess the accumulated differences in her present favour. There is no trace of grey yet in the brown hair still worn, unmodishly but attractively, long and loose; her figure remains lithe and slim, her legs shapely; the long English winter has not entirely deprived her of that deeply tanned Mediterranean complexion which so effectively frames the greenness of her extraordinary eyes; even a few freckles remain like neglected pools left by a receding tide in the clear gold of a sandy beach. She is still a remarkable woman.

Seeing her in the suede coat is quite different from seeing her in the casual apparel of the island ('Your wife,' Jim Galloway had said defensively, 'is a very beautiful woman,' as if this in itself was a sufficient explanation for their conduct) and it reminds me of ten years ago in a London that was not at all like London is now, and of my being so proud of being seen with her at first nights and parties. There is in love, I suspect, a constant longing to regain or to repossess any happiness that is lost, and with this there is the danger that we try to preserve something false and spurious as if it had the appearance of uninterrupted identity. But we are always undergoing a continual process of loss and reparation, which applies to our thoughts just as much as to our bodies, and the wise woman Diotima was right when she explained this to Socrates, so we can never really know what is true recollection and what has been implanted there to *seem* true.

How much easier it would be to dispense with recollection altogether – the paradise of sixteen years ago equally with the hell of the last year or two – and simply begin at this point of now: with the Cressida in a new coat of brown suede who stands at a window in a Gloucestershire farmhouse and is remarkable and beautiful and still desirable. But to do this one would have to waive that question – what does she see there looking out into the cold dark? What does she look at now?

It is possible that she is concerned only with the present problem. It has all been a long hammering disaster for her also. Not only the failure of the book we had counted on with so gullible an optimism, nor the economic trap sprung on us in consequence; not only the frustrations of trying to find some place for the children, lonely now in a strange environment grown alien to them and wistful for lost freedoms. She has, naturally, been very worried about the children. So have I. We cannot afford to pay for their education, and what is free is not very encouraging; the rigid bureaucratic system has only anticipated Calthrop's attitude in implacably discounting the unconventional background which was the children's richest asset: neither had sat for something called the 'eleven-plus' and in interview after interview with men soft of speech and cold of eye Cressida had learned that this non-conformity was in some way unforgivable. The children would have to go where they were put. Unless we could afford to pay for it ourselves the path to higher education was denied them. This, it seemed, was another of the penalties for jumping off the bus: again there was no bus to take you back when you were ready to go. Once you had voluntarily moved outside the fences of organized society it seemed very hard to move back inside again. We needed to be taught a lesson. And obviously there had to be punishments and penalties or every Tom, Dick and Harry would be jumping up and pulling the communication cord.

One thing to be thankful for was that Cressida and I very seldom quarrelled any more. But she was more withdrawn than I ever remembered her to be, with her emotions held on a tight rein. She seemed desperate for solitude. During the day, when the children had gone off to the rural secondary modern school to which officialdom had allocated them, she would take a book and shut herself off in the old study for hours. Going past the window of the room to fetch firewood, I would sometimes catch a glimpse of her seated at the big desk staring at nothing, her book unopened in front of her. Or she would take long solitary walks in the high woods with Harry the dog we had temporarily inherited, and sometimes at night she would go out under the frosty chink of stars to help the farmhands with the lambing on the cold hills. She was friendly with the farmhands and an old wizened gardener and a gamekeeper and the shepherd at Chestnut Farm, as if the only real accord she could find was with simple people living to simple elemental rituals. She had not turned her face to the wall exactly, but she had turned it away from one kind of reality and seemed to seek for some other reassurance elsewhere. She was not happy. Neither of us was. Miriam was right, of course. She had to be winkled out.

She turned at last and said, 'How did you get on in London?' Her voice was low and tentative.

'We'd better talk about it later,' I said, 'when the children have gone to bed. What about this celebration? Why don't we broach some of this grog?'

'Let's.' She smiled then. 'Thank you for the coat, David. I really do love it.'

Later I told her about London, not keeping anything back. 'So you see why I had to buy you that coat, don't you? It was compulsive. To prove something, I suppose, like saying bugger 'em. I don't know quite how to explain it but—'

'I understand.' She reached out and touched my hand gently. She paused. 'You said we couldn't afford it. Does this mean . . . well, do we have *any* money left?'

'Oh, a few quid still. Not much. What's the difference? It would take a bloody sight more than thirty guineas to save *our* bacon. At the moment, the coat's more important. We'll get by. The Lord provides.'

'I do hope so,' said Cressida. 'Because now there's something I have to tell you. That money you gave me . . . well, what was left over I'm afraid I blew it all on that liquor there. All I had left. Like you and the coat, I suppose. I just thought, why not?'

'Oh Jesus!' I said and we both laughed. It had been a long time since we had laughed together. Really laughed. 'It *is* terribly corny, isn't it?' I said. 'Like that awful O. Henry story. Hell, never mind. What does it matter? Something is bound to turn up.'

'Micawber!' she said, but we were very close then, happier with each other, I think, than we had been for a good many years, just the two of us together again and isolated once more from worlds that were intrusive and brutal and destructive. We drank two bottles of the Auzone, and we stayed together for a long time, on the rug where the dog and cat slept, until the fire was only a scatter of dull rubies in a pyramid of pale ash. The world outside was black and cold and howling, but it did not affect us.

By morning the snow was deep and the smoke from the village chimneys laid a pearly drift across an almost Oriental landscape, and the postman trudging up the hill pushing his bike dragged a black snaky trail behind him through the whiteness. There were a couple of letters and a heavy package for me. One of the letters was from Tom Kiernan.

> Davy:
>
> Heard you were back in the Old Dart and having a bit of a tough trot. Had intended contacting you to tell you how impressed I was by your novel. Those bastards of reviewers, though! Authors ought to be entitled to sue when pricks like that obviously don't even bother to read the book, or if they do, miss the point entirely. Or do they only write for one another, and for their little pansy cliques? This country really has gone an awful shade of grey. Anyway, I am sending under separate cover a book that might cheer you up a bit. You keep plugging, mate. And don't let 'em take your kidney fat. Salaams to Cress and the kids.
>
> Tom

The book was a beautiful and very expensive volume on Chinese art and culture – the kind of sumptuous book that always made my mouth water but which I seemed never able to afford – and when I passed it across to Cressida she said, 'Sweet Tom. What a nice thing to do.' She began to riffle through the glossy pages, and I was thumbing open the other letter when I heard her gasp, and as I looked across she whispered, 'David, *look*!' A rectangle of white paper had fallen to the rug and there was another in her fingers, and they were unquestionably £5 notes, and we were both quite stunned for a time, but later we went through the book and there were forty of the banknotes dispersed neatly through the pages – £200, but no note from Tom or even inscription on the fly-leaf.

'Well, Mr Micawber, you were right, weren't you?' said Cressida, her eyes filling. 'Something did turn up. Oh David, oh darling —' she choked on a sob as she reached out to me – 'we are lucky, aren't we? We are. We really are.'

SYDNEY, 1968

The curious thing is that what one remembers best out of the worst of times is quite likely to be the events like that, rather than the periods of torture and doubt and nightmare, which perhaps is just as well, otherwise we might find it pretty difficult to go on. So those months in the Cotswolds in Beatrice's borrowed house have now, over the years, become a time to look back to almost pleasantly, a time of apples crinkling in a big basket and beer and darts at the inn and the fruit trees a sea of blossom in the valley and the cry of the Hunt plangent in the green hills. What it was really like—the torment and the terrors, the sleepless nights, the very hopelessness of it all—is no longer recapturable.

Time has this effect—the memorizing part of our minds anyway—of changing the shapes behind us at least as much as it keeps on changing our physical bodies, or will change the shapes in store for us. In the end we have to rely on fancy for what actually happened back there along the way. For whatever *did* happen has now an imaginary existence; it is no longer what it was, it has become only an image we are able to manipulate.

I was reflecting on this today, staring into an electric radiator we have. When it is on a certain switch there is a picture in the curved metal behind the element which is exactly like a beautiful pinnacled city skyline at evening, a perfect evening, brown against gold in a wonderful luminous light. It is a city of spires and palaces and pointed roofs and gateways, serene and harmonious in this tranquil, magical light: if it were real one would like nothing more than to move across to it and walk around. It reminds me very much of the real silhouettes of real cities which I have seen at moments of such unusual splendour. Venice was one, I remember, looking across from the steps at Santa Maria della Salute; the slender spires of the Wren churches prickling a London skyline seen from the Southwark bank one June evening was another. Once in Rome, from the top of the Spanish Steps. Another of

New York in summer, from the Staten Island ferry. Now these were all completely real experiences at one time, but if they are to have any existence at all now they have to be entirely re-imagined; they have become no different from the fancied city of reflected light and metal in the electric radiator. They are no more and no less a condition of the imagination. Perhaps they are no longer even *as* real as my imagined city in the fire. At least I can evoke this one at will. And by moving my head a little from one side to the other, or up and down, I can make subtle changes in the architecture and turn spires into turrets. Erect walls. Or throw them down.

One must be careful, of course, to avoid doing this with one's own experiences.

So we shall cancel out much of what actually happened in Gloucestershire, because it led nowhere really, and was a bad time for all of us and a bad time to think about. Cressida finally was winkled out and did go to London to stay with Miriam, and it was while she was away that Calverton called. He had been to Bristol to see some young actress who had been working with the Old Vic but found she had gone on to Stratford so he was on his way there when he called in. He now had a blue Porsche and since the children were away at school he drove me in to Broadway so we could have luncheon together, doing ninety-eight on one reasonably straight stretch of the narrow road. He had grown older but very much better-looking in the two years since I had last seen him, and he drove faster and talked faster. There was some drastic and decisive change in him since Greece, but I could not at first put my finger on it. In the cocktail-bar before luncheon he drank double Scotches and chain-smoked, but his hands were steady and he had himself in good control. It was not until we were in the dining-room that I realized how upset he was by what he seemed to regard as my defection.

'You can't spend ten years of your life doing something and then simply toss it all away,' he protested. 'And what's the sense in coming back to a bloody dump like this? Do you just want to go down the dreary plughole like everyone else?'

'We were going down the plughole in Greece,' I said. The waiter was over his shoulder, impatient for us to order, but wearing the uniform mask of a polite servility. The mask was there, one realized, as shield to his own grievances and ulcers and fears and anxieties, a part of his livelihood, not merely to safeguard him from charges of living in a bloody dump and going down a dreary plughole. To test him out I looked up at him and said, 'I suppose you've got your problems too?'

'Oh, mustn't grumble, sir,' he said, with a smile as faint and unobtrusive as another button on his vest. 'May I take the liberty of recommending the trout today, gentlemen?'

'See,' I said, when he had gone off with the order and we were waiting for the drink waiter. 'He's got the right attitude. You don't grizzle. You just put up with it.'

'Bullshit!' said Calverton. 'What do you really know about *him*? He might believe in the trout. He might believe in himself, for all you know. He might have dreams of owning his own little place somewhere some time. He might be quite prepared to go on being obsequious and to tolerate bastards like you and me because one day he'll be able to thumb his nose at us whenever he wants to.' His eyes followed the waiter. 'Besides, I am an actor,' he said, 'therefore all acting is admirable.'

'Then good luck to him,' I said, and the drink waiter came, and since we were making a thing of it Calverton ordered a bottle of Pouilly Fuissé and a château-bottled Margaux, and we talked for a while about the Loire and about a trip Cressida and I had made years before to the Médoc, but obviously the subject of my defection was still gnawing at Calverton, because he cut across the conversation to say, 'You've got to get back to Greece, you know.'

'I realize that,' I said. 'I'll have to, to sell up the house, since it's the only asset we have now.'

'That's not what I meant. I mean going back there to get on with your writing.'

I shook my head. 'We tried that. It doesn't work.'

'You don't believe in yourself any longer?'

'For Christ's sake, it isn't anything to do with belief in oneself! It didn't work out, that's all. It was just a dream that didn't come off . . . the dream we all have that doesn't come off. I mean, I did give it a go. Eight years should be long enough. Now it's a question of survival.'

'Well, I'll tell you something, mate – you won't survive over here. Not in this rat-race. Not now. Besides, you opted out.'

'Funny you saying that. It's what they told me in Fleet Street. I jumped off the bus and wandered round to pick the daisies. Now they won't let me back aboard.'

'Then you be bloody thankful. Look,' he went on earnestly, 'do you know what it's really like back in this place? In this bloody jungle? Do you know what's happened to it, what's happened to people, what's happened to all of us in the last ten years? You walk around the streets now and smell what's in the air. Rot and decay and filth and corruption. The scummy values that are spread over everything like a rancid paste. You come and walk with me round Notting Hill Gate some night, or we'll take in some strip clubs in Soho. You come and take a good look at what's behind this lip-service bullshit about progress and social enlightenment. London's changed. Or maybe it's just that we've changed. Maybe it's all right if you're young, but we're not young any more, and anyway how long do you think you would last with your bloody chest in this bloody climate! Eh? In the smog with all the shit flying around!'

'I don't have very much choice, do I?'

'There's no coercion.'

'And at least one isn't an alien here.'

'No? I've got news for you, mate. When it's on the line you are. If that's what is worrying you the only place for you is back home.'

'Home?'

'Australia.'

'No, thanks. Too far. Just too bloody far.'

'You don't have much choice then, do you? You don't really have any place to go, so you'd better stay where you are. In Greece, I mean.'

I let him talk on, half listening to him, because he was only ploughing backwards and forwards over the same ground—which I had been doing myself for long enough—and the more you ploughed the more the furrows seemed alike, whether you looked backwards or looked forward. I realized suddenly what the change was in Archie which I had sensed earlier but had failed to identify. His spirit had come to a standstill. He was reluctant any longer to move forward because there was nothing ahead but a pattern of stale repetition, and whatever the rewards that went with it, it could only move him further away from youth with its hopes and bright ambitions, from dreams, from the golden sunsets. He was, I suspected, in the classic dilemma of the dislodged: he could not belong. And he was the type who never went back. He was no longer like a stone aimed with deliberate purpose, as Kiernan still was, but had become a pebble loosened on the hillside, still in motion, but falling at random with only chance to decide where it might finally come to rest. This was probably the explanation for his vehemence about me.

'What you've got to do,' he was saying, 'is to grab yourself a bit more time.'

'Yes, but it's easier said than done,' I said. 'That's really what we've been trying to do for years. Buy ourselves little bits of time. But it's hard to get. And very precious. And highly expendable.' It was the thing that got you most in Europe, that the worthwhile things about Europe, the rich and beautiful things, had all taken a lot of time to be put together, and they hadn't been made by people like Calthrop the bus-driver (or by David Meredith either!), but perhaps my trouble had been that the time I had gained I had used in the wrong way—by writing the wrong things, or by sitting in the sun drinking wine when I should have been working, or by watching the kids run, or being in love with my wife, or talking about nothing with mule-men and sponge-divers, or sitting in boats trying to work out that precise moment when the octopus turns from pink to grey at the instant the fisherman bites its eye out. Perhaps in the eight years on the island I should have made much more purposeful use of the time I was able to buy for myself. Life, after all, was more than siestas on hot afternoons, and quiet evening promenades, and night-long conversations over copper beakers of retsina; clearly if you wanted to get on there had to be a very serious intent in the employment of time. Benjamin Franklin said, 'Time is money', and founded the *Saturday Evening Post*. Without any question it was essential to be very Kiplingesque about filling the unforgiving minute if you really wanted to make a success of things.

Yet here was Calverton, who had used available time in furious pursuit of fame and fortune, now sad and disaffected and not knowing where he was going, or why, and the only peace he had known was when he had come to the island to find the healing balm of unoccupied time. And the kind of time you remembered in the end tended to be like that, the separated moments that fell away from ambition, or rejected it, or preceded it. Calverton would still have his cherished memory of the island, of himself tranquil at a table listening to the silence, just as I often thought of childhood and the sort of time that had kites drifting in the sky and I in short pants lying on the ground nibbling at onion-grass. Sometimes I saw the crimson crab, tiny as a jewel, in the rock pool at Lebanon Bay where I had made love to Cressida; at other times I remembered a spring afternoon on the island after a storm of unparalleled violence, when the sun came out and everything was hushed and still, even the birds, and every flint and stone and leaf shone in a radiance of golden magic, and it was like standing on the threshold of the beginning of the world. Benjamin Franklin wouldn't convince me that time was money; because each was only part of the eternal conflict and balance between opposites—life and death, good and evil, the *yang* and the *yin*, reality and appearance, love and hate, war and peace, matter and spirit, time and money . . . They were even bringing it up to date now, establishing new laws of difference—hallucinating instead of remembering, the psychedelic in place of the nostalgic. Not that the laws had any final bearing on the matter. In the end time had the last say . . .

It had begun to rain heavily while I had been thinking and

the room had darkened and the waiter came and switched on some half-concealed lights which printed yellow fans like mustard stains along the walls and gave the illusion of night. He walked to the window and stared out, frowning, then pulled the curtain, and this seemed to accentuate the watery sounds from outside. The wet tyres of passing cars sounded as if somebody in another room was slowly and carefully sandpapering a table ready for the french polishing.

Calverton said, 'If you were given another year on the island, what would you do. 'Have a go at another book?'

'Yes,' I said.

He nodded and examined the ruby glint in his glass of Margaux. The faintly flowery bouquet of the wine and the smell of the Gauloises he smoked and the sound of the rain made me think of France. Of Dieppe, actually, which was odd, because it had been raining at Newhaven and not at Dieppe, and at Dieppe Cressida and I had drunk *calvados*, not wine. 'Listen, then, I'll tell you what,' he said nervously. 'I'll shout you another chunk of time. Your sort of time.'

'What do you mean, you'll shout me?'

'I mean I'll kick in with the fares back to Greece for the four of you. And I'll give you a thousand quid.[8] That should see you through for a year. That'll give you a chance to find out, won't it?' He pushed the thought at me truculently, 'I mean even if it just gives you the time to make the fare to somewhere else.'

So in this way, aggressively, almost as though he hated both of us for the situation forced upon us, it was Calverton once again who came to the rescue, just as he had in that other bad time three years earlier.

We live, as someone has said, within the torn edges of our own predicaments. Sometimes we are lucky, though, and a Calverton is there with us.

Did Calverton see that David still had what David noticed he lost?

THE ISLAND, 1959

Meredith's coming back to the island from Big Grace's he arranged with some care, so that it should seem to have no connection with any suddenness of impulse. Because he wanted specifically not to surprise Cressida—fearing perhaps that surprise might work also and worse against himself—he sent a telegram in advance warning her of his intention. He carried from Georgaikis a long list of instructions, together with a good supply of the drugs he would be needing, and hypodermic syringes and needles of the type and brand specified by the physician. Grace, concealing her misgivings, drove him to Piraeus to catch the morning steamer.

A thrilling sense of excitement and freedom gripped Meredith as the trim white ship slid across the pale polish of the harbour through all the bustle and bravura of a Greek maritime morning, the whistlings and the whipping flags (why, he wondered happily, did the Greek ensign always look decorative rather than chauvinistic? why did it always seem to summon up bright brisk breezes to snap out the absolute *rightness* of its blue and white stripes?), the fussiness of island steamers and the impudence of tugs, the passengers settling with their calico-sewn baskets and parcels, and wheels of glossy bread and sesame-sticky sweets and clicking *kombollois*, and the two sorts of women, the peasant women nervous under their black headkerchiefs and the others with their jewels and sophisticated hairdos settling at saloon tables around packs of playing-cards.

But the anticipatory sense of pleasure had deserted Meredith before the steamer was abreast of Salamis; indeed, had begun to desert him at the moment of passing out beyond the breakwater, when the ship bounded forward with a sudden eager growling of engines, an unleashment of power that corresponded at once with the sharp knifing slap of the short Saronic seas as the bow swung over towards Aegina. As if it were forcing him to a commitment; as much as to say that there was no turning back now. Nor was there, in fact. The waterfront at Piraeus was no longer visible. Big Grace, anyway, would long since have climbed into her car and driven off. Even the Acropolis and Lycabettos were only fainter rubbings in the smudge to the northward. With every thud and tremor and wave-slap he was being hurried and bustled farther and farther away from the calm rituals of the quiet house at Metz, from the ordered regularities of Dr Georgaikis's clinic, from the set disciplines of healing. With every flung shower of rainbowed spray arching across the crowded foredeck he must move that much farther from that peace of mind which Georgaikis had seen as the essential nostrum.

Besides a general despondency Meredith now had a particular nervous trepidation, part of which was concerned with what he might expect to find upon his return to the island and part with what Cressida might be expected to think of this return which, in spite of his telegram, must still seem to her both sudden and unexpected. Still, the sending of the telegram, he told himself rather uncomfortably, forestalled the possibility, itself a kind of cliché, of catching them by surprise, and he hoped might prevent Cressida from feeling that it was suspicion that had dragged him back, or that he was only coming home, in effect, to spy on her. Even so, surely it would seem strange to her, strange to all of them, that Georgaikis's plan for his treatment, which had been specific enough, should have suffered so soon so drastic a revision . . .

He looked up with a start into a swarthy moustachioed smile that was offering him raffle tickets against a beguiling fan of ten giant bars of chocolate; Meredith was so relieved at this interruption to his uncomforting thoughts that he bought twenty drachmae worth of tickets; the smile became a crow of triumph as a scatter of what were claimed to be specially fortunate numbers was spread out on the table before him.

Later he went out on deck again to watch the passage through the gap between the islands just before Poros would reveal itself—he always liked to see the swirling swing of islands and mainland formally interchanging like setpieces on a revolving stage, pivoting on the buoy marking the end of the reef—and he would look up to the right, searching along the flank of the mountain that resembled a sleeping woman, above the sickle arm of Vidhi, searching for that first glimpse of the little scattering of white, like bird droppings, which was the site of ancient Troezen, where Theseus had been king. He had done this, with an almost juvenile satisfaction, and was turning to take in the Poriot scene, the spill of coloured houses down below the clocktower and the sails crowding in the narrow strait, when he heard the voice crying '*Saranda októ! Saranda októ!*' and rummaged through the raffle tickets he had stuffed into his pocket and saw number forty-eight among them. He raised his arm and called, and the swarthy smile brought him the ten great bars of chocolate which his lucky ticket had won for him, so he had to rummage again for another ten drachmae as gratuity to the ticket-seller.

His luck in winning the raffle at once banished anxiety and despondency; the feeling of self-satisfaction became a continuance of his juvenile pleasure in finding Theseus's ancient kingdom exactly there where he had expected it. Suddenly he felt happy again to be going home, and now ridiculously pleased and excited that Julian and Miranda should have as a homecoming gift from their father something as improbable, as spectacular, and as auspiciously gained as ten huge bars of chocolate. In the childishness of superstitious delight he found benevolent omens for health and well-being, prosperity, for general happiness, and this new buoyancy of his spirits prevailed for the rest of the journey and through his arrival at the island, where he was delighted to find them all on the quayside to greet him—Cressida and the two children and Archie Calverton—and even the fact that Galloway was there also, grinning at him from a discreet background, caused him no twinge of dismay. The children were suitably stirred by the sheer *quantity* of chocolate, and the others were all gratifyingly agreed that he looked well, that he looked better than for months past, that putting on a bit of weight certainly suited him, that he looked ten years younger, that his eyes were clear and his colour good, that the change in Athens had worked wonders for him, that in spite of all this he must be overjoyed to be back home again. Cressida clung to him tightly and assured him that she, at least, was very happy he was home again.

The others had the discretion to move off, and the children went on ahead up the narrow lane towards the house bearing the chocolate and the luggage, and he walked home hand in hand with his wife, convinced that he had been totally mistaken in what he had suspected but convinced, too, of his rightness in returning; those auspices which had been revealed to him aboard the ship in the completeness of their benevolence continued to seem entirely propitious.

For a week Meredith was thoroughly justified in these conclusions; the routine of his affairs seemed hardly different from what it had been in Big Grace's house; in some ways it was even more domestic because now, with Cressida giving him his needles at home, there was no need even to go out to attend the clinic. Cressida adhered strictly to the regimen which Dr Georgaikis had laid down in his meticulous list of instructions. He was allowed to do a certain amount of work on his book, but otherwise there were stipulated times for rest, for the taking of his drugs, for sleep. In the evenings he could spend an hour or so in the company of the others on the waterfront, usually outside Evangeli's tavern, where he would take a glass or two of wine, but he and Cressida would go back to the house early and after a light meal he would retire to his bed. Cressida would sit up, as he thought, to read, but one night when he was wakened by a severe fit of coughing and went downstairs to refill the water-pitcher he was surprised to find that Cressida was not there, although the kerosene lamp was still burning by the book open on the table, and it was almost midnight. He took the filled pitcher and returned to the bedroom and waited there in some agitation, standing beside the window until she returned. She came home a little before one o'clock, and he watched her approaching from some distance down the narrow moonlit lane. She was quite alone and she walked in a pondering, unhurried way. He had got back into bed by the time she came upstairs, and he said nothing to her, pretending to be asleep but watching her through the slits of his eyes as she took her clothes off, very softly crooning a song to herself. He saw that her hair was wet, so he assumed she had gone to the rocks to swim, as she often did when the nights were warm. Before his illness they had always gone together, relishing these private intimate midnights and their undisputed possession of the cool silken blackness of the rocks beside the cave, the alchemy of the starlight in the water and the misty assembly of the islands, their naked bodies aswirl in the cold fire of phosphorescence above mysterious watery continents of rock. Now beside him her body beneath the loosely tossed sheet felt cool and he imagined that he could smell the cold salty fragrance of the night sea clinging to her naked flesh. She fell at once into quiet sleep, while he thought of her slim form rising from the water at the rock steps, cascading streams of icy light, then standing in front of him, stretching her arms up to the spangled sky, a speck of phosphorescence still clinging to her thigh, bright and dancing like a diamond. The image faded, but he slept poorly, wondering and worrying.

At breakfast next morning she told him without any probing on his part that she had gone swimming. It had been, she said, a night of fantastic phosphorescence. He asked her if she had gone alone, and she said, 'I went down on my own, yes, it was so terribly hot and stuffy up here, but evidently others felt the same way, because by midnight there was almost a crowd.'

'Oh, who was there?' he asked casually.

'That young lot from the Cabana, some of them were there for a while. The girls wouldn't go in in the dark because one of them had seen an octopus caught there on the rocks.'

'The Greeks don't really care for night swimming. Nobody else there?'

'Only Jim,' she said. 'He came down just after they'd gone.'

'Then you did have some company,' he said in the same casual way. 'I didn't hear you come in,' he added.

'You were sleeping. Oh, we didn't stay there. Just long enough to cool off. It was about one when I got back here.'

He changed the subject, reminding her to write out some recipes for island dishes which she had promised to post to Big Grace.

Jim Galloway, like Calverton, had long outstayed his intentions. Calverton had come to the island originally seeking the physical anodyne of rest and some spiritual rehabilitation; Galloway's impingement had been by chance – his head-long collision with the carnival exuberance of the Hero's festival – but both men had found themselves happily attuned to the life the island had to offer and seemed anxious to postpone any return to worlds which, while more prosperous, were also far more demanding. Each man, however, had found his particular solaces. Calverton, in settling for a tranquil indolence, had moved into a kind of provisional limbo which was his escape from the prices and pressures which fame and fortune exacted and exerted. Galloway filled his new environment with an immense gusto, with vigour, laughter, virility and appetite to match his own giant proportions. He had rented a rambling, tumbling, whitewashed stone house that seemed to teeter on the lip of a great limestone crag which jutted over the little harbour: he loved the spectrum of lichens that streaked the faded apricot tiles of its sagging roof, the tangle of prickly pear and aloe that invaded askew walls as thick and white as ice-cream, the winds that buffeted around it, the rambling frugality of its big clean airy rooms, the godlike vision displayed below and around him of the picturesque harbour and the island-bossed Aegean. Here he worked furiously on his drawings and sketches of the island's architecture, with the products of his energetic labours scattered across the floors or thumbtacked in crazy collages on the plastered walls. He sought his pleasures with equal voracity. He had become an adept at the vigorous, individualistic Greek dancing, and almost every night in some tavern or another was a passionate performer. He sang, talked, laughed, jested, drank, gave parties, swam, and walked the length and breadth of the little island with no stint to his exuberance. If he was sometimes exhausting he was always kind and generous and outgiving, and with his infectious zest for life was well liked by everybody.

Consequently there was considerable surprise shown by most of the little group of expatriates gathered at midday outside the post-office, in the second week after Meredith's unexpected return from Athens, when Galloway indicated the imminence of his return to the United States.

'I figure to go early next week,' he said. 'So Saturday's the big farewell party. At my house. Everybody is expected.'

Meredith, startled, glanced quickly at Cressida and saw that she accepted the news coolly; indeed her gaze was fixed, empty and absent, on something far out to sea, as if she had not heard.

'Pretty sudden, isn't it?' said Calverton.

'I guess that's the way you've got to operate on deals like this. Wham! Make the decision and go through with it. It's been swell here, it's been terrific, but Great Sodom calls. Life goes on, and the merciless hunt for that almighty dollar. Don't worry, though, my swan song will be strident enough so you won't have to just remember my silences.'

Cressida smiled at him, gently and a little wistfully, and said, very quietly, 'We'll all miss you,' then looked across to the steps of the post-office and said, 'They've sorted the mail. I'll go and see if there's anything.'

Meredith realized that she had already been aware of Galloway's intentions: there was a kind of frozen acceptance in her expression that told him all he needed to know. He saw it quite clearly now. They had been lovers during his enforced absence in Athens, but since his return they had imposed on themselves a scrupulous morality, but one or the other of them, perhaps both, found this immaculate continence no longer endurable. Meredith had seen little of Galloway since his return, and for all his watchfulness he had detected nothing in Cressida's behaviour to which he could take exception. Even when she had gone swimming at night she had volunteered the truth and had not tried to deceive him in any way. Or had she? How could he know what had actually taken place? There had been time enough. He had only her word for it, after all. And there had been all the other nights, when he had slept, the days when he had rested, suspecting nothing . . .

The farewell party in the clifftop house had all the qualities to attract virtually every foreigner on the island. Galloway's personal popularity, his reputation as a generous host, and the nature of the occasion would have been sufficient, but Meredith sickeningly suspected that they were lured also by the unmistakable scent of drama: in a milieu as artificial, as confined, and as malicious and incestuous as this it would be surprising at the very least if the others did not know, or at any rate suspect, the illicit liaison between Galloway and Cressida[9] – it was classically expectable that the injured husband should be the last to know – and although the party had been set for an unusual hour, in the middle of the day after the post had been cleared, all the guests arrived with a punctuality that was unusual and even faintly indecent.

In one respect they were disappointed. If there was drama it remained in concealment. It was a crowded noisy party and quickly became a drunken one. Galloway had been lavish with his many dishes of *mezédes*, what he called 'the blotting-paper', but still more lavish with the liquor, having provided many large pitchers of a very strong Martini, a great bowl of powerful brandy punch, and also Scotch, bourbon and Bloody Marys, so that the normal standbys of retsina and kokkinelli and the local wines were more or less neglected in favour of these exotic and more potent dispensings. Meredith reflected a little sadly that the pattern of island parties was, like everything else, drastically changing.

Galloway was a gay and scrupulous host, attentive to all his guests. He was good-humoured and exuberant. He showed no special interest in Cressida, who seemed a little withdrawn but otherwise normal and pleasant. Yet Meredith sensed a measure of artificiality and tension in each of them; there was a hint of tautness behind their polish, a false ring to Galloway's laughter and good-fellowship, they were like actors in the last act of the last night of a failed played, playing it out for the final curtain.

After he had been there for about an hour Meredith found the situation becoming insupportable, and this made it more difficult for him to remain abstemious in the face of the uninhibited carousing.

He took Cressida aside and said, 'Listen, I'm going to push

off. This is no good for me. I should have a rest anyway, and—'

'I'll come with you,' she offered quickly, but he raised his hand. 'There's no need for *you* to come,' he said. 'You'd prefer to stay a while, wouldn't you?'

'Yes, I would, rather. If you're sure . . .'

'You stay,' he said bravely. 'Enjoy yourself. I'll go back home and stretch out for a couple of hours. I don't need a needle until five.'

'I'll be back by then,' she said. 'But I really would like to stay on a bit, if you're positive that—'

'Have a good time,' he said, and kissed her, and thanked Galloway and took his leave.

He was restless when he did get back to the house and pottered aimlessly from room to room instead of going to his bed. The children were off somewhere, the house empty, yet the quiet rooms seemed swollen by the presence of Cressida and his own absences, and in the awful hollow of these absences another figure moved, a tall strong figure, bearded and brown, with a flash of white teeth, roaring with laughter. Through the open doors he could hear in the courtyard the high-pitched *threek-eek-eek-eek* of the cicadas, chorusing their screams at him, then all stopping at once, as if taunting him to shriek a reply, and starting up again on a rising cadence of derision. He had the feeling, as he slunk through his own domain with invisible things deriding him, of skirting some awesome chasm, dark and unfathomable, and at length he identified this dreadful void, intimidating and unknown, as that secret part of Cressida, interdicted to him, which over the long years he had never known, had failed to penetrate, which had always remained beyond his reach, incomprehensible.

He went down to the cool dark kitchen and found some stale wine still left in a wicker flagon, a cheap bulk *erythros*, and poured himself a drink, and then another.

She had not returned by five o'clock, so he put water in the old saucepan and lit the kerosene burner and boiled up the hypodermic syringe and two of the needles, and when he had filled the syringe the way he had watched Cressida do it he unbuckled his belt and dropped his trousers on the kitchen floor and tried to give himself the injection. He reached behind and lunged the needle above his right buttock with a kind of sullen, violent bravado, but he struck clumsily and the needle clicked on a bone and broke off; he jumped back with a sharp cry and his clenching fingers snapped the thin glass of the syringe. He cursed aloud as he tried with a trembling hand to wipe from his flesh the sticky mess of blood and glass fragments and trickling streptomycin. Now he did feel like screaming back at the cicada chorus.

It took him some time to extract the length of broken needle and to staunch the blood and clean the broken glass and mess from his body and the floor, and by the time he had got his trousers on and set off for Galloway's house he was in a state of maddened despair.

He went by way of the back lanes and steps, avoiding the waterfront which would be crowded after the siesta, and as he limped and panted through pale ravined walls still holding the hurting glare of the summer day he suffered torments of pain and anger, misery, shame, self-pity, humiliation, and a hopeless, desperate wish to find some conclusion to his trials.

The party, he saw, had in his absence advanced as might have been expected. Some of the earlier guests were no longer present but of those who had remained all testified in varying degrees to the lavishness of Galloway's hospitality. The pitchers had been emptied. Pulp and rinds of fruit formed a thick neglected scum in the punch bowl, there was a nasty mash of soggy cigarette stubs in the silver ladle, and butts and ash littered indiscriminately among the picked-over platters of food. Galloway, who seemed not to have moved from his earlier position by the table, presided over the festive wreckage, a little unsteady but outwardly as urbane and jovial as ever.

There was an immediate and curious lull in the raucous conversation as Meredith entered, which dwindled to an instant of absolute silence. Everyone looked at him expectantly as he stared around.

'Hi!' Galloway's call was hearty and his grin welcoming as he lifted his hand, but Meredith ignored him. Cressida was nowhere in the room. Talk buzzed again for a moment, as erratic and shrill and meaningless as the pinging of an insect against a window-pane, then silence fell once more and every eye was fixed on him as he walked slowly across to the door of Galloway's bedroom and opened it.

She was by herself in the room, staring at the wall, seated on the edge of Galloway's bed, her hands folded in her lap and her sandalled feet neatly together, almost in an attitude of exaggerated decorum, quite still, her head slightly tilted as if listening to something. He closed the door gently and leaned back against it and tried to control his breathing as he looked at her. She seemed unaware of his coming, and Meredith, having expected her to start up in guilt and surprise, was shocked by her inattention to his presence. Then, as he waited and watched her, he felt weak and helpless and sick, for he saw in her eyes that secret private look he had seen only a few times before – at Lebanon Bay many years back, on the fringe of the night-moving surf, in the room at Lerici above the empty moonlit square with the crooked clock-tower when the three funny old men had piped and jigged themselves away, in Siena against the tinkling drift of Scarlatti from a distant harpsichord. Cressida's look. The look that locked him out and kept him away. She turned her head at last and smiled across at him in faint, detached recognition.

'I've come to take you home,' he said, keeping his voice steady.

'I don't think I want to go home just yet,' she replied. She spoke quietly, as if out of a reverie, spacing her words with care as she often did when she had been drinking. He noticed too that her eyes, while they acknowledged him, seemed not quite to focus on him, as if he was a point to talk at, not a person.

'I'm taking you home all the same,' he retorted. 'Come on,' he said roughly. 'Let's get going.'

To his surprise she gave a tiny quick nod of acquiescence and rose meekly from the bed. She stood with only a suggestion of unsteadiness and a fleeting smile, cryptic and personal, touched her mouth and vanished. 'Is it five yet?' she asked in a tone of calm inquiry.

'Long past,' he said curtly. 'When you hadn't come I tried to give myself the needle. I buggered it all up!' he added furiously.

She gave no indication that she had been listening. Nor did she make any move towards the door. She stood where she was, swaying imperceptibly, looking around the bare, light room as if she might memorize for ever each last separate detail of its appearance – the warps and nubbled patchings of the plaster on the walls, the broken lozenges of wood in the oiled Spanish ceiling, the wonderful irregularities of jamb and lintel, cracked tiles on a window ledge, the lopsided hang of the heavy shutter bars. She seemed to be soaking herself in the thick saturating atmosphere of something blissful but evanescent which in its physical death might still be preserved in the spirit and stored away everlastingly.

'For God's sake, come on!' he said, furious with her and flung the door wide to a sudden hush in the room without. She followed him obediently, and together they moved out through the waiting silence and the watchful eyes. She followed him like a somnambulist, staring fixedly ahead as if sighting on some invisible beckoning marker. She was a little drunk and set her feet down with a faint air of exaggerated care, as someone does when walking on a narrow plank or across stepping-stones, and perhaps because of this concentration she made no sign to Galloway as they moved across the room. Meredith nodded to him stiffly. Galloway stood rigid at the window, his mouth open. He looked as if he wanted to say something but closed his mouth instead, began to move forward, then stopped abruptly. Meredith opened the door for his wife and as he went through after her he heard Galloway call out, 'Are you two all right?'

He made no reply as he slammed the door and followed Cressida down the winding tunnel of the whitewashed steps. They took the same route through the back alleyways by which he had come to the house, and they walked home together without speaking. The silence was maintained while Cressida found the spare hypodermic and sterilized it and gave him his injection, and then the children came home from their walk to Piso, and Meredith went into the courtyard and sat beneath the thick green cavern of the summer vines while she prepared their supper.

He had retreated to the calm enclosure within the high walls because he wished to steady himself and assemble grave, implacable words and charges for the confrontation, but his mind grew more confused and frantic in the solitude; a random muddle of thoughts reared and plunged and shied away like frightened animals; he sought desperately to dwell on trivialities, grasped at every intrusion from the mundane, clutched at irrelevancies and stroked them like fingered beads. From the kitchen drifted the accustomed evening sounds, the hollow groan and gurgle of water being ladled from the great earthenware jar, the clatter of plates and dishes—that melodic *cliquetis d'assiettes* of Rabelais, he thought, clutching at digression—the whirring of an egg-beater blending with the insistent lazy buzzing of a few late noisy wasps above his head buried to their bellies in the browning grapes. A leaf, more yellow than green, fell soundlessly to the garden table, one of the old-time coffee-house tables, oblongs of mottled marble on painted wrought-iron bases, one of a surviving set of four which he and Cressida had found years before in a day of excitements and discoveries in the old junkyard at Monasteraiki. He could hear Miranda crooning some snatch of a Greek children's song all about Babayannis and his donkey and his water-jars, and then Julian's laugh came, high and bell-like, echoing the bells tolling *espéras* from some distant church. What church? Stephanos? Constantinos? Barbara? Demetrios? The Panaygia? Ioannis Prodromos? Giorgios? Pantaleminos? His fingers tightened on the cool edge of the marble table. Here he was racking his brain to recall the shapes and colours of the domes of churches when he should be facing the evidence of his wife's deceit and infamy! Steady now! Face it, man, face it! But when he tried to face it he was pushed up against a finality, because then Cressida was erased and there was nothing left but emptiness, blankness, a wall extending everywhere and blotting out the sky. In the lane a donkey pattered past with a soft creaking of leather and a boy coughing encouragement at it, 'Ho-ho-ho-ho-ho-ho!', the sound declining in a flux of bird calls and the ringing drag of a bucket against the well, and a woman with practised stridency calling home a child, 'Lefteri! *Ella*, Lefteri!' With a numbing of all other feeling and sensation Meredith waited for the child to reply, to come running home, shouting through the soft evening . . .

They were together. They were upstairs in the bedroom, just the two of them, facing each other across the full dusky diagonal of the room. He could not remember how he had got there or how it had come about that the children were no longer in the house. He was very conscious of the emptiness of the house surrounding the rigid existence of the two of them standing apart from each other but face to face.

'Yes, I have had an affair,' she was saying. Her voice was wounded and gentle, neither contrite nor confessing, the words uttered as if she suffered for both of them, yet each syllable struck and turned and twisted and stung, as if delivered to him on the sharp thin point of a knife. 'He was my lover. While you were in Athens.' She seemed to dole the terrible words out to him, measuring them one by one. 'It happened. One night . . . there was a party at Judy's . . . I didn't want it to happen . . . I thought it might and I tried not to . . . But it happened afterwards . . .' She spoke softly and recollectively, as if ruminating upon some event of years before. 'It wasn't something filthy or awful or shoddy, though, it was beautiful really, it was very beautiful . . . We knew it would have to end, and that was why . . . I would have told you except . . . except . . .'

'Except what?' he gasped hoarsely. 'Except you didn't bloody well care what—'

'It was something that I thought had to be kept quite separate from you,' she went on, as if he had not interrupted. 'It had to be quite separate. I think it still is . . .' Her voice faltered a little and she turned away to the window and looked down on the dark mat of the vines. 'There hasn't been anything since you came back,' she said. 'Not anything at all. That's why . . . I mean, it doesn't matter now, and—'

'Doesn't matter!' he cried. '*Doesn't matter!* Christ almighty, woman, what are you saying!'

'I mean it doesn't matter, David, because I still love *you*. That's why I'm saying—'

'*Love!*' He almost spat the word back at her. 'What do you know about love!'

'I know quite a lot about it, I think,' she said quietly. 'I know that this is something that's happened outside us, and our love . . . I don't even know if I can explain it exactly . . . it's not really concerned with *us*, with my loving you. We're quite separate, really, with what we've shared together and been through, and—'

'We can skip the bullshit,' he said angrily. 'I turned my back and you can hardly wait to jump into bed with someone else! I go away and you make the house a bloody brothel!' He saw her wince at that and she lifted her face to him. 'I came back this afternoon and walked around and the whole bloody place stank of *him*! And you expect me—'

'What are you talking about?' Her green eyes flashed, her body was rigid, her fingers clenched. 'Nothing happened here. Not in this house. You don't think—'

'You've had your say.'

'But you can't believe I would allow—'

'What the hell does it matter what *I* believe? Or *where* you did it! Or how often! You talk about it as if it was some passing escapade at a party. But it's been going on for weeks, months . . . It has, hasn't it? All right, so it wasn't here . . . it was up there in his place. That's why you were sitting there on his bed, wasn't it? . . . the couch of love . . . gloating over the romantic setting for your cheap, rotten little affair! That's why you were sitting there mooning, lapping it all up in retrospect, memorizing all the pleasurable little nuances . . .'

'That's where it happened, yes,' she said in a low voice. 'Up there. In his room. Nowhere else. Never anywhere else, David, and I never stayed all night with him. But it's why we went there, so nobody would see or know . . . where it could be separate, something personal and private and quite separate. Nothing to do with—'

'Shut up!' he shouted violently. He had to turn his back on

her and grasp with both hands at the window-ledge to control himself. He could see her again, sitting there on the edge of his bed, savouring every last remembered detail of their love-making so she could lock it all away in her mind like some treasured keep-sake to be taken out and dreamed over and pined for whenever she wished. But the memory she had sat there trying to impress into herself with the permanence of a delicate fossil embedded in stone implanted a second impression in his own mind, a vision haunting and more terrible because it could feed insatiably on every vivid detail of his own imaginings. Each last feature of Galloway's room to the lopsided hang of the shutter bars and the triangle of plaster torn away above the lintel of the door was fixed in his mind. He saw the room steeped in darkness, summer-scented by the night-flowering jasmine, the wick of one cheap oil-lamp turned to a low dim beam like a yellowish-brown hole bored in the darkest corner of the chamber, and Galloway's big bearded figure lay on its back on the rumpled bed as Cressida rose from beside him and it was *he* who watched her slender nakedness emerging from the bare breathing darkness into the loveliness of silhouette against the grilled window. She looked down then at the pale sleeping town as she had once looked down at Lerici sleeping beneath its tilted clock-tower, looked down on a still night pulsing with the faint music of the owl's call and the drift of goat bells, on the sleepy red and green wink of the beacons, the sleepy drift of stars reflected in the crescent blackness of the harbour, the sleepy *caïques* scattered at the moorings like split melons open to the caressing flood of night. It was Galloway who lay there relaxed in the pervasive fragrance of her love and looked across at the curves and flanks of her body etched silver by starlight. The young Cressida had star-baked on the dunes at Lebanon Bay and hoped to turn silver . . .

Meredith flung back to her, shuddering, and shouting his rage like a pummelling of fists: 'It's your bloody obsession! These romantic idiotic dreams of yours! That's it! You consider it's *your* right. *Your* entitlement. You've got to have it your way. You think you own some private bloody world of your own you don't have to give up for anyone. You talk about sharing. *You!* You won't share. You never have. You—'

'But all of us have parts of ourselves we can't share with others,' she said simply. 'You know that.'

'All I know is you've got to eat your cake and have it too.'

'You're not being fair, David.'

'*Fair!*' He approached her threateningly but she faced him without flinching, her face pale but composed in an almost expectant way. He stopped to catch his breath, and to try to control himself. She waited. 'Very well,' he said deliberately. 'Suppose you tell me in what way I am being unfair. Go on, tell me. Since you talk about adultery as if it's only a passing whim, some little personal foible . . . as obviously it doesn't matter a damn to you that you destroy everything we've ever had—'

'This hasn't destroyed everything, David. I mean, it needn't. That's what I'm trying to tell you. But I think you are being unfair when you suggest that we can possess and own and share every part of another person. We can't. We can't, darling. Look, you left Helen because there were parts of yourself you couldn't share with her, and—'

'By God, you *are* going back, aren't you!'

'But all I want you to know is what I still feel about you. About us, if you like. I realize this has been a terrible blow to you, and you can say what you like to me because you feel wronged, and you have been, but it still hasn't made any difference to—'

'No difference! You must be out of your mind!' He felt suddenly weak and bewildered, and he spoke half mechanically as if there was nothing really worth saying. For some reason the edge of his rage had blunted—perhaps for too long it had become dulled by his hackings into the dark hard woods of his imagined fears—and a miserable sense of injury possessed him to such a degree that he felt more like whimpering than shouting, and he kept moving his head from side to side as if dodging dull blows, and when finally he found words it was to say, almost plaintively, 'You don't regret anything, then? You haven't given a single bloody indication that you're sorry it happened.'

This unexpected change in his demeanour and the sudden pathetic intonation appeared to shock her far more than his anger had done, because she grew pale again and retreated a hesitant pace or two and her figure lost its proud rigidity and seemed as if it might crumple. The tip of her tongue passed slowly over her bloodless lips. 'I am not sorry it happened,' she said at last. Only a faint tremor betrayed the quiet firmness of her tone. 'I have to tell you this. I *am* sorry for you, darling. I am dreadfully sorry that you've had to be hurt. You've got to believe this. That's why I wanted it kept separate and apart, so you wouldn't have to be. But I can't stand here now and be a liar and say I'm sorry that it happened.'

The room was almost dark now, filled, it seemed, by the smothering thickness of her words as much as by the deep gloom spilling over from the impenetrable thickness of the vines. There were only two points upon which he could fix his eyes, the blurred pallid oval of her face and a high corner of one window where a last shaft of light from between the mountains made a briefly glittering pattern of amber and emerald lozenges which, while he looked, developed into a deep violet wash and at once joined its spreading darkening blot to the dismal well that was about to engulf them. He could no longer see the nebulous blur of her face, so that when his voice came he seemed to be shouting into the black mouth of some yawning hell-pit. 'You stand there,' he cried, 'without a particle of shame . . .!'

'I am not ashamed.' The low, even voice sought for him out of the menacing opacity. 'It was something very strange that occurred, and terrible in a way, and it had to happen, I think, but anyway it did happen, and it's over now and done with. And it hasn't affected my love for you or how I feel . . .'

Meredith must have rushed out then, because later he could remember nothing between his first headlong flight from the words that assaulted him from the darkness and his pushing open the big blue door of Galloway's house. It was odd that he could remember nothing of that, yet could for ever afterwards recall the appearance of the door, with a splinter of wood hanging and a knocker in the form of a painted hand emerging from a ruffled cuff and holding a tiny red apple in thin graceful cast-iron fingers. The apple thudded softly against a metal boss as he flung the door open.

Galloway was there, tying drawings and sketches into a big portfolio. All the sketches had been taken down from the walls, leaving here and there patches of broken plaster and the marks of the tacks. The room was lighted by two of the cheap brass kerosene lamps, one with a smudged and smoky chimney-glass that emitted the dim, yellow-brownish glow which his mind's eye had already seen in the bedroom. With Galloway was old Calliope, the village woman to whom he gave casual housework, who was still cleaning away the party litter.

The table, cleared of dishes, ash-trays, bottles and glasses, had been recongested by Galloway's books and papers and clothing. There were two valises open on the floor, one of them empty, the other partly packed.

Galloway, his eyes on Meredith's face, gestured a dismissal to the old woman without turning to her, and she, with a hurried frightened glance at the two men facing each other, gave a quick nod like a hen pecking and scuttled away in a mumble of incantations, making her cross as she vanished through the kitchen door.

'I figured you'd be around,' Galloway said heavily. 'I've been expecting you.'

It was this expectation that brought Meredith up sharply. What he had wanted to say had become clear in a flash between his pushing open the door and entering the room, an inexorable and unanswerable string of facts and accusations beginning with 'My wife has told me, etcetera.' But suddenly, having taken only one step towards his enemy, he stopped uncertainly, his thoughts again whirling in the most befuddled way. It was not that the words he felt he must have been rehearsing unconsciously now seemed stiff and hackneyed, like gags from a stale joke-book which went on preserving ancient vaudeville drolleries about cuckolded husbands, nor that the sheer physique of the huge American ruled out any thoughts of satisfying retributive conflict between them, not even the simple fact that Galloway's apprehension of his coming had taken the wind out of his sails. It was rather that, having got here, he was no longer sure of why he had come, or what he ought to say or do. He made a point of keeping his eyes averted from the door leading to the bedroom; he could do that by telling himself that there would not have been any preliminaries in here, they would have gone straight in there. So he allowed his gaze to travel, quite slowly and steadily, while Galloway waited, from the cluttered table to the two valises on the floor. 'Going somewhere?' he said in a tone that he felt to be both casual and ironic.

Galloway nodded carefully, and said, 'I'm leaving.'

'Next week, surely?'

'No, tomorrow. There's a morning boat Sundays. I figured on making it.'

'Good,' said Meredith. 'Take her with you.'

Galloway turned away from him and took up a grey denim shirt from the table. He folded it carefully, and reversed it so as to take the sleeves across the diagonals, then smoothed it with his fingers, and bent over to put it neatly on top of the other things in the half-packed valise. For a quite appreciable interval he stayed like that, crouched over, his head turned away from Meredith, his two arms extended down into the case, like a runner getting set in his marks, then he straightened slowly and turned to face his visitor.

'You want me to say something first?' he said. 'Hell, man, what is there to say?' His voice was thicker than usual, hoarse, and something seemed to tickle his throat because he coughed to clear it, then wiped the back of his hand hard across his bearded mouth. 'Christ, what can I say to you, man? Okay, so I'm a heel, the biggest kind of heel! Jesus, I know it! I'm the guy who comes round and screws everything up and for God's sake I do this to two people I love! I could kill myself, Davy, I swear to you, I could goddam kill myself! You've been my friends, both of you. You and Cress are two great people, swell people. I love you both, for Christ's sake! So why does a guy like me have to move into a situation like this and louse it all up!'

His voice had risen in an anguished pleading for understanding of something that defied understanding; he clenched his fists and battered a soft melodramatic rhythm at his temples; and Meredith could only stare at him blankly, half stupefied, seeing it all happening in this way he found so totally unexpected; it felt as if all his own self-pity was siphoning out, the bitter black fluid of it, siphoning out and dreamily flowing away from himself to fill the great remorse-thirsting hulk of the empty man beating at his brows in front of him. Meredith knew that if now he were to walk across to Galloway and attack him physically, for all his frailty and illness and wheezing breath, the giant would cringe away and his great shoulders would sag and his arms hang in slack submission and he would bow his head and abjectly suffer the blows without resistance. Meredith, feeling a little sick, no longer envying Galloway his physical strength and well-being, listened in a kind of trance of curiosity.

' . . . but you are my friend, goddam it, man,' Galloway was saying anxiously. 'You got to believe me when I say I never figured it'd get to this. Hell, I don't even recollect how it all began to happen. I guess we got ourselves a little plastered . . . I didn't *want* it to happen. We just—'

'The woman tempted me.' Meredith, losing patience at last, interpolated a heavy irony. 'Isn't that what they usually say? Never mind. You take her with you when you go, then you can work it out with her later, who was to blame. You two will have lots of time now to thrash it all out.'

'Listen, Davy, you got this all wrong,' said Galloway urgently. 'You're the guy she loves. It's you. *You!* Goddam it, man, it's you she's always talking about. I don't rate in this set-up. Not where you're concerned. Not with Cress.'

'That's tough titty for you then, isn't it? Because you're stuck with her, aren't you?'

'Davy, for God's sake listen to me! She loves *you*! She loves you very much, man!'

Solecism - breech of grammer or etiquette

'But I don't want her. You've had her. So you keep her.'

Galloway gnawed at his underlip and again dragged the back of his hand hard across his mouth. He shook his head and there was now a tormented glitter in the brown eyes that were usually dancing with laughter. It occurred to Meredith that the crisis had altered Galloway in every aspect. All the laughter and *joie-de-vivre* had vanished utterly, his gay zesty buoyancy had quite deserted him, his speech grown coarse, and husky, his body seemed heavier but shrunken, even his beard looked bedraggled. But as he studied him, Meredith also realized that, while he looked remorseful and anxious, he did not look guilty and he did not look ashamed. The realization brought an immediate change to Meredith's feelings; the moment of moral superiority had passed and he was acutely conscious of the awful weakness of his own position: the physical disparity between them robbed both of them of the traditional right to violence; even the clear black and white of his being wronged by this other man was blurred by the physical inequality between them. Galloway, moreover, was clearly suffering all the false emotions: in his eyes were solicitude for Meredith and a kind of martyrdom of remorse for his own failed integrity where there should have been shame and a fearful guilt; Meredith was incensed to observe that the American's conscience was less troubled by the enormity of his adultery than by the injustice and crudeness of his having played a dirty trick on someone weaker than himself, a sick man unable to assert his rights, a friend, too; the transgression a social solecism rather than a moral crime. Cressida, too, had seemed far less concerned by the monstrous nature of her sin than by her having hurt him and shown disloyalty. In fact, with both of them, their concern was less with the infamy of what had taken place than with the fact that the victim had become aware of it! Meredith, enraged, his mouth open as his struggled for breath, stepped forward threateningly, and Galloway dropped his hands to his sides, his fingers plucking at the pale blue denim of his trousers. He backed away and said, 'Look, let's talk this out man to man. Say, why don't I fix us drinks while—'

'You can stick your drinks,' said Meredith coldly. 'Why did you do it?' he said.

But Galloway had his back turned and was bent over the sideboard, fingers scrabbling as he looked for whisky and glasses.

'Why did you have to do it?' Meredith repeated.

'Do you realize how beautiful your wife is? She is a very beautiful woman.' He edged the words out one by one, as if they might explain everything.

'So what?'

'You don't strike too many dames like her. She's . . . well I guess she's kind of special. And so—'

'And so you've got to have her. Is that it?'

Galloway turned to him desperately and said, 'I keep telling you, man, I don't know how it happened. It was just one of those things.' He was breathing almost as heavily now as Meredith. Both hands were gripped tightly around his whisky glass, but although his knuckles were white the liquor still slopped about. 'We laid off when you came back,' he said. 'That's the way it had to be. She made that clear all along. She still loves you.'

'She'll get over that. When you take her away.'

'She's the most honest damned dame I ever met,' said Galloway fiercely. 'We never figured on this going on.'

'No? Well, now you can, can't you? Now you're taking her away.'

'I'm not taking her away,' Galloway said.

'No?'

'No. Hell, she wouldn't come, for a start. Not with me. Because she's loyal to you. You're the guy she loves. She'll stick by you. She wouldn't leave the kids either.'

'Don't you think she should have thought of these things earlier?'

He did not reply.

'I don't mind you taking her. I minded when I was up in Athens. But I don't mind now. I don't want her any longer.'

'Listen, feller, I couldn't take her even if I wanted to. One thing, I don't have the dough. But there's another thing you ought to know about. I've got a wife of my own, and kids, back there in Connecticut.'

'Oh, you're married. Did she know this?'

'I don't know. I guess not. It didn't arise.'

'Do you love your wife?'

'We get by,' said Galloway.

THE ISLAND, 1961

When Manolis the police lieutenant finally left, it seemed to Meredith as if the little Greek official had dropped back into his correct position in the elapsed history of a night which had come to stretch out behind him in a series of precise and separated shapes that could be run together or held apart, or even moved on with a run of little clicks, like the amber beads on a *kombolloi*. Beginning with—he counted the shapes off, as if he were sliding worry-beads through his fingers—beginning with the argument with Cressida in the early part of the evening, which had been a part of his heavy drinking and which had led directly to his smashing the glasses, which had precipitated the altercation with the interfering man in the grey flannels and tweed jacket, his consequent arrest by this gentleman in association with a very angry Lieutenant Manolis, the interminable dreary interrogation at the *gendarmerie*, his eventual release into an almost empty town, and ending up with a formal glass of brandy, supposedly reconciliatory, sipped outside Evangeli's (where the original fracas had occurred) with a by now imperturbable Lieutenant Manolis and the still far from mollified Greek in the tweed jacket.

Now they had both left him and what remained was like the re-run of a piece of old film, because the waterfront was wholly deserted, emptied of every living person save David Meredith sitting by himself at a lonely table outside Evangeli's shuttered store, and this was painfully reminiscent of the night of the festival of the Hero, two years and a month before, the night when Cressida first met Galloway, and he had sat by himself at this very table, in the empty darkness, waiting for her to come back. Now, of course, it was altogether different. Galloway was gone. Long since. And Cressida in all probability would not come back. Not after tonight.

He lifted the thick fluted glass and sipped and sucked in a vain search for a dreg of cognac; his tongue memorized but his palate could not taste the brandy. Unless he walked home for it there would be no replenishment: not only Evangeli's but every other place on the crescent of the waterfront was closed and shuttered and abandoned to dark silence and the sinister prowlings of the island's innumerable homeless scavenging cats. The cats searched for females along the walled lanes and for fishheads and offal on the mole where the moored *caïques* rocked drowsily by the lullaby-whispering sucking of the black sea: the havened vessels needed no lights or look-outs, in the black wells behind the weathercloths indistinct black bundles wrapped in blackness stirred only in response to dreams. Meredith felt alone and mortal. He felt it would always be the same as this, that there was no forgiveness.

Yet Lieutenant Manolis had, in his own stiff way, forgiven. For all his native arrogance, his stuffy priggishness, the police commandant had turned out quite human and reasonable, almost pleasant, although he had been spitting chips at the beginning and was very uncompromising during the interrogation in his office.

'It is offensive behaviour,' he had charged with implacable severity. 'Without coming to the more serious matter of your striking police officer Constantine—'

'And how was I to know he was a police officer?' Meredith protested furiously. 'How the devil was I to know *who* he was? He arrives from Piraeus today. He wears ordinary civilian clothes, swinging a bloody key-chain like any other young buck. I've never seen the fellow in my life, so when he lays his hands on me and tries to—'

'He was entitled to remonstrate with you, *Kyrie* Meredith,' said Manolis with cold politeness. 'You had thrown a wine glass at his party . . . at *my* party also, as it happens . . . and therefore . . .' He shrugged.

'I never threw a wine glass at anyone's party. That's a bloody lie! I was simply having an argument with my wife. A private argument. A purely domestic quarrel. I got mad at her. Angry, you understand. So I smashed a glass. A wine glass. I threw it down on the flagstones.'

'Two.'

'Two what?'

'Two wine glasses. You hurled two glasses at—'

'All right. Two. Hers and mine. I told you, she made me mad. I flew into a rage and smashed a couple of glasses.'

'Yes, that was regrettable. And offensive.'

'What do you mean, offensive? Why, you Greeks are always smashing glasses! Every time one of you gets a bit pissed you—'

'That is quite different,' said Lieutenant Manolis severely. 'We do not smash our glasses when we are enraged or have differences with our wives. Sometimes we are encouraged to smash a glass or two when we have *ekfi*, we feel the spirit, or we have *chará*, the joy. But in any case—' he paused and frowned—'the glass is then thrown down, straight down, at one's feet—' he gave a vigorous demonstration of the recommended action—'and not—' here he shook his head firmly, with a pout of admonition—'thrown out, as you did, in the direction of people sitting inoffensively at other tables.' Having made his point on techniques he then fixed Meredith with a look of extreme menace. 'Police officer Constantine,' he went on darkly, 'was struck on the shin by one of the glasses you flung. The second glass smashed into pieces and fragments were hurled everywhere among respectable people peacefully taking refreshment after the evening *peripató*, among them—' he mustered an expression of injury, although secretly he may have been delighted—'among them,' he repeated, 'my wife. Her leg was cut by flying glass, her stockings ruined . . .'

'Yes, I know. I am very sorry about that. I've told you—'

'Then when police officer Constantine understandably attempts to remonstrate against such very bad behaviour you—'

'I tell you I didn't know he was—'

'You seize this police officer, you grapple, you strike him.

There is, in short, an unpleasant incident, a fight. Chairs and tables are overturned. People are—'

'I've told you a hundred times I didn't *know* he was a police officer. He was just a stranger to me, a civilian, an officious Greek who was poking his nose in where it didn't belong. I resented him. Grabbing hold of me, shoving me around . . .'

'Whether he was a police officer or not he was surely entitled to object to your hurling wine glasses into his, and *my*, party. He was the one who had a right to be resentful. And then when you started to punch at him . . .' He stroked his moustache carefully and said coolly, 'You realize, *Kyrie* Meredith, that if we had not separated the two of you, you might have been very badly hurt. We were really protecting you. Police officer Constantine is young, athletic. He is strong, a *pallikári*, and you made him very angry. So it is well for you we stopped the fight. You are no longer a young man, *Kyrie* Meredith. And you are not well. So we stopped the fight and took you to the *gendarmerie* both to protect you and to allow you to cool off. So I would suggest that if in the future you are to have a quarrel with your wife you should try to arrange it privately, not where it is public, and offensive, and dangerous.'

Meredith thought about these things now in the anticlimactic quiet of the dark, sleeping town. The police commandant was right, of course: the quarrel with Cressida had been a final summing-up of failure, and Lieutenant Manolis, who had known them now for a good few years, probably was even more offended and repelled by their domestic failure than by any public manifestation of drunken truculence or just plain bloody-mindedness: it was right that Manolis should be offended and repelled; if you failed you were supposed to fail in private; it was offensive to fail in public, especially in a foreign country.

The Greeks, when you came to think about it (Meredith realized, thinking about it), were far more tolerant of us than we, in like circumstances, would be of them. Meredith had come to the conclusion that he was very tired of being an alien in a foreign country and subject to resident permits and passport examinations and the little stringencies imposed by petty little bureaucrats like Lieutenant Manolis. Yet it had to be admitted that the foreigners generally made their own rules and were often inclined to behave as if they could do just as they liked because none of their own kind was there to keep an eye on them; they didn't have to abide by the rulings of their own society or even by their neighbour's opinions; superiorities and immunities were assumed as naturally as breathing even by the most debased and miserable specimens of foreigners. But they must often have given great pain and offence to Lieutenant Manolis and his party and his wife and his compatriots. It was surprising, everything considered, that the police official was as patient as he was, or as polite, or as lenient. It was really, Meredith decided, thinking about it, a case of one law for the rich and another for the poor, because even when the foreigner was no more than a semi-destitute bum living, as likely as not, on some meagre remittance allocated solely for the purpose of keeping him out of his own country, he still in an abstract way represented 'Western' affluence and superiority as opposed to Greek poverty and inferiority; it was this superior affluence and its attendant *tourismos* that presumably must ultimately put food into the bellies and shoes on the feet of the children of Manolis's poor compatriots; so Manolis would perforce turn a tolerant gaze on many of the foreigner's excesses. He might be disgusted by the foreigner's immorality or degradation or perversion, or contemptuous of his want of dignity, he might deplore his patronizing ill-manners or crude vulgarities, he might be aghast at the distasteful scandal of the girl in the bikini strutting before the demure Greek high school virgins in their black buttoned smocks, but he would still try to be tolerant and polite. And even though he might reprimand Meredith for making a public exhibition of himself, he would do it courteously, still referring to him deferentially as *Kyrie*, mostly concerned that the Merediths were letting themselves down in the eyes of a community which for years had respected them as stable elements in the otherwise unaccountable and undisciplined world of the 'foreign colony'. (Meredith tried to imagine what it would be like if the shoe were on the other foot; in Australia among the xenophobic Australians it was extremely doubtful if Manolis, poor Manolis, would ever be as lucky in any similar predicament!)

Thus Meredith mused, disconsolate and solitary in the dark sleeping town, feeling sad and bereft in an empty loneliness, and as he mused he saw Cressida, a dim, tiny, tentative figure at the far end of the *agorá*, emerging from the inked shadows where the fish-boxes were stacked in readiness for the lanterned *gri-gri* boats to come in with their night's haul. She stood there for some minutes, searching with her eyes, then began to move in his direction, coming slowly, having seen him in the distance at the table alone in the night beneath the marble statue of the Hero, advancing with an apparent reluctance, as if drawn to him against her will.

'I've been looking for you,' she said in a low voice. 'I went to the police station, but it was empty. There wasn't even anyone on duty,' she said with an air of faint surprise.

'It's pretty late,' he suggested awkwardly.

'I looked in all the rooms. I thought they would have locked you up for the night. There were two men asleep in one room, policemen I suppose, there were uniforms hanging there, but otherwise the whole place was empty. Not even guarded. Strange for a police station.'

'Manolis let me go,' he explained, still ill at ease. 'He made us shake hands, me and the chap I had the fight with. He wasn't all that keen, the other chap, I mean . . . still . . . we came back here and had a couple of cognacs . . . then . . .' He trailed off lamely, looking at her.

'I did have to leave you,' she said. 'I had to take the children away. They were upset, of course, and rather scared, and—'

'There was nothing you could have done. I didn't expect you to get involved. Or want you to. I am sorry about the kids, though. I behaved like a bloody fool. I'm sorry they saw the spectacle.'

'Well, never mind. It doesn't matter now. I came to take you back home.'

'Well, sit down for a bit.' He was pleased and surprised, even touched, by her concern. 'It's quiet here,' he said.

For a wary interval they sat in silence, really watching each other although their eyes were fixed on the softly creaking pattern of masts and rigging black against the crowded glitter of the stars. It was a night in August, the time in the year of the meteor showers, and what looked like dislodged stars kept falling from the brilliant congestion of the firmament and plunging to extinction behind the dark bulk of the mainland hills. Meredith forced a lightness of tone to say, 'Make a wish.'

'What I wish,' she said soberly, 'is that we could talk to each other.'

'What's stopping us?'

'We are. David, we've got to talk to each other. Without tearing one another to pieces, I mean. We just can't go on like this.'

'I couldn't agree more.' He thought of what Lieutenant Manolis had said.

'What has happened to us, David?' she asked fiercely. 'Why does it have to go on *being* like this? What's gone wrong?'

'Good question. I suppose I could make the same answer you did and say we have.'

'Then we should do something about it, shouldn't we?'

'We could begin, I suppose, by not being so public about it. Manolis objects to the fact—I mean, among other things he objects in particular to the fact that we make our differences public. It seems we've lost our capacity for decent reticence. We make public exhibitions of ourselves. And the locals don't care for it.'

'Neither do I. That's why——'

'The locals don't care for it, and I can't say I blame them.'

'I wish it didn't happen in public either. I wish it didn't happen at all. But at least . . . well, tonight *was* awful, let's face it. I wish it hadn't been in front of the children, that's all.'

He nodded, accepting it, and lowering his head and poked at broken match sticks. They deluded themselves in thinking that the events of the night would have come to the children as a revelation that something was amiss, but none the less it was a bad show. And in a sense it was the position of the children that lay at the crux of the matter. Even Lieutenant Manolis had seen this. Not as an offence and injury to local opinion felt in the heat of passion, but as something considered later, at the *gendarmerie*, as an important element in the formal castigation. Nobody had thought of the children in the fury of the moment: he had quite forgotten they were there, somewhere in the vicinity, playing with the other children as they always did in the cool of the long summer evenings; and he would swear that neither Cressida nor Manolis had given a thought to the children either. But now the children had become, from quite different points of view, salient features of the problem. Meredith could understand this.

Over the years the local people had come to accept them as a family unit, in a phenomenal sense as a *foreign* family, a curious oddity of the solid, the reliable and the stable within an accreted anthropology that was intrinsically irresponsible and transient and unstable. The Meredith children went to school with their children, spoke the same language, played the same games, chanted the same patriotic poems on *Oxi* Day. Before they had come to live there the islanders had never seen foreigners with children, not foreigners like the Merediths, living with them; until then they probably thought foreigners reproduced themselves like amoeba, like some quite different form of life, splitting and dividing. Now, in public disgrace and public humiliation of the children, Meredith was made to feel he had let everybody down—himself, Cressida, the children, and the local inhabitants. Or so both Cressida and Manolis seemed to imply.

But the children had seen fights before. The Greeks themselves were great ones for passion and bellicosity and emotional turbulence; even Karagiosis, the traditional comic figure of the children's puppet shadow-theatre was always brawling. But tonight was different, when it was personal and domestic and brought out in public display. Meredith lit a cigarette and tried to think about all the fights and quarrels to which the children might have been willing or reluctant witnesses.

The first had been years before, when the children had been quite small, that first summer they had spent on the island and they had given a kind of sanctuary to Guido, the big handsome Italian gigolo who had been turfed out by his wealthy Athenian paramour Lydia. Meredith actually loathed and despised Guido, and he was secretly afraid of the Italian's flagrant good looks and his predatory tomcatting, but he tolerated him because Cressida seemed to like him and because Cressida, after the restrictions of London, was still in a state of rhapsody about the free-and-easy liberties of cosmopolitan life in the Mediterranean, and he tolerated him because tolerance towards a man of Guido's potential sexual threat was part of the self-discipline which Meredith imposed upon himself as a corrective to jealousy as far as Cressida was concerned. For three days and nights charged with high emotion Guido sulked in the sanctuary of their house, and on the evening of the fourth day Meredith and Cressida returned from the port to find the place a shambles. Guido had found and consumed a whole bottle of Metaxas brandy, had worked himself up into a state of passionate madness, and was in the process of smashing up all the pictures and furniture in the living-room, venting his rage on anything he saw. Meredith, crunching on broken glass, made a rush at him, but the maddened Italian, who had spent his formative boyhood in the back streets of Naples, kneed his host in the crotch and, as he doubled up in pain, felled him with a cruel rabbit-killer. Cressida then flew at him, and he had no compunction about punching her, then flung her to the floor and spat at her. Meredith saw all this through a daze of pain; eventually he was able to stagger to his feet and he attacked Guido with such merciless cold fury that in the end the Italian lay groaning and half senseless on the littered floor, his once handsome features a seeping bloody pulp. Meredith then crouched across him and seizing his hair in both fists began to batter the insensible head against the stone floor; it would be the only time in his life he would ever positively want to kill another human being, and perhaps he would have done so had not Cressida and some of the neighbours dragged him from his intended victim.

Not until then did Meredith realize, in a nauseous reflex of shock and disgust, that the two small children, wide-eyed and transfixed in the open doorway, had been intense witnesses to the whole of the terrible scene. Not till much later did he discover that the children had relished the sordid spectacle and, contrary to feeling shame and revulsion, had in fact been very proud of his conduct in the matter, boasted to their school friends for weeks after about their father's valour and prowess, and always remained convinced that it was he who had driven the despicable Italian from the island. They may well have been right, although it was more likely that Guido left because Lydia would have nothing more to do with him after his shameful defeat, to find a doctor and a dentist who would patch up the face that was his fortune, and a new *padrona* in the salons of Kolonaiki. You never, Meredith reflected, knew what children's reactions would be. In tonight's incident, for example, it was perfectly possible that his fighting a policeman and being carted off to gaol could have given excitement and even a thrill of delight to the children, even though the blazing row that he and Cressida had had, and which was the instigating factor in the débâcle, probably would have bored or even disgusted them.

'What are you thinking about?' Cressida wanted to know, and he told her that he had been wondering what the children really felt about it all, and she said, 'They were very upset, that's all I know.'

'They've seen fights before,' he said.

'Yes,' she agreed. 'That wasn't quite what I meant, though.'

'Actually Manolis was all right, you know. In the end he came right round and——'

'I was thinking of us,' she interrupted quietly. 'These interminable fights we have. It's been going on for so long, David.'

'I know. That's what worries you about the kids, isn't it?'

'Well, we've got to do something about it, haven't we? I mean, we've all got to try to survive together. As a unit. As *all* of us. Not just as separate individuals.'

'Yes, we have to try, I suppose. There's no guarantee we'll succeed, is there? The real trouble,' he said with sudden anger, 'is this blasted island! We've stayed too long. It's become claustrophobic. It's getting us down. It works like a trap now. Or a slow poison. It's corrosive. Destructive.'

'It has become a difficult place, I agree. But I don't think we can just sit back and blame the island. I think it's we who are at fault, really. After all, it was what *we* wanted. It was our own choice.'

'If people had left us alone . . .'

'Nobody is ever left alone. I'm beginning to believe lately that being alive is being alone, and you're always alone when you dream, but nobody is ever *left* alone. That's different.' She was thoughtful for a time, and then said, 'Anyway, what can we do? Where can we go?'

'Nowhere, that's the bloody trouble. That's what I mean, it's a trap. We're stuck here. We don't have the fare out. And has it ever occurred to you that even if we did have, we've probably buggered ourselves anyway?' He knew, of course, that it had occurred to her; it was she who had first advanced the disturbing thought that they might have subjected themselves to a kind of subtle social dismantling, that gradually their life on the island had unfitted them for any other sort of life. He had lately grown very fearful of an inexorably creeping sense of alienation, as if he watched the snapping and unravelling of all the threads that bound him to the things he had once understood and found comforting and reassuring. It had been building up to a feeling, horrible in its empty loneliness, that there was no place to go and no one to be with. Did this mean, then, that there was nothing to be done but sink unresistingly into a final despair? And did the children, also, have to be committed to it?

Cressida's reflections moved in a different orbit, and when the long silence was broken it was she who said:

'You still can't really forget what happened the summer before last, can you?'

'It doesn't worry me, not any more,' he said lying. 'That's over and done with. It's dead. At least I hope it is.' It was not over and done with, nor dead, and perhaps never would be as long as he lived, and he feared this and he knew that she feared it too. Any time either of them drank too much – Miriam was right; she may have skirted around the real issues, but she was right when she said they were drinking too much – it clawed at them, at him anyway, and he suspected that in their quarrels and recriminations this was the catalyst for all the nervous tensions, the claustrophobia of the island, the trap, failure, illness, the frustrations of his work, the sense of dislodgement, his growing irritation with the island's other foreign expatriates.

Tonight, after what had happened, he felt sobered and realistic. He began to suspect that he used the flawed image of his wife, the image he insisted on preserving as flawed, the image which in fact he *clung* to, as a reason and excuse for other disillusionments. Even, in a sense, as a kind of exoneration of his inability to achieve those aims, once clear, which were now becoming blurred. It was true that these days he was acutely conscious of a recurrent empty sense of *loss*, this hollow within himself that robbed him of will, or moral incentive, that rubbed raw everything that surrounded it: but was it not he himself who kept rubbing it raw, for ever scratching and picking at the healing scab until it bled and hurt again?

The simple fact, of course, the simple fact that Calverton had seen, was that, wherever they were going on to, he could not go on *without* Cressida. Tonight he saw this very clearly, had seen it from the moment she had appeared from behind the fish-boxes on the empty waterfront. The bond between them, frayed as it might have become, could not be broken. And if she had deceived and betrayed him, had he not deceived and betrayed her even more, and over a far longer period, by his own watchfulness and suspicion? Calverton, Jacques, Dr Kronfeld, even poor Graham Crossley of years before, even the slimy Guido . . . if all of this were submitted to reasonable judgment, might it not even be ruled that he had driven her to her defection?

There had been times since when he had wished she had lied, and made it easier for him, but Cressida never lied. And tonight he wished he could forgive, because Cressida forgave, and even a pompous little stuffed shirt like Manolis the police chief had an unsuspected gift for forgiveness; why then had *he* not been able to forgive? To forgive and forget and go on with the journey? Because, as he saw very clearly tonight, if he could not forgive then they would be united by nothing much more than time and things shared, they would become components in a journey rather than the validity of the journey, less people than points between spaces. Once Cressida had appealed to him by saying, 'But we've been through too much together to throw it all away now'; and though it was true, of course, that time itself did become a kind of cement, that one person could be held to another as much by this adhesive of shared time as — perhaps even more than — through love, this might be only because the alternative was to endure alone the terrible isolation of separate solitudes.

What he had come to fear tonight was that they were allowing a force to build up that could hold them in perpetual conflict, an obscure force drawn from hate as well as from love that would grow more powerful than either, that would divide them as it bound them together, moving them through periods of truce without ever achieving peace. This was the haunting terror — that the inflicted injury had grown chronic: if this had happened there never again would be peace . . .

'I do think we have to try,' Cressida was saying. 'I honestly do *want* to try.'

'Yes,' he said sadly.

'I mean, we could go away,' she said. 'Somewhere. Somewhere else. We could start again.'

Start again? But how could you rub out everything that had happened, the good as well as the bad, erase it all, and begin all over again with a clean sheet. Besides, you only went back to start again when there had been a false start, and he had already had his false start, with Helen, long ago, and he had had his second start, and it had been a good start, so there was really nothing to be done any longer but to push on and try to make it to the tape. It was easier, anyway, than going back and starting again: if he could no longer imagine himself as a winner, breaking the tape, at least it might be possible to see out the distance, and the worst that could happen was that you dropped in your tracks, still trying. All Cressida wanted to do was to keep on trying.

'I'm sure Miriam is right,' Cressida said. 'She saw that we're not doing each other much good here, that we do need a change. That we have to go back and see what the real world is like.'

'The rat-race.'

'Even that. What is the alternative? Australia? It's too far. And we couldn't afford it. But we could still swap houses with Beatrice. Couldn't we?'

'I suppose so,' he said doubtfully. 'It's a thought, anyway.' He pushed his chair back and said, 'Let's pack it in and go home.' In a troubled silence they walked off together through the black and silver of the sleeping town, but in the lane he took her hand and she squeezed it tightly.

After that night Meredith steadied down for quite some time and worked long hours to finish his novel and sent it off. When November came with wild winds and a steam of spray over the gulf and the rare look of steel in the bronze-age sea, and even, one morning, a light powdering of snow like a drift of fine sugar on the mainland hilltops, they took stock of their fast-dwindling resources and, with a resurgence of confidence, agreed to gamble on the book about to be published: they accepted Beatrice's offer of the exchange of houses and set off for England.

Meredith went away in some trepidation, but these days he did most things in some trepidation; at the same time he saw the venture as a substitute for a fresh start—an offering of hope, another chance. He saw it too as a kind of catharsis. He had to hope it would get the island out of his system, and the pain of the memories it harboured.

THE ISLAND, 1959

Man is very much a creature of ceremony, so I left Galloway with a profoundly disturbed feeling that I had not handled the situation well. Everything I had done had lacked ceremony. I felt robbed, as it were, of the rights of being wronged.

In the confrontations both with Cressida and with her lover, instead of standing on lofty peaks of righteous indignation I had been blundering around in the low and dreary wastelands, adrift in the bogs of uncertainty and indecision, trying to pick my way through the inconsequential messy debris of life. Where I had wanted to be the formidable denunciatory figure in a Victorian steel engraving, the betrayed husband in some huge Royal Academy canvas, I seemed to have become only another sweeping of the litter left over from Galloway's party. With Cressida there had been nothing much left but voices howling out of darkness, less accusation than a scream of pain; with Galloway an old crone scuttling off crossing herself and the villain himself calmly folding shirts into a pigskin valise. Even suggesting that we have a drink together! Where I had been entitled to display the invincible weapon of a prodigious wrath I had found myself struggling all the time against vile sensations of defeat and dismay, feeling myself to be in a false and petty position, cheapened, degraded, trapped in anticlimax, robbed of individuality, of free will, of pride, of independence. Humiliated, that was it. Struggling for dignity as much as for breath. Even, God help me, forced to rely on Cressida for a needle in the backside!

Tormented in this fashion, I had wanted after leaving Galloway to go back to Cressida solely to taunt her. To taunt her with the knowledge that Galloway, having had his fun, had no desire at all to take her with him, that in effect he had passed the buck to her for what had happened, that he too, having his own wife and children, had been involved in a double treachery. But when I reconsidered this course I could find no satisfaction in it; I even recoiled from the thought of hurting her so cheaply. Besides, I was not even sure that what I had to taunt her with was true. Maybe one day I would be obliged to thrash it out with her, because I could still not understand what she saw in Galloway, what she *had* seen in him, although probably this was one of those things that one could never expect to understand. In any case what was the point of wasting time thinking of 'one day', of some future which I certainly had no intention of sharing with Cressida?

It was not very long before I found myself on the rocks beside the sea cave, seeking refuge and solitude, close to the suck and lap of comfortless mysteries, looking across the black depths to the dim, ridged contours of the mainland, flat, substanceless, a blemish across the lower part of a magnificent celestial brilliance. By daylight the ridges were humped and solid-looking, with spines and smooth heavy flanks, so that in certain lights they sometimes reminded me of a herd of retreating elephants, comically pink as in the jokes about DTs. Now all the elephants had trotted off and vanished behind a gauzy backdrop, paper-thin. There was a semblance of solidity only here and there where the fires of the charcoal-burners glowed, baleful as the eyes of some animal quite different from the comic elephants.

The sea looked to have a thick, greasy skin on it, with streaks of starshine. At intervals, unexpectedly, the water would hump up and groan softly, in the way it does before an earthquake. There was no moon, only the extravagant scatter of stars that seemed to possess a pulsing, gigantic, flickering life of their own; frequently a bright pinpoint would detach itself and flare up and shoot itself away into black extinction, sometimes appearing to drop behind the gauzy veil of the hills; occasionally a whole fiery shower of meteorites would be released, but the vivid projectiles and the more remote myriad studs of breathing incandescence alike served only to emphasize the great cosmic indifference to the plight of mankind in general and David Meredith in particular.

I confess that in the early stages of my vigil on the sea rocks the idea of suicide crept enticingly into my mind. The thought of sinking into the soft sucking blackness, down past mysterious crusted pinnacles of cold rock into the final safety of that colourless oblivion, offered for a time a powerful temptation. The solution, moreover, was so all-embracing—it was not only escape from the fearful dilemma of my love for Cressida (which, in spite of everything, and whatever form it would have to take from now on, still, alas, existed); it was the one certain escape from the trap, from failure, from responsibility, from the unending precariousness of economic hazard, from ill health, from the whole unbearable rigour and peril of going on. There would even be a tincture, I told myself with a kind of relish, of romantic drama about it, and admirable poignancy classical in its tragic flavours . . . the struggling writer, tubercular, betrayed in love, in a foreign land thousands of miles from home, seeking the only possible freedom from trial and tribulation. Sitting alone on the dew-damp rock by the careless sibilance of the sea, a thin forlorn figure in the loneliness of night, hunched up, chin on knees and hands clasped around my shins, for a time I even gloated idly on Shelley at Lerici and Byron and Brooke, and only dislodged myself from the absurdity of such ruminations by hearing myself say aloud, and scornfully, 'Come off it, sport!'

After this it was only a matter of moments before I had discounted all prospects of suicide as a possible solution. It was just too terrifying to contemplate, too cold and sinister and lonely—and, besides, it was intolerable to think that I should not be able to see Cressida again.

This last was a queer thought in the light of what was to happen, because it must have been about this time that I came to my decision as the night began to assemble itself into different forms of definition, islands in the gulf growing more distinct while the mainland hills retreated and became almost transparent and the stars grew dim and faint nervous little zephyrs began to ruffle the surface of the water in odd patches, like the nap of fur rubbed the wrong way. Daybreak was approaching.

I walked home then, and without wakening anyone, or even looking to see if anyone was awake, I packed a suitcase with a few clothes and the necessary articles of toilet—I could send later for anything that I might find to be essential – and lugged it back to a coffee-house on the waterfront which always opened at dawn to serve the bakers and fishermen and donkey-boys and the rest of the early risers. I ordered coffee and cognac, and Pantelis, the proprietor of the *kafenéion*, yawning and stretching and wiping with his cloth, told me that the Piraeus-bound steamer was expected at seven-thirty from the next island, so I moved my drinks to an outside table to watch the sun come up out of the eastern sea and to wait. I knew that Petros the postman always came there in the morning for coffee so I spent a few minutes drafting a telegram to Big Grace which he could have transmitted for me as soon as the post-office opened. I tried various ways of explaining the situation in the telegram, but none satisfied me and in the end I simply wrote, ARRIVING PIRAEUS ELEVEN THIS MORNING. Big Grace wouldn't need more than that. She would understand. She would be there to meet me and take me home to Metz.

There was a morning chill, and as I absorbed the raw warmth of the cognac, feeling surprisingly avid and alert in spite of physical exhaustion, lack of sleep, and the intense emotional stress I had been through, I found myself taking meticulous mental inventory of each detail of the port's awakening to its innumerable small affairs. I had seen these activities many times before (there had been, for instance, five successive December mornings when Cressida and I had carried the Christmas turkey down to the bake-house for its roasting, to find Alexis before dawn stoking his great furnace with glazing pine, and afterwards we would ritually go to Pantelis's *kafenéion* to drink celebratory cognacs and wait for festive daybreak), but this, after all, would be the last time I would be here to see these things.

The donkey-men and Sunday idlers were already drifting down to watch the steamer come, and early-rising old men seeking the reassurances of daytime like stretching cats, there were bearded priests flapping their long black gowns around coffee-houses on their way to churches, and fishermen on the mole stretching nets. A line of *gri-gri* boats, gunwales almost awash, were being towed in tandem to their moorings behind a shabby yellow launch, in each boat a figure black-squatted on the hummocked nets beneath the aluminium-shielded lanterns raised in each prow on crude metal brackets like amateur models of some awkward invention. The port sailors in sloppy whites, still unshaven but with their hair greased (saving the luxury of shaving for later, when the *koureion* shops opened with their perfumes and talcs and bombast and gossip), set up the little palisade of wooden picket-barriers to fence off the landing-stage, and two of the big passenger long-boats were poled up to the steps inside the area so proscribed. Pantelis draped his wiping cloth around his mottled neck and took my suitcase across and put it down at the top of the steps inside the fence. When he came back I thanked him and he shrugged his kindness off with a brusque '*Tipota!*' and brought me another cognac and a mastika for himself and raised his glass to me and said, '*Si-yia!*' then added, mechanically, '*Kalo taxedi.*' A good journey? I supposed it would have to be, but who could say? While I was thinking of the sad implications in the phrase, some church bells began to chime and Petros came in and I called him across and I gave him the message I had written out and some money and he promised to transmit it personally with his own fingers on the key as soon as the post-office opened at eight-thirty. I offered to buy him a coffee, but he had already ordered one, and he shoved the message in his pocket, patted it, and took himself off to another table to read *Athletiki* and *Omada*. Petros, I remembered, was mad about soccer, an Olympiakos fan. There were quite a few people gathering now around the fenced-off landing-stage with suitcases and bundles and bags and baskets, one old woman with a black headscarf carrying by their claws a brace of fowls which were alive but looked as if they had been drugged. Fanuri, in his gay Sunday tie and his thin belt with the snake buckle, carved passages of bright bonhomie through the groups, writing out and selling steamer tickets from his book, stuffing drachma bills into his pocket, humming *bouzouki* tunes, twirling his key-chain, making jokes.

Galloway arrived, walking huge and slow-footed behind a very small and quick-stepping donkey laden with his two pigskin valises and a tied-up roll of cartridge paper. He had an airline bag across his shoulder and carried the big portfolio under his arm. He saw his baggage unroped from the donkey and disposed inside the fence, then bought his ticket from Fanuri and lit a cigarette and sauntered along the quay a bit, then stood by a bollard with his hands pushed into the pockets of his jeans. He seemed to be frowning away across the gulf, and the sun-glitter dusted in silver bands over the pallid dove-breast sea, as if he was anxious to be the first to see the steamer heave in sight from around the islands. It was evident that nobody had come to witness his departure. He might have given instructions to this effect, I thought, remembering his general popularity and the lavishness of the party he had given yesterday (only yesterday?), but then it occurred to me that probably he and I were the only two people on the island (apart, possibly, from Calliope the old woman) who knew that he was leaving so prematurely. He never looked once in my direction, nor indeed paid the least attention to the bustle and activity all around him.

There was quite a crowd on the quay by the time the ship came in a bouncy display of sunny white. The bow wave dropped away, the ship listed slightly as she swung, the clang of the engine-room telegraph drifted faintly across the water, a jet of steam as surprising as ectoplasm appeared in the clear sky above the yellow funnel, and a peremptory siren blast exploded gulls into the sunshine. The ship slid imperceptibly to a standstill about a hundred yards to seaward of the mole, the dark skein of the wake rolled back on the sea's skin and vanished, and in the harbour all the moored *caïques* began to lurch with a weary grunting on their ropes. There was a quickstep slap of water that eddied giddily along the mossy edging of the quay, even a few facetious jets of spray, and some men jumped into the two big longboats and spat on their hands and grasped the heavy sculling oars, the harbour-master yelled a bossy command, and people everywhere began to press forward towards the picket palisade. I sat on over the last of the cognac, watching the steadying lurch of the *caïques* and thinking back. I could see the red hull of the *Metamorphosis* there, the boat we hired for our picnics, and between her and the harbour beacon I could make out the big curves of the fat-bellied old tub from Monemvasia that always picked up earthenware water-jars from the potteries at Leonithion. Years before, Cressida and I had spent our very first day on the island looking down from the window of our room in the old Poseidon Hotel, and the big weather-pale old vessel had been moored at the quay right below us, unloading water-jars and lemons and yellow-eyed goats, and we had held each other's hands tightly and filled our hearts to brimming with the whole world.

While I called for the *logariasmós* and paid Pantelis I saw that Galloway, taller than anyone else, was already on the landing-stage handing his baggage down into one of the rocking longboats.

I walked across quite slowly. He could go out in the first boat and I would take the second. But I was in the crowd now and being pushed and jostled and hurried forward to the narrow gate where the harbour-master still shouted and Manolis the police chief stood with his official severity buttoned on. He was there on business, and unsmiling, and he favoured me with a curt nod. Galloway saw me then, inside the gate getting the ticket from Fanuri, and his hurt eyes held me in a long look, but all he said was, 'Jesus!', quite softly, and then he stepped down into the long-boat, and a great shouting was set up by somebody and they poled the boat away.

When I turned to see about my suitcase I found myself looking straight at Cressida. She was outside the fence but pressed right up against it, her hands tightly gripped on the pointed pickets, and she was just looking at me intently without saying a word. She seemed quite oblivious of the boat moving out with Galloway aboard it, she never took her eyes off me, and she was quite still, as if caught in some sort of rigid, expressionless trance. I had a vague awareness of Calverton, in the crowd pressing behind her, moving his head from side to side as if trying to catch a glimpse of something. I tried to think of some word of farewell I might say to her, but my thoughts seemed suddenly all thick and woolly, and anyway I could hear the thump and thud of feet and luggage in the boat at the steps behind me, and somebody was shouting my name impatiently. I turned to plead for a moment or two of time, but Manolis gestured at me in some irritation, so there was nothing I could do but leave her there, silently pressed against the painted wooden pickets, watching both her men moving out of her life.

The thought, coming like that, cut at me like a whip, but it was too late now and there was nothing to be done about it, because I could hear the throaty thuck of the oars on the thole-pins, and they were still shouting for me, and then I heard a voice beside me, the voice of Archie Calverton, saying, 'Go on, you hop in. I'll grab your bag and come out with you and help you aboard.'

We were rowing out then, going out in slow rhythmic jerks across the pebbles and litter and fruit rinds and rusted scraps of old cables on the harbour bottom, with Calverton standing in the boat beside me, saying nothing. The other boat was well ahead of us, squat and spread out like some huge water-beetle moving to the insectine dip and sweep and rise of the long dripping oars, but Galloway's bearded head was distinguishable above all the other passengers crowded between the thwarts, and he did not look back either. Our boat was going smoothly now, and Calverton and I stood there stiffly, aware of one another but with nothing to say, both staring ahead at the leading boat and the passengers lining the steamer's rails and the flags and the lazy curl of smoke, listening to the splash of oars and the murmurous rippling chuckle of the water flowing past. Neither of us looked back to where Cressida would have been still standing, grasping the two wooden pickets, watching everything dwindling away into the vivid radiance of the summer morning.

There was an expected swell moving outside the harbour mole and we lay to, rolling a bit, while the first boat disgorged its passengers, and the head of our boat came round as we drifted, waiting, and I looked down a surprisingly long stretch of water banded indigo and ultramarine and turquoise with a kind of pale jade selvedge to the grey stone of the quay and the clustered white houses and the burnt rocky hills beyond. The crowd at the landing-stage had all dispersed by this time, and the slow small activities were diffused along the wide spread of the waterfront, and although it was difficult to make out any particular detail with certainty I did think I saw a tiny single figure still there by the landing steps.

But the head of the longboat kept swinging around, and now I could see Galloway lifting his valises up to a deckhand standing by the open port, then the big portfolio, and someone bumped against the roll of cartridge paper and buckled it. Galloway said something and tried to punch the buckle out, then I saw him clamber inside and look this way and that way along the alleyway and then he was swallowed into the crowd. After a minute or so the boat pulled clear and our boat slid up to the steamer's overhang and a sailor seized the swinging bight of rope, and kicked a coir fender into position and warped us alongside.

'Take it easy,' Calverton advised quietly. 'Keep back from this bloody mob. Wait till last, let 'em go, there's no panic. Not to worry. I'll shove the bag on and give you a hand.'

I nodded dumbly, thankful for his custodianship and sensible authority; all I could think of was Cressida's green eyes staring out.

The passengers seemed to take a long time getting aboard, pushing and quarrelling and complaining, the women shrieking nervously, but then the last of them—the old lady with the two trussed fowls—was crawling through the port in an indecorous flurry of black petticoats and rolled-down stockings and mauve blotches of veins, and just as I began to climb on the gunwale a strong arm came chokingly around my throat and I was flung violently on to the wet floorboards. Calverton was spreadeagled on top of me, pressing my shoulders down and shouting, 'Go on, push off! He's not going! He's changed his mind! He's not going!'

He was shouting in English, so nobody could have understood what he was saying, but I heard a more distant shout and a sharper cry from somewhere, a whistle blew, I was conscious of a quickening throb of engines and a slapping rush of water, three sharp blasts of a siren, the vehemence of a screw fading behind the dip and splash of oars and the same murmurous rippling laughter of water. But now, stretched gasping on the wet floor-boards with the whole weight of Calverton flung across me and pressing me down, the water seemed to be running right along the length of my own crushed body, running through me, washing me away.

Calverton lifted himself off with a soft grunt and muttered, 'Sorry about that. Only way.' He steadied himself against a thwart and looked out and I lifted my head and saw the steamer, fussing and hurried in a toss of white crests, disappearing behind the head-land where the old cannon were mounted in embrasures. A burst of amplified music, Nana Mouskouri singing about a little cypress-tree, drifted back, a blue and white flag flicked a final flaunt, and the ship was gone and there was nothing to be seen but the same dark skein of the wake rolling and unravelling back along the milky plains of light. The wash came in ponderous groovy ridges, slapped against the tossing longboat, set a single tiny rainbow quivering and fading in the air. The oars dipped again, the boat reared up and slid on again, pointed for the landing-stage. Calverton balanced himself against the heave, then teetered off to the stern-sheets and sat down, scowling, and lit a cigarette. There were three or four strangers in the boat, peasant people by the look of them, probably passengers from the last island who had disembarked from the steamer, and they stared at me curiously enough, with darting askance glances of puzzled speculation at Calverton, but the steersman and the oarsmen paid no attention to either of us, assuming, presumably, that this was another of the incomprehensible things that foreigners were in the habit of doing and therefore no cause for curiosity and pointless to be concerned about. The church bells began to ring again and the peasants crossed themselves.

There was nobody waiting at the landing-stage.

We climbed the wet steps and Calverton took my bag and walked with me up to Evangeli's, and ushered me in to the aromatic clutter of the back room, where there were a few tables among the sacks and cheap birdcages and oil jars and earthenware pitchers and festoons of garlic.

Cressida was seated at the table in the darkest corner, alone. Calverton pushed the bag up against a sack of lentils and walked out without a word.

I had no sense of his having arranged all this. It seemed like something that was taking its own course, inevitable. We must have faced each other for some time, because I remember the church bells pealing, and a voice in the shop asking for *feta* cheese, and the ringing blows of someone beating with a hammer at the hoops of a cask.

'He made me come back,' I said at last. 'He made me.'

Still she said nothing, but she gave a quick, tight nod as if in acceptance of anything I had to say. She appeared to control a little shiver. She was not as successful with the trembling of her lips. Her eyes and cheekbones, I saw, were wet.

SYDNEY, 1968

There is no conclusion to all this. Not yet. It is quite possible, of course, that there will not be. If I had gone back to writing, if this were a novel, say, I think I would have had no conclusion, only a kind of petering out.

The trouble is that the kaleidoscope does not shake well any more. Perhaps something has gone wrong with it.

Sometimes you shake it and shake it and shake it, and all you get is a blank, a grey blankness like fog or like nothing, what one imagines nothing to be. Although it is quite hard to imagine nothing. No pattern. No colour. No design. Absence of the fortuitous as well as the intentional. Absence of oneself, too.

Mind you, it is not always blank. There are brief periods when it still comes up with perfectly clear, bright pictures, lucid little geometries, and at other times one can achieve only a kind of fragmentation of particles, a splintering, all the coloured bits flying in all directions.

Tom Kiernan had an obsession once about doing a painting of that moment when the bombs fell on Padua—was it Padua?—and blew the Mantegna frescoes to smithereens. (Of course it was Padua; they were Mantegna's first great frescoes, the ones in the Ovetari chapel in the church of the Eremitani. I was in Italy at the time, at Forli, not all that far from Padua. I knew nothing whatever about the bombing.) As I was saying, the bombs falling and blowing the Mantegna frescoes to smithereens—the pale coloured bits and pieces flying off in all directions, mouths and eyes and faces and hands and noses and bits of ears and the shreds of coloured robes and hats and whizzing chunks of bricks and plaster. He was going to call his painting *The New Renaissance*, because he wanted to symbolize a good many things; not only Padua and the lost Mantegnas, but Dresden and Coventry and Monte Cassino, and Hiroshima and Nagasaki, I suppose—because Tom intended to have the pieces in his paintings all whirling around like the inside of an atom—(if he was doing it now then Hue, also, would have to be considered) but so far as I know Tom never got around to painting it, although he spent months and months in Padua thinking about it. This is a pity, I think, because Tom would have done it well.

I must be careful in working this bit out, because it is deceptive; what seems to be very restricted and confined, practically sealed off—the people passing along the street below on their ways to and from the plastics factory clearly see it as something sealed off: you can tell from the way they look up and, should they chance to meet an eye, quickly look away—this rigidly self-contained hospital world is really quite limitless in its reach.

Last night I was painfully conscious of confinement and I remember thinking that this was a very odd place in which to be trying to tie the loose ends together, particularly loose ends like Calverton. But this morning, since I have been out on the balcony and looking down on the people passing in the street, I see it altogether differently.

Take the birds, for instance. There are so many birds that come to the hospital garden. Not only the sweet-singing natives like the magpies and currawongs, and an occasional visiting kookaburra, but the high-capped little bulbul from distant Persia (were we there together once by the water-splashing courts of Isfahan?), and mynah-birds from India, and starlings from everywhere, and English sparrows. Or the sky—the rounded heavy forms of cumulus with the infinite cerulean depth beyond: there is nothing to stop one from moving out into this and going anywhere at all. An hour ago it took me to Calcutta, of all places! Stretched out naked on my back on a flat roof in Tollygunge, staring up into the hot immensity of the same kind of ultimate mystery, watching the cumulus imperceptibly changing its form, and the kite-hawks whirling and wheeling. There was outcry in the streets around, welling and fading, frenzied when close at hand, where they were throwing at each other the coloured dusts and dyes of the Holi festival.

We are still out on the long journey from Szechwan.

There must have been a point somewhere where one could have—should have?—done something different. I am convinced of this.

This room I am in measures fifteen feet by twelve feet and has three walls painted duck-egg green and one a very pale ashy grey. One can, in fact, have a great measure of freedom here. There is a comforting security and a sense of the familiar in these encased worlds which are my present environment. The frame of the window provides the three great monoliths which stand, and often have the illusion of moving, against the sluggish drift of cloud. Rather than being impressive temples to strange gods—as in the ancient world they very assuredly would have been—they are merely the giant smokestacks of a brickworks, each notably different in size and shape, as if three different contract builders had vied with each other in reducing the principle of the ziggurat and Babel to an ultimate inhuman slenderness. All three of them are used for sacrifice, though, and trail ribbons of smoke above the corner of a disused workshop, a clump of camphor-laurel trees, sturdy though city-stunted and city-dusty, the squat cottage used by the young medical residents, and the red-brick block of the sisters' quarters, from which little Sister Lloyd is at this moment emerging, crisp-starched and beautiful in grey and white, holding her veil.

The second of the familiar framed worlds, the one I can see from my pillow without even having to turn my head, is, by odd coincidence, a reproduction on the wall of one of Tom Kiernan's paintings. It is, for Tom, an unusual subject, being an Australian scene—or rather, Tom's idea of an Australian scene, because Tuscany is there also, and a hint of the Andalusian plain, even a suggestion of the harsher islands of Greece, the Dry Sporades. I actually remember Tom talking about it soon after he had painted it, in Europe from the heartland of his long absence. (I am tickled by this typical con trick of Tom's, sneaking in so much that is exotic and alien, because all the reproductions framed on the hospital walls and in the wards are so emphatically Australian, being the gift of Rotary or Apex.) I have become very fond of the painting. It has what Tom always seems to be able to get into his best works, the sense of a recessed opening from reality, through which one might walk right into the world of his imagination, and go on and on, for ever finding one's own journey and new views and vistas and remarkable things to be examined, the same sort of mystical beckoning inside that Samuel Palmer's little etchings have. There are journeys of the spirit as well as the bodily ones, and I am beginning to think that the former are the more important. Although perhaps this is just sour grapes.

Beside the bed is the bowl of jasmine that Cressida brought in, and lying there on the counterpane is Archie Calverton, on the front page of yesterday afternoon's tabloid newspaper, below a stark headline in the bloodless blur of a halftone block. I put the paper back on the counterpane this morning after the bed had been made and the two pretty junior nurses had gone away, Jan and Jane, in their charming, old-fashioned white crossover aprons, with their kind bright faces and unchallenged laughter in the young eyes above the sterile masks. Jan and Jane are just as old as

Cressida would have been when I first saw her in the gunpit back there in Melbourne a million years ago. After they had gone I was left with the dead Calverton on the counterpane.

But what do you do with a thing like this? (It was the question I asked in the Ginza twenty-three years ago when the scared little Japanese postal clerk thrust his stamp collection on me.) I have no desire to retain the newspaper as a memento, not with all the other mementoes I have, and Calverton's gold St Christopher medallion which I still wear around my neck. Yet some superstition prevents my throwing it out, into the bin with the rest of the rubbish.

Poor Archie! The cars went faster and faster and faster. After that brief limbo on the island, his unhurried time, when the smoke from his cigarette verticled the still air and for a time he could listen to silence and be at peace with himself, he had gone back to the view-halloo and crowding pell-mell of the hunt he had to follow . . . or to lead, for whether he was huntsman or quarry I doubt if he ever discovered himself. Anyway, with his brains splashed all over the autostrada twenty kilometres outside Milan it is all one now. Was it, I find myself wondering, still the blue Porsche? I really would like to know whether it was or not, but the newspaper account is full of his fame and his scandals and the amounts of money he made and has only that he was driving a sports car, alone and late at night, and that his body had been recovered more than a hundred metres from the wreckage of the car, which appeared to have turned over five times. Poor Archie! Yet they envied him. He saw that, on the day we talked under the pines at Piso Bay, watching the others swimming. He was envied right to the very end, to this famous termination to a famous journey, for he shared his front page with nobody, not even the usual girl in a bikini. So what does it matter that tomorrow he will be in the garbage or wrapped around the prawns?

But was this, after all, the unconscious goal of his journey, a striving towards sensational obituary? Surely not? This room today is filled with journeys, fragmentations, endings, people, memories, questions. Not too many answers, though. All these drugs they give seem to cloud the passages of the mind in a certain way, so while it is easy enough to move along on a slow drift of questions, it is far more difficult to grapple with the questions, or to find answers. The questions now are mostly concerned, as they should be, with Archie Calverton. What if, for instance, he had played it safe and never gone away? Stayed in this country which is like a beautiful coloured egg from which all the meat, or almost all the meat, has been sucked away? Settled for safety and a Benzedrine inhaler instead of a blue Porsche and swift obliteration on an Italian freeway? But it is what happened in between, surely, and the undeniable final feat of getting the whole front page of the tabloid. (He is also in this morning's far more conservative newspaper – what is called a 'paper of record' – less sensationally, in smaller print; so that a hundred years from now, if anyone is interested, he can be looked up in a yellowing newspaper file and be found not to have had ultimate anonymity.) No, it is what happened in between that is important, but this is something that will dry up and vanish very quickly, like water splashed on a hot pavement, between the markers of the Benzedrine inhaler and the blue Porsche. Who was his mulatto girl in Soho? What did he do with himself and say to himself on those lonely night-wanderings, the last of which ended so abruptly on the Milan autostrada? Who *was* Archie Calverton? And *why*? A thought occurs. Teasingly. If it had been Calverton in the house at Metz the day that Morgan called he would have gone to the door at once and let Morgan in. Why did he come out in the longboat that day and force me back?

Bugger the longboat for the moment . . . we are thinking of the door. Because this is the clue, of course. Doors! It's all in the answering of the doors. The ones that are opened and the ones that aren't. People depend a lot on the doors that other people open . . .

Outside the three great monoliths are reeking in the sky, and here within the healing cube Tom Kiernan watches, invisible, from the secret far recesses of his landscape, and the Calverton General Transportation Fund has been wound up and the books put away—the young drunken voices of so long ago, banknotes long since obsolete crumpled in a top-hat on the floor, voices shouting poetry in the back seat of a car boring tunnels of light through the humid blackness of a vanished Sydney. You hardly ever see that kind of car any more.

What surprises me is that one is so terribly nostalgic now for that time we once hated so much.

Propped back here on the piled pillows is like looking down on an immense country spread out below, or an immensity of numerous countries. Sometimes they are filled with clouds and birds and people, and offshore islands; sometimes are empty as deserts. But there is no way through them any longer. No more journeys. At times I think they are not really countries at all, just old obsolete maps, no longer to be relied on.

Funny if we had the wrong maps all the time, without realizing it!

What *did* Morgan want that day? There is no doubt at all in my mind that Calverton would have gone to the door and let him in. Calverton would have found out what had been troubling him . . .

This bit is quite clear. Just as clear as if it had happened yesterday, instead of nearly ten years ago.

Calverton waited until Cressida had gone down to meet the market boats, then he went with me into the shuttered cool living-room that had developed quite a pleasant character by that time, with the books we had collected over the years and the paintings left by indigent artists who had drifted through the island. The paintings were framed in old offcuts of boxwood or a kind of makeshift *passe-partout* contrived from friction-tape, but they looked all right. The room was very different from the way it had looked after Guido smashed it up. (The day I am thinking of would have been the day after Calverton brought me back in the longboat.) He found a record and put it on the cheap little portable player—it was Mozart's Haffner symphony; I even remember that—and he turned the volume low and sprawled out on the divan covered with the old Arachova rug, with his hands linked behind his head and his eyes closed, as if all he wanted to do was to talk drowsily about nothing in particular.

There was a fly acting strangely above the slow spin of the phonograph record. It kept flying in a circle just above the disc, as if in synchronization, but also flying in a rather groggy way as if drunk with the music, and when another fly intruded it would chase it away and then come back and continue its curious circling dance.

Calverton yawned and said, 'I'm shoving off tomorrow.'

I said nothing, accepting this, wanting him to go.

Calverton said, 'I did promise I wouldn't outstay my welcome.'

'You haven't,' I said.

'You and Cress won't want me hanging around,' he said. 'You've got things to work out.'

I nodded without speaking, watching the giddy fly.

He sat up and said earnestly, 'You *will* have to work it out. You can't dodge it any longer, either of you. You've both got to a point where —'

'There are lots of things to be worked out,' I said with a touch of impatience.

'There always are. With everybody. All the time. It gets worse as you go on. I don't want to butt in, but can I say something about you and Cress?'

'Go ahead.' I managed a shrug of indifference which I did not feel.

'I've known you two a long time. I just wanted to say I'm pretty sure it had to happen. Cress and him, I mean. What happened was part of a need she had, some empty part of her that had to be filled. If it hadn't been Galloway it would have been somebody else.'

'You, for instance?' I felt cornered somehow and furious with him and I couldn't help myself. He had to be hurt too.

He shook his head slowly. 'Oh no,' he said. 'I've loved Cress almost ever since I've known you two, been in love with her, I mean. But not that way. You don't have to worry. No—but I imagined somebody like him, with all that zest and laughter, that great appetite for life. He was a simple sort of bastard, really, an innocent . . . he had a capacity for wonder. Actually he wasn't a bad bloke, all things considered.'

'If that's what you wanted to say, let's skip it,' I said angrily. This time it was Calverton who shrugged, so I said, 'I didn't qualify, you mean? Is that it? I didn't stack up? In other words, it was my own bloody fault?'

'I didn't say that. In fact, though, I think quite a lot of it was,' he said calmly. 'In anything of this nature, of course, there are two sides to everything, but —'

'Three in this case.'

'Just two, I think. Just you two. You've both been keeping things bottled up inside yourselves for years. Burying things away. Neither of you wanting to hurt the other, perhaps. I don't know. But both of you have been building walls and hiding behind 'em.'

'*Both* of us? She does, I agree. That's because she won't face realities.'

'Pig's arse. And anyway who are you to talk? You don't face realities yourself.'

'Is that so?'

'Listen, years ago, when the three of us were in London together, Cress sometimes used to talk to me in a way she never seemed to talk to you. I often wondered about it, but it was one of the reasons I liked being with her . . . the way she would talk, I mean. There was a kind of magic in it, a warmth, an innocence, if you like . . . and an excitement, as if she had found some very precious substance that she desperately wanted to show to someone. To share with someone. One day I did question her and she told me she didn't talk the same way to you any longer because she was scared you might get it wrong or misunderstand.' He paused. 'There were times —' his reminder was gentle — 'when you did misunderstand.' He stopped then, waiting, I think, for me to tell him to shut up.

'Go on,' I said, with a heavy patience. 'You've got the floor.'

'I just think both of you, in your different ways, have been over-reaching to buggery. Striving after something nobody can ever really hope to attain. Trying to impose form on something which by its very nature is formless. Now your particular unreality—because you're the one we're dealing with—was that you wanted too much from *her*. You demanded of her a kind of perfection that was only the shape of perfection the way you saw it. Not just because she was your most cherished possession and it had to be flawless, but I think as a kind of compensation for your own self-doubts, your shortcomings, your setbacks, even for your own weaknesses, in a way. You even resented her being ill. That was an imperfection. She wasn't allowed to have imperfections.'

'It seems I was bloody wrong, wasn't I?'

'It beats me how you could ever have expected to be right. People really want mercy and escape, you know, they're not looking for justice and truth.' He hesitated. 'You tried to wall her in. It stands to reason that eventually she would have to break free and get out . . . if only to try to find what she felt she had lost. What I find astonishing is that she was able to keep it up for so long.'

'I'll tell you how she kept it up,' I said furiously. 'She kept it up by retreating into her bloody dream world! Into unreality. She's the one who shut herself away. She locked *me* out. Ever since we've been here in Greece she's lived in some romantic damned delusion that life goes on in a balmy golden haze. She's everlastingly searching for some lost Golden Age where she can be a barefoot pagan kid running around the sand listening to the sea.'

'Well, who's to say she's wrong? She could be right, you know.'

'Bullshit! It's nothing but a romantic bloody dream! She won't face facts. She won't look at reality. She will *not* be practical.'

'I can't believe you really mean that, Davy. At the moment you're all steamed up, but if you look at it rationally you just can't mean it. Not after the way she's back-stopped for you for years. Not after what she's gone through and put up with. And why? I'll tell you why. Because you've had *your* dreams too. She has her dreams, sure. Why not? She's entitled to them. None of us makes any sense at all if we don't have dreams. For Christ's sake, man, you've got to be fair.'

'Fair! That's bloody rich, that is! Listen to me, you don't know Cressida. No one bloody well knows her. No one's allowed to. There's a part of her that no one can get at. No one, I tell you. You talk about this *need* of hers, this empty part of her that I'm not able to fill but this other bastard apparently is. Well, whose fault is that? You tell me. Whose fault is it?'

'Look, Davy, you're mad to go on like this. It's got beyond the point of recriminations and blame and all that shit. If you take my advice you—'

'I don't want your advice. I didn't ask for it. I'm just telling you that she's secretive. She's always been secretive. You can't get *at* her. She listens to a music that only she is allowed to hear. Nobody else. It's private. Totally private. It's this mad romantic dream world of hers, this bloody escape into unreality.'

He gave me a long, quizzical look and said, 'Yes, I know about this.'

'What?'

'This music of hers. She's talked to me about it.'

'Talked to *you* about it?'

He nodded. 'Quite often, as a matter of fact. Maybe she talked to Galloway about it too. Maybe he was able to understand it. Maybe that's the whole point. It's something very important to her, you see, and she has to share it with someone. Can't you see this? I suppose it's what makes her Cressida . . . it's her soul if you like, her belief, her poetry . . . it doesn't matter really what you call it . . . it doesn't really matter whether it's right or wrong. It's the music she hears. It's *hers*.' The symphony was over. The needle scratched and whispered around the groove. The fly still circled. 'Do you ever hear it?' Calverton asked softly.

'What?'

'This music of hers.'

'How can I? I told you, I'm barred.'

'Perhaps that's the trouble. I mean, if you did hear it, just once . . . if you both heard it together and understood it and . . .'

'It's a damned sight too late for that,' I said.

'Yes, perhaps it is.' For the first time he seemed unsure of what he wanted to say, even embarrassed. 'Anyway, it's just my bloody impertinence,' he said. 'It's really a private thing between you and Cress, isn't it?'

'Surely it's all a private thing between me and Cress?' I said tartly.

'That's right. You could have always told me to shut up, you know, to mind my own business.'

'I wanted to hear what you had to say.'

'Well, what I have to say is quite simple, really. Whatever has happened had to happen, because it's been building up to happen for a hell of a long time. But now it has happened it's something you have to live with. Both of you.' He reached across and took the disc off the record-player and disturbed the still-circling fly. 'You only have each other,' he said.

It doesn't worry me particularly that I shall never see the islands of Greece again. I don't think it *worries* Cressida either, although I am certain she misses some things passionately at times.

The very first time I saw them was below, far below, from an aircraft during the war, black in a silver glitter in the moonlight, lovely and haunting. Flying north, we were. The last time I saw them was from another aircraft, the same nocturnal alchemy of black and silver, again far below. Flying south. In between were all the years.

Sailing those waters we were once wise in what had to be done in a night of storm, should a beautiful woman rise on the tempestuous waves lashing at the boat and cry her aching question: 'Where is Alexander the Great?' Quick as a flash one had to be ready with the reply: 'Alexander the Great lives and reigns!' If this were shouted out the woman would vanish, the storm-wind quieten, the seas subside, and sunrise would come over an Aegean innocent again. To neglect that response, that cry of affirmation, was to be doomed. We knew that. We were warned about it,

Cressida and I, the first time sailing off Santorin, another time coming in to Patmos, with the sun rising behind Samos like the gold embellishment on an icon.

Greece's, of course, is a fatal beauty. It always has been, I suppose. So how important it is to understand the hazardous, breathtaking mysteries, to grasp at wisdoms in the moment of peril, to stand upright and shout with loud and confident authority into the very howling mouth of danger, 'Alexander the Great lives and reigns!'

Except to go to the near-by washroom, Meredith never moved from his comfortable tilt-back window-seat in the airliner on the flight back to Australia. He accepted a few drinks, smoked many cigarettes, ate what was presented to him from time to time on the plastic trays. Once Athens had dropped away he could look down on the black and pewter gleam of islands in the moonlight until they were sucked under a hazy height, not thinking about anything very much now, and while they were stubbing cigarettes and fastening seat-belts and coming in to Cairo over the darkly glimmering Nile – a flick of polish here and there as if the night had been rubbed with black Nugget – he asked a steward if it would be all right for him to remain in the airliner during the twenty-minute stopover. The steward was momentarily surprised, then reassembled his imperturbability and said, 'Just as you wish, sir. Makes no difference to us. No smoking, of course, on the ground. Does get jolly warm in the aircraft, sir, that's all.'

He must have said something to the stewardesses about this dopey bastard who insisted on staying in his seat, because they gave him curious glances as they followed the other passengers to the exit doors, and Meredith was left by himself in the huge empty plane, thinking of Cairo and the madly futile way he had once pursued the tantalizing Faisa, the pretty Syrian dance hostess who had worked her pitch at Doll's Cabaret on Melika Farida.

Airports and air terminals were everywhere much of a muchness, aside from the gimmicks on the tourist stalls, and besides he had been in all the cities on the route – been in them properly and involved, even if it was a long time ago, the way he had been in his frustrated chase after Faisa. He smiled at the wry memory, then seeing himself solitary in the plane's emptiness he made himself laugh aloud. It sounded forced and foolish.

He did not leave his seat at Karachi either, or Calcutta, or Singapore—having reassured the stewardesses that he was perfectly all right, and not ill—but sat quite alone after all the other passengers had trooped out, breathing the stifling humidity and the smell of insecticide. He tried not to think about the future, and was able to do this fairly successfully by thinking about the past or re-reading Cavafy's poems. Just before going out to the airport at Phaleron Cressida had given him the volume of Cavafy's poetry, but he had not unwrapped it while they sat with Tom Kiernan, talking and waiting, so the plane had been, appropriately enough, almost over Alexandria, where Cavafy had lived, before he saw that Cressida had written a sentimental little epigraph on the fly-leaf and had transcribed the final lines from 'Ithaca':

Without her you would never have taken the road.
Ithaca has given you the beautiful voyage.
But she has nothing more to give you.

And if you find her poor,
Ithaca has not defrauded you.
With all the great wisdom you have gained,
With so much experience,
you must surely have understood by then what Ithacas[10] *mean.*

He read the words many times, finding curious ambiguities in them . . .

Yesterday was a full day, when you come to think of it—Cressida's visit, and then the shock of seeing Calverton on the front page of the newspaper, and the doctor telling me I can go home next week.

The doctor used almost the same words that Calverton had

used, although in a quite different context, of course. 'You just have to learn to live with it, that's all,' he said, after he had told me that the condition arising from the lung damage and the surgery was irreversible. 'But at least you can go home next week and get on with living,' he said cheerfully. 'You look after yourself, and with a bit of luck we can stop this in and out of hospital business.' He seemed to search around for some other seed of satisfaction or encouragement. 'Where you're more fortunate than most is in being a writer. I mean, after all, you *can* go back to your work.'

As if nothing had happened. Gavin Turley quoted Kafka to me in his untidy room back there in Melbourne twenty-three years ago. ' "And then he went back to his work as if nothing had happened," ' he said. And I had ranted at him and he had waved the stump of his arm at me and said, 'Why not, cock? What else?'

Whatever happened to Gavin Turley?

Coming in to each landing Meredith would look out of the window hoping to identify some familiar old landmark: not necessarily the brothel in Karachi from which he and Major Baer had been forcibly ejected, but at least some recognizable evidence of what at one time he had felt to be significant segments of his life. Calcutta came closest to giving him something . . . the slimy crowded tanks and the jungly Hooghly-clammy vegetation, skinny figures around muddy buffaloes, the dull yellow river reaches with steamy patches like banks of drying clay. Coming in, he had been able to pick out Chowringhee and the Maidan, where he had often gone with Kay, the American Red Cross girl, and this set him thinking of Betty Boyce, the prostitute in Carya Road, so that when the plane touched down with a thump and screech and the whining scream of jets Dum Dum seemed hardly changed at all. Even from within the plane he could smell the familiar smell of it and the heat. Yesterday, in Athens, there had been sleet and snow. During the refuelling it became almost unbearable inside the plane, but he resisted the temptation to go out and walk around.

Once he had flown out from here in the old DC3s – where were all the old DC3s now? – out to Comilla or up to Assam and then across the mountains to China, and this seemed a more real and more reliable thing to be doing than to be in a great modern Boeing jet flying all the way back to Australia. Yet it had to be done. Cressida had agreed about this. They had talked about it being 'in the nature of a reconnaissance', that if he found Australia all right then – and only then – he would arrange for her to follow him out with the children. Neither of them had dared admit that there was no longer any other course open to them. The island had long since played itself out, both of them recoiled from the thought of tackling England again, there were the children to be considered, his state of health, the simple economics of making a living. There was nowhere else to go. They might keep up a pretence that other avenues of retreat were still open to them, but it was no more than a pretence: the only possible movement now was back the way they had come. The additional time on the island that Calverton had given them had not been entirely wasted; the book he had written had been better than others he had done and more successful – at least it had done what Calverton had predicted, it had bought the way to somewhere else – and by selling the house in Greece he would be able to pay for their passages back to Australia and perhaps have enough to get themselves re-established and even pay back some of the money he owed. With luck they could all be together again back home, pretty much where they were before they had set out fourteen years before, only that much older.

It would be an anticlimactic ending to it all, in a way, Meredith reflected, but sometimes it seemed to him that this had always been on the cards, predictable, a kind of calculated anticlimax, as if they had been damned from the very beginning by what they thought was liberating them . . .

Meredith sighed and thought of the old DC3s droning up to Assam.

Flying out over the Arakan his thoughts focused again on the war, the war which had brought the violent horror of death to thirty million human beings and the qualified horror of living to even more, the war that people hardly ever thought about any longer because too much had happened since; and at Singapore the passengers marched back to the plane like mercenaries bearing loot, laden with transistors and cameras and watches and portable TV sets and tape-recorders, their faces glistening with sweat and acquisition.

The man in the seat next to Meredith, a friendly, fleshy Australian businessman with grey hair cut very short on a brick-red neck, chided Meredith good-naturedly. 'You know, you were a bloody goat not to come with me, like I said. You wouldn't believe what they got there, you know. Everything duty free, you know. You know, you could spend a bloody fortune. No risk. Every bloody thing you can imagine. You know, Jap stuff. German. Swiss watches. Mind you, you've got to be awake up. There's some cunning bastards, Chows most of 'em, try to put things over. You're right, though, if you look for the reputable makes. Go for the name brands, that's my policy. Then you just can't lose. Look, I paid ten quid for this transistor, ten sterling. Back home I can get forty or fifty for it. Jesus, I'd have grabbed a bloody ton of the stuff if I thought for a bloody minute I could get it through.'

Meredith nodded and closed his eyes and when he opened them again the businessman was scribbling calculations in a little note-book, and Meredith saw the straits below being sucked away in haze and heat and he thought about bombs and Changi and people he had once known.

He thought of his father also. And of the old round army biscuit which his father had sent back from Cairo in 1915 and which had been kept in the glass dome on the top of the pianola. On top of the piano first and later the pianola. He thought of his dead father who once had been in Cairo too, and perhaps had chased a Syrian dance girl through the Wazir, and he would have seen the Greek islands on his way to Gallipoli, and known the fields and the big-rumped white horses of Picardy. But afterwards these experiences had come to mean nothing to him nor to anyone else. What *was* the meaning of experience, Meredith wondered. If one could live backward instead of having to press on and go forward, would one want to do it? And where would one choose to stop? Had it ever occurred to his father to want to live backwards?

He rested his head against the seat and half dozed. The Cavafy book lay closed on his lap, and perhaps this was why quotations went on drifting through his mind, other quotations, Hemingway's 'The people and the places and how the weather was,' and Horace's 'You can change your skies but not your soul,' and Herder's 'We are carried ever forward; the stream never returns to its source.'

But here he was, high over the Spice Islands, certainly being carried ever forward, rushingly, at almost six hundred miles an hour, but being returned to his source just as certainly. Yet how far it was away . . . how terribly far away . . .

Meredith fell asleep, thinking of the seas and oceans in between, and all the islands.

Cressida took the clean folded pyjamas and stowed them in the locker and rearranged the bowl of jasmine and said, 'You'll hardly know the house when you come out next week. All the trees are going like mad. We'll be surrounded by bush. Already you can hardly see the neighbours' houses.' Before she left she said, 'What I'm mostly thrilled about, though, apart from your coming home, is Julian,' and he smiled at her, sharing her delight, although after she had gone he found himself wondering what he really thought about Julian winning the poetry prize at the university and deciding he wanted to be a writer.

It would be quite different for him, of course; he didn't quite know in what way it would be different although he saw that everything was different for Julian's generation, even though he couldn't really understand them. He didn't at all subscribe to the common belief that they had it easier, but he did have the feeling that they probably had a better chance of not ending up the way he had, neither demonstrably a failure nor demonstrably a success, a kind of in-between man. Surely the obvious thing, anyway, was to go for the safe way and chase security? It was odd that this was the one question he was never able to answer.

He was still trying to puzzle it out when the night nurse came with the sedatives. If he didn't take the sedative he could stay awake listening to the old DC3s taking out the newspapers.

Outside a strong gusty north-easterly had blown up and there were tossing shadows in the room from the branches of the camphor-laurels. He hoped the young trees surrounding the house were firmly staked. Something loose, a shutter, a window frame, a faulty latch, rapped and rattled, like someone knocking . . .

Almost all the lights were out in the airliner when Meredith wakened, and he was gripped by a frantic excitement as he pressed his head against the cool plastic of the window and looked down on the Australian continent. Even in the darkness it had a murky, brownish look. Brownish and dry and wrinkled, like old leather. It lay six miles below, lonely, featureless, enormous, without sign of light or life. Or landmark. Or purpose. He was seized by a shiver of uneasiness. It was so forbidding, so desolate and empty, so utterly unwelcoming. There was no sense imparted of arrival or return, no feeling that he or anything human could have sprung from this: he thought of crowding Europe and the human maggot-heap of Asia. He had a sharp spasm of panic that now this huge blind heedless thing would have to be confronted.

The man beside him was tilted right back, snoring gently, his mouth open. Could he too have been spawned by this, with his tape-recorders and the quids he was able to make? Meredith felt he ought to waken him.

Instead he crouched by the window, watching the dark and terrifying pattern repeating itself until his attention was distracted by the light in the east. A glowing funnel of flamingo-pink, gilded silkworms crawling on a huge flat leaf of night, then the reddest and biggest sun he had ever seen—bigger than the orange moon at Lerici—jerking up from behind the rim of the earth. A tremor of something atavistic passed through his cramped body: the lurking monster had been evaded.

Meredith looked down upon a country quite foreign to him. You are an alien here too, he told himself. You are an alien everywhere, because alienation is something you carry inside yourself, and all you can do is fashion little enclaves and try to live inside them. You are an alien because there is no one you will ever really know, not even yourself . . .

They were gliding down now over dark forests and inlets and estuaries and wide rivers and indeterminate grey bruisings and the scars of red rooftops spread out like cheap and threadbare hearth-rugs. There were formal arrangements of winking little lights and gassy flares of blue, which began to cluster into vivid scatterings of gems and brilliants. In Hyderabad once an Indian rajah had flung down in front of Meredith's eyes, on a billiard table covered with black baize, a prince's ransom of jewels and gems and brilliants. But they were circling in lower now over a congestion of factory buildings, and the gems and brilliants had all turned into advertisements and traffic lights.

The sun had still to reach the grey world waiting below when Meredith clipped his seat-belt and sucked on a piece of toffee and prepared to come home.

NOTES

A small number of notes is provided here mainly to point out differences between the novel and the biographical actualities of Johnston's life. This does not mean that the remainder of the novel is autobiographically accurate; only the more significant departures are noted here.

1. Bernard Brewster, who also appears in *My Brother Jack*, is drawn from several of Johnston's editorial superiors at the Melbourne *Argus* over a number of years, including R. L. Curthoys, E. A. Doyle and Errol Knox. Doyle seems to have supplied Brewster's physical appearance, and Knox his dictatorial manner.

2. Since Archie Calverton is in some parts based on Johnston's friendship with the actor Peter Finch, there is a temptation to connect all Calverton's activities to Finch, but this would be a mistake. Here, for instance, it is highly unlikely that this represents the first meeting between Johnston and Finch. That was more likely to have taken place in Sydney around 1947, possibly at the Journalist's Club. See also notes 7 and 8.

3. 'Lebanon Bay' is a reference to the NSW coastal town of Kiama, where Charmian Clift was born. The name connotes the large Lebanese cedars that are a feature of the town.

4. The character of Tom Kiernan is based on the painter Sidney Nolan. It is probably the least fictionalized and most affectionate of Johnston's characterizations.

5. These 'Notes From an Expatriate's Journal' are taken almost verbatim from a notebook kept by Charmian Clift of her travels through Europe with Johnston in 1952. It is more than likely that Clift agreed to their use here, but puzzling that no acknowledgement is made that the observations are hers.

6. This refers to Clarisse Zander, mother-in-law of the painter Carl Plate. Mrs Zander had actually been to Hydra in her travels, and recommended it to the Johnstons as an ideal and inexpensive place to live as a writer. She was introduced to the Johnstons by Sidney Nolan.

7. Again, because of the connection between Calverton and Peter Finch, some have presumed a possible affair between Clift and Finch, but there is nothing to support the idea.

8. This has been taken by some (for instance, Elaine Dundy, author of the biography *Finch, Bloody Finch*) to mean that Peter Finch gave the Johnstons 1000 pounds to get back to Greece in 1961. He did not. Johnston borrowed the fare from an old friend in England, Vic Valentine.

9. The affair between Cressida and Galloway is not a representation of a particular affair that Charmian Clift had. Indeed, Jim Galloway is a fictionalized character, an idealized lover, and more a substitute for, rather than a composite of, the several men in Clift's life in Greece.

10. Some translations make this reference to 'Ithacas' in the final line singular, but the word in the original is 'Ithakes', and should be read as plural.

ALSO PUBLISHED IN THE IMPRINT CLASSICS SERIES

MY BROTHER JACK

GEORGE JOHNSTON

My brother Jack does not come into the story straight away. Nobody ever does, of course, because a person doesn't begin to exist without parents and an environment...

In *My Brother Jack*, George Johnston traces the lives of brothers David and Jack Meredith. He focuses on their childhood during the First World War, growing up in a patriotic, suburban Melbourne household, and describes the events that help shape their very different lives. Through David and Jack, Johnston explores two Australian myths: that of the man who loses his soul as he gains worldly success, and that of the tough, honest, 'Aussie' battler, who sees the justification of his life in the realization of his ambition—to serve his country during the war.

My Brother Jack is a deeply satisfying, complex and moving novel. It is an Australian literary masterpiece in the true classic mould, and is introduced here by Brian Matthews.

SEVEN POOR MEN OF SYDNEY

CHRISTINA STEAD

The trees raged in the park; they lifted their arms and tossed in the darkness of the under-cliff. The souls of the trees are freed in storms, they struggle, arise and commingle in the lower air...

The threads of the mesh appear and are woven of the bodies of flying men and women...Thought flies along their veins, they move and gesticulate with old motions lost in memory.

From the Endpiece, *Seven Poor Men of Sydney*

In this poetic and impressionistic novel, Catherine Baguenault and the seven men of the title are held together by the tenuous associations of their city, by the fickle bonds of love and friendship, and by an encompassing, and defeating poverty. Their inner landscapes are as tangible as the city and as intense as the elements.

Reprinted here with a new introduction by Margaret Harris, this classic novel presents a Sydney that is at once daunting and familiar.

RETURN TO COOLAMI
ELEANOR DARK

Coolami. Coolami. A word, thought Susan, and a mass of pictures. A word and an ache of memories, a chill of many fears.

Bret has come to take Susan back to Coolami. They have 300 miles to drive, two days in a car, time enough for the fears and secrets of the past to be revealed. With them are Susan's parents, themselves caught at a moment of regret and evaluation. Outside, the bush is silent, mysterious, beckoning.

Introduced by Barbara Brooks with Judith Clark, *Return to Coolami* is part thriller, part romance, and a serious enquiry into the nature of marriage.

Letty Fox: Her Luck

Christina Stead

When *Letty Fox* first appeared in 1946, opinion was divided. Some readers recognised it as a 'worldly, ribald and magnificent tale'. For others it was 'trashy and obscene', and a slur on womanhood.

In this classic novel by Christina Stead, published here with a new introduction by Susan Sheridan, Letty Fox tells her story as a self-styled sexual vagabond in New York's world of passion, love and sexual bargaining. As a bright, uninhibited daughter of the middle class who believes that the world is her oyster, Letty Fox tells it all—family secrets, social scandals, her desires and self-deceptions.

Launching herself as a free woman in a great city, Letty discovers that the pleasures of modern love are matched by the pain and exhaustion of a game that men and women play unequally: 'The woman looking for love is like a little boat meeting waterspout after waterspout. She is tired of steering, rowing, looking for land, hanging up old shirts for sails and the rest of it. But the pirates, they are not tired at all. They don't care if they don't make landfall in three years; they live off little craft.'

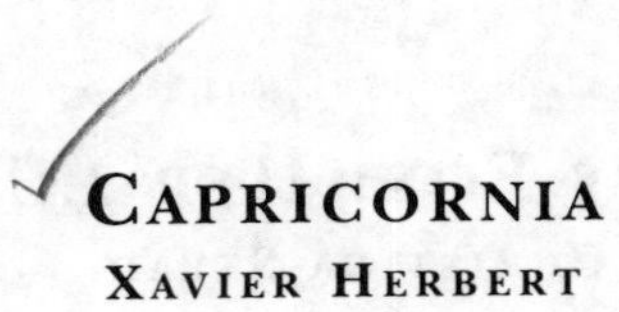

CAPRICORNIA

XAVIER HERBERT

Although that northern part of the Continent of Australia which is called Capricornia was pioneered long after the southern parts, its unofficial early history was even more bloody than that of the others. One probable reason for this is that the pioneers had already had experience in subduing Aborigines in the South and hence were impatient of wasting time with people who they knew were determined to take no immigrants.

And so *Capricornia* opens with a sweep as vast as the territory it covers. First published to controversy and acclaim in 1938, the novel brings to life a cast of memorable characters in an epic stretching fifty years.

In this edition, Aboriginal critic and writer Mudrooroo Nyoongah reassesses this classic novel of race relations in a new introduction.

Come in Spinner

Florence James, Dymphna Cusack

We were both pretty steamed up about the problems of women on the home front, so we decided to pool our wartime experience and tell the truth about what the war had done...how it had thrown decent people off balance and exploitation had become the name of the game.

Florence James, on writing *Come in Spinner*

Come in Spinner was an immediate sensation when it was first published in an abridged edition in 1951. Set in a beauty salon at the Hotel South Pacific in wartime Sydney, it revolves around the life and loves of three women, Deb, Guinea and Claire. Their romantic entanglements are further complicated by the tensions of war, with American troops in 'occupation' and where anything could be obtained—for a price.

'To lose oneself in *Come in Spinner* is indeed a stirring and memorable experience.'

The Sunday Times

Come in Spinner was recently highly acclaimed as a two-part series on ABC Television.

THE TIMELESS LAND
ELEANOR DARK

First published in 1941, Eleanor Dark's classic novel of the early settlement of Australia is a story of hardship, cruelty and danger. Above all it is the story of conflict: between the Aborigines and the white settlers.

In this dramatic novel, introduced here by Humphrey McQueen, a large cast of characters, historical and fictional, black and white, convict and settler, brings alive those bitter years with moments of tenderness and conciliation amid the brutality and hostility. All the while, behind the veneer of British civilisation, lies the baffling presence of Australia, a timeless land that shares with England 'not even its seasons or its stars'.